Flora Pearce was born in Heath End, Staffordshire, the Midlands village which is one of the settings for *Essie*. Her parents kept the local shop and it is her father, George, former miner and coal merchant, who by his wonderful recall supplied much of the background detail for this and her first novel, *No Work Today*.

Flora Pearce now lives in Dorset with her husband, Dennis.

Also by Flora Pearce from Futura:

NO WORK TODAY

Essie

FLORA PEARCE

Futura

A *Futura* Book

Copyright © Flora Pearce, 1988

First published in Great Britain by
Futura Publications 1988
This edition published by
Futura Publications 1994

ISBN 0 7088 4049 3

Printed in England by Clays Ltd, St Ives plc

Futura Publications
A Division of
Macdonald & Co (Publishers)
Brettenham House
Lancaster Place
London WC2E 7EN

Life was full of surprises.

Her son had a new life ahead.

Essie remembered so well the day her new life began.

To my darling Denby
and our lovely family,
Garth, Davina, Gemma
and Dulcie.

Chapter One

'I'll say when you can get out o' bed.'

'Our Essie starts work today.'

' 'Er's thirteen. Old enough to get 'erself off.'

'It's all right, Mam. I'm up.' Whimperings, heavings and cursings had been going on all night from the double bed she could touch from where she lay, and Essie was wide awake. She was amazed that her mam, not famous for her spunk, had the temerity to voice any sort of protest.

As she clambered over her snoring sister a coat slid to the floor. Essie wrapped it tightly around Clara and reached across for her own coat from the opposite side of the mattress they shared. She shivered as her feet touched the draughty floorboards. By pressing her back to the wall there was just enough space to enable her to inch sideways to the dark creaky staircase which led directly into the kitchen, their only downstairs room. The houses in Long Row were back-to-back one-up-and-downers. Its real name was Double Row, but most people referred to it as Long Row because it seemed to go on for ever.

Essie breathed heavily on the kitchen window in order to scrape away a patch of frost sufficient to peep outside at the deserted road that led through the village of Heath End, or Cod End, as it was nicknamed.

New Year's Day, 1913, and she was about to escape all this. Escape! She hugged the word to her like a hot-water bottle. A new day. A new year. *A new life.*

She turned back into the drab room, to where Sidney, her seventeen-year-old brother, snored and snuffled with the catarrh that also plagued Clara, his narrow bed pushed against the wall behind a dingy sofa.

The only other furniture in the room was an old chair tucked under a rickety table. Beneath this was an enamel bowl containing a tiny square of carbolic soap, and a galvanized bucket. There was about half a pint of water left in the bucket. It should have been filled last night. That was Sidney's job; he had forgotten again.

Dampness from the cracked quarries slithered like a snake into Essie's bare feet, searing up through her body until her teeth chattered.

Washing hung on lines strung across the kitchen, some of it as dry as a board from the fire that had smouldered all night. Smoke dried, thought Essie. The thicker garments, like her navy knickers, were still damp. She hung them over the oven door and draped her grey serge frock over the string line beneath the mantelpiece.

The raker smouldered in the grate. Essie would have liked to have knocked it up; she would have loved to see the flames dance into life, but she knew she risked a clout from her dad if he should come down and see that some of the fire had already burned away.

Going into service couldn't be worse than this, whatever Clara said. 'They treat yer like dirt,' she had warned Essie. Clara, a year older, had stuck it for a month; now she scrubbed doorsteps or sorted coal at the pit head.

The one cheerful sight was a big cast-iron kettle, bubbling on the tiny black hob. Essie brought the enamel bowl to it.

Grasping the scorching handle with a piece of hessian that served as a towel for them all, she poured some of the steaming liquid into the bowl, revelling for a moment in the warmth from the steam rising up into her chilled face. She stood as close as possible to the warm grate, holding the bowl to her body for a moment before placing it on the table. The water continued to sizzle. She couldn't wait for it to cool, and there was no point in getting scalded on her first day of freedom; there was nothing for it, she would have to add all of the precious cold water from the bucket.

She stripped off the grey flannel nightie that barely reached her knees and washed herself down, glancing from time to time to make sure that Sidney was still asleep. If he awoke he would sit up in bed leering at her.

The navy knickers and grey dress felt warm and comforting despite their dampness, as did her black stockings and lace-up shoes. One comb, shared by all of them, lay on the mantelpiece. She ran it through her hair, ineffectually tugging at the knots. She had a brand-new comb in the hessian bag she had roughly stitched together for her belongings; the comb she had bought with some pennies earned by baby minding.

She must fill the bucket or her mother would be in trouble. Dare she wake Sidney to ask him to go round to the tap in the big yard? There would only be a row and even then he might refuse. Oh well, this would be the very last time she would have to do it.

After tipping the water she had used for washing into the bucket to take to the drain, she wrapped herself into her black coat, bought from a jumble and several sizes too big.

Yesterday's sprinkle of snow had frozen solid in the night. Essie slipped and slithered past the dozen or so terraced houses tacked on to their own before she reached the communal yard. Houses backing on to theirs faced the yard.

11

The one communal tap was frozen! Her heart sunk to the hole at the bottom of her boots as she glanced desperately along the row of houses, seeking for one light, one door she could knock and ask for hot water to unfreeze it. Nothing stirred. What would her dad say when he discovered there was no water in the house?

Quarter-to-six was not usually too early for Heath-Enders to be up. But last night being New Year's Eve there had been lots of booze-ups and the men would be sleeping them off. Her dad had come home roaring drunk. Not that that was news; it happened most nights. Oh, trust it to be New Year's Day! Normally the miners' wives would be astir, already having got their men off for the morning shift. But today the pits were off. Not a single light!

She bit her lip in frustration. Water she must have if she was to save her mam from another good hiding. She knew that if this tap was frozen it was more than likely that all the other taps in open yards would be the same.

Suddenly she remembered that the Brooks, who kept the village shop, had a tap inside a brewhouse. Would the shop be open at this hour? She breathed a sigh of relief as the door yielded to the latch and Mrs Brook appeared in response to the sound of the tinkling bell. Bustling and fresh as always, her soft shiny hair piled on top of her head, she smiled at Essie, noting the bucket.

'You're abroad early, love.'

'Could I have some water from your brewhouse? I'm startin' work today and I 'ave to hurry up. I'm supposed to be there for half past seven, at the Mellish Road, in Walsall.'

'You haven't much time, then.'

'Is . . . is your tap froze, Mary Ann?' Everyone called Mrs Brook Mary Ann, even the children; she didn't seem to mind.

'No, it's all right, love. I left a bit of fire under the boiler in there last night. Help yourself. I expect most of Heath End will be turning up with their buckets today.'

Essie was very conscious of the lack of time to spare, but she always felt she wanted to linger, to talk to this clean, homely woman. She was about the same age as her own mam, but what a difference! Here was Mary Ann, alert, erect, bright-eyed, with lovely fresh skin and a warm smile. And there was her mam with her sunken, grey eyes, bony, grey face, apathetic manner and shaky hands.

Of course Mam had her dad to contend with. But Mary Ann had a boozing husband as well. Nearly died of drink, he did. Cod End men liked their booze. Yet most of the women seemed happy enough. But not her mother; she could not remember ever having seen her smile. Essie promised herself she would never be saddled with a man. Never.

'Your Paul called in to see us last night. He's back from Canada, then? He looks well, don't he?'

'He's a sight for sore eyes.' Mary Ann smiled. 'It was a wonderful surprise to see him walk in last night. And he says how well your brother Arthur is doing out there, Essie.'

'He brought us some money from Arthur. I expect me Dad'll get his hands on it. It'll all go to the pubs. Well, I'd better be off. Don't want the sack before I start, do I? Thanks for letting me 'ave the water.'

Mary Ann brought out four silver threepenny bits from the till. 'Here you are, dear. Best of luck.'

Essie flushed. She wished she did not have to accept it; Mary Ann had helped them so much already. But she could not afford to refuse. 'Thank you, Mary Ann, and for everything else you've done for us.'

'You're welcome, love.'

Essie had never owned so much money before.

It was difficult not to spill any water from the heavy bucket; some of it slopped on to her boots as she slid on the

13

icy road. Any moment she expected to lose the lot but she arrived with most of the precious liquid intact and the three-penny bits deep in her pocket.

Once back in the house she checked over the contents of the carrier bag she had made from an old piece of sacking sewn up with big, untidy, woollen stitches. The handles were pieces of string.

She counted out four aprons, two white and two black, and two caps. She had made them herself at school, from bits of calico gleaned from Mary Ann's 'bundles'. Mary Ann went regularly to the rag market at Brum. All Cod End would watch for her return, knowing there would be bargains and some free gifts as well. But she often kept some oddments back, for Essie.

A bundle had also provided the material for a dark blue blouse with a white collar which she now withdrew from the bag with a sense of pride. That blouse had nearly driven her scatty. The needlework mistress had insisted she unpick the sleeves and collar at least six times before she got them right. But it had all been worth it in the end, for when she had shown it to Mary Ann she had said, 'Well done, Essie,' and had slipped a tape measure round her tiny waist. Mary Ann's daughter, who was a dressmaker, had made her a lovely skirt as a gift. Light grey, it was, with flecks of blue exactly the shade of the blouse.

Essie re-folded all the garments carefully and returned them to the bag. The only other things she had to take were a couple of sludge-coloured, over-washed nightdresses someone had given to her mam. She wished she had a spare pair of knickers, and wondered what chance there would be to wash and iron the ones she was wearing.

Ah, here was the new comb. She decided to try it out; it felt good. It had all its teeth, not like the one on the mantel-piece. It was a pretty lavender shade; she had spent ages choosing it.

14

'How many more times yer gunna check them things?'

She had forgotten all about Sidney and nearly jumped out of her skin. He was still stretched out on the bed but was fully dressed.

'That's the last time.'

He indicated a stained brown teapot stewing on the hob. 'I med sum tea, if you want it.'

She poured some into an enamel cup and hurriedly ate a chunk of bread she broke off from a loaf on the table.

'I must be off now.'

'I've gotta come with yer.'

'Whatever for?'

'Me Dad said last night.'

'There's no need.'

'Me Dad said last night,' he repeated sullenly.

'Well, get a move on then, if you're coming.'

'I'm ready, ain't I?'

Essie guessed her dad had insisted on Sidney accompanying her, not because of any concern for her, but out of spite for Sidney, to get him out of the house, into the cold. She knew he would sulk throughout the journey. She would have been far better off without him. Nobody went with her when she was interviewed for the job, thank goodness.

She hesitated at the foot of the stairs. She wanted to call, 'Ta ra, Mam. Ta ra, Clara.' She wanted somebody to wish her luck, as Mary Ann had done. But she could hear thumps and moans still going on up there and decided to leave it. She handed her bag to Sidney.

'You might as well make yourself useful, if you're coming.'

Anxious to put as much space as possible between herself and Long Row, she raced his legs off for the first mile. The bits of felt she had tacked on to the heels of her boots helped grip the icy surface, but Sidney slipped several times. Suddenly he stopped.

15

' 'Ere, 'old on a minute. My side 'urts.'

He did look poorly, a right sight with his boils and pimples standing out bright red on his ashen face. Stick thin and bent, nursing his side, he was like an old man. Essie knew he must be frozen in his thin jacket, far too small, with the sleeves halfway up his arms. Her jumble-sale coat would have held him as well, and two besides. It looked ridiculous, she knew. She had wrapped it round her body twice, and it completely covered her legs. It was made of thick woolly material. She felt quite warm, what with the coat and the exertion of hurrying.

'We'll sit on this wall a minute,' she conceded.

She took the bag so that her brother could put both his hands under his jacket after he had blown on them. He was panting and his breath was like a fog on the frosty air.

'Why don't you rest here for a while and then go home?'

'Me Dad says I 'ave to see where you're workin'. Just in case you don't bring your money 'ome every month, 'e said.'

'Oh, he did, did he?' Essie felt infuriated with herself, boasting after she had been for the job. On Christmas Eve it was, and the place where she was going to work had smelled lovely, the house's large kitchen bustling with festive preparation.

'Five-and-sixpence a month,' she had announced proudly, 'and all found.' She should have said half-a-crown. She kicked the wall now in exasperation. What a fool she had been.

'But yer will come 'ome, won't yer, our Essie?'

'No fear. I'm never coming back there again.'

He was sniffing and snuffling like an old horse. She brought out a square of clean cotton, hemmed round the edges. She had made several with material left over from the white aprons.

She thought back to that never-to-be-forgotten day when

16

she had started school. At the end of morning service the head teacher had seated the small newcomers on the floor of the big room while the rest of the school stood watching. She instructed the little ones to hold up their handkerchiefs for her inspection. The more affluent proudly waved their small squares like Union Jacks, some of them prettily embroidered by fond grannies or sisters who knew the school routine.

No one had warned Essie. She had to stand facing the assembled school as the teacher pinned a large piece of clean rag to her jumper. The other children nudged and sniggered as she was publicly admonished never to forget her handkerchief again. And she never did. She had clutched that first piece of rag to her all night, frightened to go to sleep in case she forgot it next day. She was to feel guilty for the rest of her life if there was no clean hankie in her pocket. Since then she had collected every piece of material she could lay her hands on to make into handkerchiefs.

Sidney was blowing his nose like a trumpet. She waited a few more minutes until he looked better. 'Are you coming, or not?'

'Can we slow down a bit?'

'All right.' They trudged for several minutes in silence.

'When are you going to get yourself a job?' she enquired from the lofty heights of one who is about to be employed.

'When one turns up,' he replied sulkily.

'Jobs don't just turn up, Sidney. You have to go after 'em. Like our Arthur did. Remember how he kept goin' round the pits? He'd wait for hours to see if he could stand in for somebody who hadn't turned up.'

'Oh, ar. I remember our Arthur. I remember the fuss you made when 'e 'opped it to Canada.'

' 'Cos I missed him, that's why. And he didn't just 'op it, as you call it; he went to get more money. He's got guts, 'as our Arthur.'

17

''E couldn't-a missed you, could he? 'Cos 'e ain't cummin' back like Paul Brook 'as. Don't bother about lookin' after you, does 'e?'

'I can look after myself, thank you.'

Sidney continued to drag his feet, sighing and clutching at his side, until suddenly a shot of life was injected into him by a glorious, pungent aroma, wafting on the cold air and serenading his empty stomach.

'What's that smell?' he asked, his sore nose twitching like a rabbit, his short-sighted eyes unable to discern what Essie saw. A wiry little man was pushing an oven on wheels; she could see the coals glowing brightly beneath it.

'It's the hot potato man,' she said.

The thought of warmth of any kind livened Sidney's pace considerably, and they were soon walking alongside the man, luxuriating in the heat emanating from the side of the contraption. The tempting smell of baking potatoes was enough to turn both their stomachs; it seemed a long time since the stewed tea and bite of bread.

The potato man drew up where a side street formed a convenient corner to park his machine. 'It's a sharp 'un today,' he said, stamping his feet and banging his arms across his chest.

Sidney huddled as close as he could to the burning coals.

''Taters ain't quite ready yet,' explained the man. 'Won't be long.' He grinned. 'Yoh can be 'avin' a warm while yer waitin'; looks like yoh could do with one.' He explained he was on his way to get a good position at the fair. 'I've got plenty o' time, though. Doh mind standin' 'ere for a bit. Might catch a customer or two.'

A few people were appearing from side streets, women cleaners and two or three railwaymen. Sidney's face was funereal. He knew that it was very unlikely he would get a potato without the necessary halfpenny. He blew like a trumpet into Essie's handkerchief and looked as if he was about to cry.

Essie dived into her deep pocket and from beneath the neatly folded handkerchiefs brought out one of her silver threepenny bits. 'Here you are, Sidney.'

Her brother's eyes widened as much as his slitty eyes could. 'Where did you get that?'

'Never mind. Buy yourself a couple of potatoes. You could eat one and hold the other under your jacket on the way back to keep you warm.'

He had never known how to smile, but his pale eyes crinkled in gratification. 'Can I keep the tuppence change?'

She nodded, wondering if she would regret her rashness later. 'You needn't come any further. Mellish Road is only just a bit further on and round the corner. Am I right, mister?' she consulted the potato man.

The little man nodded in agreement. 'Posh road, the Mellish.' He assumed a funny swanky voice. 'I am not residing there myself at present.'

'I will be at the second house from the corner,' Essie informed Sidney. 'So you will know where to find me.'

'Got business in Mellish Road, 'ave yer, duck?'

'I start work there today,' Essie stated proudly. 'I'm goin' into service.'

' 'Ow old are yer, then?'

Essie drew herself up to her full height, which wasn't much. 'I was thirteen in December.'

The man calculated the odd little figure in her long black coat, clutching the disreputable-looking bag, and thought, 'Poor little sod.' Big brown eyes stared back at him from a small pale face. All eyes, she was. 'They'll work yer to death, gel. I'd turn back with 'im if I wuz you.'

'No fear!' She recognized the pity in the man's eyes and knew she was tougher than he gave her credit for.

Sidney was still gazing in awe at the threepenny piece,

now in the palm of his purple hand. 'Ain't yoh gunna 'ave a tater, Essie?'

'No time for that.'

'Well, thanks, our kid.' He shuffled awkwardly. 'Ta ra, then.'

'Ta ra, Sidney. You can take it easy on the way back.' He would never find her. The second house round the corner was quite a trek from her destination; the place she was making for stood well back, behind tall trees, away from the main road.

Poor old Sidney. He had to go back to Long Row and their dad. She was never going back. Never.

'Careful 'ow yer go, duck,' the potato man shouted after her. 'And don't let 'em turn yer into a slave.'

She turned and smiled at him. He was surprised at how different she looked when she smiled.

'I'll manage,' she said.

'Am I on time?'

Mrs Vincent's cook-housekeeper cast a startled glance at the strange-looking child in the dracula-type coat. Tufts of short hair sprouting out from her head like surprised straw showed signs of having been cut with a knife and fork by the school nurse. She could guess at the reason, too; they would have to watch out.

She wondered what on earth had possessed her to agree to take the girl on! The bonhomie of Christmas Eve must have blurred her judgement. She had hardly had time to study the girl then anyway; also, just as she was searching for excuses, they *had* heard that the regular daily was to go into hospital at New Year. Then of course there had been that letter of recommendation from the school-marm to Mrs Vincent, who thought the girl should be given a chance. Mrs V. had not seen her, though, had she! What on earth would she think when she did? It must be made absolutely clear to the girl she was on a month's trial, although she doubted whether she would survive as long as that.

She sighed deeply. Nevertheless her voice was kind when at length she replied, 'Yes, you're on time. Just! I expect you would like a mug of cocoa?'

'Ooh, luvley!'

'My name is Mrs Lake.'

'Oh yes?'

'So it's yes please, Mrs Lake.'

'Yes please, Mrs Lake,' repeated Essie with a smile that went right up to her huge brown eyes. She looked quite appealing when she smiled.

'Those your belongings?' That disreputable-looking bag told a story as well!

'Yes, Mrs Lake.'

'Put them down while you have your drink, and hang your coat behind the scullery door.'

Essie sipped her drink, appreciatively, entwining her fingers round the hot mug. She did look happy, conceded Mrs Lake; you could say that for her. What a tiny thing she was without that great coat. The dress fitted a little better, but it was obvious it had not been ironed.

At the same time Essie was studying Mrs Lake, apple-cheeked and round as a pumpkin, with snowy hair piled in a bun on top of her head. Essie liked her. She glanced around the vast kitchen with its huge, coal-fired cooking-stove and an enormous table in the centre of the room, scrubbed white. There were lots of cupboards and shelves and a tall dresser.

'Your name's Essie, isn't it?'

'Yes, Mrs Lake.'.

'And what do you know about scrubbing and polishing, and laying fires, Essie?'

There had been very little scrubbing or polishing in Long Row. Essie hesitated, only for a moment. 'I can do fires,' she said brightly, 'and clean up ashes.'

21

'Clever girl,' sang out a merry voice. 'Let's all pack up and go home.'

A girl of about eighteen bounced in carrying a box of cutlery which she adroitly slid into the dresser. She was smart in a starched white cap and apron over a dark blue dress. Her shiny brown hair was wound around her head in thick plaits, reminding Essie of the gypsies who sometimes parked on Pelsall Common.

'This is Essie,' Mrs Lake explained almost apologetically.

'How are you, Essie? I'm Ivy. Have you come to join the happy band of workers?' Ivy beamed at her from a round, cheerful face.

Essie grinned back. 'Hope so.'

Mrs Lake decided now was the time. 'You do realize you are on a month's trial, Essie?' she asked briskly.

'You mean?'

'That if you don't get things *exactly right* you will have to go,' Mrs Lake stated firmly. Best to get that straight, from the start.

Essie placed the mug on the table, feeling sick in the stomach as the image of a return to Long Row and her dad loomed threateningly, but it lasted for only a moment. She would do anything, anything, rather than go back.

'I'll get it right.' She only meant to think it but she must have said it out loud because Ivy said, 'Of course you will, love.'

'Drink up your cocoa, then, and get started. The hearths must be scrubbed and the grates cleaned before you lay the fires. The fires on this floor have to be lit before the family are up. But remember, wait until the bedrooms are vacated before you lay the fires upstairs. Ivy will put you right.'

Mrs Lake produced an elasticated black cap to cover her hair, while Essie foraged in her bag for the long black apron. Ivy pointed out the drawing room, morning room, dining room, study and library. Essie had never imagined such big

22

fireplaces, or that folk had fires in bedrooms; much less that there could be eight fireplaces for attention in one house – and every one as dead as a doornail. These people had evidently never heard of rakers.

But she cried out in surprised delight when she discovered that she only had to turn on a brass tap in the scullery for hot water to gush from a huge wall tank. After scrubbing the hearths she put every bit of strength she had into polishing the brasses and fenders; she must get everything *exactly right.*

Mrs Lake, inspecting her downstairs fires, seemed pleasantly surprised, but she was cautious in her praise. 'A very good try,' she said. 'But you must try and not get covered in ashes.'

There were three bedroom fires to lay; they were to be lit just before supper. The rooms were furnished with grand furniture, highly polished. Ivy said the room with the two narrow beds, lots of toys and a sturdy brass fireplace belonged to Mrs V.'s two little lads; the long bedroom was still catering for Christmas guests, and the pretty room that smelled lovely belonged to Mrs V.

'Is there a Mr Vee?' Essie enquired, misconstruing the letter V for the name of her employer.

'I'll say! He's in the army. He went back from Christmas leave yesterday.' Ivy rolled her round hazel eyes expressively. 'Thank God!'

Before Essie could ask why, she had hurried away. As Essie sat on her heels before her last firegrate she wondered where she would be sleeping that night.

At last she was about to find out.

With her coat and bag slung over her arm she followed Ivy up some narrow backstairs. It had been a long day. She had scrubbed floors, prepared vegetables, cleaned windows, tidied cupboards, all with a vigour and determination that had finally drenched her in weariness. Her legs ached and the

23

stairs seemed endless. How was she to know that they were leading up to heaven? At last Ivy pushed open a door, handed her a candle she had been carrying and said, 'This is your room.'

Open-mouthed with astonishment Essie was not conscious of the coat and bag slipping to the floor. 'A room of my own! All to myself?'

Disbelief, mingled with a yearning for it to be true, created such agony in her chest she thought she would burst. She was never to forget the thrill of that moment.

Ivy, an only child, who had all her life taken a room of her own for granted, was startled by the starry-eyed excitement in the new girl's face. Was it possible she was going into a trance like the woman in the spiritualist chapel?

She watched, bemused, as Essie wandered around the room, speechless, incredulously fingering the little three-drawer chest, gently exploring the shelf with its china figures, marvelling at the pink jug and bowl on the wash-stand, peeping curiously behind curtains that disguised a hanging space in the corner. She ran her hand along the bed-stead, across the back of the pink bedroom chair, along the tiny bedside table. She stroked the artificial carnations. It was as if she must touch everything to be certain it was not all a figment of her imagination.

'I made the flowers for you on my afternoon off.'

Essie sank into the chair and Ivy perched on the bed.

'Oh, Ivy, it's like a dream.'

'My room's much the same, except that it is blue. There's just you and me up here. We're in the roof. That's why the ceiling slants a bit.'

Essie hadn't noticed. 'It's all luvely,' she breathed.

'Mrs V. likes her maids to be comfortable. By the way, don't let Mrs Lake frighten you. She has a heart of gold really. But she does like things to be just right. It's nigh impossible; there are so few of us now.

'When I first came there were maids for upstairs, maids for downstairs, a maid for waiting at table, a kitchen maid, a part-time sewing hand, and a nanny. They've all gone, one by one.'

'Why?'

Ivy lowered her voice to a whisper, although Essie felt that, with all the stairs they had climbed, they must be miles out of earshot. 'I don't think Mrs V. can afford any more staff these days.'

'But she must be rich to own this house.'

'Well, that's my opinion anyway. Because now it's just down to you, me, Mrs Lake and Joe.'

Essie had met Mrs Lake's husband, Joe, when they all supped their evening cocoa together. He was the gardener-handyman. He was a tall man, a bit round-shouldered, with a pleasant weather-beaten face, thinning hair and a nice smile; he had winked at her over the top of his mug.

'Where do Mrs Lake and Joe sleep?'

'They have the housekeeper's flat on the ground floor, on this side of the house.'

Ivy turned to leave. 'I had better be off now.' She picked up Essie's bag and coat and placed them on the bed. 'I shall be just across the landing should you need anything.'

Her chubby face broke into a big smile. 'You made a good start today, Essie. You'll be all right. I'll help you.' She put her arms round Essie and gave her a hug. No one had ever hugged Essie before and she could have wept with joy. But she never wept, so she just grinned back at Ivy.

'It will be nice to have someone up here in the 'gods' with me. It's been a bit lonely at times. Now don't sit up too late mooning about the room. We have to be up bright and early in the morning.' She indicated an alarm clock which was ticking away companionably. 'I wound up your clock and put the alarm on for five-thirty. I filled your water jug too. Just for tonight, as it's your first.'

'You are good. Thank you, Ivy.'

'All part of the service,' Ivy smiled. ' 'Night, Essie.'

' 'Night, Ivy. Thank you, Ivy.'

Essie, still trembling with excitement, inspected the room again after Ivy had left. She ran her hand disbelievingly along the shiny walnut lowboy, pulling out each drawer, one by one, noting the clean white lining-paper in each; she supposed she had Ivy to thank for that too. Behind the prettily-sprigged curtain in the corner she found a shelf; a hanging rail and some brass hooks fixed to the wall.

She sighed in deep content. What a lot had happened today. She had stepped into a new world inhabited by kind people, and for the first time in her life she felt really clean, for, before their bedtime cocoa, Ivy had unhooked a large tin bath from the scullery wall and placed it beneath the hot water tank.

'Bath night tonight, Essie,' she sang out in her cheery voice. 'We have a bath in here once a week and it's tonight. You can go first. There's a hose on the cold tap over the sink and you can use as much of the hot water from the gas tank as you like.'

Essie had felt almost too tired to bother, but soon she was revelling in the luxury of her first bath. She rubbed at her skin with a large cake of yellow soap until it glowed. And she was able to wash her hair in *hot* water.

Always before she had had to wash it under the cold water tap in the big yard. The school nurse had never understood why she could not get rid of the nits. How could she know she had to use the same comb as Clara, who, since she left school, had not bothered whether she had nits or not.

Essie shuddered as she remembered the humiliation she had suffered time and time again when she had to wear the dreaded linen cap in class and sit well away from everyone else. There had never been enough soap in their house to wash out the awful stuff the nurse plastered on her unfor-

26

tunate head. At last, in desperation, Nurse had cut off nearly all her hair, and one day she said, 'I think we have won the battle, Essie.'

Now she would be able to wash her hair every week in *hot* water. And she had her very own new lavender comb.

She bounced from the chair suddenly, all tiredness forgotten in her eagerness to unpack her belongings. They would have all fitted quite easily into one drawer but she enjoyed the luxury of spreading them out. Her coat she hung on a hook behind the curtain. The white aprons and caps went into the top drawer, the precious blue blouse and skirt into the middle one, and everything else into the bottom, her black aprons, her handkerchiefs and spare nightdress; the other she placed on the bed. It looked grubby against the snowy-white linen sheets and pillow.

All the time she was unpacking she was expecting to come across her new comb. She turned the bag upside down and shook it frantically. Nothing!

Gooseflesh crept along the skin that had been warm and glowing from her bath as she realized what she had done. She remembered taking the comb out of the bag to try it this morning before she left, enjoying the luxury of using it for the first time. Her lovely lavender comb, left behind for Clara and Sidney to use. Her dad, too! That prospect made her feel sick.

She stood on the chair so that she could see herself through the small round wall-mirror hung high above the set of drawers. Panic-stricken eyes in a pale, pointed face gazed miserably back at her. Hair, tufted and knotted as it always was after a wash, stuck out wildly from her scalp. She tried to separate it with her fingers but that only made it worse.

She climbed down dejectedly, her knees weak. It was all spoiled. The lovely room. Everything. How could she face

27

Mrs Lake in the morning looking like this? She might be given her marching orders on the spot! Where would she go? Not to Long Row; she couldn't bear the humiliation. But where? Her head was spinning with the uncertainty of it all.

Then she remembered Ivy saying, 'If you need any-thing . . . ', and a glimmer of hope stirred. But Ivy might be fast asleep by now. She dithered on the landing before summoning up enough courage to knock on her door prior to opening it quietly, as she had been taught at school.

Ivy was seated in front of her mirror, which was hung lower than Essie's. She was brushing her hair. It was loose now and hung to her waist, thick and shiny and springy, billowing out with every stroke of the brush. She appeared to be counting and did not notice Essie immediately. When she became aware of her quiet scrutiny she dropped the hairbrush in astonishment.

'What on earth is the matter?'

She had left her in seventh heaven fifteen minutes ago. Now she was shaking like a leaf and her lip trembled as she explained. 'I forgot my comb.'

Ivy burst into peals of laughter, while Essie stood down-cast, biting the trembling lip. 'I thought at least you had been burgled. Here, take your choice.'

She opened her top drawer. Neatly arranged were boxes of hairpins, several hair ribbons, a box with beautifully-embroidered handkerchiefs, two pairs of gloves, two white collars and four combs. *Four combs!*

'Which one would you like, Essie?'

'Oh, you say.'

'Well, the little red one fits nicely into my purse. And the white one's my best. How about the pink one? Or the black?'

'The pink one, please,' Essie stated hastily. The black would contain too many memories of a mantelpiece in Long

Row. 'I'll buy one and let you have yours back, Ivy.'
Thank heaven for the threepenny bits.

'No need. Really. I have some more at home.'

'Oh, thank you, Ivy. I'll never forget it. Never,' gasped
Essie, dizzy with relief.

'You are a funny little thing, Essie.' Ivy closed the drawer
and continued brushing her hair. 'Fancy getting so worked
up about a comb!'

How could someone with more than *four combs* possibly
understand, thought Essie. 'I wish my hair was like yours,'
she said.

'You should brush it, Essie. Every night. A hundred
strokes. It would help it to grow, and make it shine.'

'Would I be able to buy a brush for ninepence?'

'I would think so.' Ivy tied her hair back with a blue
ribbon. 'I would brush yours for you now but . . . ' She
flushed suddenly. She couldn't say that. Poor kid!

Remnants of shame made Essie blush too. 'It's all right,'
she stated quietly. 'We got rid of the nits. My hair's clean
now.'

'Oh, come on, then,' Ivy said kindly. 'Not a hundred
strokes tonight, though. I'm too tired. Here, sit in my
chair.'

She brushed the short mop vigorously for a few minutes
until all the knots were out, shaping it with the hairbrush
round Essie's small face. 'You will have pretty hair if you
look after it. It's a lovely colour.'

Essie, watching the process in the mirror, could hardly
believe the difference a few strokes could make.

'You are kind to me, Ivy.'

'That's what friends are for. Go and get some sleep now.'

A friend! Essie returned to her own room, glowing again.
Her own room. Her own friend!

What a beautiful white nightie Ivy had been wearing; it
made her own appear even dingier by comparison. But as

29

she snuggled between the crisp sheets and clean blankets her spirits soared. She did not need the black coat on the bed tonight. No more of her dad touching her in ways she did not like. There were things about her dad she could not have told anyone. Things that made her blush with shame.

She could see the outlines of the furniture from the faint glow of the moon. She could smell the candle she had just blown out. She could feel the freshness of her bed. But she could hear nothing except the ticking of the clock. No snufflings, no whimperings, no curses or bangings from the next bed.

Marvellous magical silence!

It was all so wonderful. Being in service was wonderful. Her sister Clara did not know what she was missing. Essie closed her eyes with a sigh of contentment. Long Row was a thousand miles away. She must get everything exactly right so that she could stay here for ever.

Chapter Two

Few shoppers looked as radiant as Essie on the cold January day she first thrilled to the sights and sounds of Walsall market, its fascinating array of stalls snaking from the centre of town to the top of Market Hill where the parish church presided over the town.

She was wearing her new blouse and skirt for the first time, and felt wonderful. Ivy had lent her a belt to pull in the tent-like coat, Joe had shown her how to polish her shoes until they shone like new, and never had she felt so fit, so clean or so confident. There were so many things here she would like to buy, but she must budget her ninepence carefully.

She lingered at every stall, pausing to admire the Staffordshire pottery, the linen stall with its mountains of sheets and tablecloths, the tiered displays of greengroceries, the mishmash of pots and pans and the dazzling array of dress materials. She stayed for some considerable time, gazing down at a square of lino on the ground, overflowing exuberantly with a variety of buttons, cottons, velvet squares, curtain remnants, elastic, tapes, laces, safety-pins, pots of ointment – and what was that, in the centre of the display? A hairbrush!

Last night she had washed her hair again, this time making a lather in an old basin, as Ivy had advised, rather than rubbing the soap directly on her hair. Ivy had let her use her hairbrush and it had worked wonders. Essie reached across the jumble of items to pick up the hairbrush; it just fit into the palm of her hand.

The man in charge of the lino square called over to her. 'Best bristle. Only sixpence to you, love.' Essie took one last lingering look before replacing it on the ground. 'Yer won't gerrit cheaper anywhere else,' the man shouted to her retreating back.

She would have loved to have bought it. Just as she would have loved to buy books from the second-hand book stall. She had a passion for books. The teacher had read *A Christmas Carol* to them just before she left school. Here were some books by the same author, *Oliver Twist* and *The Old Curiosity Shop*. Essie had read the latter, bit by bit, in Library time at school. Some of the pupils had been allowed to take books home, but not Essie, even though she was the best reader in the class. That had been her dad's fault. As a reward for getting her head clean she had been lent a lovely book called *Black Beauty*.

'What's this?' her dad had bellowed.

He had caught her trying to catch a few minutes' read in between ironing his shirts, while the black smoothing iron heated over the coals in the grate. He swayed toward her menacingly, his eyes wild, his hair unkempt, his buttonless shirt revealing masses of black hair. 'What do y'er think y'er doin'?'

'Just reading, Dad.'

'Reading!' A page of the open book tore as he snatched it away from her.

Essie cried out, panic about the book giving her sufficient courage to protest. 'Oh, please! Don't tear it!' Whatever would the head teacher say tomorrow?

The book hit her head with a terrible force.

'Don't tear it. Don't tear it,' he mimicked cruelly. 'Tellin' me what to do now, are yer?' He aimed another blow at her head before deliberately tearing out a couple of pages and dropping them on to the black iron, where they smouldered away slowly, curling into charred scrolls, tighter and tighter, like Essie's heart.

Her dad held the book over the fire, threatening to burn that too, enjoying tormenting her. Automatically she said the only thing that might have any effect. 'You will have to pay for it.' At that he hit her again with the book, now hot from the fire, before throwing it at the wall in disgust.

'Don't bring such rubbish 'ere again,' he screamed. 'Get on with my shirt.'

Next morning he accompanied her, deliberately late, to school, marching her by the ear into the Head's classroom without so much as knocking the door. To Essie's everlasting mortification, in front of sniggering classmates he bawled, 'Don't let 'er bring any more 'o these time wasters. We got two books in our 'ouse already.' The books he referred to were a family bible which propped up one corner of his bed, and a dog-eared Sunday school prize with a dirty cover, once awarded to her mother. It was called *To School and Adventure*. Essie had read it several times, surreptitiously, beneath the bedclothes.

The head teacher looked her father up and down with considerable disdain, not even deigning to reply, causing Essie's cheeks to burn with embarrassment.

Her father blundered on, shouting, 'Ask 'er about the couple o' pages 'er ripped out and burned.'

A pin dropping would have seemed thunderous in the silence after he departed, every pupil holding his or her breath. And none so much as Essie herself.

'You may sit down, Essie,' was all the head teacher said before continuing with the lesson. At break she was told to remain behind. Her hands shook as she placed her writing on the little shelf beneath her desk, wondering what was going to happen now. Every nerve in her body was tensed as she was called to the teacher's desk. She could hardly believe her own ears when she heard the teacher talking kindly, suggesting she might like to stay in and read during break.

'Every day?' Essie breathed.

'If you want to,' the teacher smiled.

Essie murmured her grateful thankyous, overcome with relief. Someone trusted her enough to disbelieve her father! She would work doubly hard for this teacher, and made up her mind there and then never to go out at play-time again.

So eager was she to read as much as she could in the fifteen-minute breaks she soon became the fastest reader in the school.

Now, here in the market, were books galore and she could not afford them. But she would. She would.

Essie managed to push through the crowd of women who were sorting out bargains in the eager way she had seen them rummage through Mary Ann's bundles at the shop in Cod End. She joined them, and frantically turned over a mound of children's liberty bodices, men's ganzies and shirts, women's corsets and hats without any success.

'What yer after, duck?'

'Have you any, er, knickers?'

The stallholder dived under a pile of outsize combinations and waved two pairs at her, one pale blue and one navy, like the ones she was wearing. 'For yerself, are they, duck?'

Essie nodded.

'Just yer size. The blue, do yer think?'

Essie hesitated. 'They look a bit big.'

'Just right, they'll be, luv,' the woman laughed. 'Keep 'er knees warm, won't they?' she shouted to the crowd.

' 'Er tits an' all, I should think,' called one woman to raucous shouts of laughter from her companions.

Essie would have liked the pale blue but they would have fitted Mrs Lake. 'How much are the navy?'

She could hardly believe her ears when the woman replied, 'Tuppence to you, duck. 'Ere, catch.'

Essie caught them with a grin, stuffed them into her pocket, handed over a threepenny bit and received a penny change. She still had sevenpence left! She hastily retraced her steps towards the hairbrush. Oh, please let it be there still. Oh please! Why hadn't she bought it before? But how was she to know she would get a pair of knickers for tuppence? The knickers demanded top priority as each week they had to put their laundry into a laundry basket for it to be pounded in the dolly tub, and tomorrow was the day. She knew she would be the one to do the pounding but was equally sure that Mrs Lake would check the contents of the basket carefully beforehand.

She began to despair of ever finding the square of lino with the hairbrush until a voice called to her above the heads of the people examining the oddments. 'Ah, I knew you'd come back, gel. Couldn't find anythin' cheaper, could yer?' The stallholder reached for the brush and handed it to her, above the bent heads of the crowd.

Nothing could embarrass her today. She smiled happily at the man and handed over her sixpence. He was quite taken by the large, sparkling eyes. 'Why ain't yer at school?'

'I'm workin'. It's my afternoon off.'

'A workin' gel! Well! See yer next week, then, duck.'

But it would be no use coming next week. She would have to wait until she had worked a month before she could have any more money to spend. She could always come to look, of course; to size up what she would buy when she had the cash. Yes, that is what she would do.

Who would have thought that those threepenny bits from Mary Ann would have gone so far, and she still had a penny!

As she was about to leave she saw some packets of ginger snaps, all curly and golden; she bought a packet to take back for Ivy. Ivy had been so good to her. Not only had she introduced her to the merits of the hairbrush, but had insisted on making her a present of a toothbrush, something that Essie had never considered before. Since then she had treated her teeth to a hundred strokes each night, in her desire to have teeth as pearly as her new friend.

'Are you looking forward to going home on your day off?' Ivy had enquired one day, her eyes widening in amazement when Essie replied, 'I'm not going home.'

'Don't you think about your family a lot?'

'I don't think about them at all.'

Ivy's eyes became even rounder. 'I can't wait for my afternoons off,' she confided.

'Do you go home every week?'

'I'll say! Couldn't exist for more than a week without seeing my mam.'

As Essie made her way back to Mellish Road she thought about that. How differently Ivy must feel toward her mother than she felt toward hers.

What a lot had happened in a short time. Mrs Lake had kept her at it constantly. But it had all been worth while. Essie had watched and listened and learned a lot already, and she hadn't been hungry for a week. Always there was Mrs Lake's cooking to look forward to, succulent meals such as she had never tasted before, to give her new strength.

Sometimes she could hardly manage to drag her feet up the long winding staircase at night. But one look at her room justly rewarded her for all her efforts. She could not bear the thought of losing this job. It opened up a whole new world to her.

It had not been quite true when she told Ivy she did not think about her family, because each night when she sat in her precious room she compared it with the house in Long

Row. Ivy, Mrs Lake and Joe she compared with her sister and brother, her apathetic mother and her bullying dad. And when she had washed herself in unrationed warm water she had brought upstairs in the pretty pink jug, she snuggled between the sheets and prayed out loud, like they did in School Assembly. Her prayer was only slightly different.

'Please, God, help me to do everything *exactly* right. So that I don't have to leave at the end of the month.'

So it was with quaking heart that she heard Mrs Lake call to her from the kitchen immediately she entered the scullery, after her visit to the market.

'Essie! There you are! Slip upstairs straight away and tidy up. Mrs V. wants to see you.'

Essie had not met her mistress yet. Why had she sent for her? What could she have done wrong? Alarm riveted her to the spot until Mrs Lake's pumpkin figure appeared in the doorway. 'Get a move on, girl,' she said impatiently.

'Yes, Mrs Lake. Where will she be?'

'*Your mistress* is in the library. Let's have a look at you.' She considered her critically. 'Just slip up to your room and brush your hair. Wash your hands and face and wear one of your white aprons.'

In trepidation Essie gently tapped on the door of the library, her face flushed from the exertion of running up and downstairs in double-quick time. She was glad she was wearing her new blouse and skirt beneath the white apron.

The lady working at the desk turned round immediately Essie entered. Essie gaped in amazement. She had never seen such a vision of loveliness. Beautiful, violet eyes shone compassionately from a perfect, pink and white oval face. Dark wavy hair, neatly caught into two bunches, was tied with lavender ribbons that matched her dress. Lavender, the exact colour of the comb Essie had left behind at Long Row. As she moved forward Essie recognized the perfume she caught a whiff of every time she attended to the fire in her mistress's bedroom.

She took Essie's hand in both her own, which were soft and smooth. 'At last we meet, Essie. Do sit down.' Her face broke into a lovely smile. Essie had never imagined a mother of two boys could look so young. 'I am so sorry I haven't been able to welcome you sooner. My Christmas visitors did not leave until today.'

Essie was tongue-tied. This elegant lady apologizing to her!

'How are you settling in, Essie?'

Essie's heart was beating an anxious tattoo in her throat. What if she was about to get her marching orders? She must speak up. 'I am trying very hard.'

'So Mrs Lake tells me. She is very pleased with you.'

Amazement showed in Essie's face.

'It is your afternoon off, isn't it?'

'Yes, Mrs Vee.'

The enchanting face dimpled as she laughed involuntarily.

'Have I said something wrong?'

'No, Essie. No.' But it was obvious she was amused about something. 'What did you do this afternoon?'

'I went to the market.'

'Did you see anything interesting?'

'Oh yes!' Essie's face shone with enthusiasm as she remembered. 'Lots of things.' She forgot her anxiety. Her employer caught first sight of the real Essie as she described the various stalls, the noises and the smells. 'There was a second-hand bookstall,' she ended nostalgically.

'You like books?'

'Oh yes!'

'Did you buy one?'

'No. But I shall when I have my first wages.'

'What will you buy, Essie?'

'If it is still there, *Oliver Twist*.'

'Meanwhile, my dear, you shall borrow it.'

Essie had been so intent examining the gorgeous face in front of her she had quite forgotten the rows and rows of bookshelves all around them. Mrs Vee quickly found what she was looking for, and in a moment a beautiful leather-bound copy of *Oliver Twist* lay in her hands.

Essie gasped. 'You mean? I can take this to my room?'

'Of course. Keep it until you have read it, Essie; then return it to me.'

Essie, open mouthed in wonder, handled the lovely volume as if it were the crown jewels.

'When will you find time to read it?'

'On my afternoons off.'

'You'll not go home?'

Essie shook her head determinedly. 'No.'

'Well, let me know what you think of it. I hope you will be happy with us, Essie.'

'But I will. I *am*.' Two huge eyes overflowed with gratitude as Essie floated on a cloud toward the door. She paused and turned, remembering the manners that had been hammered into her at school. 'Thank you. Thank you very much for the book; I'll take care of it, Mrs Vee.'

Once again the lovely face broke into an amused smile, but this time she did not laugh. 'If ever you are worried, or in any sort of trouble, don't hesitate, come and see me, Essie,' she told her gently.

Essie caught her breath. How could there be people like this in the world and she never knew?

It was a few days later before Essie knew the reason for the amusement. She was once again in the library. Ivy was dusting the tops of the bookcases from a tall ladder while Essie gently smoothed a clean duster over the bottom row of book covers in the way Ivy had shown her. It was a lovely job because she could read the titles, smell the leather and feel the embossed gold lettering beneath the thin duster. So engrossed was she that she was not even aware that her mistress had entered the room and selected a book until she was on her way out.

'Enjoying that job, Essie?'

'Yes, Mrs Vee,' she replied cheerfully.

Ivy, perched on top of the ladder, found the duster in her hand frozen in mid-air. 'Essie! What did you call Mrs Vincent?' she whispered in a horrified tone as soon as the door closed.

'Mrs Vee, you mean?'

'That's awful bad form, Essie.'

'Why? What's wrong?'

'Well, it's like calling Mrs Lake Mrs L. The balloon would go up with a bang, wouldn't it?'

'You mean? You mean that she's not Mrs Vee?'

'V is just her initial. Her name is Mrs Vincent.'

'But you all call her . . . '

'Between ourselves, yes. But never, never, to her face. It's . . . Well, it's so rude, Essie.'

The alarm in Ivy's round eyes transferred itself to the pit of Essie's stomach. It travelled up her spine in a wave of sickly embarrassment. It stuck in her throat, making it as dry as the dust they were shifting. The thought of being rude to the lovely lady who had been so wonderful to her made her feel physically ill.

'Why didn't somebody tell me?'

'We all assumed you knew the name of your employer, Essie.' This time Ivy did not laugh away Essie's anxiety.

Essie put down her duster and made toward the door. 'I must go and see her.'

Wait!' Ivy slid down the ladder, her round face unusually serious. 'You can't do that. Not without being sent for.'

'But she's not going to send for me, is she? And she told me I was to go to her if I was worried about anything.'

'You must get permission from Mrs Lake first.'

'Oh, please don't tell Mrs Lake. Say you won't, Ivy, please.'

'Well, all right, if you don't want me to. But you can't go barging in to see Mrs Vincent any old time. You can't Essie! It isn't allowed.'

'You will be taking afternoon tea in soon, won't you?' Ivy nodded. 'Let me take it instead. Oh, Ivy, please!'

'You! Essie, I can't. I was here a year before I was allowed to do it. Mrs Lake would kill me.'

'She often has an afternoon nap, you know she does. If she says anything you can tell her you are teaching me what to do, in case you are ever away.'

'What shall you say to Mrs Vincent?'

'I shall apologize for using the wrong name, of course.'

Ivy lost the worried frown and her usual smile creased her homely face. 'You've got a cheek, I must say, madam. But quite a bit of pluck to go with it.'

So it was Essie, with scrubbed face and hands, and crisp white cap and apron, starched as Mrs Lake had shown her how, who carried in the tray with its silver pot and jug, its blue china cup and saucer and its plate of home-made biscuits, while Ivy hovered anxiously in the hall.

'What did she say?' she asked as Essie emerged, flushed and smiling.

'She just laughed and said she rather liked being called Mrs Vee. She asked me to continue to do so.'

Ivy's rosy mouth rounded into the shape of her surprised eyes. 'Well I never! All I can say is, don't let Mrs Lake hear you.' And later, 'Mrs V. must have really taken to you.'

All Essie could think of was that she would never ever be scared of Mrs Vee. She was the most wonderful person she had ever met and she was going to work even harder, if that was possible. If Mrs Vee could not afford to take on more servants then Essie would do the work of two.

She kept to her resolution. Mrs Lake had never had a scullery maid so eager to learn, nor so quick on the uptake. She never seemed to mind the early mornings, nor the long hours. She asked countless questions and remembered the answers. She was always quizzing Joe about his gardening. Whenever she had a spare moment she helped him. She loved the garden, never having been in one before, and Joe said she was more help than a garden boy.

Mrs Lake became quite fond of her young charge. Under her expert eye Essie learned how to make first-class Yorkshire pudding, how to make sure that a cake never sank in the middle, how to roast, boil and steam meat, the odours and flavours of which were a recurring discovery. She learned how to stuff poultry, how to recognize that fish was fresh, how to make soup from left-overs.

Not that there were ever any left-overs as far as Essie was concerned; she ate everything put in front of her with a relish and gratitude that did Mrs Lake's heart good. The stews she ate now could not have been more different from the handful of highly-salted potatoes, carrots and swedes thrown together and boiled on the hob at Long Row, although that was a rare treat at the time.

And to Mrs Lake's satisfaction the effects of good food showed. Essie's face and body began to gently fill out. No longer did she have that awful grey look. In fact, after an hour or two gardening with Joe her skin positively glowed, and although she did not chuckle in the uninhibited way of Ivy, she had a wry turn of humour and a nice smile. Mrs Lake counted herself lucky to have two such good girls in a house that was as hopelessly short-staffed as the Vincents'.

The housekeeper thought it strange that Essie never wanted to go home to see her mother. She was content to spend her free time helping Joe, browsing round Walsall market, or reading. Mrs Lake had never known such a girl for reading. Even the *Book of Household Management* came down from the high shelf in the kitchen.

Essie was well into another Dickens novel kindly lent by the mistress, and as Mrs Lake told Joe later, she had never seen anyone looking so thrilled as on the day Essie came back from the market clutching a battered copy of *Moonfleet*, bought from her second month's salary, along with a pair of black stockings and a second-hand coat knitted in a pretty shade of lavender. It was obvious that it was the book that had put the sparkle in her eyes, the first book she had ever owned.

Mrs Lake was pleased that Ivy had taken the younger girl under her wing, and one week, when Mrs Vincent took the two boys to London to meet the master there for a few days, she allowed the two maids to take the whole day off together so that Ivy could take Essie to her home.

Ivy's mam was an older version of Ivy, with the same round hazel eyes in a dimpled face, the same sunny disposition. In spite of it being a crisp March morning she was standing at the gate, looking out for them, and came forward to greet them as soon as they appeared into the lane. 'So this is Essie,' she called warmly before she reached them. 'Hello, love. Ivy talks about you such a lot.'

She linked arms with them both until they were inside the cosy house. 'Make yourself at home, Essie. Kettle's boiling. We'll soon have a cup of tea. Ivy, take Essie's coat.' She took a knitted kettle-holder from a hook near the fireplace and poured boiling water from a singing kettle into a brown pot warming on the hob.

Ivy held Essie's enormous black coat aloft for her mother's inspection. 'This is the coat we are hoping you will alter, Mam.'

'Yes, of course, if Essie would like that. Would you, Essie?'

Essie grinned. 'It is a big big.'

Ivy had told her how clever her mam was with a

43

sewing-machine. She earned money from sewing, but would do Essie's without charge.

'Pop the coat into the sewing room, love,' she said to Ivy. 'I'll take a look later.'

The room they were in was a testimony to her skill. There was a wealth of crocheted mats, with pretty pansies round the edges, standing up as if they were growing. There were gaily-covered chairs, a tapestry-topped footstool, a beautifully-embroidered tea cosy and a partly-knitted pair of socks lying on a little corner table.

All three of them sat in a comradely fashion round the fire, sipping their drinks. 'What shift is Dad on?' Ivy enquired. Her dad worked on the railway.

'Earlies. He will be here midday. Now! What's all the news from Mellish, love?'

Essie sat bemused, listening in amazement as they exchanged news and confidences. She had not known such closeness could exist between mother and daughter.

Ivy explained how they had started spring-cleaning yesterday after the mistress had left with the boys for London. Then she confided how the lad who brought the eggs from the farm had asked her out. Her mam said it wouldn't hurt to go once, to see what he was like. She was only eighteen when she had first gone out with Ivy's father, and look how well that had turned out, she said.

Did marriages ever turn out well, Essie wondered. She supposed that Mrs Lake and Joe got by, but even so Mrs Lake seemed to boss Joe about a lot. That had been a revelation to Essie; she thought it was always the other way round.

The room they were in was not much bigger than the downstairs room at Long Row, but this was so different, with its lovingly-polished wooden floor, its colourful pegged rug on the hearth and a crisp white tablecloth, beautifully embroidered round the edges.

In a recess formed by the chimney were shelves filled with books. 'I can see you're itching to get your nose into those,' Ivy chuckled. 'They're Dad's travel books. He says when he's spent a couple of hours with one of those it's as good as visiting the countries.'

'Help yourself, Essie,' invited Ivy's mam kindly, 'while I go and unpick your coat.'

'And I'll go and prepare the meal.'

Essie's offer of help was brushed aside by Ivy. 'You have a rest while you can. This is the first time since you started work that I've seen you relax.'

Tucked inside a book about Canada was a folded map. After a diligent search Essie found Moosejaw, the place where Arthur lived. Arthur had been the only one who had meant anything to her. None of the others missed him like she did. They were only interested in the money he sent home, she mused, which led her to think of Sidney. She wondered if he had been looking for her to take her money to their dad. She could not help a little mischievous grin as she settled down to read about Arthur's Canada.

She was deep into the prairies where Arthur was working when she heard a man's voice rumbling from the kitchen. Essie felt a little apprehensive. Fathers, in her experience, were not much cop.

Yet, earlier, Ivy had described how her dad used to take her out for trips along the canal in a boat lent by one of his workmates. And how, sometimes, just the two of them would cycle round the country lanes. Essie wished there was just one nice thing she could remember about her own dad. She tried but all she could recall was disappointment and fear. One occasion in particular stood out in her mind.

It had been nearly dusk as Essie had slipped out of the house at Long Row that early October evening. She could hear excited screams and shouts as hopscotch slates slid along the chalk-marked numbers on the blackened bricks of the butcher's yard.

Essie was immediately accepted into the game. She liked the gloom of evening, when dirty knees, tatty shoes and knicker legs which fell down without elastic were less noticeable. Not that it ever mattered here. Cod End kids were never snooty toward each other in their own domain. It was only when they were dressed up for school or chapel that some of them took on a few temporary airs and graces.

They had formed two teams for hopscotch. Albert Arrowsmith, who was good at sums, was chalking up the scores on the wall of the abattoir. Both team leaders squabbled about who was to have Essie, for she was a worthy hopscotch player, being wiry and nimble. The idea was to get round the hopscotch squares with as few hops as possible, so it was the team with the least points that won.

Albert decided that it should be Aileen Eldridge's team to claim the new member, as they were hampered by Aileen's five-year-old brother and his pal among their hoppers. After a few goes Essie soon reduced the number of hops for Aileen's team. She and Aileen stood talking companionably while someone else had a turn.

Aileen was excited about the fair coming to The Common the next night. 'Shall you be comin', Essie?'

'Don't 'spect so.' Essie kept her voice casual.

'Why not? There ain't any babbies to mind in your 'ouse, are there?'

'No, but . . . ' Essie bit her lip.

'If yer ain't got any money, Essie, you can 'ave one o' my halfpennies to come on the swing-boats with me. We'll get it goin' high, you and me.'

Essie looked up into Aileen's eager face gratefully. She was flushed with the success of bringing Aileen's hopscotch team in sight of victory. And now a chance for the swingboats! She permitted herself to hope. 'I'll 'ave to ask me Dad.'

As she said it a heavy hand fell on her shoulder and the gruff voice of Caleb Connor sounded close to her ear. 'And why didn't yer ask yer Dad about comin' out tonight, eh? Instead o' creeping out without a word.' He shook her violently.

The hopscotchers stopped their hopping and stood looking on helplessly as Essie's dad grabbed her ear and spun her round to face him. They all feared Essie's dad's temper almost as much as she did.

'Yer comin' 'ome with me.' He sensed the nervousness of the crowd of youngsters and it boosted his ego no end. He gazed round at them all contemptuously before bringing his face down beside Aileen's, who immediately shrank away with a little cry. 'I'll say when 'er can go out,' he spat. 'And it ain't tonight, nor tomorrow night. I'll see to that.'

He dragged Essie away from what just minutes before had been such a merry band of players, now standing silently with ashen faces. Essie was scared out of her wits. She knew her mam was out visiting a relative in the sanatorium, and her sister and brother had been sent on errands. She dreaded going back with him to an empty house.

She protested loudly all the way home. Mothers who appeared on their doorsteps to see what all the commotion was about merely tut-tutted and remarked what a naughty girl that young Connor could be; she played up whenever her dad fetched her in.

How could they guess what was in store for her?

Essie shook her head at the painful memory. Even brief moments of pleasure such as hopscotch glory and anticipation of a swingboat ride could be terminated so swiftly and spitefully by the appearance of her father.

No, there was not one nice thing she could remember about him.

47

She was brought back to earth by Ivy's mother calling her into the sewing room. Across a tiny dividing passage was a room with a treadle sewing-machine beneath the window, a tall mirror on a stand in the corner, and a work-table in the centre. On the table lay the unpicked pieces of her black coat.

'We can make a lovely coat out of this, Essie,' Ivy's mam enthused. 'It's good quality material.' She ran a tape round Essie in several places and measured from neck to hem.

'Can I watch?'

'Of course, if you want to, love.'

'I was never very good at sewing at school.'

Secretly she was longing to get back to the travel book but she never allowed a chance to learn anything pass her by. It was fascinating to see how swiftly Ivy's mam worked. She cut paper patterns from thin brown paper, occasionally fitting them against Essie; she pinned the pieces to the black material, and finally hacked away confidently with huge scissors.

'I expect you are puzzling what to call me,' she observed with a smile.

'Yes; I don't know Ivy's surname.'

'Call me Mabel. And my better half's George.'

'Don't you mind?'

'Of course not. More friendly than Mister and Missus.'

She chatted away as she worked, telling Essie how, when she was employed as dressmaker at the home of a very distinguished gentleman, she made all the clothes for his wife and five daughters.

The tacked pieces were soon being fitted on to Essie, inside out. She could not help wondering whether the coat would end up looking better or worse than before; it looked so odd.

'Don't worry, love,' Mabel smiled reassuringly. 'It will be all right. I am going to start machining now until Ivy calls us for our dinner. You get back to your book.'

'You mean, it will be finished by the time we leave?'

'It had better be, hadn't it, lovie, on a cold day like today?' Mabel chuckled.

During their meal of shepherd's pie and treacle tart Ivy and her man and dad joked and teased one another the whole time, including Essie in their conversation as if they had always known her. Meals at Long Row had been taken in complete silence, or else accompanied by her dad's ravings. Usually they were taken standing up, his lordship being the only one considered entitled to a chair.

Ivy's dad, George, was a big broad-shouldered man, with a round country face and laughing eyes. He could have been an older brother to Ivy and her mam, they were all so similar. After the meal he explained how he had collected his precious travel books from second-hand bookshops, over a long period of time. Mabel again disappeared into her sewing room and George went to give Ivy a hand with the washing-up, insisting that Essie had a rest; he had heard how hard she worked, he said.

Every now and then Essie would hear laughter from the scullery. To her it seemed as incredible as a man going to the moon. A girl laughing with her father. And the father helping with the dishes!

She had never envisaged that such warmth and camaraderie could exist among members of a family and now understood why her friend always looked so happy.

At four o'clock Ivy made a pot of tea and said they had better start back before dark. It was then that Mabel brought in the newly-fashioned coat for Essie to try on. What a transformation! The coat no longer needed a belt, for it fitted tightly into her tiny waist, and fell softly into a full skirt. The bodice buttoned snugly to her neck. Mabel had found a scrap of silver-grey fur which felt warm and expensive round the collar. It was just the right length.

'It's beautiful. I can't believe it!'

49

'Ooh, Essie, it *is* beautiful. Mam, you are clever!'

Mabel beamed in satisfaction. 'Come and look in the long mirror, Essie.'

Essie was tongue-tied as she gaped in disbelief at her own reflection. It was like a stranger gazing back at her, the coat hanging gracefully, emphasizing her small, gently-rounding figure, her cheeks pink from the fire, her eyes shining with excitement.

'You are a very pretty girl, Essie,' said Mabel, the first person ever to tell her that. 'I've made something else for you.'

She produced a tam-o'-shanter hat made from triangles of left-over material which she had edged with a strip of fur to match the collar. Mabel placed it on Essie's head, slightly to the side, so that wisps of blonde hair, growing at last, hung just below it.

Essie cried out in delight as the little family crowded round in admiration. It was a dream come true – that is, if she had ever dared to dream anything as wonderful as this. She was bursting inside but could not find the words to tell them how she felt. Perhaps they knew from her face because they all started to laugh in sheer delight, and Mabel said Ivy had better look out or the farmer's lad would be transferring his affections.

She kissed them both and said Essie must come again soon. Both parents stood at the gate, George's arm resting fondly round Mabel's shoulders, watching and waving until the girls were out of sight as they turned into the main road where they caught a tram.

'They're lovely, Ivy, your mam and dad. You are lucky.'

'Don't I know it! Now remember what Mam said, Essie. You can visit them any time, whether I am with you or not. You know the way now. I don't expect we shall be allowed time off together very often. If ever.'

How generous she was. Essie wondered, if she had a

mother as nice as Mabel, whether she would want to share her with anybody.

There was a biting wind and a flurry of snow when they reached the town, but as they walked back to Mellish Road Essie felt snug as a bug in a rug in her warm, fitted coat, with the luxurious, unfamiliar feel of fur round her neck and a warm, unfamiliar glow round her heart.

Chapter Three

Essie's triumph at outwitting Sidney was short-lived.

Feeling cheerful and confident in her newly-designed coat and hat, her March salary reclining richly in her pocket, she was happily browsing round Walsall market on her afternoon off, carefully weighing up the merits of a brooch from the jewellery barrow against a bottle of lavender water from the now familiar lino square, as a present for Ivy's mam. Suddenly she froze at the sight of a well-remembered scarecrow figure. Her first instinct was to run. She turned swiftly to do just that, but was too late.

Sidney's voice drifted after her, choking breathlessly on each word. 'Ai, our Essie!' He still wore the thin jacket with the sleeves halfway up his arms; there were no buttons on it and underneath was a dirty, well-worn, collarless shirt. As he shuffled toward her in his down-at-heel shoes she noticed that the boils and pimples, bulging bright red on his pasty skin, were worse than before. She continued to walk away from him.

He shouted again, this time so loud that passers-by stared. 'Ai, our Essie!'

She paused at the corner of George Street, which led off

Market Street halfway up the hill, resigned to the inevitable. As a result of all his shouting Sidney had to pause due to a paroxysm of coughing. She could have bolted then, but feeling sorry for him, she waited.

Breathless when he reached her, he hesitated, still doubtful of her identity. 'It is our Essie, ain't it?'

'My name is Essie, but I'm not *yours* any more.'

His mouth stayed open in astonishment. He gave a snort and rubbed his nose on the back of his hand. She automatically reached for a handkerchief. It was a pretty one Ivy had embroidered for her.

'I doh want that. I ain't no pansy.'

He peered down at her, his short-sighted eyes crinkling to nothing. 'Cor, Essie. Yer doh 'alf look different.'

He looked different too. Dirtier than she remembered, with a stubbly chin; time he started shaving. She could smell he was dirty. Goodness, did she used to smell like that? She shuddered. No wonder the teachers sat her well away from the rest of the class.

They continued to scrutinize one another in silence until she asked, 'What do you want, Sidney?'

'What do I want! You nearly 'ad me murdered, tellin' me the wrong 'ouse. Me Dad med me go back and knock on nearly every door in Mellish Road. Until a bobby appeared and sent me packin'.' He gazed at her, full of resentment.

'It ain't no laughin' matter, our Essie,' he sniffed as he observed a puckish grin starting at the corner of her lips. 'Any road, you can look out. 'Cos me Dad's cummin' to find yer 'isself. Startin' where I left off, 'e is. An' if the bobby appears 'e's gunna tell 'im that 'is daughter ran off.'

That cut short Essie's smile before it had a chance. 'What does he want?' she asked, knowing full well.

'Yer wages o' course. What yer think? 'E knows yer 'ad yer money yesterday. 'E vows 'e'll find yer tomorrer. Yer can just imagine the mood 'e'll be in, can't yer?'

53

She could. Just thinking of him was like a body blow. She felt as breathless as Sidney looked. The vision of her dad presenting himself to Mrs Lake produced a pain in her chest. She could envisage his swearing, his scruffy clothes, his bloated, drunken face. How would she feel if Ivy saw him. And oh, what about Mrs Vee? She would rather run away and die. He had mortified her so many times before. Christmas Eve in particular was still painfully etched in her mind.

'Good King Wenceslas' had always been Essie's favourite hymn ever since she could remember. But she had never heard it sung with such joy and enthusiasm as on that chill December night under the lone village lamp in Heath End square.

Essie stood in the shadows beyond the edge of the arc of light cast by the lamp, away from the main group of on-lookers, yet longing to belong. A kindly Heath-Ender, whom the children called Aunt Sal, was the only one to notice the lonely figure and edged toward her.

'Ain't it great, love? Our Ruth's got a drink and mince pies laid on for them when they've finished 'ere.'

Mince pies! Essie's insides groaned.

'Mr Carter's in fine voice tonight.'

'Who is Mr Carter?' queried Essie.

'Don't you know, my duck? He's the chief chorister at St Michael's. Every Sunday I go 'specially to hear him.'

Essie felt ashamed she had never been inside a church in her life.

'Mr Carter works in the bakery,' the woman explained in a hushed voice, in a break between carols, when the choristers stamped their feet, consulted their music sheets, and chatted quietly among themselves. Mr Carter was the only grown-up in the choir, the rest being boys between eleven and fourteen.

'Mr Carter's always in the back, baking,' Aunt Sal

continued. 'So you never see him. He makes lovely dough-nuts. We always ask for his, do you?'

Essie shook her head. Chance would be a fine thing.

After a rousing rendering of 'While Shepherds Watched', the choir sang 'Holy Night', so sweetly and softly that it caused little shivers to slide up and down Essie's spine, and she saw one or two of the female listeners wipe their eyes with the corners of their aprons.

She took in the peaceful scene, the joyful faces of the choir members, the rapturous expressions of the villagers, mostly older children, with a spattering of adults, mainly female. They were totally absorbed, transported into another world.

If this was Christmas Eve Essie was all for it, although she knew there would be no exchange of gifts at their house tomorrow. She had not even sampled a halfpenny dip from the village shop. It did not seem to matter now. This was enough. Enough to make Christmas.

Next the choir struck up boisterously with 'Hark the Herald Angels Sing' and Aunt Sal began to hum the tune as the choristers sang. One by one the onlookers joined in. The singing was swelling to a joyful crescendo when Essie's heart missed a beat.

Into the arc of lamplight, from the direction of The Red Cow, staggered her father. His voice, rough and coarse and bellowing, repeated the first line of the carol, over and over again, in a drunken stupor. Essie could hardly bear to look; she covered her face with her hands. The woman at her side stopped humming. One by one the rest of the singers subsided, all except Mr Carter who ploughed on man-fully.

Essie watched fearfully, through splayed fingers, as her father lurched toward the smaller man, still singing, right to the end of the carol, without a single tremor in his wonderful tenor voice. 'Glory to the new-born King.'

He simply ignored Caleb Connor's blusterings.

'What the 'ell do yer think yer doin'? Keepin' everybody awake. Disturbin' the peace!'

As the carol ended his heavy hand came across the singer's throat sharply, sending him sprawling. 'That'll put paid to your singin' for a bit.'

Mr Carter's choirboys and some of the women tried to pick him up. Essie could see a trickle of blood oozing from his mouth and heard someone say, 'We shall have to get a doctor.' Her dad shuffled from the pool of light, having wrecked the peace and happiness of Christmas Eve.

Aunt Sal placed a gentle arm around Essie's shoulder. 'I'm sorry, luv,' she said.

Essie could still feel the shame of that night even now. She could not bear the prospect of seeing him again. She reached into her pocket, now re-designed and smaller than before. 'Listen carefully, Sidney. You tell our father if he as much as sets foot in the garden where I work I shall lose my job. Employers don't take kindly to servants having visitors. Then there would be no more money, except perhaps an odd shilling for scrubbing steps, like Clara. I did get my pay yesterday, and here it is.' She counted three shillings and sixpence into his grubby hand.

'*Five*-and-six, you said you was gonna get.'

Essie had a sudden inspiration, remembering something Ivy had told her about a friend of hers in service. 'They keep two shillings a month for uniform.'

'What about next month?'

'I'll meet you here, at this spot, on the first Tuesday of every month.'

'Are you sure there's no more?'

'I am sure. And you be sure to pass on that message. Or I'm out on my heels and there will be no more three-and-sixpences. Remember to tell him that.'

'I ain't gonna risk a clout for you. Tell 'im yerself,'

Sidney sniffed. 'Any road, 'e'll want to know what you've done with the two months' wages you've had before.'

'I had to buy some clothes. They would have sacked me if I hadn't smartened myself up a bit.'

'Same time next month, then? That's if 'e ain't murdered you afore then.'

'I'll be here.'

'Our Essie, you ain't the same.'

Essie wept inside as she watched him shuffle off down the hill; not for Sidney, nor even for herself, but because she had longed to buy a really nice present for Ivy's mam. Now it would have to be just a tablet of Melrose like Mrs Lake used on her hands when they were rough. She did not have the heart to even peep at the bookstall, and goodness knows how long it would be before she had saved enough for a pair of new shoes.

That night she dreamed that her sister was snuffling and fidgeting beside her; that there were thumps and curses, whisperings and protests from a bed too close to hers. She dreamt that her dad came and took her away.

When she awoke she lay trembling, afraid of losing all the kind people who had made life worth living these last few weeks; Ivy and her mam, Mrs Lake and Joe. And her lovely lavender lady.

It was a very subdued Essie who tackled her work next morning, going about her tasks in such a mechanical way that Mrs Lake was convinced she was sickening for something and wondered what on earth she would do without her if she was taken ill.

She gave her permission to take a couple of hours off. 'Have a lie down,' she said. But Essie preferred to join Joe in the garden. He pointed out the daffodils and crocuses that were just coming through; he showed her how to prune the roses. He allowed her to plant seeds in boxes. The lovely names Joe told her rolled off her tongue deliciously: lobelia, alyssum, nemesia, marigolds. She studied pictures of them in Joe's garden book which he kept in the greenhouse. There must be some kind men in the world, mustn't there, because she had met Joe and Ivy's dad. But when men were bad they were awful, awful in ways that only men could be.

She hoped she was still here to see all these flowers bloom, she thought despondently. Last night's dream and Sidney's threats had really frightened her. Finally, she worked off her frustration by raking and spiking the lawns, before going in to do the ironing.

It was Ivy's day off tomorrow. That night Essie tapped on the door across the landing, noticing for the first time that Ivy's room had a lock and key. She handed the little packet of Melrose to her friend, for Mabel.

'Wish it could have been something better, Ivy.'

'Mam doesn't expect anything.'

Essie perched on the edge of the bed and watched as Ivy gave her hair its customary hundred strokes, as she had done on that first night. 'Tell her I like my coat.'

Ivy had been aware of an anxiety in Essie today. 'Why don't you take the present and tell her yourself. They would both like to see you, Mam and Dad.'

'I will go later.' How could she explain she would no longer be able to afford the tram fare? If she walked it would not be possible to be back before dark; anyway she felt too depressed to make any such plans. Was she ever going to be free of her dad?

Sidney's threat with regard to her dad finding her filled Essie with gloom. But as the days lengthened she did walk to Mabel's, often glancing around nervously, expecting her dad to pop out from every field-gate or clump of bushes. Mabel always welcomed her with open arms. Remnants of material bought cheaply from the market were greeted with cries of delight and swiftly transformed into blouses. It was much more fun learning to sew from Ivy's chuckly mum than it had been at school. Once they made a dress together from a piece of gingham which had only cost sixpence-a-yard new. It was in fresh lavender and white check and Essie loved it; it reminded her of her lovely lavender mistress.

She felt very humbled and overwhelmed by such kindness, but found it difficult to put into words, and well nigh impossible to return Mabel's hugs. To show open affection was something that Heath End families just did not do; among her family there had been none to show. But Mabel was more than rewarded by the gratitude in the girl's face.

With the help of Joe, who repaired her shoes as expertly as any cobbler, she found she could budget her two shillings a month quite cleverly. She even managed to save enough to buy another book. This time it was *Rose in Bloom* by Louisa M. Alcott; she bought it because she liked the title. It wasn't the usual stallholder, but a curly-haired youth not much older than herself. He did not seem to mind how often she picked up books to examine them. Sometimes she would read several pages before putting them down again.

She was getting bold enough to bargain. 'Seems a lot for this,' she commented, indicating the price pencilled just inside the cover. 'The book was only half-a-crown new, I see.'

'That's because it's a first edition. Those are the sort you should be collecting. Fetch a fortune some day, they will.'

'What does first edition mean?'

The lad explained patiently and told her what to look out for. She bought books to read, not to make a fortune; still, you could not afford to ignore that sort of information. Her big brown eyes were so filled with gratitude he knocked threepence off the price.

So it was with a light step she went to meet Sidney on that August Tuesday. He was usually waiting for her on the corner of George Street, but today she was there first. There was no sign of Sidney shuffling up the market hill, but as she scanned the crowds she thought she saw someone she knew, a tall figure striding purporsefully toward her. At first she thought she must be affected by the sun; she could not believe what she saw until they were face to face.

'Will I do instead of Sidney?'

'Arthur!'

Despite the depth of emotion which flooded her body she could not respond to the kiss her older brother planted on her cheek. She was embarrassed by the curious stares of passers-by as he hugged her; he had never hugged her before he went away to Canada. When at last he let her go he stood back to appraise this new attractive little sister in the fresh gingham dress.

Essie's corn-coloured hair now almost reached her shoulders, curling softly at the ends. Her tiny, pointed face was blossoming into a pretty oval, now flushed with excitement, and she was taller than he remembered. She had always had those attractive eyes. Heaven knows where she got them from; the rest of the family, including himself, looked as if their eyes were permanently half-closed.

'You look lovely, Essie,' he stated simply.

'So do you.' He did; so fit and bronzed. 'I thought you were in Canada.'

'I have to go back there quite soon.'

Her face fell.

'But not today. Come on, I've booked us a table at Allisons, for tea.'

The first thing he said when they were seated, after ordering a pot of tea and cakes, was, 'I am married now, Essie. Did you know?'

She shook her head.

He explained that he had married Liddy, the daughter of his Canadian boss. 'And you know Paul Brook?'

She nodded. 'He brought home twenty pounds from you on New Year's Eve. And his mother, Mary Ann at the shop, has helped me a lot.'

'Well, Paul is getting married to Liddy's sister, Meg, at Pelsall Church, on Saturday. And Mary Ann particularly asked that you should come. Will you, Essie?'

She immediately shook her head, quite firmly.

'Your new sister-in-law would love to meet you.'

'Where is she now?'

'She stayed behind to give Meg a hand. Anyway, we both thought it would be nice for you and me to have a little talk on our own. Do try and come, Essie. There's something we want to show you.'

'I don't get time off on Saturday, Arthur.'

'Not even a couple of hours if you explained? Or maybe you would like me to come and explain? We return to Canada just a couple of days after the wedding.'

She would not have minded Arthur coming to the house, would have been quite proud of him, but she shook her head. 'I am not going back to Cod End, Arthur, ever. You haven't been in a hurry to return to it yourself.'

'Can't deny that,' he conceded as he poured tea for them both. 'Then if you won't come to Cod End how about coming to Canada? It's a wonderful place, Essie, and you would love the farm.'

'I am all right here,' she replied firmly, while imagining the relief it would be to be the other side of the world, away from the clutches of her dad for ever.

'I am not so sure that you are all right, Essie. Germany's flexing its muscles for trouble. There's mounting tension in Europe. There could be a war.'

A war seemed very remote. The only impact the word made was to register the fact that Captain Vincent, Mrs Vee's husband, would be one of the first to go, being a regular army man.

'What was it you wanted to show me in Heath End?' she asked curiously.

'Sure you won't come and see for yourself?'

'Certain.' Arthur remembered that tone from when Essie was little.

'Then I will tell you. Liddy was horrified when she saw the conditions the family were living in. I'm afraid I copped it badly. She would not rest until she had found a cottage being renovated, down by the stepping bridge. It's quite nice: two bedrooms, parlour, kitchen and scullery. Running water.'

'When do you think they will be moving in?'

'They're in.' He chuckled at Essie's startled face. She could not believe all this had happened since she saw Sidney last month. It seemed impossible to imagine them anywhere but Long Row.

'Doesn't let grass grow beneath her feet, my Liddy. She badgered the workmen until they were glad to get it finished. Folk have rallied round with pots and pans, curtains, bed-linen, crockery. Clara has a bedroom of her own and Sidney has the front parlour.'

'How will they afford the rent?'

'That's all settled. We shall pay the rent directly into the bank for the landlady.'

Essie hadn't realized you could do that, but thought it a brilliant idea; otherwise the pubs would have had it.

'Tell me what you have been doing with yourself, Essie.'

He watched the expressions of pride and delight flit across her animated face as she described the people she had met, the beautiful home she looked after, particularly her bedroom, the books she had read. She showed him *Rose in Bloom* and told him what the bookstall lad had said about first editions. It all took ages; it was lovely having Arthur to chat to.

'They are lucky to have you, Essie,' he said when she had finished.

As he paid the bill at the little glass office there was time to glance around Allisons elegant tea-room and to study the well-dressed people supping tea.

'How about a stroll to the arboretum?' Arthur suggested. 'It's such a lovely day.'

Seated on a bench beside the arboretum lake he talked with great enthusiasm about Canada; its vastness, the hundreds of lakes they had passed on their long train journey from Toronto to Moosejaw, the flatness of the prairies, the fishing, the breath-taking beauty of the fall, as he called the autumn. He said how Liddy was kept busy.

'She does all the cooking for the farmworkers,' he explained. 'The McNabs employ a lot of extras in summer; that's how Paul and I started.' He said how he and Liddy liked to ride off on the horses whenever they had a break from work. She thought of how she had enjoyed working in the garden with Joe; she could imagine Arthur as a farmer.

'It must be better than the pits,' she commented.

He went on to tell her how his father-in-law had set him up with a holding of his own, how he had helped him build a house. 'Like you, Essie, I've discovered some wonderful, generous people. Promise me, if you ever change your mind, you will come out to us. I could send you the fare. There will always be a welcome, Liddy told me to stress that.'

He smiled wryly, 'She thought you would refuse to come to the wedding. She doesn't like Heath End either. Fortunately Meg, her sister, loves it and has made lots of friends already. She will make Paul a wonderful wife.'

'Come back with us, Essie.'

Essie shook her head. She ached to escape from her dad for ever. But going to Canada would mean leaving Mrs Vee in the lurch. She could not do that. Yet would her dad leave her alone, after Arthur had gone back?

She fell silent. Part of her wanted to confide in Arthur. Although the sun was shining, birds were twittering happily and sweetly-fragrant roses surrounded them, reminding her of the title of her new book *Rose in Bloom*, and it was lovely to be sitting here, talking like this to her brother, the very fact that he *was* here highlighted the danger there would be after he had gone back. Arthur. Arthur's money, tied up in the rent in a way her dad could not get at it! Would her three-and-sixpence be enough to keep him away? She doubted it. Should she tell Arthur? Could she tell him about the day she had stood at the bottom of the staircase, trembling at the sound of a row which she knew would erupt into violence? Clara was out, Sidney was lounging on the sofa and she, herself, had just walked in from school. Her mam and dad were upstairs.

'Where's Arthur's money? It should 'ave bin 'ere days ago.' Her father was shouting at the top of his voice.

'It must be late comin',' her mother replied nervously.

'It's never late. I reckon you've spent it.'

'No!' A crack across the face.

'What 'ave you spent it on?'

'It ain't come!'

Another crack. 'Where yer 'iding it?'

'I 'aven't 'ad it.'

'I'm tekkin' my belt off.'

'No, Caleb!' Her mother's pitiful cries as the belt descended catapulted Essie up the stairs. She had no idea what she planned to do except that she had grabbed the poker from the hearth. She was holding it aloft as she reached the top step. It was immediately ripped from her hand.

'Just what I could do with,' her dad sneered. 'Better than a belt.' He picked Essie up by a leg and an arm and with great force threw her downstairs.

'You asked for that,' said Sidney, annoyed at being disturbed by the commotion.

But he pulled her into the kitchen and clumsily attempted to bathe her cut face with some hot water from the kettle and the piece of hessian that served as a towel.

Within a minute their father reeled downstairs, still insisting the money had been received. He tipped the small amount of tea from a can on the mantelpiece on to the table, together with the cupful of sugar Essie had been sent to borrow that morning, in case the money was hidden in either container. He tipped the coal from the bucket on to the hearth. He picked up the piece of carbolic from the bowl Sidney was using. 'I'll wash 'er mouth out with this. Telling me lies!'

It was Sidney's turn to find a bit of pluck. 'The money ain't come, Dad. The postman never come today, nor yesterday, nor the day afore.'

His dad's arm was just about to descend on him when Clara appeared, home from her scrubbing. In her hands she carried a package postmarked Canada.

'This was delivered to Lizzie Althorp's by mistake.'

Her dad grabbed it from her. The swipe intended for Sidney descended on poor Clara, as if it was her fault. 'I'll kill that postman.'

Back from the pub late that night he recalled Sidney's 'interference', and locked him out for the night. It was filthy weather. He had to shiver in wet clothes in somebody's entry, and looked so bad next morning that Essie thought he was going to die. When her dad finally came downstairs for his midday boozing session he boxed her ears for letting Sidney in and making him a cup of hot tea.

Sidney never found the courage to speak up for his mother again.

It was best to say nothing to Arthur, Essie decided, as she returned to the present with a jolt. As it was, their precious

65

time together ran out far too soon. Essie brought out the three-and-sixpence she had put aside for Sidney. 'Will you deliver this for me?'

Arthur's hard brown hand closed over hers. 'Buy something for yourself, Essie. I'll pay it.'

'Oh Arthur!' But still she proffered the money. 'Give this to Mam, then. Tell her I am pleased about the house and to buy something for it.' He hesitated and she read his mind. 'Go on, take it. It won't be the same if *you* give it to her,' she insisted.

'I will tell her, Essie,' he agreed. 'I feel sure her life is going to be transformed from now on.'

Essie had her doubts about that. Their mother still had their dad to contend with. No new house was ever going to compensate for that. And was the new house going to keep him away from herself? She shuddered. She felt that she knew the answer.

She and her brother exchanged addresses.

'Keep in touch, Essie,' Arthur said. 'I'm not much good at corresponding, but Liddy will write. If I remember rightly you were always top of the class.'

It was nice to know someone remembered.

Chapter Four

Essie almost ran back to Mellish Road. She was so eager to tell Ivy all about her exciting afternoon. She had never felt so elated, already anticipating Ivy's wide-eyed pleasure for her.

They would never stop talking tonight after they finished work. Ivy would be able to repeat it all to Mabel tomorrow: all about Arthur, the tea-rooms, and their walk to the arboretum; about Canada and the wedding of her brother's friend to a Canadian girl who had agreed to live over here.

She knew that George would be interested to hear about Canada. Then of course there was her new book and the conversation she had had with the bookstall lad. And she had a new Canadian sister-in-law.

She was bursting with anticipation as she entered the house through the scullery, but instead of Ivy meeting her at the door leading from the scullery to the kitchen it was Mrs Lake who greeted her anxiously.

'Thank heavens you're here, Essie. Hurry up and get changed. You will have to serve tonight.'

'Why? Where's Ivy?'

'Her dad came to fetch her. Her mother has had a stroke.'

'No! Not Mabel. Not Ivy's mam!' She froze where she stood, all today's joy oozing out of her.

'Get changed, Essie,' said Mrs Lake quietly. 'There's nothing we can do.'

Essie never knew how she got through the next few days. There was so much to do and she missed Ivy more than she had imagined she could miss anyone.

Joe cycled over to see how things were. Mabel was home but could neither move nor speak. Ivy said she would not be back for ages, if ever. Joe went to see Mrs Turner, the Vincents' former daily cleaner, now totally recovered from her operation and eager to return. So Mrs Turner took over most of the menial tasks that Essie had performed, and Essie did Ivy's work.

There was a huge chunk of unshed tears in her chest whenever she thought of Mabel, the welcoming hugs, her merry chatter, her kindness and how she would stand at the gate waving her off until she was out of sight.

When she went to bed she lay awake thinking of Ivy and her mam; of George too, and how he had stood with his arm resting fondly along his wife's shoulder on that first visit, and how Mabel had put her arms round him and kissed him when he came home from work. It didn't seem fair; why did the happiness of this family have to be destroyed? She thought about Arthur; she had not had chance to tell anyone about the afternoon they had shared. He and Liddy would be on their way back to Canada by now.

The only good thing to come out of all this was that Essie saw more of Mrs Vee, who seemed to understand just how she was feeling and helped her unobtrusively whenever she was stuck, like on that first evening when Mrs Vee had guests and Essie had forgotten from which side Ivy had told her to serve. When she knew that Ivy had asked Joe if Essie could take her belongings on her afternoon off she offered to take her in the pony cart.

Essie had felt so sad, packing the things into Ivy's hold-all: the pretty cotton nighties and embroidered underwear, her dresses and the contents of the top drawer, neatly-laid-out collars, handkerchiefs, gloves, hair ribbons, and finally the hairbrush and combs, reminding her of how insurmountable the loss of her comb had seemed and how Ivy laughed and generously offered one of hers. It seemed so final, this packing.

Mrs Vee loaded fruit and eggs into a large basket, together with a chicken pie Mrs Lake had baked. Essie helped Joe pick an armful of flowers. The small trap was filled, what with Ivy's holdall and the two little boys, Justin, a fiery, unpredictable little redhead, just two years old, and Robert, aged four, smiling and patient, with lovely violet eyes like his mother.

'I know how upset you must feel, Essie,' said Mrs Vee as they cantered along the lanes, where the hedgerows were ablaze with wild flowers of every hue.

'They have been so kind to me. And I do miss Ivy.'

'Don't despair. Ivy may be back sooner than you think. People who have strokes often do get better.'

Mabel was seated in a wheelchair in the little strip of front garden, Ivy perched on a low stool nearby, shelling peas. Ivy was quite excited; her mother had moved one arm that morning. Mabel could not speak, but Essie could tell by her eyes that she understood what they were saying and that she was pleased to see them.

Ivy talked all the time to her mother as though everything was normal which Mrs Vee said later was the best thing she could do. She promised Ivy that her job was open any time she wanted to come back, however long it might be. Ivy smiled and said she was grateful but she would never leave her mam while she needed her.

She pushed the heavy wheelchair to the gate for Mabel and herself to watch them down the lane, giving Essie a hug big enough for both of them. 'Don't wear yourself out,' she said.

'I will see that she doesn't,' Mrs Vee promised.

As Essie bent to kiss Mabel, so still and lifeless, so unlike the Mabel she knew, she felt that the tight knot of tears would burst her chest.

Inspired by Ivy's cheerfulness, Essie continued to work enthusiastically. She threw herself into her new tasks. Mrs Vee sometimes left her in charge of the little boys and they played together in the garden. One day she was entrusted to take Robert to the arboretum. They watched young men proudly rowing their girlfriends across the lake, they saw the tennis players leaping and grunting, they laughed at the boastful peacocks strutting with fan-like feathers.

'I like you, Essie,' Robert confided as they made their way home, hand in hand. 'Will you be able to play with me when my father comes on leave? He will be here soon.'

'We'll see.'

But Captain Vincent forbade it almost as soon as he arrived a week later. Essie took an instant dislike to him when Mrs Vee introduced him. Green cat-like eyes slid over her body in a way that made her blush. He had thin red hair and beard to match. He reminded her of a slimy snake with green and orange bands that had startled her once in Pelsall woods when she and Clara were collecting firewood. Whenever she served dinner she could feel the sly green eyes upon her.

One day he suddenly entered the dining room where she was bending across a table energetically polishing. He strode over swiftly before she could straighten up and ran his hands slowly and impudently over her buttocks.

His thin lips curved sarcastically as she snapped, 'Don't do that!', an angry flush mounting her cheeks.

'Little spitfire, eh?' He spun her round to face him, holding her tightly. 'Daring to tell *me*, "don't!" As I pay your wages I have the right to admire your tight little rump, my dear.' With finger and thumb he insultingly flipped at the nipples of her small young breasts, making her hot with shame. 'These as well,' he added.

Trapped between the man and the table Essie glanced at the door as if someone had entered. 'I'm coming, this minute, Mrs Lake,' she called. The Captain drew back swiftly, like a scalded cat, giving her the opportunity to dart away, her heart beating fearfully in her throat.

She thought she had escaped all that when she left Heath End. It brought it all back, the insulting ways in which her dad had touched her, the fear, the shame.

Mrs Lake could not fail to notice her heightened colour as she ran into the kitchen. 'Anything the matter, Essie?'

'No.' She felt too ashamed to say anything, as if it was all her fault. Men! He was no better than her dad.

Mrs Vee repeated the same question that evening as Essie served the meal without her usual bounce and impish smile.

'Anything the matter, Essie?'

'No, thank you, Mrs Vee.'

She was painfully aware of the narrowed green eyes following her every movement, while keeping her own eyes averted.

'Here, what's all this *Mrs Vee*?'

'Ah, that's a secret between Essie and me,' Mrs Vee answered gaily. 'Isn't it, Essie?'

But even that did not bring forth a smile. Her young mistress looked so lovely tonight, in a dark blue velvet gown with a matching bow in her hair, smiling at her husband with such devotion and trust. Essie could not imagine how his eyes could ever stray.

She remained constantly on the alert for all the places he might be lurking, avoiding him as much as possible.

Only twice did he catch her unawares. One Tuesday afternoon she was returning from a visit to Ivy and her mam. The nights were drawing in and she was hurrying to try to beat the darkness when he drew up beside her in the pony trap, so close he almost knocked her over.

'Get in.'

'I can walk, thank you.'

'*Sir.*'

'I can walk, sir.'

'You can ride quicker. Get in.' Because he looked as if he would haul her up forcibly if she refused she climbed into the trap, sitting as far away from him as possible. He wanted to know where she had been, and asked politely after Ivy and her mother. He talked in the same disarming manner about what a good maid Ivy had been and asked to be remembered.

Essie began to think she had worried over nothing. Maybe he had offered her a lift in order to make sure his supper was ready on time. But when he drew up in the stableyard he sprinted round to her side before she could get out, and lifted her down, forcing her body to slide slowly and sensuously against his own before releasing her. She felt sick. And even more sick when she realized that Joe had seen them. Did she imagine cold suspicion in Joe's eyes when they drank their cocoa together in the kitchen that night? Again she felt guilty, as though it was her fault, just as she always felt guilty about her dad.

The second time was when she was alone in the kitchen one afternoon when Mrs Lake had gone for a lie-down. Mrs Lake was feeling her age lately and finding it difficult to get through the long day without a rest. Essie was rubbing fat into flour for pastry, but she was also reading the latest Dickens novel from Mrs Vee.

Suddenly he was blocking the doorway. He was dressed for riding. As he stood considering her through narrowed eyes he fingered his riding crop.

'Well! So the child can read!' he sneered, striding over arrogantly to pick up the book. His sandy eyebrows drew into a straight line. 'What are you doing with this?' he demanded angrily. 'My book!'

'Mrs Vincent lent it to me.'

'*Sir.*'

'Sir.'

'I must have a word with Mrs Vincent, your *Mrs Vee*. I wonder what she would have to say if she could see it lying among all this . . . this mess.' He indicated the remaining ingredients, neatly laid out, apples, apricots, a pot of jam.

Essie had placed the book on a piece of clean linen, well away from anything that could mark or damage it.

'I am always very careful with books, – sir.'

His eyes travelled over her insultingly. She felt her cheeks burning with indignation. 'God preserve us from educated servants,' he spat out sourly.

She moved to the sink under pretext of washing her hands. Almost instantly she felt the riding crop swish across her shoulders, making her flinch with pain.

'That's nothing to what you can expect if you ever walk away from me again, girl.' Essie could sense his annoyance that she did not find him irresistible. He turned at the door, holding the book aloft. 'You can earn the loan of this before I leave.'

Essie felt annoyed with herself. It was the first time she had ever brought one of the precious books into the kitchen. She had been so curious to know what happened next; there had been little time for reading lately. She would explain to Mrs Vee as soon as she had the chance, after that detestable husband had departed. She was apprehensive about what he had said but consoled herself with the thought that his leave must be almost at an end.

That night she slipped into the white cotton nightie Ivy had passed on to her before Mabel was taken ill, first embroidering the letter E on the collar. 'So you will feel it is really yours,' she had remarked kindly.

Essie had bathed in the scullery tub and the nightie felt cool against her glowing skin. As she lay, never failing to appreciate the clean sheets and cosy blankets, she thought of Ivy struggling to keep her mam cheerful, and how lovely it had been to have a friend across the landing. She was just about to blow out the candle when she heard footsteps on the stairs.

No one ever came up to the attic except herself. During the first few weeks Mrs Lake had laboured up the narrow staircase to inspect her room, but had soon realized it was unnecessary. It was always like a new pin.

The footsteps ceased on the landing. Essie tried to force herself out of bed, in order to reach something, anything, with which to defend herself, but she was riveted by fear as the door creaked slowly open and the Captain hovered there, focusing his eyes for a moment before lurching toward her bed. He smelled strongly of drink.

'Waiting for me, were you, darlin'?' Made you a promise, didn't I?'

He reached for the candle and held it over her. 'That won't do at all, m'dear,' he leered, as she pulled the sheet even more tightly up to her chin. 'Loosen up.'

As the candle swayed dangerously close Essie lost her hold on the sheet but found her voice. 'Be careful, you fool. You will set the bed on fire.'

He replaced the candle unsteadily on the bedside table. 'A fool, am I?' he muttered through gritted teeth. 'We shall see about that.' He tore wildly at the bedclothes and within a moment he had rent her nightdress from top to bottom as

74

she struggled ineffectually. His weight pinned her down, his hands darted greedily over her body. 'Mm, not bad,' he murmured gruffly. 'Room for improvement.'

She hated him slopping all over her, his moustache rough against her chest, and she was incensed about her lovely nightie. Gasping for breath, she wrenched one arm free and found the candle. It was her turn to bring it toward him. 'Get off me this minute, or you might get burned.'

'You wouldn't dare!' He lurched to grab it from her and they both smelled singeing. He screamed in panic.

'My hair's on fire, you baggage!'

He heaved far enough away for Essie to roll out of bed on the other side and run for the door. But where to go?

A moment of hesitation on the landing brought him right behind her, cursing loudly. He clawed at the back of her nightdress, leaving her naked.

She darted into Ivy's room and locked the door; she had remembered that lock just in time.

'Little trollop, I'll get you.' He was pushing at the door so wildly she thought he would burst it open. Mustering all her strength she dragged Ivy's heavy set of drawers against the door. He rattled the knob a few more times.

'Open this door immediately or you're dismissed. Do you hear me? Sacked. First thing in the morning you can clear off. Out. You understand? *Mrs Vee* will be told how you invited me up here. You're finished.'

At last she heard his uneven footsteps descending the stairs. She lay back on Ivy's bed, breathless and trembling.

Out! Where could she go? Back to Cod End? To the new house? To her dad? She shuddered. All men must be like this. None of them could be trusted. The only difference between this one and her dad was that one smelled of beer and the other of whisky.

She remembered Mrs Vee saying that if ever she was in trouble to go to her. But that would be cruel. From the way she looked at her husband you could tell she adored him. Anyway he had said, 'Mrs Vee will be told how you invited me up.'

There was nothing she could do. If only Ivy was here! At that moment she felt the loneliest person in the world.

She pulled the covers round her and lay, alert and listening all night, afraid to go back to her own room in case he returned. As dawn broke she plucked up courage to dart across the landing, a blanket clutched tightly round her. She ran back with her clothes, locking the door immediately.

When she was dressed she sat on the edge of the bed, wondering what was to happen to her. How could she tell Mrs Lake she had to leave? What would Mrs Vee think of her? Would she even be allowed to see her before she went? Essie felt bruised and angry at the injustice of it all.

She had no idea how long she sat there. An urgent knocking caused her to jump up, startled. She must have dropped off, for she had heard no footsteps. She was preparing to move the set of drawers to the door again when she heard a familiar voice. 'Unlock the door, Essie. It's only me.'

Essie's hands were trembling as she turned the key and opened the door to find Mrs Lake, puffing from the exertion of the stairs, carrying a mug of steaming tea. The little bedroom chair creaked as she wearily lowered herself into it.

There were dark rings under Essie's eyes, making them appear larger than ever. Her face was devoid of colour, reminding Mrs Lake of the state she was in on the day she arrived to start work. She recalled the black tent of a coat, and her own doubts, despite the girl's eagerness. They had all grown attached to her since that day.

'It's all right, lovey.' She set the tea down and held her arms wide. Essie went into them with a deep, sobbing sigh, confused but daring to hope that her world had not come to an end yet. Those arms were a port in a storm.

'How did you know?'

'The Captain shifted a lot of drink last night and Joe thought he heard him shouting later.' Essie guessed that would be when his hair was singed. 'Joe decided to come to see if you were all right. He was on the stairs when he saw you dash across the landing.'

'Mrs Lake, I didn't let him . . . he didn't . . . '

Mrs Lake patted her hand. 'We know, love. We know. He fell down the bottom set of stairs and cut his head on that broken patch of stone floor. Joe had to doctor him up and put him to bed. He was filled with indignation and cursing like a trooper because he hadn't got what he wanted.'

Essie felt a flood of relief. Whatever happened at least they knew that. 'He said I have to leave today.'

'Did he now? We'll see what Mrs Vincent has to say about that. Poor young lady, having to put up with such a man. Now sup your tea, lass, and then try to get some sleep. Later Joe will fix a good strong lock on your bedroom door.'

Essie wondered whether Ivy had had to have a lock fitted for the same reason.

But Essie was not allowed to sleep, for soon after breakfast the Captain sent a message for her to present herself in the library.

It was Mrs Vee who called, 'Come in, Essie,' in answer to her timorous knock. She was seated at the desk, very upright, yet looking white and strained. The Captain stood staring through the window, his hands behind his back. He rounded swiftly toward Essie as she entered.

'Is this the maid you trusted so implicitly, my dear?'

Mrs Vee did not reply, nor did she take her eyes off Essie's face.

'The same girl who invited me to her room last night.'

77

The Captain laughed hollowly. 'Willing to trade herself for the loan of a book.' His eyes ran over Essie contemptuously. 'Then, when I went up to lecture her on her dangerous foolishness, she, in a fit of pique because I was not prepared to succumb to her invitation, deliberately tried to *set me on fire*!'

Essie, the vibrations of her heart almost choking her, could no longer bear the pain on her mistress's face. She dropped her eyes to the floor.

There was a long pause before the question she was dreading came. 'What have you to say to all this, Essie?' Mrs Vee's gentle voice was even quieter than usual. 'Essie, look at me, please.'

Essie met the lovely violet eyes which were as troubled as her own. What could she say? If she denied it, could her word be taken against that of an adored husband? Was it fair on such a loving wife to even raise a doubt about him?

Essie dropped her eyes again without replying.

'Haven't you *anything* to say, Essie?'

Essie shook her head.

'Of course she hasn't,' expostulated the Captain. 'You only have to look at her; there's guilt in every line.'

Cold silence seemed to fill the room, broken suddenly by nine sharp chimes of the mantel clock. 'You're sacked,' he said curtly. 'Be out within the hour.'

Essie's world caved in at that moment. Where could she go? How could she get another job without a reference? She could not go back to Heath End. No, no! Not back to her dad. A low moan escaped her lips as she turned toward the door. As she reached it she heard the Captain say, 'My God! If she throws herself at men now, what's she going to be like at eighteen?'

She stumbled into the kitchen where Mrs Lake was waiting just inside the door. One look at Essie's face told her what had happened.

'He says I have to pack my bags. Now.'

'Oh no, child. No!'

Mrs Lake again held out her arms, but Essie turned away to go to her room. This time nothing could comfort her.

Upstairs she folded her clothes from the drawers and hanging rail and put them into her bag, all the time wondering what she would do. Arthur had asked her to go to Canada. If she could only have foreseen this she would have gone. She knew he would send her the fare if she asked, but what to do during the weeks of waiting?

When her bag was packed she automatically reached for one of the dusters she kept upstairs and cleaned her room, stripping the sheets and pillowcases from her bed and folding them neatly. She sat on the little pink chair when she had done, her mind now a blank. Waiting. She knew not what for.

It seemed hours later when Mrs Lake puffed up the stairs and tapped on her door.

'Essie, the mistress came to the kitchen to talk to me.'

Essie's eyeballs seemed too leaden to raise in query. When she did not speak or move, Mrs Lake continued. 'She has persuaded the Captain to allow you a week's notice.'

'Oh, no! That will mean I shall have to face her again. And him. Oh no!'

'Be sensible, Essie. At least it will mean another week's wages. And a week's grace to think about what you are going to do. They will be out for the rest of the day. And tonight, when Joe comes in, I shall ask him to tell the mistress exactly what the Captain admitted to him last night.'

This was sufficient to enliven Essie. She sat up straight, alert, startled. 'He mustn't do that, Mrs Lake, *please*. He must not do that,' she repeated emphatically.

'But, child, it is the only way . . . '

'No! She must not be told that about him.' It was as if

Essie had taken charge as Mrs Lake sat silently. 'But you are right about the week's grace. It will give me time to think of something.'

Mechanically she began to unpack the battered old bag.

The following day Captain Vincent was recalled from leave, and two days later war was declared. It seemed that Arthur had been right in his prediction. There had been much talk of war lately, but Essie had been too preoccupied with events at Mellish Road to give it much attention.

In spite of Mrs Vee being upset at the recall of her husband, towards the end of the week and without consulting Essie, Joe told the mistress exactly what Captain Vincent had admitted when he had put him to bed after his fall down the stone steps. Mrs Vee immediately sent for Essie. 'Joe had been to see me, Essie,' she said sadly.

'Oh, Mrs Vee! I'm sorry.'

'It is I who should be apologizing. Why didn't you tell me, Essie?'

Essie looked up into the beautiful face, into the violet eyes clouded with anxiety, and said the first thing that came into her head. 'Because I didn't want you to be unhappy.'

Mrs Vee took both her hands in her own. 'My poor Essie! I am sorry you were mistrusted, even for a moment. Can you forgive me that, and will you consider staying on?'

'What about the Captain?'

'You must leave that to me. Will you stay on, Essie? For my sake?'

Essie smiled. 'For your sake? Oh, yes. Please.'

Young market stallholders eagerly joined up straight away, along with thousands of others, and the number of stalls gradually decreased. One raw autumn afternoon Essie, already late, hurried past those remaining on her way to meet Sidney. As usual he was waiting at the corner of George

Street. But today he looked startlingly unfamiliar in a khaki uniform as many sizes too big as his own clothes had been small.

'You passed your medical, then?' Essie was frankly amazed. She immediately noticed her brother was already standing straighter and snuffling less, probably due to the first warm clothes he had ever worn.

'I'm not A1,' he replied. 'They're gunna give me a non-military job, perhaps in the kitchens.'

'Good for you, Sidney. Where are you stationed?'

'I'm at Lichfield Barracks. But we're movin' on any day now,' he informed her importantly. 'So I won't be collectin' your money from now on.'

'Who will collect it?' she asked, her heart in her throat.

'You might get a visit from the man 'imself, I shouldn't wonder. 'E's never forgiven yer for what yoh did. I'd look out if I was yoh.'

'On the other 'and,' he continued airily, 'they've all got jobs now. 'E's back in the pits and Clara and Mam have gone into a factory starting up in munitions. They might just tell yer to stuff yer measly three-and-sixpence.'

Essie laughed with a bravado she did not feel. 'That would be good news, wouldn't it?'

'You ain't like yer used to be, our Essie,' he told her for the hundredth time.

'You won't be when you've gone away for a while, Sidney.'

'Don't 'spec I'll be gone long. This war'll soon be over. Then we'll all be out o' work again.'

'This war will change everything. It will be a land fit for heroes. You'll see.' Essie had had long conversations with Joe about it. She held out her hand. 'Good luck, Sidney.' They shook hands awkwardly.

She watched as he set off jauntiily down Market Hill, recalling the day almost exactly two years ago when, bent almost double, he had huddled close to the hot potato machine. She watched until her last link with Cod End was out of sight, not knowing whether to feel sad or relieved. One thing was certain, even a yelling sergeant would be better for Sidney than their dad.

As she hurried back to Mellish Road she thought of Ivy, who was helping part-time at a farm from where some of the younger hands, including Ron, who was courting Ivy, had gone to war. Ivy had to fit in with her dad's shifts so that there was always someone at home with her mam, and Essie went whenever she could on her half days.

Mabel could move, with great difficulty, on one side only. She could say a few indistinct words. She looked tired and old. It pleased her when Essie sat beside her with some sewing in her hand; she could nod approvingly or shake her head to indicate whether her former pupil was doing the work correctly or not.

It had begun to snow as Essie arrived at Mellish Road. A scout was ringing the front doorbell. She knew that Mrs Vee would be fetching Robert from school and Mrs Lake would be resting so she took the telegram he held in his hand. 'Please give it to Mrs Vincent,' he said.

Later, Essie watched helplessly as Mrs Vee's lovely violet eyes filled with tears.

'Oh Essie! Captain Vincent has been, has been . . . ' A deep sob escaped her as she whispered brokenly, 'Killed in action.' She sank into a chair, pressing a handkerchief to her lips. 'Oh, my love. My dear, dear love.'

Essie longed to cry out, 'Don't cry. He was never worth your tears.'

As if she had spoken her thoughts aloud, Mrs Vee continued softly, 'I loved him, Essie. In spite of everything. I loved him.'

'I know that. It shone out of you.' Her mistress's distress was tearing her heart from her body. She placed a small hand firmly on the young widow's shoulder. 'Don't worry. I shall look after you,' she promised fervently. And meant it from the bottom of her heart.

Several weeks elapsed before things were sorted out at Mellish Road. Mrs Lake muttered angry curses against the dead man, for gradually it transpired that he had gambled everything away and was heavily in debt. He had borrowed from army colleagues and relatives who were now demanding their dues. Solicitors came and went, often in consultation with Mrs Vee for hours on end, while Essie took charge of the boys.

The mistress was determined to pay back all she could, which meant she could no longer keep the house. She claimed only the personal items she already owned before her marriage, insisting that the rest of the house contents be disposed of to help pay off what was owing. Some loyal friends rallied round and paid top prices for furniture and pictures they admired. The rest had to be sold by auction.

There came a day when the whole house seemed crammed with a wide variety of people: auctioneers, canny dealers who merely raised an eyebrow or fingered a coat button when they wished to place a bid, and less experienced mortals who called out or waved their catalogues in their eagerness to catch a bargain. And there were those who came simply out of curiosity or because they fancied a day out. Essie found herself categorizing them as she glanced around. It was the first housesale Essie had witnessed. She stood on tiptoe, and although saturated in sadness for Mrs Vee and all that this must mean to her, she could not fail to sense the interest and excitement of the buyers and the tenseness of the atmosphere. It fascinated her.

Later that evening she stood beside Joe in the darkening garden. They watched despondently as a cart pulled out with what must surely be the last load.

'What a sad day, Essie.'

Essie swallowed hard. 'What's to become of you and Mrs Lake, Joe?'

'We're all right, the missus and me,' he assured her. 'We have an eye on a little house to rent.'

Essie tried to summon a smile. Joe's voice gave him away. She knew there would be little left of their wages to put aside for the proverbial rainy day that had now arrived.

'Time we retired,' added Joe flatly. 'It's all been too much . . . '

Essie's eyes followed Joe's bent figure, fork in hand, as he walked away. What was to become of her? She thought of all the good times there had been with Mrs Lake and Joe, dear Ivy, and, most of all, with her mistress and the boys. What would her future hold without them?

With a sigh she turned to walk down the drive to close the gates behind the dray. There, only five yards away, stood the swaying figure of her father. He held a belt in his hand, the brass buckle glinting menacingly. Essie felt the blood drain from her face.

'You've been tellin' me lies.' Each word was enunciated like a growl.

Essie stood and stared, rooted in horror.

'No one tells me lies.'

She could smell his body odour, the beer on his breath. How had he got there? Dear God, why was her body riveted to the ground?

A heavy hand fell on her shoulder. 'Got yer! Movin' house, are they? Thought you'd escape me, did yer?' He shook her. 'Yer'll never escape yer dad. Never.'

Essie dug small sharp teeth into the red fist which by now was stifling her mouth, causing him to curse sharply. He jerked to his full height, lifting her off her feet and carrying her behind the thick rhododendron bushes that skirted the garden near the gate.

'Make one sound, gel, and it'll be yer last,' he threatened. Essie could not have raised a scream if she tried. Nor could she move away from the swinging belt before it hit her. The disgust she felt at his proximity was as hard to bear as the searing pain from the belt, which made her gasp while nausea suffocated her and prevented her from crying out.

'Yer pay two shillings a month for uniform, do yer?' His huge crimson hands tugged at the black apron she wore to help Joe in the garden. 'This is the uniform? This smart outfit? Two bob a month?' He spat on the ground, just missing her.

'Miss High and Mighty, Sidney said you was. You're no better than the rest of us, remember that, my gel. And I'll soon prove it to yer.' Again he lashed out at her, this time with the buckle end of the belt. Essie's terror was entrapped in her chest; in spite of the agony of the buckle biting into her skin, the scream in her throat could not escape. Only her small fists were mobile, lashing out at him ineffectually as his voice changed to a horrible, wheedling tone. He pulled her close toward him as she stumbled on the ground. 'C'mon. Be nice. Then no 'arm shall come to yer. I am yer dad after all. Yer know what yer mam's like.'

Essie's hand had landed on a large stone. She only realized she had aimed it at him when he let out a cry like an enraged bull, yet his next words were quiet and menacing as his hands sunk into both her shoulders, again lifting her up towards his bloated, ominous face. 'Right, gel. I'm tekkin' you home.'

'No!' Was that really her voice, escaped at last? She found herself screaming pitifully, as when he used to take her away from her playmates. 'No! no! no!'

He swung at her again, this time the hard buckle biting into her shoulder, the pain intense; this time it seemed nothing would quell his anger. Essie could feel her eyes misting over, her senses drifting.

Suddenly she heard a howl of agony from her father and the belt came no more. She turned her blurred eyes upward to see Joe, fork in hand. Her father was clutching his thigh. His hands were covered in blood.

She heard Joe speaking with an authority he had never used before.

'Get out. Get out. And never come back.'

Her father turned and hobbled toward the driveway, leaving the cruel belt lifeless where it had fallen. 'I'll get you both,' he rasped.

Joe kept the fork ominously close to her father's chest. Essie watched, not daring to breathe, as the anger and tension hung heavily between the two men. On any other occasion she suspected the strength of her father would have been too much for the bowed figure of Joe, but she noticed with relief her father's glazed eyes move uncertainly from his hands to his injured leg and back toward the rock-steady fork.

He continued to edge toward the outer gate, putting a distance of some twenty paces between himself and Joe. Essie pulled herself unsteadily to her feet, flinching at the pain from the beating.

Her father halted and glared at her with murderous eyes. 'I won't forget this,' he said with unnerving calm. 'I shall be back for you. And there'll be nothing he nor anyone else will be able to do about it.'

With that he limped away into Mellish Road and was gone. Essie knew that it was more than her very life was worth to ever let him find her again.

Joe told Mrs Vincent what had happened as she gently bathed Essie's wounds later.

'I think it is time we both moved on, Essie,' she said.

86

Chapter Five

Pure magic it was.

Framed by a back-cloth of tall trees lush with new growth, the little pink-washed cottage that was to be their home tucked itself comfortably into a hillside that tumbled down to the sea.

Straight ahead, beyond the river lazily slurping its way to the ocean, gentle Stonebarrow Hill and lofty Golden Cap vied for attention as they glittered in the sun. A soft haze hovered in the dip between distant hills, shrouding Portland across the bay. To the right stretched Lyme Regis, a huge uncut emerald, ducking and weaving down to where the grey arms of the Cobb curved protectively around a colourful harbour.

And immediately below where she stood, lay the quiet sea at Charmouth, reflecting will-o'-the-wisp tufts of gossamer gliding leisurely across a satin sky.

That's how it was, the day Essie first saw Charmouth. She would never forget it.

'Told you you would adore Dorset, didn't I, Essie?'

With an effort Essie tore her eyes from the panorama stretched before her. Life had stood still for a minute. Now it had to accelerate to catch up.

Mrs Vee had paid the drayman who had transported them with their bags from Axminster station. The heavy luggage, which had been sent on ahead, he had placed in an outhouse behind the cottage. The boys had already bounded inside and were whooping with the joys of discovery. Essie was light-headed with relief. Her dad would never find her here.

Inside the cottage was much the same shape as Ivy's home and only slightly bigger, with a room on either side of its tiny entrance hall. The two front rooms were backed by a small kitchen and scullery. Miraculously there was a water closet, under cover, near the scullery door.

From both upstairs rooms they could see a narrow road snaking between hills on either side, to the left and slightly inland. Mrs Vee said that the road led to the town of Bridport, five or six miles away. Axminster, about the same distance, lay on the other side, just in Devon.

This was the cottage, she said, where she had spent many happy holidays as a child. A friend had offered to lend it to her at a peppercorn rent for as long as she liked. The same friend had recommended her to the headmaster of the village school, who was short of a teacher owing to the only other man on the staff going off to war.

'I thought you and the boys could have these two rooms, Essie. I will make a bed-sitting-room-cum-study for myself in the room at the right of the hall downstairs.'

'But these rooms are bigger . . .'

'The other will suit me very well. It already has a desk and a sofa bed. There I shall disturb no one when I am working late.'

'Besides,' she added with a teasing smile, 'if the boys wake they can toddle across the landing to you.

'Now! What shall we do? Clean up, eat up, or go to the beach?'

The beach won.

It was deserted except for an elderly lady walking her

dog. The four of them scrambled excitedly, hand in hand, down the grassy slopes from the cottage before picking their way painfully across mounds of pebbles to a strip of firm sand near the water's edge. Here they perched on a boulder to remove shoes and stockings, the boys whooping with delight, skipping and jumping along the edge of a gently-lapping sea.

Essie clasped Robert's hand while Justin hung on to his mother and complained that the water was too cold.

With the afternoon sun on their heads, sand between their toes and pure untainted air in their lungs, they could forget about the war, about the tall house they had had to leave, and about Cod End, while they leaped and played in gay abandonment like children in paradise. For Essie it was the first taste of childhood she had known.

Later they stood on the wooden bridge spanning the river which separated Charmouth into two beaches, watching as the swans proudly marshalled their five young cygnets while dozens of noisy ducks chortled their approval.

They hunted for fossils separately, each collecting a handful, until a sun like a giant orange began to sink slowly over Lyme, shedding a rosy glow over sea and sky.

Back at the cottage Essie found bread, sausages, bacon and eggs she had packed that morning. She fried the meal on a new-fangled primus stove while her companion unpacked the bed-linen and made up the beds.

'I could have done that, Mrs Vee,' she protested as they sat down, all ravenously hungry, squashed together like sardines round a small table by the window.

'I have made beds before,' Mrs Vee twinkled. 'It will have to be all hands to the pump here. And that includes you two boys.'

'By the way, Essie, as we shall be living as a family now, let's do away with the Mrs. Just call me Vee.'

So Vee it was. It did not seem impertinent. It felt quite

natural, for Vee seemed more like an older sister than her boss, and now that Essie was turned fifteen the age difference did not seem half what it had been.

She discovered that the young widow was only twenty-seven. She looked even younger.

'Living as a family,' was what Vee had offered.

'I won't be able to pay you much, Essie,' she had warned when they first discussed the move to Charmouth. 'Perhaps sometimes nothing. But I shall earn enough to keep us all from starving. And you would love Dorset. But consider it carefully.' It had taken Essie half a minute to make up her mind.

After the fry-up, out came a delicious fruit cake, Mrs Lake's last offering before she and Joe had left the day before for their little house, not far from Ivy's. Essie felt pleased about that, for she knew they would visit Ivy's mam.

Relaxed from the food and too tired to move away from the table, they sat gazing at the quiet sea, now merging mistily with the sky, eliminating the horizon, dreamlike in the subdued light of evening. They were to sit here many times, watching the moon cushioned in velvet, its rays turning the sea to silver, but now it was the last of the sun, toppled from view behind mysterious hills, which lent its reflected glow.

'That's where I found my first fossil, near the river,' Robert pointed out, breaking the silence.

'And I got my feet all slicky.'

'Sticky you mean, Justin,' Robert corrected his brother, laughing.

'Slicky's a more descriptive word,' mused Essie. Vee gazed at her thoughtfully. It was not the first time she had imagined how rewarding it might be to educate Essie. But for a time she would be fully occupied polishing up her skills at the village school.

Vee began teaching at the junior school the following week

and Robert joined the infants' department on the same site, as a pupil.

The first task Essie set herself was to cultivate the neglected vegetable patch behind the cottage, where apple trees were in full blossom. She had brought potato sets, cabbage plants and marrow, all of which Joe had packed into a cardboard box, along with seeds in carefully-marked white packets, peas, broad beans, runner beans, lettuces.

It was important to grow food; everybody said so. Shortages were feared if the war went on. She had filled a little notebook with vegetarian recipes gleaned from Mrs Lake or *The Book of Household Management*. Even if they had no meat they could survive.

This little home was so easy after Mellish Road, despite Justin nurturing the kitchen floor with a watering can after she had cleaned it, or transforming her neatly-made beds into sailing ships.

The sparsely-furnished cottage was enriched with small items Vee had been allowed to claim: her pictures, a pretty secretaire, a small regency table which came apart into two fluted trays, a collection of ink stands, miniature paintings, porcelain figures and hand-embroidered samplers; these last items fascinated Essie most of all. She imagined 'Elizabeth Geddon. Her work, 1766' as someone who could not put a foot wrong – or to be more precise, a needle wrong, – while she wondered if Emma Flemming had been reprimanded in 1801 for reversing the order of L and M and missing the W out altogether in the alphabet she had painfully embroidered.

A carpenter from the village fixed bookshelves in Vee's study, in the boys' room and in Essie's. Surrounded by books, Essie was in seventh heaven. Sometimes she would take one to the beach, to read while Justin amused himself in the rock pools. Vee bought newspapers, too, which Essie devoured with interest; she had never had newspapers to read before. There was a lot of war news, most of it optimistic - it seemed no country could beat the British - and other interesting items, book reviews, ladies fashions, politics, all fascinating stuff.

Life was filled with interest. At weekends she walked the boys along the beach to Lyme Regis, stopping every few yards, to search for small pieces of coloured glass, washed smooth by the tides. They would return home triumphantly, their pockets bulging with treasures of all kinds; sparkling 'jewels', blue, green, cream, brown, amber. It was a cause for celebration when one of them found a much rarer red.

They climbed Stonebarrow Hill from the beach. The boys would sit on top munching apples, while Essie enjoyed the sweeping coastal views all the way round Lyme Bay to Portland.

The sea was not always as calm as on the day they arrived, but she loved it in all its moods. She laughed at the cheeky gurgling waves, determined to be heard above everything else, resolutely pounding on the door of the cliffs below, persisting with their knocking, however many times they were thrown back. She philosophized when the ocean was a mass of tense scrolls, all anger subsiding when they reached the shore. She thrilled when mountains of froth reached for the sky and angrily tossed the beach pebbles against the sea wall.

How she loved the spray on her face, the salt on her lips, the changeable river Char, which sometimes surged, swift and wide, eager to join the sea, and at other times slurped lazily into two or three narrow channels, leaving islands of sand between. Geography she had learned at school came to life before her eyes. She had vainly tried to imagine seas and rivers as she had drawn them on her maps. She had tried to picture cliffs that sometimes rumbled slowly into the sea. Now it was all here, to see and enjoy every day.

During school holidays Vee joined them on their walks. Together they sailed out with the fishermen, bringing back fresh mackerel for tea. They climbed Granny's Teeth, old roughly-hewn steps which led to the top shelf of the Cobb harbour wall at Lyme Regis. Vee taught them all how to swim. They travelled by dray into the market towns of Bridport and Axminster.

The vicar's wife passed a bicycle on to them very cheaply, and both Essie and Vee had fun learning to ride it. They took it in turns to ride along the quiet paths of Langdon forest, where there were carpets of bluebells and where ponies came to nuzzle a greeting, where meadows rippled like the sea, and where, in deep dells below them, sheep and goats grazed peacefully, and through the trees flitted tantalizing glimpses of Golden Cap and the ocean below.

In such a setting it was difficult to remember that a war was raging, and that men were being robbed of the privilege of ever being able to enjoy anything like this again.

Vee encouraged Essie to explore on her own, and the market at Bridport was her favourite choice. Stalls were diminished in wartime but there were still some second-hand books, odd remnants of material and bric-a-brac. Second-hand hatpins were cheap and plentiful. Essie polished the ones she bought and soon had an attractive collection, displaying them in a porcelain hatpin-holder given to her by Vee for her sixteenth birthday. The boys had given her a vase they had made by painstakingly glueing their precious pieces of glass from the beach to the outside of a large jar.

She was thrilled one day when she found an embroidered sampler she could afford. It was not old enough to be valuable but it was in perfect condition. House, garden and the alphabet had been worked by a girl with her own Christian name. 'Esther Wilkes,' it said, 'Her Work. Aged 11. 1899.' The same year Essie was born.

At about the time that Essie was buying the sampler from

the market, Vee waited expectantly for the five-past-four train at Axminster station. The train was late and with each passing minute she was concerned that Essie would return from her afternoon at Bridport, and wonder at her absence.

At last it arrived, steaming and hissing, filling the small platform with noise and smoke.

She did not see him at first. His hat was drawn at an angle over one eye and he was carrying a leather portmanteau. She heard his quiet, formal voice. 'I am so pleased you were able to meet me.'

She smiled, remembering how she had always admired his calm and cultured manner.

'You don't look a day older,' he said. 'If only I could say the same for myself.' They stood, uncertain whether to shake hands or hug each other; in fact they did neither.

'I've kept the cab,' she stated briskly. 'Mind you, it's so close, your hotel, it might have been just as quick to walk.'

She watched as he handed his bag to the cabby and took off his hat to run long fingers through his blond hair. He looked so attractive; more attractive than she remembered.

'Is your business in the area going to take long?'

He had worked for the Foreign Office since the outbreak of war. Vee wondered what he was doing down here, but would ask no more questions.

'No longer than a couple of days,' he replied.

'I would like to invite you round, but it would be difficult . . . ' Her voice trailed away. She could just imagine how upset Essie would be if she thought she was trusting another man.

'This is just a snatched half-hour,' she added.

'Don't worry. I shall be fairly tied up anyway. I am grateful for you booking the hotel.' He smiled. 'Maybe you could snatch another half-hour tomorrow?'

'Maybe.'

'Or better still, come to see me sometimes?'

It was her turn to smile mischievously. 'We'll see.'

In such an idyllic existence it would have been easy to forget about the war, despite growing casualty lists in newspapers, and troop traffic going through Charmouth for Southampton. Essie had joined a group of ladies who met at the vicarage and did knitting for the troops, and she often wondered about her brother Sidney. She had never felt much affection for him, but she hoped he wasn't hurt.

At the tiny village post office they were used to her bringing in her Canadian letters to be weighed and stamped; she was never short of news for Arthur and Liddy.

Her happy smiles and genuine desire to learn more about their local area endeared her to the villagers, and also ensured adequate supplies of cheap stewing meat from the village butcher.

Despite Justin's naughtiness Essie missed him when he started at the school where Vee taught. It was at about this time that Vee offered to tutor her and Essie accepted gratefully. After the boys were asleep they would settle down to work, side by side in the study, Vee setting her willing pupil some work before she started on her own marking and lesson preparation.

When they had both finished she would check Essie's work, and they would discuss at length a wide range of subjects, English language, literature, history, art, simple mathematics and travel.

No wonder the years rolled by so fast.

One day Vee said, 'I think you are catching up with me, Essie. You absorb everything like blotting paper. What else can I teach you?'

'How to talk like you,' Essie replied immediately.

'Oh, Essie! Is that necessary? You have said yourself that you love to hear the Dorset dialect. Accents are attractive.'

'Not the Black Country accent. Now, doh denoi it, are kid,' she quipped broadly, exaggerating each word.

Vee laughed. 'Very well, if you are quite sure. We will start by pitching your voice lower, Essie . . . '

It took time. But they managed it.

Essie was gently bullied into taking some time off during school holidays. Vee insisted she needed her room because she had a friend coming to stay. 'I have regular breaks and you must,' she stressed when Essie argued that she did not need a holiday.

Vee's 'breaks' were spent in London. Sometimes she took the boys; at other times she left them with Essie. She usually returned with gruesome tales of injured troops at crowded railway stations, and for a while they would talk about the war and wonder if it would ever end.

Essie took her holidays at Ivy's. Although not able to join properly in the conversation Mabel loved to listen to the chatter of the two girls, and George said that Essie's visit was better than a tonic from the doctor.

It was lovely to feel the sincerity of their welcome, and nice to be able to visit Mrs Lake and Joe nearby, but soon after she arrived Essie was hankering to be back by the sea. She missed Vee and the boys. She missed the rolling hills, the 'sweet retired bay' Jane Austen had written about, the fresh clean air. Black Country murkiness irritated her nostrils now; strange how she had never noticed it when she was breathing it all the time. And she was too close to her dad for comfort!

While Essie was in the Midlands Vee again met her friend at the station. This time the train was not late, there were no strained formalities, and she had not booked him in a room at a hotel.

'Hello darling,' he greeted her simply after their lips had met for a long time. 'I have not been able to get you out of my mind since we said goodbye at Waterloo.'

She was unable to suppress a laugh at the happiness she felt. It was going to be a wonderful weekend.

In the summer of 1918 Essie was bridesmaid at Ivy's wedding during Ron's first leave for two years. She stayed on to look after Mabel until the newly-weds returned starry-eyed from a three-day honeymoon at Blackpool, full of plans for 'after the war', when they had dreams of a little farm of their own.

'Married life is marvellous,' Ivy confided as Essie prepared to leave. 'Ron says you will be snapped up before you know where you are. He says we couldn't have had a prettier bridesmaid. You won't be able to stay on the shelf for long, mark my words.'

'No one is going to get me off that shelf.'

'Rubbish! You don't want to be an old maid, surely?'

'If there is no alternative to marriage, yes, I do.'

'But why, Essie?'

'Let's just say I don't trust men.'

Ivy appeared crestfallen until Essie added, smiling, 'Except your Ron, of course. He's the tops.'

Ivy chuckled then. 'He is, isn't he? I am so lucky.'

'Marriage will be wonderful for you and Ron, Ivy. You will live happily ever after. But it's not for me; I don't need marriage.'

'Hm. We'll see, madam.'

It was November 1918. The war had been over for only a week when Vee dropped her bombshell.

Essie had been in the church hall since dawn, helping to prepare for the celebratory end-of-war supper. It had been the idea of the knitting circle and had been eagerly embraced by the vicar and the parish council.

Red, white and blue bunting lay piled high in a corner; it had last been used for George V's coronation in 1911, and needed to be carefully untangled before being hung between the high beams of the ceiling.

Trestle-tables were being noisily constructed by a group of enthusiastic scouts; four members of the Women's Institute, laden with cakes and clutching snowy-white table-cloths, were anxiously awaiting their opportunity to lay out the first table. The vicar's wife, beaming broadly at everyone, was counting cups.

Essie was gazing round, caught up in the joyous relief and expectant happiness of the occasion, when she caught sight of Vee. Instantly she felt concerned. Vee was struggling through the entrance with a stepladder almost twice her height, and looked in pain. But as Essie watched, the ladder was lifted from her hands and laid expertly against a wall by one of the taller scouts; yet Vee's expression had not altered.

'Have you been overdoing things?' Essie enquired anxiously.

Vee shook her head abruptly. 'Of course not.' There was something in her tone which brought to Essie strange pangs of insecurity which had laid dormant for years.

'I think everyone is going to be splendid,' she remarked, in an attempt to sound more cheerful than she felt.

Vee's eyes looked slightly glazed as if she was concentrating hard.

'Essie,' she said, 'I have something important to tell you.'

Once the words began they came in a torrent. She intended to re-marry in the new year, she said. She had decided to marry the friend who came to stay while Essie was away and whom she had been meeting in London. Surely she had guessed already? After all, the boys had talked about their uncle who had taken them to the London parks and to Lyons for tea.

Essie was shattered. How naive she had been. It was her turn to fall silent and struggle for words, which finally tumbled out with a wavering harshness that surprised her. 'Why didn't you give me any warning?' she asked. 'And why leave it until now to tell me here?'

Vee glanced round guiltily at all the activity; no one else in the hall seemed at all aware of the importance of their conversation. She had been wondering how to broach the subject for days. Now it had happened involuntarily.

She tried to explain gently. 'I am afraid that I am very different to you, dear,' she said. 'I need a man in my life, someone who will take care of me. I *like* male companionship.'

Essie could feel a hot blush suffuse her cheeks. Of course Vee needed some male companionship and more excitement than she cound find here. She was still young, intelligent and very beautiful. But marriage! How could she ever think of marrying again after her experience with that awful husband?

'We have been friends since childhood,' Vee was explaining as Essie struggled to grasp the situation, amid the distracting bustle in the hall. She leaned back against a trestle-table as Vee continued. 'Our mothers were friends. I went to school with his sister.

'He is a good man, Essie. Thoroughly trustworthy and reliable.' It was the only oblique reference she had ever made to the fact that the Captain may have been otherwise. 'It will be good for the boys, too. They need a man.'

'You seemed so happy here . . . '

Vee placed an affectionate arm around her shoulder. 'As happy as I have ever been, believe me.'

'Is the cottage his?'

Vee nodded. 'Shared by the family. They offered it immediately they heard of our predicament after . . . ' She paused before pleading, 'You will come with us, won't you, Essie? My future husband's work will take him away a lot. The family home is up north. We would still be able to spend much time together, you and I. We would all very much like you to come.'

'I must think about it carefully, Vee.'

Essie felt she could no longer remain in the hall with its ardent activity around her. She left instantly, consulting no one, to walk briskly toward the sea.

The vicar's wife watched her departure in surprise; Essie was not one to leave a job half finished. She shrugged; the end of the war coming so suddenly had affected them all in different ways.

Essie knew the answer to Vee's invitation before she went down to consult the sea. The waves were in turmoil, like her heart. They reminded her of politicians, mighty authoritative waves, pushing others less energetic out of the way, racing, heaving, lording their power, until at last it was their turn to lap insignificantly on the seashore, or, gasping with exhaustion, to be sucked into oblivion by the great jaws of other, younger, more powerful masses following in their wake.

She recalled the mood of the sea on that first, heavenly day when they arrived. It could not always be like that. There had to be change. Charmouth had given her the chance to live a childhood she had missed. Now it was time to grow up and be on her way. To stand alone.

She was more mature, more knowledgeable, more attractive than the thirteen-year-old Essie who had confidently stepped out into the world on that New Year's Day almost six years ago. Why was it that the young Essie had felt so much braver? Maybe because she had no emotional ties then. She had been able to leave parents, brother and sister, without a single backward glance.

Now she felt this awful ache, this sense of loss.

She should have been warned by the light in Vee's eyes, the joy of her laughter, whenever she returned after time away. She had foolishly supposed it was because they were

100

together again. She herself always felt elated when she returned; it was like coming home. She had come to regard Vee and the boys as part of her life. A mistake. Oh what a mistake!

She groaned inwardly. How she had changed. She must re-capture the toughness of the former Essie and never lean on anyone again. 'Never, never, never again, Essie, do you hear?' she admonished herself severely, throwing her words into the wind, together with the biggest pebble she could find, which winged far away into the threatening sea.

By Christmas she had found a place to live above a corner shop, in the little market town of Axminster, just over the border in Devon. Previously storerooms, the place smelled fusty, but it was roomy and light, with two windows, one overlooking the cattle market, the other with a view over a narrow lane which led downhill to some auction rooms. There was a poky kitchenette with an earthenware sink, a cold tap and two gas rings.

Another tiny dark room, filled with cobwebs, led off from the kitchen. The owner suggested that it could be used as a bedroom, but Essie decided she would put a bed in the corner of 'the barn', as she had christened the main room.

Vee bought linoleum and together they laid it to hide the cracks in the floor. Together they removed cobwebs, cleaned windows, and made curtains from cheap cotton gingham. Essie brought her books, her sampler by Esther Wilkes and her collection of hatpins, which she placed on the mantelpiece. The precious vase which the boys had made with glass from the beach, now filled with cheerful red-berried holly, stood on the window sill, a permanent memento of their happy jaunts.

They painted the dingy walls pink and the ceiling white. As they sat in a couple of second-hand armchairs Essie had picked up at the auction rooms, they surveyed their handiwork with mutual satisfaction. Essie's heart sank as she realized how much she would miss Vee's wonderful companionship.

She had it in mind to move on New Year's Day; it seemed appropriate. New Year's Day had been the start of her new life when she had left Heath End six years before. Vee tried to persuade her to stay in the cottage throughout the winter but when she saw that she was determined she decided to move on the same day herself.

The boys were sent to their grandparents for Christmas. Essie wondered if 'the friend' might appear, but they were able to spend Christmas Day alone together, just the two of them.

On Christmas morning they left a chicken in the oven while they climbed Stonebarrow Hill. It was a mild, clear morning; they could see all around the coast, from where gentle hills dipped and rolled round Lyme Bay, to Portland Bill. After pausing to enjoy the scene they walked on to the top of tall Golden Cap, where they stood breathlessly admiring the undulating cliffs glinting gold in the winter sunlight, their valleys carpeted in every shade of green. Fluffy clouds chased one another across the sky, a suspicion of haze hovering over Portland. Waves as dozy as summer reminded them both of the day they first arrived.

Vee sighed. 'I shall miss this place.'

'Me too.'

'You will still be able to come.'

'So will you if you use the cottage for holidays.'

Vee shook her head. 'It is to be sold. The family were on the brink of selling when our needs arose.' Essie noticed the violet eyes filling with tears. She could not allow that.

'Race you home,' she said.

Home! After their Christmas meal she gave Vee an old map of Dorset she had bought from a bookstall. 'Happy Christmas, Vee.'

'Thank you, my dear Essie. It is lovely. But I am afraid you will have to wait until New Year for your present.'

New Year arrived all too soon.

Together they had packed the belongings that Vee had brought with her to the cottage. A man arrived with a hired van. He was also going to take Vee to the station. Essie had offered to stay behind for a final clean-up.

'We must write to each other regularly, Essie. I shall want to hear . . . '

'No!' The word exploded emphatically, startling Essie herself. 'A clean break, Vee. Please!'

'If this is what you want. Oh dear, Essie, are you sure?'

Essie's heart jerked uncomfortably at the pain in the eyes of the kindest person she was ever likely to meet. But Vee's voice was as gentle as ever as she took a printed card from her bag. 'The address of my bank, Essie. They will send mail on to me, wherever I am. If ever you need me, please do get in touch.' She wrote swiftly on the back of the card. 'My new name.'

It was agony saying goodbye. This was not the tough little Essie who had left Heath End on that icy January morning; it seemed a world away from the milder South. A world away, all of it.

'Are you sure you have enough money?'

'Quite sure.' Tears in her throat were forced to stay there.

'Oh, Essie! What will you do?'

'I shall manage.'

After waving until she could no longer see them, Essie returned to the tiny fireplace, holding the card Vee had given her tightly between clenched hands to stop them trembling. Then, without even glancing at it, she dropped it into the dying embers of the fire. She must stand on her own feet, and must not be tempted by an address to do otherwise.

When she moved into her own rooms later they were all there; all the things she had helped pack earlier. The small regency table that came apart into two trays, the pretty secretaire, inkstands, porcelain figures, paintings, hand-embroidered samplers, workboxes, a clock - all neatly set out in the room they had decorated together.

The pictures had been left for her to hang them herself.

A note on lavender-scented paper said:

> Dearest Essie,
>   Please accept these with my love.
> I know how fond you are of each and
> every one of them, but don't hesitate to
> sell them all if need be.
>   Ever your friend,
>   Vee

The bicycle they had shared was parked in an outhouse at the back of the shop.

Chapter Six

The first few weeks were awful.

Essie missed the life she had enjoyed more than she would have believed possible: Vee and the boys, the companionship and shared hobbies, the caring, the comforts of the warm cottage, the sight of sea and downs from its windows. Most of all she missed being needed.

She had thought she would have no trouble in getting work. She possessed so many more skills now than when she first started. She could cook, sew, garden, decorate; she knew quite a lot about Art, Literature, Geography and History, and she talked properly. But it had been easier to get a job when she knew nothing.

She tried the bakery, the post office, the shops, all in vain. Men were returning from war and women were willingly giving up their jobs to make way for them. She answered advertisements for cleaners and cooks. Employers were suspicious of anyone looking as pretty as a picture and talking like a lady.

Some days she gave herself up to walking to Charmouth, strolling along its beaches, exploring the woods and climbing the downs bordering the shore. She was reminded of a poem she had enjoyed with Vee.

> There is a pleasure in the pathless woods,
> There is a rapture on the lonely shore,
> There is society, where none intrudes,
> By the deep sea, and music in its roar.

But there was no rapture now and she could not bear to go and look at the cottage.

She still haunted the markets in Axminster and Bridport. It reminded her of the days in Walsall when she could only look and not buy, for now she was watching her decreasing funds with trepidation. Rent day rolled round with the speed of light. It cost a lot to heat the barn-like room which became damp as the weather worsened and it seemed almost as expensive buying food for one as it had been for four.

She regularly attended the auctions in the sale-rooms nearby, fascinated by the atmosphere of excitement as people bid against each other, some poker-faced throughout, others unable to contain their delight when their bid had succeeded. She noticed that items such as Vee had given her fetched high prices. Recognizing them on the stalls at Bridport later, she realized that the stallholders were asking far more than they had paid for them.

Suddenly she had only enough money left to keep her rooms for two more weeks. She re-read Vee's note, 'Don't hesitate to sell . . . ' At the time she had never dreamed she would even consider selling anything, but now she realized she might have to. Maybe if she sold just one or two things on Axminster market she could buy from the auction with money she had made and re-sell at a fair profit; then she would not have to part with any more of Vee's precious gifts.

Axminster market did not boast an antiques stall, yet there were always bustling crowds in the town on market days, and a lot of money changed hands. Farmers came to buy and sell while their wives wandered around the stalls, and floats from outlying villages came, packed with families determined to have a merry day out.

The more she thought of hiring a stall the more she liked the idea. She felt elated when she had made her decision; this might be the start of a successful venture.

Her first day as a stallholder wore on and she became more and more frustrated. She was cold, hungry, and she had not recuperated a penny toward the cost of hiring the stall, which was nearly as much as a week's rent for her rooms.

She had resisted calling out in the way that the seasoned stallholders did in order to advertise their wares but at last, in desperation, she found herself hailing a group of chattering farmers' wives whom she had watched buying curtain materials and wellington boots. 'Are you interested in a bit of quality, ladies?' The women wandered over, smiling back at her good-naturedly, their cheerful country faces glowing like ripe rosy apples.

She had brought two of her samplers along; they fingered them and remarked on the embroidery. 'A bit amateurish,' one of them commented critically. 'Not very colourful,' said another. They handled her delicate pieces of porcelain quite roughly; Essie could hardly bear it. They barely glanced at the pictures, the beautiful carriage clock or her little regency table.

'I've lots of stuff like this at home, m'dear,' one of the women remarked, not unkindly. She was round and neat as a new pin.

'Same hee-er,' her friend, a younger woman, agreed in her soft Dorset burr. 'We 'ave Oswald's grandmother's junk now, to find houseroom for. It's new stuff I'm arfter.'

'Fine chance you have of getting anything new, Amy,' her companion laughed. 'Your old man will at this minute be spending all his wealth on pigs, if I know him. 'Fraid you're stuck with Gran's junk, my dear.'

'I will take all Gran's junk off your hands and give you a fair price for it. Then you will be able to buy all the new you want.' The women swung round to see a man, square-shouldered and handsome, with an engaging smile and impudent eyes.

'Well! If it means you're thinking o' comin' yourself I will certainly consider it,' Amy laughed.

'What sort of things do ee buy, young man?' asked the older woman.

'Anything that's worth buying'.'

The women appeared interested.

'I'll be under no obligation, mind, young man.'

'Me neither, madam.'

He produced notebook and pencil. 'Tell me where you lovely ladies live and I'll be there tomorrow, without fail.'

Several of the women, charmed by the midnight-blue eyes beneath thick curly lashes, and the deep dimple in the square chin, wrote down their addresses for him.

'Be sure and come when my old man's out,' said Amy, chuckling.

'Knock three times and ask for Bo,' said another. They had surrounded him; it was as if Essie and her wares were invisible.

After careful instructions as to how to find them and a bit more banter, they were off to seek their husbands. The man turned his attention to Essie, aware of her irritation, yet smiling as bold as brass while stripping her with his eyes.

She flushed with an annoyance she had not felt in years. She had seen him earlier in the day, buying from the old man who sold second-hand toys from a barrow. He had bought the only things of any value, a musical box shaped like a barrel-organ, a miniature oak bureau, beautifully carved, a colourful silk parasol. She had vaguely wondered if he had children, but later as his keen eyes searched the pottery stall critically, before quizzing the stallholder, she guessed he was buying to sell again. There was a familiarity about him which was faintly disturbing. She tried to remember where she had seen him before. Was it at the auction rooms?

She puzzled over it now as he faced her across the stall.

'How dare you come barging in like that,' she demanded angrily. 'Just as I was about to make a sale.'

His head went back as he roared with laughter. 'You're kidding, love. You didn't have a dog's chance. Those old farmhouses are stately homes in miniature, packed with more antiques than you've ever seen.'

'Even if some of them are pushed into the barns,' he added drily.

'How do you know what I have seen, you interfering busybody. And don't call me love!'

She reached hastily for the cardboard box at her feet and placed it on the trestle of the stall with a bang.

'Tell you what, just to make it up to you, I'll take the lot.'

She ignored him as if she was deaf, as she dismantled the fluted trays of her beautiful regency table, folding the delicate legs carefully against one another, before placing it gently in the box. This was the last thing she wanted to part with really, but she had decided last night that if she could just sell this one item she could hang on to the rest, for the money from the table would keep her going for weeks, by which time a job may have come along.

He scrutinized her face as she wrapped each piece of porcelain in a piece of newspaper. 'Did you hear me, spitfire? I said I will buy the lot.'

'Thank you, Mr . . . '

'Joss Berridge. Just call me Joss.'

'Thank you, Mr Berridge,' she continued coldly, 'but I have decided to sell no more today.'

'But I saw you set up your stall this morning. You haven't sold a thing.'

'And you decided to wait, thinking I would lower my prices, I suppose,' she retorted angrily.

'As if I would do that! Miss, er?'

She continued silently to pack the rest of the things, her small lips compressed. She tied the pictures together with string.

'Do you live far?'

'No.'

'If you won't take my money at least let me help you with these.' He scooped the box from the stall before she could object and tucked the pictures under his arm. 'Lead the way.'

Several stallholders were already watching with undisguised interest. A sea fret was blowing up, the crowds were thinning out fast and they were ready for a diversion before packing up themselves. So Essie held her tongue, stepping out smartly in front of him, seething inside at her own stupidity in not selling him at least one item. Pride would not pay the rent. And she would not dream of missing the rent, for the old couple who kept the sweetshop below, and who sub-let the rooms, barely made a living themselves. The shop was away from the main thoroughfare and did not do much trade, especially on market days when big bags of sweets were sold from stalls for next to nothing. They had talked lately of closing the shop, and living with a daughter.

The stranger followed her in as she unlocked her door. He placed the box on the floor and propped the pictures carefully against the wall. 'They're good pictures. You should wrap them. They're worth more than a bit of old string. Do you realize what they're worth?'

She did not reply. She crossed to the hearth.

The fire was almost dead. She automatically reached for a

square of coal from the brass scuttle; there were only two lumps left.

The man glanced round the room, noting how sparsely furnished it was, and how scrupulously clean. 'A bit chilly in here, isn't it, love? Short of coal?'

'I forgot to order some, that's all. Now, Mr Berridge, as I do not feel the need of any more of your advice, goodbye.'

'Maybe more advice another day then?' he grinned and was gone.

Essie returned her treasures to their usual places with a mixture of relief and disappointment. She had set off this morning with such high hopes of starting a profitable little business. The rooms felt empty and cheerless. It was the coldest March since she had come south. Or was it just that she missed the carpeted cosiness of the Charmouth cottage?

She poked at the fire sharply, feeling suddenly lonely. Even arguing with the irritating Mr Berridge had been better than having no one to talk to. 'Snap out of it, Essie,' she reprimanded herself sternly. 'You are going to stand on your own two feet, remember.'

She washed her face and hands with the first kettleful of hot water and made a pot of tea with the second. She had just laid a tray and he was back, tapping a tune on her door.

He stood there, holding a huge bulging sack. 'A peace offering.'

'I don't need one.'

'You need these.' He lifted the bag lightly, quickly easing himself past her into the room, and straight away began packing the coal scuttle with logs, first ramming a couple into the fire-grate, one on either side of the almost lifeless lump of coal. Immediately the logs began to spark and burn. 'Good dry logs, these. I had them given to me today. Only taking up room in my van.'

'Where would you like me to put the rest of them?'

'There is a little room off the kitchen.'

He carried the sack through. She heard him washing his hands under the tap, before he returned to the hearth.

'They should last you for a while, until you've ordered the coal.'

'Thank you.'

He smiled, glancing at the tray. 'Do I deserve a cup of tea, then?'

'I suppose so.' She felt too cold and dispirited to argue any more. 'Take a seat.' While she fetched another cup he pulled the two easy chairs close to the fire which was already throwing out a welcome warmth.

'Take the weight off your feet, love.' He held up his hand to forestall her protest. 'If I'm not to call you "love" I need a name.'

'Essie.'

'We shall both feel better after a cup of tea, Essie.'

Her legs ached from standing in the cold all day. She was disappointed and hungry. It was good to see a fire, which was beginning to bathe the room in a rosy glow; the logs smelled nice, too. She was surprised that he was capable of sitting still; he seemed so volatile. They quietly sipped the scalding tea; there had only been enough milk for a dash in each cup.

He was completely at ease, his legs stretched out toward the blaze. She studied his face. Striking, it was, even in repose, with a stubborn chin, deeply dimpled, thick black brows and lashes, dark blue eyes that seemed permanently amused, and a firm mouth, now serious, making him appear older. An impudent face, yet strong. A familiar face. Again that niggling, disturbing feeling that she should be able to fit him into a time and place.

It was strangely comforting to have a companion sharing the warmth of the tea and fire. She realized that he was the first visitor to enter her new home since Vee. She recalled how they had sat warming their hands on the mugs of soup, and how Vee had left the treasures for which she had not been able to drop even a line of thanks.

'You don't want to give up your treasures, do you?' he remarked, as if reading her thoughts, his voice no longer bantering.

'They were given to me by a very dear friend.'

'There's no room for sentiment in business, Essie.'

'I am not sentimental.'

'Good. Glad to get that out of the way.'

She recognized a familiar twang in his voice. 'You are a Midlander.'

'Indisputable accent?'

'Yes.' She smiled.

'And I spent four years at an expensive finishing school in France trying to get rid of it.'

'Army?'

He nodded briefly and changed the subject. 'That's the first time you've smiled at me. Those big brown eyes have been mournful all day. You should smile more, Essie. You are very beautiful now, all flushed from the fire. And smiling at me.' He leaned forward to touch her cheek.

'Don't push your luck.'

'I won't.' He laughed good-humouredly, drawing back instantly. There was a pause as he pondered her thoughtfully. 'Well, it takes one to know one.'

'Meaning?'

'Meaning you can recognize a Midlander. So you are one yourself?'

'I worked there for a time. Before the war.'

'Where?'

'In Walsall.'

'My stepfather used to keep a bookshop there.'

She sat up with a jerk. She was back in Walsall market on the day Arthur came instead of Sidney. She had it! The time and the place. The curly-haired lad not much older than

113

herself, handing out advice even then. 'These are what you should be collecting,' he had said. 'First editions.'

The day she had bought *Rose in Bloom*, forerunner to all the other first editions that now graced her shelves. She almost blurted it out, then decided it would keep. 'So you own a van? Where is it?'

'In the yard at The George. I'm booked in there for the night. I've booked a good hot supper as well. How about joining me, Essie? I would like to make amends.'

'I thought you already had,' she replied, indicating the crackling logs.

'It's roast beef and yorkshire . . . '

Her stomach groaned for it, but still she hesitated. 'I don't eat out. And I don't know you.'

'You know my name and where I come from. Isn't that enough to be going on with? If I walk away now you'll never know me. What's worse, I'll never know you. And I've a mind we may be able to do business together. I haven't any bad intentions, if that's what you think.'

'It would be all the same if you had.'

It was stimulating to have someone to fence with. She had not argued with anyone for so long. It was as if the spirit of the younger Essie was being resuscitated.

The thought of a good meal and conversation, even with a stranger, appealed. Yet somehow the man did not seem like a stranger, sitting close, sharing the fire with her. Maybe it was because he was a Midlander and there was a trace left in her.

Could she trust him? She doubted it. Not with that cheeky grin and those eyes that seemed to burrow straight into your soul and know what you were going to say before you said it. Right now she guessed that he felt certain she would say yes. For that reason alone she would have liked to refuse.

'Say I can pick you up at half-six.'

'To take me to The George! It is only five minutes walk,' she stalled.

'So?'

'I will meet you there.'

'I will pick you up at half-past-six.'

The meal was served immediately they sat down, succulent beef, lashings of it in steaming gravy, baked potatoes, roasted parsnips, mashed swedes and carrots. Essie did not speak until she had cleared the plate, eating slowly and concentrating in order to appreciate every mouthful.

Joss attacked his meal with enthusiasm. He grinned at her now; it had been a joy to see her eat. 'I needed that,' he said.

'Not half as much as I did,' Essie rejoined frankly, knowing she was giving nothing away he could not deduce for himself.

She did not join him in the apple pie and clotted cream; there was a limit to what an unpractised stomach could stand after weeks of bread and boiled vegetables. The landlord invited them to be seated before a roaring fire. Joss ordered cider for himself and coffee 'for the lady'. The only other diners, three businessmen, went along to the bar, and Joss began to talk of his ambitions. His older, serious face was back.

There were lots of businessmen in the Midlands who had been made rich by war, he said, foundry-owners, manufacturers, colliery managers, soon to be pit bosses again when the government turned over the mines back to them.

'The new rich. They've bought their big houses, and now they're looking for something else to invest in that can't be taxed. Things that are going to gain in value.'

'Like antiques?'

He nodded. 'The money's burnin' a hole in their pockets, Essie. That's the place to be sellin', and down here's the place to buy. You were trying to sell ice cream to the eskimos today.'

She pulled a face at him, and he laughed.

'Farm-owners down here may not have much in their pockets, but, believe me, their houses and their barns are stuffed with ancient valuables. Handed down from generation to generation.

'There are a lot of retired rich down here, as well. When they died whole houseloads go up for sale. Sometimes there are hardly any bidders.'

'So you are buying down here and taking it up to the Midlands to sell?'

'That's my idea. But I can't be in two places at once. I need an agent down here to buy from the auctions and housesales when I am engaged elsewhere.'

He sipped his cider, watching the varying expressions flitting across her face, his dark eyes dancing. 'What do you say? Do you fancy the job? As my agent?'

Her mind was racing excitedly. It sounded attractive and she did need the money, but she replied evenly, 'I would have to think about it.'

'There is yet another market as well,' he continued. 'Thousands of soldiers returning from war. Setting up homes in Viscount Addison's new houses "fit for heroes to live in". Unlike the industrialists who stayed home, there's been no chance for the heroes to make their fortunes. So they are looking for reasonably-priced, good second-hand furniture.

'The *nouveaux riches* want that out of the way. And quickly. Black Country folk don't hoard; you will know that. It's off to the rag-and-bone man before you can say knife. So I have to beat the rag-and-bone man to it. I've got that little business nicely off the ground already.'

'You sell second-hand?' He nodded.

'Where do you sell from?'

'From what was the bookshop.'

'What happened to the books?' She could not resist asking.

'Oh, they're safe. All the ones of any value anyway.

'Have you ever been to an auction?' he enquired suddenly.

'Lots.' Essie replied airily.

'Then you could attend the auctions and housesales for me. Quality antique furniture is what I'm after, as well as small stuff. There is enough space in those rooms of yours to store whatever you manage to obtain until I come down again. I am willing to pay rent for storage space. We could start with what I bought today.'

'What did you buy today?' she asked curiously.

'A couple of nice Georgian chairs. Some silver. Glass. Hoping for more tomorrow. I shall be off, bright and early, to look in at Chard, Crewkerne and Honiton, in addition to calling on the farm ladies. Don't fancy carting such a precious cargo around with me all day, especially the silver. That may get lifted. What do you say? Will you store it for me?'

'Strictly business?'

'Strictly business.'

It sounded like the answer to a prayer, but she replied cautiously. 'You can leave your purchases with me tonight. As for the rest of your proposition, I will consider it and let you know tomorrow.'

'Over supper?'

'If you like.'

He grinned, carefree and boyish again. 'In that case I will book in here for another night.'

But they did not eat at The George the following evening. Joss was back from the farms early afternoon, parking his van within sight of Essie's window. It was square and

117

sturdy, like Joss himself, canvas-covered, with large wheels and chunky mudguards. Like an elated schoolboy he related his 'finds'. He chatted away racily, excitedly, poised for flight, one eye always on the van.

'From the first house a dresser, oak coffer and oak stool,' he recounted in answer to her question. 'All sixteenth-century. A seventeenth-century box-seat settle from the second house, plus a Gothic-type oak food-cupboard, being used for corn in the hen-house. And from that cheeky lass . . .'

'Amy?'

'That's the name. From Amy, a Queen Anne walnut settee; perfect it will be when I've restored it. I had to sweep off three cats and a sleeping puppy before I could examine it properly.' He chuckled at the memory. 'There's a lot of good stuff there Amy would like to be rid of, but she has to ask Oswald's permission first, she says.' He grinned cheekily. 'I think she wants to get me back there, that's the top and bottom of it.

'In her kitchen she was using some Georgian mahogany library steps.' He laughed again; evidently the whole episode had been a source of amusement. 'She was easily persuaded to part with them on the understanding I found her some new steps. So there's your first task, Essie.'

'You seem to be taking an awful lot for granted. And how do you recognize all this furniture for what it is?'

'Books. And keeping my ears and eyes open.' He took one sip at the tea she had handed him. 'The point is,' he continued hurriedly, 'I would like to unload all this and leave it with you, love.'

'Now?'

'Now. Because even more successful, Essie, was the business I conducted this morning. I went to Chard first, and there was no need to go elsewhere. I walked straight into a housesale. A Frenchman's home. No family.

Executors' sale.' His eyes were dancing with satisfaction. 'I bought a whole lot of Louis XV furniture. I know just the buyer in Birmingham. So I want to get it up there tonight.'

'Do you think you could give us a hand? I've a lad watching the van. He will help me carry the stuff up. You only have to guide us upstairs, see that we damage nothing.'

'But I haven't said I agree . . . '

She had prepared a speech about the terms and conditions under which she would agree, but he was giving her no chance to deliver it.

'Hurry up and make up your mind,' he interrupted, 'because I have to be back at Chard to get the goods removed before four o'clock, or the place will be closed. You are only agreeing to rent me a space at this stage. Surely there is no risk in that? And you can use the furniture while it is here.'

She found herself doing as he asked, on the one hand resenting his tone of authority, and on the other having to admire the agility and strength with which he manoeuvred the furniture up her awkward staircase, which turned at the top.

He skipped up and down the stairs surprisingly quietly for such a well-built man. The whole operation was performed swiftly, without fuss or noise; nevertheless Essie was glad she had mentioned what was happening to the old couple in the shop below.

On his final trip up her stairs Joss produced some thick slices of home-fed bacon and a dozen large brown eggs. 'A present from Amy,' he explained. 'I am afraid there will be no time for The George tonight, Essie. Sorry. We shall have to dine here. I shall be back before five. Do you think you can have it ready by then?'

He was gone before she could say yes or no. What a nerve the man had, inviting himself! Nevertheless she had to admit to a feeling of excitement as she admired the furniture he had left, re-arranging some of it in her room, pushing the heavier pieces with her back.

All the furniture from the first house, the oak coffer with iron carrying-handles, the magnificently-carved dresser with a cupboard and roomy plate rack, and the oak stool, had been well cared for and lovingly polished. Essie guessed they had come from the older woman.

The other items needed attention, particularly Amy's settee and steps. The settee was skilfully worked in wool and silk petit point; it would be very pretty when it was cleaned. And Essie was fascinated with how the library steps folded down into a table. The mahogany was badly scratched. She felt like getting out her polish and rags, but decided that Joss Berridge would have his own very definite ideas about restoration.

They ate bacon, eggs and crisply-fried bread in front of a brightly-burning log fire and surrounded by strange furniture. With obvious satisfaction Joss described the furniture he had bought from the housesale: a walnut, kneehole dressing-table, an ornate hanging cupboard, a marquetry commode, a beautifully-grained beechwood canapé, a silver display cabinet.

'All Louis XV?' queried Essie, trying to sound knowledgeable.

'All of them. And all bargains.'

'Even so, you must have got through a lot of money today.'

'Practically all I have. But there's some left for you, sweetheart.' He put down a sovereign. 'There's some rent in advance, for storage. I'll be back in about a week. And there are a few sovereigns for you to gamble with at the auction; I see they're holding one down the road before I come back. You know the things I'm after. See that you buy well. Also I want you to promise me that if the logs run out you will use some of the money to buy coal. I need this place warm and dry for the sake of the furniture.'

'What! After it surviving the hen-house and a farmhouse kitchen!'

'Well, let's say that I don't want the damp getting at you. All right?'

'The logs you brought will last more than a week.'

'Promise.'

'If you will promise to persuade your rich Birmingham buyer to purchase a couple of my pictures.'

'Are you sure that's what you want?' he asked, surprised.

'They are already packed.' She handed them to him, wrapped in clean pieces of old sheeting. 'And I would like to discuss our business arrangements.'

'Certainly.' He gave a little mock bow. 'But not now. I have to be off. To get more money to buy again, sweetheart.'

'Don't call me sweet . . . '

But he was already at the door, laughingly blowing her kisses. 'Isn't it all exciting?' he said as he left.

It was. She could not deny a sense of elation. Her world was on the move again. She had plans. Plans to make money, and plans not to get emotionally involved with anyone, ever again. And certainly not with Joss Berridge. Nor any man for that matter. Her dad and Captain Vincent had seen to that.

Chapter Seven

She put her hair up to make herself look older and more responsible. The auctioneer smiled indulgently, recognizing her as the slip of a girl who had been haunting the sale-room for the last few weeks, and who had only once made a bid, for a pair of tatty armchairs no one else wanted.

Essie had visited the sale-rooms to view on the day before the auction. There was a wide assortment of furniture of all types, some of which she studied closely, feeling reasonably sure that Joss would have been interested. But she had not the money to bid for good-quality furniture. She discovered some pretty porcelain, divided into lots, and racked her brains to remember what similar pieces had fetched in previous weeks.

She had done her homework as far as she could, studying and copying the marks from the bases of her own porcelain figures. Vee had explained briefly what they meant, but she wished she had more knowledge.

A selection of Meissen, identifiable by their crossed swords, fetched far more than the money alloted to her. Her second choice, a set of Chelsea jugs and plates, beautifully-decorated with flowers and leaves, went for only half-a-crown more than her five pounds limit, which had seemed such a fortune when Joss had dropped five sovereigns on to her table. 'Something to gamble with,' he had said. It was galling to have bid so close to the final figure, and lost; at the same time exciting still to have money in her pocket.

She was consulting the list she had made yesterday, to decide what to try for next, when the auctioneer made an announcement. 'We will leave the porcelain for the time being, ladies and gentlemen, while we take a look at these.' He held aloft two small gold boxes, ornately decorated. 'Louis XV snuffboxes,' he said. 'And beautiful.'

Louis XV! Joss had been so excited about the Louis XV furniture. Maybe his Birmingham buyer would be interested in some smaller items from the same period.

'Who will start me with a half-sovereign for the two?'

A nod; a slight movement of a catalogue; two gentlemen alternately bidding until the price rose to four guineas. They shook their heads as the auctioneer attempted to push the price up by another couple of shillings. Essie raised her hand just before the hammer came down. They were hers for four pounds six shillings.

'Name?' the auctioneer enquired with as much surprise as he ever registered.

'Connaught. Esther Connaught,' she replied clearly.

Her name was Connor, but she had just decided to change it. She did not want to use her father's name any more.

'You have a good buy, Miss Connaught.'

Almost at the end of the sale, when most people had gone, she bought a pair of perfume bottles for five shillings.

Back in her rooms she studied the snuffboxes with a certain amount of trepidation, wondering whether she had been wise. But whatever Joss might say they were quite lovely. She turned them over and over in her hands, marvelling at the workmanship and design. One was in-laid with mother-of-pearl, tiny pixie people beside giant toadstools and drinking vessels. The second snuffbox was covered with delicate pink and blue porcelain flowers nestling inside gold triangles.

The scent bottles she had bought because she liked them so much. They had tall necks and stoppers and were decorated with pale trailing leaves and flowers in delicate colours. If Joss Berridge did not want them she would find some way to buy them herself.

In an unused exercise book she wrote on the left-hand page: 'Received £5.' On the right-hand page: 'Snuffboxes £4. 6s. 0d.' Below that: 'Scent bottles 5s. 0d.' And 'Balance 9s. 0d.' She totalled both sides to five pounds in the same way she had kept housekeeping accounts for Vee.

Would Joss Berridge say that she had wasted his money? 'See that you buy well,' he had said. How could she know?

He turned up a week later. 'Well, how did things go at the auction?'

She handed him the snuffboxes, hardly daring to breathe. Would he deride her for foolish buying? He stood at the window to examine them in the fading afternoon light.

'Will you be able to sell them to your Birmingham customer?'

'He couldn't resist them, darling. Just right for his display cabinet. We must fill that for him, Essie. How much?'

She told him. 'Hm. About right,' he commented guardedly But it was the scent bottles that excited him. 'These are Rockingham!'

'What does that mean?'

'Rockingham were a firm who were only in business for sixteen years, during which time they made some very fine porcelain. So it means, my pet, that there won't be much of it about. What did you pay?'

'Five shillings. For the two.'

'Five shillings!' He grinned broadly, lifting her off her feet and swinging her round, ignoring her protests. 'I knew you would be a natural.'

'Even if you can't sell from a market stall,' he added, chuckling.

'I suppose I lack your gift for bullying people into buying. Or selling!'

'No need for bullying. The secret, Essie, is to know what people want and to provide it for them. Speaking of which, did you get the steps for Amy?'

'I . . . I haven't been able to find any yet.'

'Where have you tried?'

'Several places.'

'Essie!' he exclaimed in mock horror. 'Your face tells me you forgot.'

Essie felt herself blushing uncomfortably with guilt and exasperation. 'All right, Joss Know-All. What if I did?'

'Then isn't it fortunate that there are some nice new steps inside my van?'

It irked that he had anticipated she would forget. She was annoyed with herself.

'Don't worry about it. I shan't.' He cocked an eyebrow. 'Last time I was here you said you wanted to discuss business arrangements.' He seated himself at the table after drawing a chair out for her. His eyes were twinkling with amusement. Trust him to choose to talk business now, just as he had caught her at a disadvantage. He made her feel embarrassingly naive, in a way that she never had before. She had to remind herself firmly that now was the moment to obtain the best possible terms, although she was painfully aware that his obvious experience highlighted her lack of it. How she wished she had some means of learning more about antiques.

First she showed him her account book. He seemed amused, but pleased. 'I have stumbled on a bookkeeper as well, have I? What a nose I have for staff!' She felt that he was teasing again; she changed the subject.

'Did you make a lot of money from your Louis-XV business?'

He laughed out loud. 'Enough to take us both out for a good meal at The George tonight.'

'Providing I agree to come.'

'Providing you agree,' he repeated quietly.

Then, 'What have you done to your hair?' he asked suddenly.

'What business is it of yours?' She was flushing again.

'I loved you better when it hung down your back, like spun silk.'

She knew he was only being flippant but she stood up impatiently. 'You're impossible, Joss Berridge.'

'And you're immovable, Essie . . . er? I suppose you do have a surname?'

'Connaught.'

'Why not relax and have fun, Essie Connaught?'

'We agreed our arrangements were to be strictly business, I remember.'

'All right. *All right!*' Five pounds a week to represent me in this area, plus rental for storage. Will that do? I can't exactly make you a partner until you've proved your worth, can I?'

His words took the wind right out of her sails. She had supposed she would have to negotiate for a paltry commission.

'Some weeks I may not be doing any business for you! It is . . . too much.'

'Oh dear! Suspecting me of ulterior motives now, are you?' He sighed.

'I wouldn't put it past you. But it's not that. I haven't enough knowledge or experience to accept . . . '

'You will learn pretty fast if I'm any judge.' He counted

out twenty sovereigns. 'Four weeks in advance,' he explained. 'I may not be down again for some time.' Then he placed two five-pound notes in front of her. 'Sale of two pictures.'

'Ten pounds!'

'The best I could do, I'm afraid. One was by a fairly well-known Dutch artist. But the other . . . '

'I did not expect half that amount.'

'Never say that when you are selling, Miss Connaught. Always expect twice as much. Relate it to how much it will buy. Ten pounds isn't a fortune.'

Her experience with five pounds at the auction had proved that, but Essie was relating it to one hundred weeks' rent, when so recently she had been wondering how she could stay another two weeks.

Joss rose abruptly. 'I will take this off your hands tomorrow,' he said, indicating the furniture she had stored.

He strode toward the door. 'Are you dining with me this evening?' he asked casually, without glancing at her.

'No. Thank you.'

'In that case I will be away, to see Amy.' He laughed. 'She may be kinder to me than you are.'

He did not repeat his invitation and she told herself that it did not matter. She had to admit that she would have enjoyed another good meal at The George, but she had enough money to buy one for herself now and she did not want to become dependent on Joss Berridge and his favours.

It was the following afternoon before he returned, brisk and business-like. He wrote down dates of auctions in the area, one in Crewkerne, one in Chard, two in Bridport, and suggested she watch the local press for housesales.

'I have an account at Crewkerne Sale-rooms, and at Moreys, Bridport. Just give my name; they will deliver here. Here is forty pounds for Chard and anything else that might crop up.'

Essie had never seen so much money at one go. It never occurred to her that he should not trust her. 'You have a week before the first auction. Here's a bit of homework for you meanwhile.'

He handed her a slim volume entitled simply *Porcelain* and a fat book called *Antique Furniture*.

Essie's delight glowed in her face. Just what she had longed for. 'Thank you, Joss,' she breathed. 'I'll take good care of them.'

'Well! Of all the strange women! I dazzle her with wages in advance, money from picture sales, cash to play around with, an invitation to dine, and the only way I can get a smile is by lending her a couple of books!'

'I can learn a lot from these.' Essie flocked through the pages, impatient to settle down with them.

'True. But even more from these.' He stroked the corners of her eyes lightly and gently placed a sturdy hand over each ear. 'Keep your ears and eyes open, Essie. Far better than books. Although there are plenty more where they came from.' He felt her draw back from his touch as her smile faded. He withdrew his hands immediately.

Her room seemed emptier than ever after Joss took the furniture. But there would be some more. Meanwhile she had studying to do. Something to get her teeth into. She felt that her feet were on the first rungs of a ladder which would lead to a coveted goal; to know as much about antiques as Joss did.

Life developed a strange, routineless pattern; never dull. It was a life that suited Essie very well. She soon regained her previous fitness and alertness. Cycling to the various towns provided plenty of fresh air and exercise; she ate properly, and within a few months was saving regularly with Lloyds Bank.

Visits to the auctions, the markets and housesales kept her mentally alert, as did the books on history and antiques regularly supplied by Joss. He was quick to let her know when she made mistakes and she was equally quick to learn from them. As he had forecast, she needed practical experience to supplement the book-learning.

Soon she knew how to recognize quality porcelain and had memorized the various makers' marks. She bought handsome Doulton vases, pretty Dresden figures, a Delft tea kettle and one day a whole set of early Meissen soup plates. Sometimes Joss would ask her to look out for specific items, such as candelabra, work-boxes, mirrors, jewellery. She concentrated on the smaller items, leaving the furniture buying to Joss. Occasionally she accompanied him to auctions, where she observed his skilled bidding methods, his apparent lack of concern, his timing.

He popped up at varying intervals, often when least expected. Sometimes he would be gone for only a few days; at other times she would be left wondering if she would ever see him again. After one such period he turned up late one night, carrying a sleeping-bag.

'The George is filled with bank-holiday visitors. I shall have to bed down here tonight, Essie, my love.'

'You will do no such thing!'

'Would you have me sleep in the van? Particularly when you have a spare room.'

'A *what*?'

'The little dark room off your kitchen. A bit cell-like but I don't mind that.' He indicated a lovely Georgian day-bed she had been storing for him. 'I can push that into the spare room; I'm not fussy.'

'Certainly not! What would the old couple in the shop below think?'

'They would think you're a very lucky girl. Anyway, since when have you minded what people think?' He chuckled. 'You need not worry. I promise to keep the kitchen between us. And behave like a gent. It's too late to get a bed for the night now, Essie.'

'Just for tonight then.'

But he stayed the week. And to her surprise he behaved. Not only that, they had a lot of fun together. It was his holiday, he said. Business had been good and he was treating himself to a week off.

They swam in the sea at Charmouth, among the holiday crowds, and, from the beach, she pointed out the little pink cottage far above them. She did not feel she wanted to take him to look at it from close quarters; it was something too precious to share.

They paid one shilling each for best seats at The Electric Palace in Bridport to see *Prisoner of Zenda* and Charlie Chaplin in *Easy Street*; Joss imitated him when they returned home, causing Essie to laugh with an abandon she had seldom shown before. Bank-holiday crowds were surging through the town on that day, motor cars, carriages and traps streaming along the road from Bridport toward West Bay from morning until late at night. Thousands of people thronged the harbour and east and west beaches were crowded with visitors picnicking on the sands. In the evening, after Joss and Essie came out of The Electric Palace, they joined the crowds making their way to the mound, to participate in the dance arranged by the Bridport Volunteer Band; it had been glorious weather and the day brought a return to pre-war festivity.

She was surprised how well Joss danced, resulting in her booking herself into some dancing classes at the Greyhound Hotel, where every Tuesday she learned how to waltz, foxtrot and veleta.

They enjoyed *Maid of the Mountains* at the Drill Hall, and a concert given by an Australian band to raise money for widows of their soldiers residing in Britain.

They walked along the coast to Beer, sitting on Joss's jacket on the mossy banks of Beer Head to rest and to enjoy the magnificent coastal views; the luminous sky emphasized the plunging and rising of the hills linking Devon with Dorset, making them stand out like three-dimensional, glossy cardboard cut-outs. Essie could imagine Herculean hands chiselling away with giant scissors until quite satisfied with the panorama they had created.

The glistening sea far below showed no signs of such manipulation. Self-willed as always, it bounced mischievously, teasing the small craft and sparring with the seagulls. Joss breathed in deep chunks of pure air.

'Wonderful,' he enthused. 'Wish I could load some of this on to my lorry.'

'I used to walk over the hills like this with my friend Vee,' she said. Perhaps it was the glory of the day reviving happy memories that made her tell him all about Vee and the boys and the joys they had shared at Charmouth. He listened attentively, letting her talk without interruption. When she had finished he reached over and covered her hand with his own, strong, square and warm. 'There is still plenty left to enjoy, Essie.'

She smiled and nodded, but withdrew her hand immediately.

The next day, very early, they travelled along the quiet Dorset coast to Weymouth. Suddenly, as Essie was absorbing the twin pleasures of rolling seas and quiet countryside on either side of the road, Joss braked and climbed out of the van. 'Move over,' he said, in reply to her startled enquiry. 'You will be able to buy something of your own soon. It would be handy to know how to drive it, wouldn't it?'

'You mean I can have a go?' She hooted in unaccustomed excitement. 'You will entrust your precious van to me?'

'I would entrust my life, Essie darling,' he replied lightly, a wide grin minimizing the importance of his words. She was used to his exaggerated statements by now, so merely replied, 'And I shall be entrusting my life to you, it seems,' as she eased herself into the driving seat.

So on a high coastal road, beneath a fresh morning sky, with the sun climbing swiftly and seagulls as elated as herself, swooping over the cliffs, she had her first driving lesson, Joss alternatively teasing and bullying, approving and reproachful. Mastering the gears was the worst thing, but soon she was experiencing the puffed-up sensation of Mr Toad himself.

'How does it feel?'

'Better than a bike,' she chuckled.

She was able to cover many miles before Joss took over as they approached the town. She found herself laughing unrestrainedly as she had never done in her life – and again, when flouncing about on the gaudily-painted horses and swingboats at the fair, and when watching Punch and the humorous sand-sculpture man.

They munched gingersnaps as they explored the harbour, pausing to contemplate the fishermen gutting their catch and to wave to the steamer *Victoria* as she chugged off to Sidmouth and Torquay. Later they lunched in style at the Royal Hotel.

The coast road was busy on the way home, with charabanc-loads of singing holidaymakers, but Joss promised other driving lessons in quieter spots later in the week.

'Enjoyed yourself?' he asked, glancing across at Essie's animated face, polished by the sun in spite of the straw hat she had worn on the back of her head all day, her corn-coloured hair being allowed to hang down her back in the way that he liked it.

'Wonderful, wonderful.' She threw back her head and laughed again in the way that gave him so much pleasure.

After arriving home from Weymouth they washed bread

and cheese down with a bottle of cider Joss had bought. Then they sat silently by her window watching the occasional late drinker tipsily wending his way home after bank-holiday revelling, and young couples congregating beneath a gas-lamp, giggling or arguing, or merely clutching shyly at each other's arms.

Joss broke the silence. 'I wish Rebecca could have shared what we saw today. That magnificent coastline! Those skies! The sun setting over the hills on our way home. The sea and the sands, the crowds; she would have loved all that.'

'And who is Rebecca?'

'Was,' he corrected. 'Rebecca, my mother. Me mam.'

Beneath the bantering tone she detected a seriousness which made her say impulsively, 'Tell me about her.'

'There was just Rebecca and me until I was ten. Great fun she was. And dotty about me. A right spoiled little brat I must have been.' He paused, smiling reflectively. Essie could sense he was recalling a time as cherished as her time at Charmouth with Vee and the boys.

'Then she married Arnie, my stepfather. A man much older than herself.'

Essie recalled the kind, elderly man who ran the bookstall.

'She worked for him part-time for years, in his bookshop,' he continued. 'She used to take me along in school holidays. He was always good to me. Left me his shop. Good to her, too. But it wasn't until after she was married that she became dotty about him. I wasn't used to sharing her, never having known a father. I resented that no end, all the fuss she gave him. But that was Rebecca. Never did things by halves.'

'She's . . . she's died?'

He nodded. 'While I was away in the army. Only forty-one, she was. They said it was the worry of me being reported missing. But it was only a month after Arnie died;

133

I'd wager it was him she pined for. He gave her the only security she had ever known.

'There is so much I could have done for her now.'

He stood up impatiently, as if to shake off this show of sentiment.

'What about your parents?' he enquired. 'Still around?'

'Yes.'

'Do you see them?'

'Never.'

'Pity. You don't know how lucky you are.'

She had recognized the bitterness in his voice when he said he had never had a father. She would have liked to have explained that it was he who was lucky. But she could not talk about her dad. And memories of her mam were nothing like those of Rebecca.

So she stayed silent. And he asked no more questions.

Despite his casual manner and bantering tone she never felt entirely safe with him. Sometimes she caught him looking at her with barely-concealed desire smouldering in his dark eyes.

She did not mind staying up late and he liked to rise at the crack of dawn so their toilet arrangements were such that she bathed at the sink after Joss had gone to bed, and the little scullery was his for his ablutions first thing in the morning.

One day she was up earlier than usual. A Chinese screen, one of the items she had stored for Joss and which he said she could keep, gave privacy to the corner of the room where she slept. She dressed swiftly behind the screen.

The scullery was still filled with steam from the water he had washed in and she could smell the soap he had used. He had left a kettle singing on one jet for their morning tea. Essie was concentrating on frying bacon and eggs on the other jet when she felt steely arms enfolding her from behind and the rippling muscles of Joss's bare chest on her back. His voice was muffled by the softness of her hair. 'Essie, you are so lovely. Even at this time in the morning.' An old nightmare of the captain creeping up behind her made her snap in panic and self-preservation.

'Take your hands away at once. Unless you want me to throw this!'

He dropped his hands and stepped back as if from an exploding gun. 'OK. That's not the way I enjoy breakfast, thanks.'

She spun round, holding the pan aloft, her face flushed with indignation.

'Sorry, ma'am,' he said with an exaggerated bow, and disappeared into the little room to finish dressing.

Over breakfast she warned, 'Don't ever do that again, Joss.'

He stared at her keenly, a puzzled frown creasing his brow. 'My poor Essie. Something must have upset you very badly.'

But he heeded the warning and the rest of the week went smoothly.

'I wasn't such a bad lodger, was I?' he twinkled as he prepared for home.

She shook her head, smiling.

'Why not extend our holiday and come back with me to the Middies? You could see your friend, what's her name?'

'Ivy.'

'Well?'

She was relaxed after a week of fun. Ivy had recently given birth to a baby girl. It would have been easy to agree. But Essie felt that she and Joss had been long enough together. It was time to get back to their former business footing.

He read her mind as always. 'Business as usual, is it?'

'Yes. Back to business. But thanks for a lovely week.'

'What don't you like about me?' he asked quietly, his dark eyes unusually serious.

'It's not that, Joss.' She tried to explain. 'I don't want to be dependent on anyone. For company, nor anything else.'

He shrugged and his usual impish grin returned. 'As long as it applies to the rest of the world.'

'It does.'

Before he returned a month later she had fallen hopelessly in love.

Chapter Eight

'If you've no intention of coming back with me you may as well pay a visit to Eden House,' Joss had said. 'It will be the most exciting auction you have attended yet.'

It was. For it was at Eden House that she first saw Francis. She noticed him as soon as she entered the music room, packed with hot bodies and dark formal suits. He had found himself an oasis, away from the general hubbub. Tall and elegant in a cool, pale-blue linen jacket, his blond hair brushed smoothly, his gentle, sculptured features reminding her of a Greek god, he was totally removed from his surroundings, engrossed in studying a painting hanging immediately above him. There was an air of breeding about him; at the same time an ethereal quality, like someone she had met in a dream. She followed his gaze to the work of art which was absorbing his whole attention.

Earthily rural, yet fanciful, it was of an avenue of trees skirting a wheel-marked cart track, lush green meadows on either side. In the distance was a farm and a church, beyond them the blurred outlines of a village. The stony track gave the impression of continuing beyond the village into the swirling clouds. The painting offered an invitation to step along the track to discover what lay beyond the far horizon.

Essie dragged her eyes away, forcing them to concentrate on the glossy inventory on which Joss had marked items he wished her to bid for, with the prices he was prepared to pay.

'A charming residential estate, only one mile from Exeter station,' she read, 'comprising dwelling-house, cottages, orchards, stables, coach-house and gardens. All contents.' The contents were listed under the rooms they occupied. The brochure was several pages long. The main auction was to be conducted in the music room, china and glass in 'the long dining room'.

She had been excited at the thought of travelling further afield, and of being entrusted, for the first time, with buying quality furniture. One of Joss's well-off Midland customers had a fetish to furnish his whole house in walnut; Essie was to try to obtain either the George I walnut bureau cabinet or a neat Queen Anne secretaire.

And for the Louis XV collector, Essie was to bid for an ornately-decorated corner cupboard, listed as an *encoignure*, a sofa, described as a *duchesse en bateau*, and a two-tier *étagère*, which turned out to be a cabinet with unenclosed display-shelves.

Walking from Exeter station had seemed a long mile, the drive leading to Eden House even longer, so eager was she to arrive. It was all more fascinating than she had imagined: the beautifully-manicured lawns and shrubs, the graceful building, the smartly-dressed buyers, chatting knowledgeably, many of them recognizing acquaintances; the magnificent furniture, carpets, china, glassware and pictures. The owner must have been extremely rich.

The tall, slim man moved at last and walked quietly from the room, not lingering to talk to anyone.

The first items to be auctioned were the pictures. Before beginning, the auctioneer announced that the picture *An*

Invitation to View had been bought privately and was thus withdrawn. There were murmurings of disapproval and one man strode off, claiming that his journey had been nothing but a waste of time.

It was mind-boggling to hear the astronomical prices bid for the pictures; it appeared that every one was a masterpiece. The furniture came next. Essie was left with an overwhelming sense of disappointment as each piece she had hoped to bid for was sold for far more than the pencilled figures in her brochure. She did not manage to obtain a single thing.

Despondently she made her way to the long dining room.

Soon after she arrived a piece of Meissen was held aloft, described by the auctioneer as a rare example, two lovers at a sewing table, mounted on a Louis-XV ormulu base. Essie gasped at the sheer beauty and artistry of the piece: the lady in a crinoline, ornately decorated with flowers; her partner in a blue coat, braided with gold decorated cuffs, blue breeches and white stockings with gold-buckled shoes.

Courageously she made several bids, but it was knocked down to the gentleman in the pale-blue jacket. He glanced over at her apologetically and then again he left the room.

It was not until it was time to leave for her train that she realized a summer storm had erupted. From where she stood on the wide entrance steps, dressed only in an apple-green gingham dress and straw hat, it looked as if the wet drive had grown an extra half-mile since her arrival. It was then that she saw him again. His car was drawn up beneath the stone canopy which covered the entrance; he was carefully placing parcels on the back seat. He returned to the house to collect several pictures, neatly packed in cardboard containers.

'Quite a storm,' he remarked as he noticed her standing on the steps. 'Do you have any means of conveyance?'

'Only these,' she smiled, lifting one small foot.

'Where are you making for?'

'The railway station.'

'And you plan to *walk*? I am staying in the city. Please allow me to give you a lift.'

'I shall be all right. I expect the storm will soon be over.'

'Please! Allow me to make amends.'

He smiled, and it was then that she became aware of the brightness of his wide, blue eyes, the sort of blue she had seen in pictures depicting Mediterranean skies. It was a slow smile, so unlike Joss's quick grin, but it lit up his face as soon as it began.

'What is there to make amends for?'

'The Meissen.'

'Oh, that! I expected it would be way out of my reach.'

'Please!' He was holding the car-door open on her side, while extending his other hand to help her in. She noticed his slim white fingers. Everything about him was fresh, and calm. And perfect. There must be a snag.

He settled her comfortably into the passenger seat and started the engine.

'I love the picture you bought, *Invitation to View*. It was you who bought it, wasn't it?'

He smiled. 'Yes, wonderful, isn't it? Perhaps I should introduce myself, Miss . . . ?'

'Connaught.'

'I am Francis Jameson. I buy for a famous gallery. They would have scalped me if I had failed to get the Meissen. Otherwise,' the slow smile began, 'I just might have let you have it. I saw how disappointed you were. I am sorry about that.'

'I also buy for someone else,' she explained, 'and I didn't get a single thing today.'

'We all have days like that, Miss Connaught. There were

a lot of well-heeled London buyers today. Don't be discouraged.'

She was conscious of his voice right from that first meeting; it was so quiet and cultured.

'What were you hoping to buy?'

She told him.

'In that case you may be more successful at a sale to be held on Thursday, in a little village about fifteen miles from Exeter. An antique shop is closing because of the death of the owner. His wife had to make a decision quickly, owing to the lease. I don't think it's generally known.'

Essie sat forward with lively interest. 'Is there any form of transport out of Exeter? Train? Or bus?'

'Afraid not. It's a bit off the beaten track.'

She sat back in her seat. 'That lets me out, then.'

'I shall be going myself. I would be happy to meet you off the train and take you along.'

He was waiting for her at Exeter station. Essie had dressed with care. She was wearing a light-grey skirt, with a short, checked bolero nipping tightly into her tiny waist. A crisp white blouse and a wide-brimmed, grey hat trimmed with white daisies completed a pretty picture.

He was immaculate in a lightweight grey suit and brilliant white shirt.

'You look very fashionable.'

'Snap.'

He raised a blond eyebrow quizzically, and she indicated the matching colours of their outfits.

'Telepathy?'

'Maybe.'

His car was luxurious. She was able to settle down to enjoy the countryside without feeling she had to make conversation; there was a comfortable quietness about him. She judged him to be in his late thirties, again noticing the long slim fingers, the intelligent forehead and wide, sky-blue eyes.

He drove smoothly along narrow country lanes which gradually descended into a picturesque combe. As they approached the village he pointed out things of interest, a quaint pottery-studio built into a hillside, a bakery in the centre of a field, surrounded by piles of cut tree-trunks, gurgling fountains bouncing into fast streams where trout leaped, a tiny church built high on a hill. Thatched cottages clustered together on either side of the road, leaving just enough space for the car to inch its way through.

The antique shop was on the extreme outer edge of the village. Its modest exterior gave no hint of the spaciousness inside, where beautiful furniture was arranged stylishly, and lovely pictures adorned the walls. Her escort had explained there was to be no auction here, but that everything had been marked down to the lowest possible figure. The owner had died and his wife wished to dispose of everything quickly before the renewal of a lease which was almost due.

A gracious, elderly lady with a sweet smile came forward to greet Essie's companion fondly; it was obvious they knew one another well. Essie was introduced and it was explained what she was looking for.

'We have always been rather attached to French furniture,' the lady remarked amiably, guiding them toward the back of the room, to where there was a good selection of Louis-XV furniture, including several corner cupboards and two sofas. There was also an early Georgian walnut bureau, very attractive with fascinating, secret drawers.

Essie's heart beat excitedly; this was like Aladdin's cave, and all to themselves! Discreet little tabs proclaimed prices far less than those obtained at Eden House.

With unassuming tact Francis Jameson helped her choose between the two sofas before he was ushered away to see some paintings put by for his inspection. Essie chose a corner cupboard and decided to buy the walnut bureau. A quick calculation revealed that she had not spent nearly as much as Joss had allocated. Two walnut corner chairs caught her eye, which she guessed the collector would like because they were so unusual; also a pair of more comfortable chairs with walnut arms and needlework seats in exceptionally good condition. Later Francis informed her that they were of the Queen Anne period and a very good buy.

Having decided on her essential purchases Essie wandered around the shop, admiring the craftsmanship and creativity that had gone into the making of such lovely furniture, savouring the delicious colours of the various woods, and the quiet elegance of the shop.

She became absorbed in a hanging sampler, fascinated by the name of the embroiderer. 'Eden Cornish,' it proclaimed, 'aged ten. His Work. April, 1680.' What a coincidence, having been to Eden House so recently. Beneath the usual alphabet was a wide border of beautifully-embroidered pictures, cricket bats and balls, a chestnut horse, a cluster of trees.

'Unusual, isn't it?' The proprietor was standing close behind her, alongside Francis Jameson.

'The first I have seen worked by a boy,' Essie replied.

'Maybe he was an invalid who took it up as a pastime,' the elderly lady suggested.

But Essie preferred to think of him as a healthy little boy, playing cricket, riding horses and climbing trees.

No little price tag was visible. She was about to enquire when Francis said, 'Fascinating; I'll take it.'

Essie felt a sense of disappointment as she watched it brought down from the wall, rolled like a scroll in tissue paper, and handed to her companion, together with two wrapped canvasses. She was assured there would be no problem about transporting her order to Axminster, and paid her bill.

'Thank you for giving us first viewing, Dorothy.'

'My pleasure, Francis. Michael would have wished it.' The lady smiled. 'I am glad you both found something you liked.' She accompanied them to the door.

'So that's why we had the shop to ourselves. A private viewing!' Essie exclaimed when they were again seated in the car. 'Weren't we lucky?'

'Indeed. Dorothy does not normally open until the afternoon.'

Essie had wondered how such a shop came to be situated in so modest a village, but, driving out a different way, she noticed they passed several flourishing farms, and country estates with tree-lined drives similar to Eden House. It was obvious that the area was more prosperous than she had first supposed. The cottagers from the village doubtless supplied the labour for these palatial residences.

They drew up at a thatched-roofed country inn, and were soon being served with delicious trout and home-made bread spread with thick yellow butter.

'Are you pleased with your purchases?' her companion asked over coffee.

'Delighted. Thank you for taking me, Mr Jameson.'

'Francis, please!'

'Then thank you, Francis.'

'Are you to remain Miss Connaught?'

'You may call me Esther.'

'Essie' did not seem quite right for a friendship with anyone as sophisticated as Francis Jameson. 'Thank you,' he said quietly, his slow smile transforming his serious face and making his eyes appear bluer than ever.

'There is an auction at Crewkerne on Tuesday, Esther. Will you be going?'

'At Crewkerne Sale-rooms?' Joss had an account there.

He nodded.

'It is one of my haunts.'

'Then could I pick you up?'

'There is no need, thank you. I can get there quite easily.' For the first time she felt ashamed of her accommodation in Axminster. She did not want him to see it any more than she wanted him to call her Essie. She resolved to go on her bicycle so that she would not have to accept a lift home.

They drove leisurely through country lanes back to Exeter. He described the pictures he had bought, while Essie listened enraptured, fascinated by his quiet, harmonious voice.

As the train was moving off he placed the tissued scroll in her hand through the open window. 'Just a little thankyou for today, Esther.'

'Oh no! I couldn't,' she protested, but the train was gaining speed and the tall slim man waving her off could not hear her protestations.

She unrolled the sampler carefully, gently tracing the embroidery with her little finger. Eden House. Ten-year-old Eden Cornish. Francis Jameson. His friend's antique shop. It gave her pleasure to think of them all. Separately and together. A sense of peace. And trust.

That was how it started. There followed a glorious month of visiting stately homes which were selling up for one reason or another, followed by visits to theatres, museums, new eating-places, new towns, Bath, Plymouth, Dartmouth, Salisbury. Once they travelled as far as Penzance, putting up at an hotel for two nights, where Francis, in his gentlemanly way, had booked bedrooms on different floors. She felt safe with him. Safer than she had ever felt with any man.

Essie gained invaluable knowledge from him. He helped her choose several pieces of porcelain, and would have made presents of some if she had allowed him. For the first time since Charmouth she felt completely happy, totally unthreatened, at ease with her undemanding companion. He often bought her flowers. She felt respected, feminine, totally safe. The only time they touched was when he helped her in or out of the car. Gradually she began to realize she was falling in love with this unpretentious man, so well-groomed, so knowledgeable, yet so unassuming.

She dreamed of him holding her ever so gently. She began to wish he would kiss her. But the time came for him to leave Exeter before he had shown any intention of extending their relationship beyond friendship. They spent their last evening dining at his hotel.

Across the table he placed a hand lightly over hers. 'Shall we write, Esther?'

She nodded dumbly, her body crying out to him in a way she had not believed possible.

'Have you ever been to London?'

'No.'

'I would love to show it to you some time.'

'There is a direct line from Axminster to Waterloo,' she found herself suggesting boldly.

'Then maybe we could meet some time.' He smiled. 'Meanwhile, are you going to let me drive you home tonight?'

'No. Please! Just take me to the station.'

As the train drew in he brushed her cheek with his lips. 'Take care, little Esther. I will write.' It was such a sweet kiss; she was to re-live it often.

On Joss's first visit after Francis had departed he was immediately aware of the change in Essie. There was a new softness in her large brown eyes, a serenity in her smile. And she smiled much more often.

But as the weeks went by without a line from Francis she became more business-like than ever. Joss had been delighted with the furniture bought from Francis's friend, which he thought came from Eden House; somehow Essie did not want to tell him otherwise. He was filled with admiration for the extra knowledge and confidence she was gaining so rapidly. He told her so when he increased her monthly salary, and one day he suggested they form a partnership.

'That's generous of you, Joss. But there could be no partnership without me putting in some money, and I have something else in mind to do with my savings.

'The old couple below are giving up the shop to live with their daughter and family. I have asked them to recommend me to the landlord. I would like to rent the ground floor in addition to this.'

'What! To sell sweets?'

'No, to sell furniture. I think I could do the same as you do in Walsall with regard to second-hand. After all, there are young couples down here also, setting up new homes, who would be interested. To say nothing of the farm ladies you are regularly stripping of their antiques.

'So if I continue to obtain antiques for you to take up, will you agree to bring me some good second-hand furniture?'

'I sell to a bigger population, Essie. And do you think you are in the right position to catch trade here, on the edge of the town?'

'With the right sort of advertising, definitely. I shall aim at attracting people from surrounding towns, in addition to Axminster.'

He shrugged. 'If that's what you want to risk your money on. I don't mind giving you a start, my love, if that's what you want. And I usually come down with an empty van; I could fill it for you.'

He agreed to help her with the conversion she had in mind, which was to knock the shop into the present ground-floor living space, by permission of the landlord.

Essie had convinced him that a big showroom would render his property much more valuable.

With unerring instinct for choosing the right people Joss enlisted the help of Len, the son-in-law of the old man who had kept the shop, recently out of the army where he had served with the engineers. Len was fit, middle-aged, with two growing children, out of a job and willing to do anything. He was a quiet man who worked swiftly without fuss. Together he and Joss made a good team. They lost no time in knocking out the offending walls. Joss insisted on leaving one small room for himself on the ground floor as an emergency bedroom and Essie could hardly protest in view of all that he was doing. It was not much bigger than the one he had used upstairs in the summer holiday, but it did have a window.

Essie decorated the walls while Joss panelled a little corner of the showroom in half wood, half glass, which became her office and cash-desk. She had recently taught herself to type on a second-hand Remington, which had come complete with instruction book. She still kept meticulous accounts for herself and for Joss. Recently a new name had appeared on the 'wages' list: Joy Burnett. Essie wondered about her. When she questioned Joss as to who she was and what was she like his eyes twinkled mischievously. 'My new assistant at Walsall. Not quite as pretty as you, Essie, my love, but quite glamorous. A definite acquisition to us both, I'd say.'

An outside scullery and toilet was brought under cover from the main building by a newly-built corridor. The two men plumbed in a small hip-bath and hot and cold water.

There was a well-built coach-house in the yard where Joss's stock could now be stored without it having to be manoeuvred up the awkward staircase. They whitewashed it and checked the roof for leaks.

The first consignment of furniture Joss brought down for

her was a good mix: sofas, armchairs, sideboards, together with a selection of bedroom and kitchen furniture. Essie had laid plain lino in an acorn shade which toned with anything and now arranged the store to resemble separate rooms, an innovation which drew whole-hearted approval from both Joss and Len. She learned from Joss how to move furniture without undue strain. Being fit and agile she found she could cope with this quite well.

'You will have to offer delivery,' he pointed out.

'I know. There is a second-hand van for sale in Beaminster. Will you look at it for me, please, Joss?'

'Let me look at you first, baby.' He swung her round to face him squarely, his strong hands warm on her shoulders.

Her face was flushed with exertion. Her hair, wound casually into a coil, was falling prettily out of place, her nose smudged with dust, her body belted into a voluminous white apron. She looked young, vulnerable, in spite of the resolute chin and grave, brown eyes.

'We are partners, Essie, whatever you say. Two halves of a whole.' He took her neat little chin into his hard square hand. He was very close, his dark eyes penetrating, searching, longing. She knew it would only need one word of encouragement to find herself enclosed tightly in his arms.

Sidestepping deftly, she murmured, 'I'd be grateful if you would look at the van.'

He laughed sarcastically. 'I wonder!'

However he did inspect the van. He also managed to persuade the owner to accept eighty pounds instead of ninety, including delivery, and insisted on giving Essie a few more driving lessons before he left for the Midlands with his latest cargo of antiques for his prosperous customers.

Now all was shipshape Essie placed a large eye-catching advertisement in *The Bridport News, Axminster Herald* and *Pulmans Weekly.* 'GRAND OPENING. SECOND-HAND

149

FURNITURE, at Connaught House, Axminster. Newly extended. Bargains in household furniture from quality homes all over the country. Customers cordially invited to walk round. No pressure to buy. All classes of furniture on view.'

On the following Saturday customers arrived by the score, many just to wander around and look, but others bought, and her stock was well depleted after the first day. She was on tenter-hooks in case Joss did not come again for some time to replenish it.

But he did appear quite soon with another varied load. He announced that he would be staying for a week and had other alterations in mind if the landlord agreed. First he fitted out the little ground-floor bedroom for himself with a single bed, wardrobe and table.

That evening he joined Essie for a meal. When the table was cleared he spread out a plan for altering the room they were in, which they called the barn. It showed a small entrance hall with wall-pegs for outdoor clothes. Leading off were two doors, one into a bedroom, the other to the living room. The fact that there were already two windows, one each end, simplified matters.

'It looks wonderful. But won't it be terribly complicated and expensive?'

'Not at all. With plasterboards I have brought with me, and Len's help, it could be done in a couple of days. You can choose some wallpaper and we will decorate the walls together. You and me. How does that appeal, my little tycoon?'

When she enquired how he could spare the time, he replied simply, 'Joy will cope.'

They explained the scheme to the landlord who immediately dropped a bombshell. 'It's all right by me. There is only one snag. I shall be selling the place soon; I'm off to America to live with my brother.

'The asking price will be more than I had originally thought by the time you two have finished,' he chuckled. 'And then, will the new owner let you stay? . . . '

Regardless of the fact that all her money was now tied up in stock, Essie was off to see the manager of Lloyds Bank the following day. The impact Connaught House had made in the town had not escaped him, but it did not make him any keener to lend money to a woman, especially one so young and presumably inexperienced. But he agreed to come to the shop, to see for himself.

The well-documented accounts impressed him, and when Mr Joss Berridge offered himself as guarantor he promised to give favourable consideration to a loan should the property come on to the market at a reasonable price.

By the end of the week the top floor was transformed. Joss had hung wallpaper while Essie cut and pasted. Her bedroom walls were now decorated in a pretty pink-and-white rose design, the lounge and hallway in pale green.

Essie wandered round what was now a suite of rooms. A white bath Joss had picked up cheaply was plumbed into the little room which led off her kitchen. The living room was still a fair size. The sampler by Eden Cornish, which she had framed, hung on her wall, a constant reminder of the fascinating, village antique shop. Her bedroom was cosy, private and pretty, with the flowered walls, deep-rose curtains and matching rugs either side of her bed. All the presents Vee had given her were there, the little regency table, the small secretaire, set out with the inkstands and workboxes. Her one remaining picture, a delicate seascape, hung on the wall.

As they admired their handiwork Joss suddenly announced. 'I am off back tomorrow, early.' He grinned. 'The lovely Joy can't bear me out of her sight for too long.'

Essie felt a pang of unreasonable jealousy. She had

experienced a wonderful feeling of camaraderie working alongside him, but after all, she had no claim on him, nor would she want any. He would demand a far greater commitment than she could give. But she could not but wonder about Joy Burnett and whether she shared Joss's house, or even his bed.

There had been no time for jaunts or meals out. Every available minute had been taken up with working against the clock. Certainly there had been no time to wonder about Francis. It was only when she went to bed at night that she longed to hear his voice, and in her dreams re-lived the wonderful month they had enjoyed together and the gentle kiss at the station.

Her body ached with exhaustion, although she felt mentally alert and elated. Joss looked as fresh and energetic as the day he had arrived.

On the morning of his departure he sprinted lightly up her stairs.

'Post!' he called as he swung through the door.

She entered the living room from the kitchen where she had been making morning tea, dressed in a soft cream dressing-gown, tightly belted into her tiny waist, her sunny hair falling loosely on her shoulders, her eyes still slumbrous with the look of an appealing child.

'My God, Essie,' Joss breathed. You are beautiful.' His dark eyes bored into her with a naked craving that stripped her down to her skin.

Suddenly it was no longer Joss Berridge's handsome features she saw, but the pit-marked face of Caleb Connor, her dad. It was as if ice trickled slowly down her spine, and she was afraid.

Joss reached out to take her in his arms. She was immediately on the defensive, wide-eyed and resistant, moving smartly away from him to the other side of the table.

'Did you say post?'

He handed her two letters, one from Canada, the other postmarked London. She tore the London letter open eagerly, warmth returning, oblivious to Joss's scrutiny. He watched the colour flood her face as she read; he saw her eyes brighten, her small mouth, so determined a moment ago, soften.

Francis wrote in neat, perfect copperplate. He explained that he had been travelling round the country and in France. He was back in London now for a time, so would she like to meet him? If so he would leave it to her to suggest the day and time.

Suddenly aware of Joss's intent gaze she folded the letter, put it back in the envelope and into her pocket.

'Something important?'

'No.'

It was obvious that no explanation was forthcoming so he wasted no time on goodbyes.

'Thank you, Joss, for all your help,' she said when he was safely on the landing. 'You have worked so hard.'

'Perhaps I'd have done better writing a letter,' he remarked drily as he ran down the stairs.

She watched through the window as his van disappeared down the street. She was aware that, at present, he was her only source of supply for the sort of goods she wanted to sell, and decided that this was too risky; it placed her under obligation.

So when she went to housesales, on Mondays when the shop was closed or on days when Len stood in, she found herself looking out, not only for antiques for Joss, but for furniture from maids' rooms, housekeepers' flats, and kitchen furniture. She could buy these in job-lots and re-sell cheaply. She also bought good bed-linen and voluminous curtains which could be cut down to make smaller sets. Pauline, Len's wife, was glad to do this for a few shillings.

She re-read Francis's letter repeatedly. She was too busy

getting her business off the ground to take time off, and after a week or so she wrote to him and explained. A prompt reply arrived, congratulating her on what she was doing, and expressing the hope that they may meet in the future.

News soon spread that there were real bargains at Connaught House. People who did not buy first time invariably came back later. Towards Christmas business hotted up, and for the first time she had difficulty in supplying all that her customers were looking for. Joss had not been for above a month; she supposed he was just as busy at Walsall.

Essie delivered the goods in the evenings after the shop had closed. Len was always willing to help her load. He also proved to be a first-class mechanic and kept the van in good order. He had a few jobs with local builders, but he did not mind coming in on odd days or being called upon at short notice.

One day he arrived with a request from someone to hire the van for a day to move house. So another advertisement was placed, 'Connaught's Van Hire. With or without driver.' After that the van more than paid its own way.

Len and his wife and their two girls became her good friends. In order for the old couple to move in with them they had had to give up their front room, leaving just one room to live, cook and wash in, so in a way the cramped cottage reminded her of Heath End, although it could not have been more different, for Pauline kept it as clean as a new pin, while Len kept it in good repair.

Essie gladly agreed to give extra tutoring to Molly, the older girl, who was hoping to sit for a free place to Woodroffe High School. It brought back memories of how Vee had patiently tutored her.

She invited them all on Christmas Day, Len and Pauline, their daughters and the old couple. Hoops, decorated with coloured paper, and holly and mistletoe she had picked herself from Langdon woods gave the new room a festive air. Round the fire, after a turkey meal Essie had cooked in her new gas-stove, the old folk reminisced about other Christmases they remembered, their granddaughters asking innumerable questions.

Later the girls sang a little duet they had learned at school, their grandfather performed a funny monologue, and Len, usually so quiet, surprised them with a few magical tricks. The flat, for they could no longer call it a barn, received a real housewarming and at last it felt like home.

'Just wish that Joss could have been here to enjoy all this with us,' Len said as they prepared to depart. Essie did, too, in a way, for Joss was responsible for the transformation of her barn-like accommodation into a cosy suite of rooms.

But most of all she longed to see Francis and wondered where he was. As if in reply to her thoughts, a letter arrived a few days later. 'Sweet Esther. Missing you more than I can say. Hope to see you early in the new year. Francis.'

She held the letter to her cheek, trying to draw from it the tranquillity she felt when she was with him. Early in the new year, he said. She wondered how long it would be before she saw him again.

Before she did, Joss arrived. On New Year's Eve, the anniversary of Essie's move from Charmouth. Like herself, his businesses had done well in the run-up to Christmas and again on Boxing Day, when wives brought their husbands on their day off.

'What did you do on Christmas Day?' she quizzed, after describing the Christmas Day party she had held with Len and his family.

'Ah, now that would be telling, my sweet,' he replied lightly, which annoyed Essie as she had given him such a detailed description of their little get-together.

'Did you spend it with Joy?' she asked curiously.

'As a matter of fact, my dear, I did. Jealous?'

'Of course not!' She was annoyed with herself for probing.

He swiftly changed the subject to describe the 'new line' he had introduced at his Walsall store; second-hand baths and toiletware, bought from well-off industrialists who were improving their bathrooms. They sold like hot cakes, he said, to do-it-yourselfers who had no baths at all.

'We can afford to celebrate, partner,' he grinned. 'And you don't have to travel in a furniture van tonight.' He led her to the window and indicated a brand-new Ford car with soft top, in the street below. 'I thought we may as well start the new year in style,' he laughed when Essie exclaimed in surprise.

'You are taking it for granted I am coming tonight?'

'It is New Year's Eve, love, and I have come a long way to celebrate it with you.'

He already had tickets for a gala meal and dance at a hotel in Honiton. It would have been churlish to refuse.

'It hasn't been a bad year for either of us, has it, Essie?' he smiled as they finished their meal.

Essie had to admit it had been quite a year. She recalled the despair she was beginning to feel about rent and warmth during the cold month of March when Joss appeared on the scene and rescued her. Now she was a property owner. Her former landlord had gone to live in America, as he had forewarned, after offering her the premises at a very fair price. The bank manager, who by then was convinced of the business acumen of his young client, had willingly agreed to lend the money. Property owner! Sometimes it seemed an incredible dream, yet she had documents to prove it.

From across the table Joss contemplated the varying expressions flitting across her face. Her cheeks were pink from the wine and the warmth of the room. She wore a soft green dress in the new, figure-hugging crêpe-de-chine, and her hair was tied back with matching ribbon. 'You look terrific, Essie.'

'You don't look so bad yourself,' she permitted herself to say, protected by the table.

But later, as they danced, he held her much more tightly than was necessary, and at midnight, when Old Father Time had wended his weary way through one door as a young white sprite appeared at another, amid chiming bells and greetings of 'Happy New Year', he kissed her full on the lips, passionately and long.

Hemmed in by New Year revellers, laughing and jumping to catch balloons and coloured streamers, there was no escape. Enfolded closely in his arms, his lips hard on her own, Essie experienced a stirring that was frightening in its intensity. She shut her eyes and tried to imagine it was Francis who was kissing her; that way she was transported to paradise.

Joss was especially solicitous as he wrapped a rug around her for their journey home. He would have taken her into his arms again if she had not protested firmly.

'Thank you for taking me out, Joss,' she said as they reached her landing. 'Goodnight, and a Happy New Year.'

'What! Here and now? You are not inviting me in?'

She yawned. 'I'm tired.' All she wanted was to get into bed and imagine it had been Francis holding her and kissing her in the way Joss had done. 'You danced me off my feet,' she said lightly. 'See you tomorrow.'

'You will see me tonight, Essie.' He scooped her up into his arms as if she were a feather and carried her inside.

'Put me down this minute,' she demanded furiously.

He stood her on her feet but continued to enclose her tightly in arms of steel. 'How much do you think flesh and blood can stand, Essie?'

'Let me go. Immediately, Joss Berridge.' There was panic as well as annoyance in her voice.

He released her then with a puzzled frown. 'Why?'

'Because I hate it.'

'Tonight, when I kissed you, Essie, you responded. I know you did.' He searched her angry face. 'You didn't hate it then, did you?'

'Only because I was pretending you were someone else,' she replied heatedly. She had turned away from him. He spun her round to face him.

'You were *what*?' he shouted.

'You heard what I said. Joss, you're hurting me.'

He loosened his grip on her arms, but continued to hold her so that he could see her face.

'Tell me! Who was I standing in for?'

'Someone I met.'

'Where? Where did you meet?'

His voice was quiet now, but intense, demanding an answer.

'If you must know! At the auction at Exeter.'

'So he was one of those smart-alec Londoners you said were there.'

'I did *not* say they were . . .'

'No, but they were, weren't they?'

'*No*! What right have you to say that? You're the smart alec!'

'So he's the one who wrote the letter that came from London.'

'I don't see that it is any of your business.'

'You said you didn't want to depend on anyone, for company or anything else.'

'I don't want to depend . . .'

'But you've fallen for him?'

She did not reply.

'You said it applied to the whole world.'

'That was before I met him,' she sighed, as if explaining to a child.

158

'*I* love you, Essie, you must know that.'

'Sure it's not lust, Joss?'

'How can you say that, when I've waited all this time and never touched you. All these months! Could he be as patient?'

'More so.' Her voice rose. 'He's not like that. He's *different*. He's gentlemanly.'

'What's that supposed to mean? He can't love you as a *woman*?'

'He doesn't try to *paw* me,' she whispered under her breath, talking only to herself, but he heard.

'And I do?'

'Well, you must admit that it isn't for the want of trying that you haven't . . . *touched* me, as you put it.'

He released her so suddenly she almost toppled over. She watched as the anger slowly drained from his face and the hurt was replaced by controlled indifference. He shrugged before he turned on his heel and strode toward the door.

She followed him. 'Joss!' He waited, his dark eyes unfathomable. 'I'm sorry.'

'Don't apologize, dear. As one door shuts another opens, as they say in our part of the world.'

'We are good business colleagues, aren't we? Can't we leave it at that?'

'No, we can't. But don't worry about your *business*, Essie. I won't let you down. Just make sure that *he* doesn't.'

She felt shaken by the argument, and guilty when she recalled all that he had done for her. At the same time she was annoyed at letting herself be provoked into disclosing how she felt about Francis.

Her heart cried out for someone to love her, but not with the physical intensity that Joss would put into a love affair; that would remind her too vividly of her dad. And Captain Vincent. She could not think of either of them without a sense of revulsion.

She tried to draw on the memory of Francis's calm serenity. But she did not sleep at all that night, and in the early hours she heard Joss leave his downstairs room and drive away in his new car.

Chapter Nine

She knew that Francis would come soon. Throughout the first cold days of January she had willed him to come. So it was no surprise, one dark customerless afternoon when she had decided to shut shop, to see him stepping from his car, tall and graceful. He paused to check the name above the store. Then he was walking toward her from across the road, that long, slow smile lighting up his serious face when he became aware of her gaze from the other side of the glazed door.

He took both her hands gently into his own, his bright blue eyes searching her face. He seemed to find the answer he was looking for in her happy, welcoming smile.

'All this is looking very prosperous,' he remarked, indicating the neatly laid-out store.

'Not today it isn't,' she laughed. 'I think all customers have hibernated since Christmas. Spent out, I suppose. Joss warned me it would be a quiet time from now until March, when people will begin to think of smartening up for Easter.'

'Joss?'

'The man I was buying the antiques for.' She could have

bitten off her tongue for mentioning Joss so soon, remembering what had happened on his last visit when she had talked to him about Francis. But Francis just said, 'I see. Joss-the-boss?'

'Not with regard to this store. This is totally my affair.' She realized that was not strictly true. Wasn't she already anxious in case Joss kept her waiting too long before his next consignment? And hadn't he given her invaluable help with the conversion?

'You're a brave lady.'

She gave him a quick tour before taking him upstairs to her flat, no longer ashamed to do so. She made coffee, then sat on the hearth-rug at his feet, her back resting against his legs; it seemed the most natural thing in the world. She was totally without guile, and felt she could trust him implicitly.

'I want to hear about everything you have been doing.'

She told him about Christmas, working backwards to the first advertisement she had placed in the local press. She had longed to talk with him, and now he was here, close, as she had known he would be. 'Now tell me all your news.'

'Oh, I do much the same things all the time. Examining beautiful, precious things for the gallery and buying some of them. Only the venues are different.'

'What a fascinating task.'

'Yes, I am fortunate. But I have had something more important on my mind lately.'

'What's that?'

'Esther Connaught.'

She turned round to look up at him.

'I have not been able to get you out of my mind, Esther.'

'Did you want to?'

'Certainly I wanted to. You interfere with my work.'

She dimpled. 'Oh! Sorry.'

'You're not at all, Miss.' He pressed her small nose teasingly, then gently touched the top of her shining hair.

'Would you . . . ?' He hesitated. 'No, perhaps I shouldn't ask.'

'Would I what?'

'Would you untie your lovely hair?'

As she removed the comb which had held her hair firmly in place, it cascaded exuberantly round her shoulders.

'You make a beautiful picture, Esther. If you could be painted now, sitting there, like that, people would flock to buy.

'Many London ladies are having their hair cut. You won't do that, will you?'

'Not likely! It was far too much of a chore growing it.'

He laughed. 'You are so natural. You're good for me.'

'And you for me.'

They sat quietly then, as if both of them were half-afraid they had said too much, but it was a comfortable silence, as it had been on their journey to the village in the combe. It was enough for Essie just to feel he was there. Later he explained he had to go on to Exeter; he was meeting someone first thing in the morning.

'How long will you be staying?'

'It's a flying visit, I am afraid. I have an appointment in London on the following day.'

Her face clouded.

'How about coming next weekend? Business is slack, you say.'

She considered for a moment. 'I suppose I could come on Sunday; I'm closed on Mondays and could travel back then.'

'I will book you into a hotel adjoining my apartment.'

That was how Essie's London visits began. He would meet her off the train and take her back to Waterloo on Monday afternoon. On Sundays they lunched out, after which they walked in the parks, often pausing to listen to speakers expounding various political opinions, or they

163

visited St Paul's, the Tower, some famous little churches, or an afternoon concert.

In the evening Francis would cook something unusual for her in his luxurious apartment. They listened to records on his new gramophone; sometimes they discussed books they had read. At other times they sat quietly, she with her head resting in the crook of his arm. He would silently stroke her hair, or run his fingers lightly from her chin to the base of her throat; sometimes she would feel a kiss on her cheek or forehead as light as butterflies' wings. Sweet gentle caresses. At last an undemanding man who loved her for herself, not just for her body. This on its own would have endeared him to her, without all the other gentlemanly qualities she admired.

At night he escorted her to a nearby hotel and said goodnight on the doorstep. On Mondays they visited the art galleries, where every one seemed to know Francis and greeted him with a sort of awe.

Sometimes, if he had tickets for a play or ballet, she would stay on until Tuesday morning, having arranged with Len to take charge of the store if she had not returned.

Her weekends were oases of tranquillity which stayed with her throughout the week as she conducted her business. She continued to search for antiques for Joss, and he delivered a couple of consignments of furniture for her. He was both impersonal and watchful, aware of her visits to London, for he had turned up one weekend when she was away, and had questioned Len closely. They were studiously polite to one another as they exchanged invoices and cheques.

She still felt faintly guilty about Joss, but could not let anything destroy the serenity she felt from her visits to Francis. Yet her body was stirring with an almost imperceptible yearning for something more, and one day, when Francis suddenly asked, 'How old are you, Esther?' she surprised herself by replying, 'Old enough to be kissed on the lips.'

'I am forty next birthday. Almost twice your age, I would guess.'

'You feel old, do you?' she chided teasingly.

'Younger than I have ever felt, my little Esther, since I met you.'

'That's all that matters, then,' she replied softly.

It was then that he took her into his arms and placed his lips on hers, not in a bruising way, like Joss had done, but fondly, sweetly, making no demands. It was because he made no demands that she wanted to give herself freely to him. Her arms went round his neck, then into his hair, holding him closer to her when he would have drawn away.

Suddenly she was aching to feel his gentle lips on her body; to feel his body as part of her own. She felt the thrill of response surge through him, his need answering her need.

'Please, Francis. *Love me.*'

'Are you sure?'

'Quite, quite sure.'

He made love to her shyly and gradually. She wished the gentle caresses and soft kisses could have gone on for ever; it was heaven to be held so reverently, like all the best dreams she had ever known. But when the real lovemaking began she felt a sense of terror flood through her and was relieved when it was over, and they were able to lie still and quiet, enfolded in each other's arms.

At last Francis spoke. 'My dear little love. I never intended this should happen.' He stroked her face tenderly. 'You were afraid.'

'Ssh. Don't say anything,' she whispered. She *had* been afraid, as visions of traumatic childhood experiences engulfed her. This was not her father, though, was it, but her gentle Francis. She loved him. She belonged to him now, and he to her, for ever. He buried his face into the soft strands of her hair. Then, taking her on to his lap, he said, 'Esther, there is something I must tell you. You have to know.'

She tucked her face beneath his chin. 'I love you. That's all I need to know.'

'Oh, my dear!'

The misery in his voice caused her to sit up anxiously. 'What is it? Francis, what is it?'

First turning her face away as if he could not bear to watch her reaction, he said in a strangled voice, 'I have a wife, Esther.'

The dream crashed into a thousand pieces. She closed her eyes against the deafening impact of its destruction.

'A wife! Where? Where is she now?'

'At our home in Yorkshire,' he replied hoarsely. 'Dear little Esther. This should never have happened. I'm sorry.'

'It's my fault.' She stood, her legs feeling jellified as if after a long illness.

'You said just now that you love me.'

'And you love her?'

'I thought I did.'

'Have I spoiled it?'

'Believe me, darling, you are the first woman I have ever truly loved. I did not know what it was until now.'

'Oh, Francis! Neither did I. But it's wrong, isn't it?'

'Yes, it is wrong. I shouldn't have allowed it to happen. I'm sorry, darling. I tried to keep away. That is why I didn't write for so long. But I could not forget you, Esther. I had to see you again. I had to.

'Then when I did see you, you were so sweet, and so innocent. I felt we could go on like that . . . '

'It was my fault that we didn't.'

'No, no. Mine. I wanted both worlds.'

'What are we going to do?'

'What do you want to do?'

'Catch the early train in the morning to Axminster. And think about it.' She thought about it throughout a sleepless night.

As he kissed her goodbye next morning he said, 'Whatever you decide, my darling, remember I love you.'

Joss was there when she arrived. He was chatting to Len in the store. She nodded briefly to them both.

No sooner had she taken off her coat than he appeared in the flat beside her. 'What is the matter?' he demanded.

'Nothing's the matter. What do you mean?'

'Oh, Essie!' He stood her in front of a mirror. A pale, haunted, unfamiliar face stared back. 'Look at yourself. And you say there is nothing the matter!'

He sat her in a chair and made coffee. She entwined cold hands round the hot cup and sipped slowly. She had no recollection of the journey, or of driving from Axminster station in a hired cab, only of the image of Francis saying, 'I have a wife', and the memory of a deep numbing pain which blotted out all other thoughts.

Joss put a match to the fire, already laid. As the warmth from the flames penetrated her outer, chilled body she became conscious of him sitting opposite, watching her closely, questioning her only with his eyes.

He had to strain to hear her first, miserable words. 'He's married.'

She expected sarcasm or disgust, but he showed no surprise and only said, 'So he's married. Then you have had a lucky escape, haven't you. No damage done.'

'Damage to my heart.' Her voice was only just audible.

He chuckled then in his usual fashion, as if there was nothing the matter. She could have hated him if there had been room for any emotion in her heart other than this deep sense of loss.

'It will pass, Essie. You've been dazzled by the Big City, the City Gent.'

'It wasn't like that at all.'

'No. What was it like, then?' She ignored that.

After a moment's silence she whispered, 'I feel so guilty. About his wife.'

'Nothing to feel guilty about if you didn't know. You say he showed you only – um – *gentlemanly* conduct. That can't hurt her. Or you.' He sounded more like the normal Joss now. 'Or didn't he remain *gentlemanly*?'

The instinct to hit back flared in spite of herself. 'You couldn't understand that, no doubt. But yes, he did. He did.'

Her voice rose and he laughed out loud. 'Good! There *is* life after death you see. Now what you are going to do, my girl, is jump into the bath, give yourself a quick scrub to get the circulation going, doll yourself up, and we are going out to celebrate.'

'Celebrate!' She stared, horrified.

'Yes, celebrate. You are footloose and fancy-free again, my love. I can recommend it; it has its advantages.'

'You're heartless! I wish I had never told you.'

'So you want to sit and mopse do you?' He caught hold of her wrists and pulled her up out of the chair. 'Now, are you going to get into the bath yourself, or do you want me to help you?' He ushered her to the bathroom and turned on the taps.

'Get out.'

'I am going. I shall be the other side of the door and I want to hear plenty of scrubbing, or I'll be in to do the job myself.'

It was amazing how the hot water helped to de-frost and relax her. As numbness receded, thought returned. Her brain called out one thing, her heart another. Repeatedly they contradicted each other.

'Whatever you decide, remember I love you.' Francis's quiet voice, leaving the options open, leaving her to make the decision. She closed her eyes and lay quite still, listening to his voice in her mind. 'I wanted both worlds.' Both worlds. Francis had another world, a world she had known nothing about. A world that was important to him. 'I thought I loved her.'

'Keep moving,' another, louder voice called. 'Keep moving, or I'll be in.'

They should have fixed a lock on the door when they made the bathroom. She resolved to ask Len to do it tomorrow, as she splashed water about to make a noise.

She nearly jumped out of her skin when he rattled the doorknob a few minutes later. 'Essie! I want to hear you getting out now. Your bathrobe is just outside the door.'

What a nerve! He must have rummaged in her bedroom to find it. But she was glad to be able to slip her arm out to retrieve it and put it on, surprised to find that he had warmed it in front of the fire. She had not realized how cold she had been, a chill not brought on by outside temperature, but by the pain in her heart.

'That's better,' he said when she emerged pink and warm from the bath. 'Now for the glad rags.'

She shook her head. 'No more bullying, Joss. I don't feel like going out.'

'Have you eaten today?'

She was surprised when she realized she hadn't.

'I thought not,' he said, reading her face. 'You are coming out to eat, Essie, if I have to carry you all the way to The George. I am not leaving you to blubber about a man who did not have the guts to tell you he was married before now.'

'I don't blubber and he's not short of . . .'

'I don't want to hear what he is, or what he isn't.' He glanced at his pocket watch. 'I shall pick you up in an hour.

Don't dress in mourning, and do put a bit of rouge on.'

He turned at the door. 'Be ready,' he commanded. 'Or I shall invade your wardrobe and dress you myself.'

The very thought of it sent her scurrying into her bedroom as soon as he had gone. First she considered the green crêpe-de-chine, but it reminded her of New Year's Eve; Joss's remark about mourning put her off a smart black suit she had made herself. Finally from her weekend bag, still unpacked, she brought out a cream, lightweight woollen dress which Francis had chosen for her in London, and laid it carefully on the bed. Beautifully-cut, it was the most expensive dress she had ever owned. The skirt swirled gracefully and the bodice was fitted tightly with little buttons covered in brown velvet, with matching velvet belt and hairbow.

She sat in front of the mirror to brush her hair, untouched since early morning. Suddenly she was back in Ivy's bedroom, looking like a little scarecrow, being advised by her new friend to give her hair a hundred strokes a day. She opened her drawer, now neatly laid out with handkerchiefs, ribbons and gloves, as Ivy's had been. There, among the rest, was a pot of rouge her friend had sent her for Christmas, still unused.

She dabbed the tiniest pink spot high on each cheek, blending it with her little finger until it almost disappeared. The faint sheen remaining emphasised her eyes, making them appear larger than ever.

'Oh, Ivy!' she whispered, dropping her head on to her hands. 'What am I to do?'

Straight away came a firm reply. 'Pull yourself together, Essie. You'll manage.'

When Joss arrived he looked her up and down appreciatively. 'What a transformation!' he exclaimed. It was the only reference he was to make to her previous distress.

As they walked to the hotel he talked about their

respective businesses, reminding her that Easter was only one week away. 'You need to get a new advertisement in immediately,' he advised. 'Offer something new. Sale prices. Free cider. Anything to grab their attention. Folk like to have somewhere to go on a bank holiday; if you make it attractive enough they'll come to you.'

Essie did not feel like eating until the food was put in front of her, when she surprised herself by polishing off the lot, and noticed that Joss smiled in satisfaction.

'There is much to think about,' he said. 'I have a list of special orders as long as my arm. One lady is anxious to get her hands on some quality china, as antique as possible, no limit on price. Right up your street. So pull out all the stops to find some, my sweet.' He grinned. 'You are still my official agent, you know.' He piled on the instructions until her head was spinning. She knew he was deliberately trying to push all other thoughts from her mind. He must have succeeded in part, because, once home, she found herself writing out a memo for herself, as well as composing an advertisement to take into the newspaper offices the next day. Free cider was a good idea, she decided, and she would get Pauline to make tea for the ladies.

She had been in bed some time before she was relaxed enough to re-live Francis's gentle introduction to a loving she had never believed could be for her. She knew that if he was by her side now she would give herself to him again, if he wanted her, wife or no wife. But she preferred the gentle caresses without the other, more violent, thing.

Chapter Ten

Morris dancers and a rollicking Bank Holiday Fair brought crowds into Axminster, and in to the store for a free drink. Brisk trade over Easter meant that Essie was delivering until late at night for a week. Going into people's homes she came to know customers personally, and sometimes was able to buy things they were glad to be rid of.

When a lull came she decided to go in search of Joss's requirements. She enjoyed driving, and went as far afield as Exeter in the one direction and Weymouth in the other; visiting all the likely auctions, markets and housesales she could find. Seasoned dealers had long ago lost the resentment they had shown at first toward such a 'raw youngster and female at that'. They had learned to respect her for her shrewdness and good humour. Now there was always someone who came over to chat; in fact many a man would have gone further if she had given the slightest encouragement. Sometimes they dropped hints as to where were the best places to find what she was looking for.

She threw herself enthusiastically into her work, but it never diminished an aching sense of loss, a hungering to see Francis, to hear his voice, to feel his gentleness. She had received one letter telling her that he would be away for a few weeks, giving her the date of his return. The letter ended: 'I miss you terribly, my darling Esther. I shall always love you.'

A letter also came from Ivy, proudly announcing she was pregnant again. 'And you have not seen our first-born yet, Essie,' she chided. 'She is a bonny, bouncing girl now, ten months old, and eager to see you. Mam too. And me, of course.'

Essie read the letter through several times, feeling guilty. She had been considering buying another van. The one she had was always in demand for one thing or another. When a local church had booked it for a Sunday school outing to Sidmouth Len had ingeniously made benches which could be fitted or removed in minutes. Word soon spread, and various organizations such as public houses, Women's Institutes, fishing groups and skittles groups applied. Most wanted a driver. She realized she could not keep calling on Len. He had various building jobs; his time was becoming limited.

So Essie made several decisions. She offered Len a regular full-time job which he readily accepted. She bought a brand-new Ford van for £250 and decided to run it in by driving to the Midlands. She would visit Ivy, take the goods she had obtained for Joss, and hopefully collect a consignment of second-hand for herself. Owing to Joss's unusually long absence her stocks were becoming sadly depleted. Then she could hurry back, before she had chance to bump into her father.

It was late afternoon when Essie arrived in Walsall, after a very early start. For the first time she appreciated the distance Joss had driven so often, always arriving as bright as if he had done a mere couple of miles.

She had stretched her legs at Gloucester where she ate her

173

sandwiches standing, overlooking the river, faintly discouraged by the number of miles that still lay ahead. The new gears were stiff and her arms and back ached. The last few miles were a depressing stretch of dark streets and black-walled factories belching smoke, some of them mere shacks with corrugated roofs and no windows.

But it was well worth while as she drove through the centre of the town with the satisfaction of knowing she had not once lost her way.

She found Joss's place easily, not that it took much finding. It was in a prominent shopping quarter known as Townend Bank, an area not far from the station and right opposite the impressive building of Her Majesty's Theatre. A large board proclaiming JOSS BERRIDGE'S WALK-ABOUT assured her she was in the right place.

A three-storeyed double-fronted building, blackened by the industrial revolution, was compensated by attractive bow-windows on either side of a front entrance. She could picture it as a bookshop.

She drove under an archway which linked the premises to an almost identical property next door, wondering curiously if the glamorous Joy Burnett would be on duty today.

A huge yard ran along the back of both properties. Under a roughly-constructed cover was an assortment of baths, basins, sinks, taps, piping, toilet pans and, scattered haphazardly about the open yard, a wide assortment of hardware, including enamel buckets and bowls, sturdy yard-brooms, roof tiles, slabs, garden implements, and plumbing materials.

As she jumped lightly down from the van Essie was immediately aware of a man and a woman trying to find a lock and key that matched from a jumble of assorted door furniture in a large, square cardboard box. The woman, aged about fifty, was as wide as she was tall. Every few minutes she would emit a hearty chortle. The whole of her body laughed with her, her generous bosom and fleshy arms bouncing up and down in unison. The customer, although clearly impatient to find his lock and key and depart, was joining in the merriment, and Essie could see why. She found herself chuckling when yet another too-small key slid through a lock like a greased dart and the infectious laughter peeled out again.

'Like to tek a look round inside while yer waitin', duck?' called out the woman in broadest Staffordshire. 'I woe be a minute. We've only bin 'ere all day!'

Essie wandered through the open back door, from whence a narrow hall led directly to the front entrance, splitting the house in two. There were two rooms on either side of the corridor, one locked, the others open for inspection. There was hardly enough space to walk among the clutter of a wide variety of second-hand furniture amid a mish-mash of everything else.

Timber off-cuts, thick wooden posts, kitchenware, picture frames, all jostled for attention alongside ornate sections of oak panelling, reminiscent of stately homes.

Nothing was displayed neatly as in her store, but she did recognize that there was a certain kind of attraction in rummaging among the confusion, hoping that from the jumble you may untangle some treasure that others had failed to spot.

There was no sign of Joss nor of anyone else, but now the plump lady bustled in, still chuckling.

'Do yer need any help, ducks?'

'I was hoping to find Mr Berridge.'

'Joss? 'E's out buyin' today, duck. But where he's gonna put it among this lot, God knows.

'And 'e's not telling,' she added, irreverently.

'Is Miss Joy Burnett about?'

'Yer lookin' at her, duck. Joy by name an' joy by nature, my old man always used to say. What can I do fer yer?'

Essie was dumbstruck for a moment before laughing aloud. So this was Joss's glamorous Joy Burnett! It did not matter that she laughed; it was just taken as part of the general merriment.

'I have travelled from Devon today with a . . . '

'You're Essie! Well, why didn't yer say, love? I bet you're in need of a cuppa tea. Tell yer what – just cum into my place an' we'll 'ave one together. I was just thinkin' o' closin', any road.'

Essie hesitated. 'There are furniture and oddments to unload from my van.' She glanced round. 'Although, as you say, I don't know where . . . '

'Ah, but that'll be a bit o' good, won't it, duck? That'll go in 'ere.' She produced a key from her pocket and unlocked the fourth room, which housed a few choice items of furniture, leaving plenty of space for Essie's consignment.

'We'd best unload it, then, my ducks, afore I lock up.'

With amazing agility the short round woman hopped into the back of the van, after exclaiming on its smartness, asking how much it had cost, and congratulating Essie on a good buy. Together they carried in Essie's latest finds: a Louis-XV ornamented clock, an elegant three-tier dumb-waiter, two walnut wing chairs, upholstered with embroidery on canvas, and a beautiful silver-topped table with matching silver-framed mirror and candle-stands.

'Don't know much about this lot, love, but I expect Joss'll be over the moon.'

Essie carried in the precious porcelain herself; she would have been unwilling to entrust it to anyone. For the moneyed lady, who Joss said would pay anything, she had acquired an early Meissen set of teapot, milk jug and sugar basin, each piece decorated with silver mounts; a whole set of Meissen soup-bowls, and a fine-looking table candelabrum, its base decorated with tiny porcelain dancers. There were also two early Chelsea crinoline ladies, and a blue and white Ming flask for which Essie had had to bid above the figure she had in mind.

'Ah, now this is somethin' I do know summat about.'

To Essie's horror Joy picked up each piece separately, and held it up to the light.

'Fantastic, my love. Early Meissen for a guess.' She turned over the handsome teapot to check the makers' marks. 'Hm. Thought as much. "Right again, my gel", my Jim would 'ave said.' Again that deep throaty laugh that shook her body, and Essie feared for the teapot. Her apprehension was not lost on her companion. 'Don't worry, my ducks. I was handlin' this stuff afore you were born. Never bin known to drop anythin' worthwhile yet. Altho' we've crashed a bit o' pottery in our time, I can tell yer.'

Changing the subject swiftly she opened a door at the far end of the room revealing a staircase. 'That leads up to Joss's living-quarters, and one or two more stockrooms. Got a library up there an' all; kept all Arnie's best books, 'e did. He'll be right put out, not to 'ave bin 'ere to greet yer. But cum wi' me to my 'ouse, an' I'll soon 'ave kettle on.'

Essie was torn between wanting to stay and arriving at Ivy's before nightfall. 'How far is it?' she asked. 'I am staying with a friend tonight.'

'Oh, it's p'raps too far for you, then, duck,' Joy chortled as she locked the gates of the archway and, tucking a plump hand beneath Essie's elbow, guided her to the back door of the house adjoining, into a large scrupulously-tidy kitchen, with a gleaming up-to-date gas-stove, on which a kettle was soon singing.

'I didn't realize you lived next door.'

'Hasn't told you much about me, has he, duck?' Joy laughed, as she piled home-made cakes on a tray with the tea things. 'Follow me,' she invited cheerily as she pushed open a door with a chubby foot, now shoe-less.

She sank into a deep, soft chair, depositing the tray on a low table at her side, and immediately put her feet up on an upholstered stool. 'Ah, that's better,' she sighed. 'Been on me pins all day. Take a pew, my ducks.' She indicated an identical chair opposite.

The room was large and bright and extremely comfortably furnished, with a preponderence of inviting armchairs, scattered with plump cushions, covered in plain good-quality linens, or flowered cretonnes, with red predominating. There was a thick, red hearthrug in curly wool, while attractive mirrors and pictures, mainly landscapes, adorned the walls. A display table was filled with a variety of china knick-knacks, and an archway of recessed shelves held some fine porcelain pieces.

'What an attractive room!'

'I like pretty things,' smiled her companion as she poured tea into delicate china cups. 'Get stuck into the cakes, my ducks.'

Now that Essie could study the other woman face-to-face she could see that Joss's tag of 'glamorous' must have applied once. Joy Burnett had a round cheerful face with wonderful clear skin, wide-apart, attractive grey eyes that sparkled merrily and neat even teeth in a wide generous mouth; a face full of geniality and good nature. Silky grey hair tucked into a bun at her neck and she wore a simple loose-fitting shift in pale blue-and-grey sprigged cotton.

She was aware that she herself was also being subjected to careful scrutiny. 'So you're Essie! Joss has talked a lot about you. I must say 'e's got a good choice. Yes, you'll be good for him.'

'There's nothing like that,' protested Essie, flushing. 'We're just business partners, Joss and I.'

Her companion laughed. 'Wouldn't be too sure about that, if I were you, ducks. 'E usually gets what 'e's set 'is 'eart on, does Joss. And 'e's set 'is 'eart on you, mek no mistake.'

'No, I can assure you . . . '

A plump warm hand squeezed her own. 'Sorry if I've embarrassed you. Don't mind me, love. I'm straight from the horse's mouth.' She laughed again. 'Take a bit o' gettin' used to, I do. But believe me, 'e's a good 'un, is Joss. Don't come any better. 'E's bin golden to me since my old man died. Given me summat to occupy me mind. And 'e's keepin' my three scallywags in order.'

'Your three . . . ?'

'My three lads,' she explained. 'One's at university. Bullied along by Joss, or 'e'd 'ave never made it. The middle one's at night school. Doin' general studies, 'e is. Clever lad.' She glanced at the clock. 'And young Jim, the little 'un, will be givin' 'em an 'and at the paper shop by now. Keepin' 'em all busy and out of mischief, is Joss. I think they might 'ave run a bit wild otherwise, after their dad died.

'Do you know, he even came round to us on Christmas Day? 'Cos it was our first Christmas without Jim. A pretty miserable lot we'd 'ave bin, otherwise.' She chuckled. 'Got us all organized, 'e did. Even played our old Joanna.' She indicated another room with her thumb. 'In parlour.'

'Joss plays the piano?'

'I'll say! His mam sent him to lessons when he was quite a little kid. Piano, dancin', swimmin', she had him taught the lot, did Rebecca. Nothin' too good for 'er kid. Had him tutored for grammar school. Then he left afore he needed to, didn't 'e?' She tutted. 'Independent little devil. Said 'e wanted to make 'is own way. Just because 'e was 'avin' to depend on Arnie for extras, uniform and so on. Arnie was 'is step-dad, you know.'

'So you've always known Joss?'

'Oh yes, bless yer life. I got on well with his mam. It was

me that introduced her to Arnie next door; that started her housekeeping for him and lookin' after 'is bookshop. Never thought she'd marry 'im, though. You could 'ave knocked me down with a feather. He was a lot older. Not that they didn't make each other happy; they did. He was a good man, was Arnie. And she deserved somebody like that, after all her hard work. But Joss could never quite accept it. He'd 'ad 'er to 'isself for so long, you see; they doted on one another.

'But 'e was always a good lad. From when he was quite a little 'un he used to come and help me and Jim on our crockery stall up the market. He loved it. Couldn't get our own lads interested. But he loved it.'

'So that's how you know about porcelain!'

'Well not exactly.' The whole of her soliloquy had been punctuated by chuckles, and she chuckled now. 'Didn't sell much o' that sort of stuff on Walsall market. It was bargains they wuz after, and bargains we found for 'em. A right entertainer, was my Jim. He pulled in the crowds. They would stand ages listening to his patter. A right comedian he was. And once he started to sell, they'd buy; with little Joss wrapping it all up for dear life in pieces o' newspaper he'd cut up aforehand.'

Essie could remember the crowds round the pottery stall; she had often stood in them herself, listening to the tall, moustached man who always wore an eye-catching woolly hat and scarf. So that was Jim. And Joss would be toiling away somewhere in the background. She had no recollection of Joy; maybe she was slimmer then.

'He'd help anybody on the market, would Joss. We gid 'im a bit o' pocket money, and I suspect some o' the others did an' all. A little sharp 'un, Joss. So quick. And willing.

'Jim went round all the markets; took Joss with 'im when Rebecca would let 'im go, in school 'olidays. I looked after our pottery shop, 'ere. Sold the lot when Jim died; had no stomach for it any more.' Her face fell, just for a moment. 'Right misery, I was. Until Joss jerked me out of it. Mm, 'ard as a nut on the outside, that one; soft as a marshmallow within.'

Essie's eyes had strayed again to the collection of porcelain, which was carefully arranged into various groups; a variety of dainty Chelsea ladies, baskets of china flowers, a wide assortment of Wedgwood, and one whole shelf given over to a pair of lovers carved in a delicate cream biscuitware which Essie could not identify.

'French, my love,' volunteered Joy. 'And very rare.

'Do you like my Wedgwood? That's where I learned me trade. Started at Josiah Wedgwood's when I left school; had a thorough training there, from bottom to top. Later, when I went into Sales I had to know all about the competition we faced. They sent me abroad and all over the country. That's how I met my Jim. We'd both got skilled jobs, but as soon as my first-born was on the way I hankered to come back to Walsall and me family, and eventually we did. That's when I bumped into Rebecca. She'd got Joss, a little lad, by then.

'She never did divulge who 'is dad was. Never.' She shook her head in puzzlement, then laughed again, 'And me her best mate! Never bothered with anyone else. Entirely on her own, she was.'

'How did she manage for money?'

'Oh, Rebecca had always got jobs. Very determined, she was. She sewed, cooked, cleaned, helped on the market. Took Joss everywhere with her. Never short of money; at least that's what she said. Very independent, was Rebecca. Joss takes after 'er, I reckon. Independent, and never short o' money.'

Essie could have sat and listened to Joy all night, and said so as she got to her feet. 'I feel you could teach me a lot.'

Joy chuckled. 'About Joss?'

'About porcelain,' Essie replied firmly. 'But I must go. My friend will think I got lost.'

'Before you go, look at this.' She ushered Essie through to what had been her two front rooms, now in process of being joined together by an archway. Workers' tools and dried cement littered the floor. 'This was our china shop. When it's finished it will be knocked through to join Joss's place. Fine big showroom he'll have then.'

'You don't mind?'

'Mind?' Joy laughed. 'Bless your heart, we don't need a place as big as this now. And Joss is paying me good money for it.

'Come and have a meal with me tomorrow, about midday. I'll be on my own; Joss won't be back until the day after.'

'I would like that,' Essie replied. 'But I can't promise until I see what my friend has in mind.'

It was as if she was meant to go. Ivy was committed to accompany her mam to the hospital for her treatment, while her mother-in-law had been promised she could take charge of baby Emma, who looked like being as curvaceous and smiling as Ivy herself, with the same round hazel eyes and rosy cheeks. For a moment, as she had observed the sleeping child, Essie had longed for it to be Francis and herself holding hands and proudly peeping into the crib, as Ivy and Ron were doing. But try as she might she could not imagine Francis gazing at a baby with the same reverence as he would give to an admirable portrait.

Joss Berridge's Walkabout was buzzing with people, some of them trying to catch the attention of Joy, who was darting about the yard, either helping load baths into customers' own transport or writing down instructions for later delivery.

' 'Ello, ducks,' she called out when she caught sight of Essie. 'I forgot it would be market day. We're always overworked and undermanned on Tuesdays. Mek yerself at 'ome.'

Inside, folk left to their own devices were picking their way gingerly through the furniture, opening drawers or peeping into wardrobes.

' 'Ere, Tom,' an excited voice called out. 'This is just what our kid could do with in 'is room; and ever so cheap.'

Others were gleefully shuffling commodities from one pile to another until they came up with just the right thing. 'Just what I've bin after for the hen-'ouse, Mavis. It's even got the hinges still on it.'

'Ar, but 'ow long 'ave we gorrer wait to pay? Joss ain't 'ere, and 'er outside is runnin' around like a fly in a bottle.'

'There's a gel settin' up a table in passageway,' came another voice. 'Yoh tekkin' orders, our kid?'

'Kid' nodded, smiling. 'Just come this way,' she said, reaching for pencil and notebook from her bag.

It was nearly two o'clock before the rush of customers had departed. Joy appeared at the door, blocking out the light. 'Bless you, my child,' she said, chuckling. 'Now, 'ow about some dinner, my ducks?'

'That would be nice.'

'But I ain't 'ad time to cook, 'ave I?' She hooted with laughter. 'Ain't I a right 'un, inviting you to dinner on market day; ought to 'ave 'ad more sense. Tell you what; did you notice that fish and chip shop just down the road?'

'As a matter of fact I did. It looked so clean and spacious.'

'First-class, their fish and chips. Can't fry like that down your way, Joss says.'

She thrust some money into Essie's hand, ignoring her protest. 'My treat. You fetch the fish and chips; I'll lay the table and pop a morsel of apple pie in stove.'

It had been a long time since Essie had thought about the fish and chips that used to be sold from a small wooden hut in Heath End. The only person in their household allowed a fish was her dad. The standing order was fish and chips for him and one pennorth of chips between the rest of them. Sometimes Sidney would meet her to make sure she did not wriggle her finger between the folds of newspaper for a long golden chip to eat on her way home.

Children, crammed together like fried sardines, used to sit on a bench against a wall made wet by steam as thick as November fog. The odours of boiling fat, pungent vinegar and coke fumes mingled with the aroma of fried food, causing desperate young stomachs to rumble.

Often they had to wait as much as an hour until all adults had been served. Not that they minded the waiting, for they were warm and could enjoy the constant repartee between old Isaac and his missus, the only woman in Heath End who dared to stand up to her husband; and in public too. Essie used to fantasize on the possibility of her mother having the courage to speak out in the way that Isaac's wife did, whereupon her dad would have a heart attack and die on the spot.

What a contrast it all was from the gleaming white walls and sparkling counter of the shop she had just entered, with neat tables and chairs in the corner, and assistants in white linen jackets.

'I think we can ease off now a bit, Mr Connor,' said the woman who was serving the only other customer beside herself. 'Bet you've not worked so hard for a long time. Never mind, Eric will be back tomorrow.'

The bulky man who had had his back to Essie turned round to assess the situation, and she was face to face with her brother.

'Sidney!'

The man showed no sign of recognition and at first she

thought that perhaps she was mistaken. Sidney had always been tall if he stood up straight. Now his body had thickened, his face no longer thin and sickly grey, but fleshy and florid, obviously some of his colour heightened by working so close to the hot stove. Unchanged were the small, grey short-sighted eyes, now threatening to bounce from his head as realization dawned.

'It *is* Sidney, isn't it?'

'And you're Essie,' he replied at last.

He turned to the assistant at his side. 'My sister.'

'The one you tried to find?'

'The same.'

'Well I never!' the woman exclaimed, addressing Essie. 'We don't usually see Mr Connor until he comes to collect the takings, do we, Mr Connor? He helped out today because we were short-handed. You wuz meant to see one another.'

Sidney was divesting himself of his white overall, under which he wore a smart brown suit. He lifted the hinged flap which separated customers from servers. 'Come through,' he said shortly.

In a yard at the back of the shop was a car equally as elegant as the one she rode in with Francis.

'Shall we go and eat? Somewhere we can talk in comfort?'

He opened the car-door and she climbed inside.

'I can't. We shall have to talk here.' He stared stonily ahead, resentful animosity emanating from his set face and rigid shoulders. 'I am sorry, Sidney. I have promised to eat with a friend.'

'With some of your fish and chips for our meal,' she added, suddenly remembering. 'How long have you had the shop?'

In the same flat voice he told her how he was invalided out of the army in the early stages of the war, how he rented a front room to start, how he now owned four fish saloons, two in Walsall, one in Wolverhampton and one in Willenhall. 'All in prominent positions in busy thoroughfares,' he concluded proudly.

'That's wonderful!' Essie enthused, thinking how unimportant her one store would sound. 'That's wonderful, Sidney.'

'Sid. Everybody calls me Sid now.'

He would never seem like Sid to her. But maybe he would say she did not look like a Connaught. 'I suppose it suits you better,' she conceded. 'I couldn't be sure it was you. You are so different.'

'We're all different. You most of all. Yet I suppose underneath we are all still the same.'

'Heaven forbid!' Essie shuddered involuntarily before asking, 'Why were you trying to find me?'

'I thought you might like to know our father is no longer with us.'

'Do you mean he is dead?'

'That's just what I mean.'

'Who killed him?'

'He killed himself. He walked into a moving charabanc.'

Essie stretched her arms above her head and leaned back against the seat, expecting to savour the first moment of awakening from a lifelong nightmare. But she felt nothing. Nothing was any different. She had removed herself from him physically years ago; the emotional scars he had inflicted were still there.

'Shall you honour our mam and Clara with your presence now?' her brother was asking sarcastically.

'Today, Sid. Would that please you?' She smiled at him.

He shrugged, continuing to stare ahead. 'It might please our Clara. She's not clapped eyes on you since you walked out for good without so much as a ta-ra.' Essie recalled the thumpings and moanings that had caused her to hesitate at the bottom of the staircase, afraid to call goodbye on the morning she was to start work.

'Don't go today. Clara's nursing at The General. It's her day off tomorrow.' He handed her a printed card. 'That's where I live if you ever feel like callin',' he said airily. 'I won't send *you* to the wrong address.' The card announced that the private residence of Mr Sid Connor was an address in Mellish Road, just a few doors from the house where Essie used to work.

She studied the man at her side, a man whose eyes slid away from hers as they always had, a man with a voice tonelessly dull, a man, for all his apparent prosperity, constantly on the defensive. Inside the fleshy exterior of flamboyant assurance she could detect the presence of the scrawny, apprehensive youth she used to meet on the corner of George Street. Just as the old Essie surfaced from time to time, the old Sidney was still there. Underneath we are still the same, he had said. Perhaps, after all, he was right.

'I was just goin' to send a search party,' exclaimed Joy. 'Plates are so 'ot they'll be crackin'. But never mind, you're 'ere now.' She held out a hand to take their fish and chips. When Essie said she had met someone she knew and had forgotten all about them, Joy laughed until the tears ran down her cheeks.

The corner house, opposite the stepping bridge, Sidney had said. Crisp net curtains adorned gleaming windows; the front step was scrubbed white. What a contrast from Long Row! Clara came to the door. Clara, whom Essie had never seen smile, was smiling at her. Clara, whom she had never seen clean, was immaculate in navy skirt and starched white blouse with navy bow.

'Our Essie! Come in.'

Essie stepped into a highly-polished front parlour.

187

'Sid told me you were coming. I've looked forward to it all morning.'

'So have I.' They shook hands. Never having embraced they could not do so now. Sisters, yet strangers, they contemplated one another curiously. Clara's voice, in spite of its broad Midlands accent, was low and well modulated, a voice that patients would find soothing, yet would not have to strain hopelessly to hear. She wore glasses now. They seemed to give her face an even longer look, while making her grey eyes appear larger and luminously attractive.

'Come and see Mam,' she said, ushering Essie quietly into the kitchen.

The rest of them may have changed, but her mother had not. She looked exactly the same, the same lifeless eyes, the same grey skin stretched tautly over bones that if anything were more prominent than before, the same deadpan voice.

'Who is it?' She peered at Essie without recognition.

'It's Essie, Mam. You knew she was coming.'

'You've cum 'ome at last, 'ave yer?'

'I've come to see you, Mam, yes,' replied Essie. Taking the dry hands into her own she felt no response whatsoever.

'There's no need,' the thin voice droned. 'Our Sid sees I'm all right. And our Arthur, even if 'e is t'other side o' the world.' She sniffed. 'Good job I 'ad two lads worn't it? 'Cos the gels ain't done me much good.'

Clara emerged from the adjoining scullery with tea for them all. She handed their mother the first cup. 'There you are, Mam,' she said kindly. 'And there are your tablets. You like to take them with your tea, don't you?'

Their mother sipped her tea noisily, eyeing Essie with the same resentment she had sensed in Sidney. Just seeing her again, the stretched grey skin, the slitty eyes, the hunched bony shoulders, the undisguised hostility, caused a cold sweat to break out between Essie's shoulders. She was not here, in this neat clean house, but back in Long Row, with the cold from damp quarries striking up into her thin legs and a constant nagging in her heart. She was relieved when her mother announced she needed her afternoon nap.

She went without a backward glance at her long-lost daughter. Clara returned after settling her down. 'I think she misses him,' she remarked, seating herself opposite Essie. 'She lies thinking about him, talking to him, before she drops off to sleep.'

'Misses *him*! Never!'

'Didn't he do some awful things to us, Essie?'

Essie looked hard at her sister to make sure she had understood her correctly. 'You too?'

'Oh yes.' She raised her eyes. 'And I know he did it to you. He told me. Not that you could believe half he said. But I knew that was true. It was a sort of boasting. Yet we could never talk about it, could we?'

'Have you ever told anyone?'

Clara shook her head. 'This is the first time in my life I have spoken of it. I have always felt too ashamed. As if it was my fault.'

'I know what you mean.'

'It's such a relief to talk . . . '

'It's all over now, Clara,' Essie replied, knowing that it wasn't.

It would never be all over.

'Do you enjoy nursing?'

Clara nodded. 'It's hard work but I do like it. I was in munitions at the start of the war. Later they were asking for volunteer nurses. I went to get away from home, and *him*. For the first time I was doing something I enjoyed, so I took the entrance exam. It wasn't easy; you were always the clever one. I lived in the Nurses' Home; it was wonderful to be free of him. But mother had a sort of mental breakdown after he died. We can't blame her for the way he

189

was, can we? She was just a pawn in his hands. She needed help, so I moved back here.

'Back to Cod End!' she murmured with a sigh.

'I came on the tram today as far as Rushall,' said Essie, in an attempt to change the subject for the second time. 'The hedgerows in Rushall Lane are filled with wild flowers. I enjoyed the walk, so I went on, through Heath End, past Long Row . . . '

'Looking as grim as ever,' Clara put in. 'Still one tap in the yard between the lot.'

'I walked on further, Clara, over the common. It is lovely, isn't it? With the trees in full leaf, the birds singing, the ducks on the pond. So fresh and quiet. Long Row is almost next door to it. How is it we never noticed? The few people who were about all chatted to me; they were ever so friendly. Maybe we never saw Heath End as it really is.'

'You don't see anything other than Long Row when you have to live in it,' said Clara, shuddering visibly. 'Our eyes were too full of things forced upon us; things that girls our age should never have seen.'

It seemed that now she had been able to put aside her inhibitions she was determined to talk about it.

'It is all behind us now, Clara.'

'You do talk posh, our Essie.'

'I'm sorry.'

'Oh, don't say that. It's nice. I wish I could change my accent.'

Essie remembered expressing the same wish, resulting in the elocution lessons from Vee.

'Has there ever been anyone you thought you might like to marry, Essie?' asked Clara suddenly.

'Yes,' replied Essie quietly, Francis's face filling her heart and mind. 'But it isn't possible.'

'I couldn't ever marry, either,' breathed Clara, misunderstanding. '*He* put me off for life. There was a soldier who wanted to walk out with me seriously. I went out with him a few times; I quite liked him. But no, I couldn't have married him. It wouldn't have been fair.'

Essie would have liked to reassure her sister that physical love could be tender, but there was no way she could have explained the overwhelming passion that had made her plead with Francis, 'Love me.' And anyway the physical act, even with Francis, whom she loved so much, only brought revulsion and fear.

'Our father was such an awful man. It's such a relief to talk about it,' Clara repeated.

But Essie could not talk about it. Even now, faced with one who had known the same repugnance, the same distress, the same anxieties. She hated talking about it; she hated being reminded of it. She felt suffocated by it. She longed for fresh air, and it was with undeniable relief that she heard the voice of Joss at the door asking for her.

He came in and chatted with Clara, offering to give her a lift to see Essie any time she wanted. There was a visible shrinking from such a suggestion as Clara replied stiffly that she would use the train.

Essie climbed gratefully into the car beside him. She had left her van in his yard ready for loading, telling Joy she was visiting her mother and sister. But she still could not work out how he had found her and enquired curiously.

'Easily,' he replied. 'I know Heath End. All I had to do was to enquire where Mrs Connor and her daughter lived.'

The conversation with Clara had depressed her more than any of the traumatic events she had had to deal with; Vee's departure, her subsequent loneliness, hovering on the breadline, learning that Francis was married. She had found strength to cope with all these things, whereas there was no panacea for the wound Clara's reminiscing had re-opened.

She was so preoccupied with her own thoughts it was much later before she realized that Joss had said Connor instead of Connaught, the name she had assumed. It was also some time before she recognized they were travelling in the opposite direction from Walsall.

'It's such a glorious afternoon, I thought we would take a walk on Cannock Chase,' Joss explained.

'Can you spare time for that?'

'To be with you, my love, all the time in the world,' he replied with a grin.

The chase was replendent in its autumnal oranges and golds. Stepping smartly along deserted tracks, breathing deeply the bracing air, was just what she needed. With every breath she was getting rid of Sidney, Clara and their mam.

On the edge of some woods Joss halted suddenly. With fingers on lips he indicated a herd of deer slipping silently through the trees; they waited quietly until they had disappeared into deeper camouflage.

They paused near the falls at Seven Springs, leaning over a rickety wooden bridge to watch champagne-water bouncing from huge stones into the stream below, churning the pebbles as it hit them from a height. She felt the tension oozing from her body. It was only when she had visibly relaxed that Joss began to talk.

'It was a pleasant surprise to discover you came such a long way to see us, Essie.'

'I came to see Ivy.'

'Of course. How is she?'

'Flourishing.' Essie smiled for the first time since he had picked her up at Heath End. Ivy had been thrilled to see Essie again, as were her mam and dad who lived next door. Last night she had sat on Essie's bed in the old way and they had chatted, about the baby, about Ivy's parents, Ron's smallholdings and Essie's business.

'Tell me about Joss. Is he special?' Ivy had quizzed.

'Only as a business partner.'

'No man in your life yet then?'

Essie shook her head, smiling. 'Sorry. No wedding bells. Nor will there ever be.'

'I wouldn't be too sure about that. My Ron says you are far too attractive to get away scot-free.'

'I didn't get away scot-free,' Essie whispered to the walls when Ivy had left. And then, 'Oh, my dear Francis, where are you?'

While she had been ruminating on last night's conversation Joss had lain his jacket in a hollow beside a tree. She hesitated when he offered her his hand to help her down the slope. 'It's all right, kitten. You can have the jacket all to yourself.'

Nevertheless they were very close as they rested their backs against the tree trunk. She could feel the warmth from his body and was conscious of rippling muscles beneath his thin white shirt.

'Do you like my glamorous assistant, now that you've met?' he asked, his eyes twinkling.

'Joy? She is every bit as lovely as you said, Joss. She showed me the building extension. Business must be good.'

He quirked an eyebrow. 'And, according to the brand-new Ford in my yard, things aren't too bad for you, my sweet.'

Careful to keep the conversation on a business footing she told him how the van-hire business had taken off, how she had employed Len full-time; they discussed the consignment she had brought for him and 'a houseful of furniture' he had loaded ready for her to take to Axminster the next day.

She felt quite composed by the time they walked back to the car and was reminded how Joss had calmed her once before, on the day after she had learned of Francis's marriage.

They had not driven far when he pulled into a curved driveway which led to a large square house built in a mixture of red brick and stone, attached to which was an attractive, domed conservatory. The house had tasteful mullioned windows either side of an impressive oak door.

Joss brought a key from his pocket. 'I would like you to see this house,' he said. The door opened into an oak-panelled hall, with a central staircase leading off on either side to galleried landings. Bright light poured in from a wide window on the first landing.

Joss ushered her into a huge front room which overlooked the driveway, and from there into another room equally impressive, with its ornately-decorated ceilings in gentle tasteful colours. The rooms were empty, with windows front and side.

'Wouldn't this make a marvellous antiques centre, Essie?'

'Antiques centre! Would people come out this far?'

'The sort of customers I'd be aiming at would. It may feel as if we're out in the wilds, but Stafford is only four miles away and Brocton Golf Club just down the road. Golfers may even drop off their wives to browse while they play golf. Ardent collectors will travel miles, Essie, if there is a chance of finding what they are after.'

'But come and see the rest.'

A relaxing, oak-panelled library, lined with bookshelves, looked out on to heather-filled rockeries at the side of the house. Overlooking the back garden were a roomy kitchen and scullery, and two good-sized rooms separated by a sturdy oak divider, which folded smoothly on to itself. These could be dining room and sitting room. A door in the corner led into the conservatory she had noticed from the front drive, with its domed glass ceiling, its vines and peach trees, and wrought-iron garden furniture, painted white. The garden was laid out with shrubs and rose beds, and fascinating paths leading to quiet corners. The whole house was light and airy with warm, wooden floors.

'It's perfect,' Essie murmured involuntarily, responsive to the warm welcome the house exuded.

Joss led the way back to the ground floor; pointing out a cloakroom and hanging cupboard beneath the stairs, either side of the wide staircase.

The two front rooms they had not previously inspected were almost identical to the rooms on the opposite side of the hall, one room leading into another through an inviting archway. But whereas the first rooms had been empty these were furnished with lovely antiques.

'Do sit down, madam,' invited Joss, indicating a graceful French armchair. He sat beside her, quite close.

'I am sure the owner would object to us sitting in these chairs.'

'The owner is honoured, I assure you.'

'You mean? You?'

'I bought all this from an auction here yesterday.'

'They let you leave it! Joss, it is beautiful. *All* this furniture? You bought it *all*?'

'Plus the house.' He laughed, enjoying her amazement.

Essie gasped. '*The house?*'

'Isn't it lovely, Essie? Imagine the four front rooms filled with really first-class stuff. Rare furniture, valuable porcelain, ancient silver, glass, unusual clocks, antique jewellery, maybe even old musical instruments. This place could become a showpiece for the Midlands.

'And there would still be sufficient rooms facing the garden at the back to make a comfortable home, with a gardener in a nearby cottage who has promised to keep an eye on the place for me, and his wife willing to do the cleaning.'

'You intend to live here?'

'That depends on you.'

'On me! Why me?'

'Because, my dearest love, you are the woman I want to share it with. Will you marry me, Essie?'

'*Marry* you?' She gazed at him in astonishment.

He held up his hand. 'If you are thinking of saying no, don't say anything at all. At least consider it first. It will be several months before I have the place ready.'

'Quite apart from anything else, Joss, have you forgotten I have a business of my own?'

'That could all be arranged to suit you, Essie. You could keep it or sell it, whichever you wished. But I know, and you know, you would find it far more exhilarating dealing in precious old things, such as these, than trading in second-hand modern. Think about it, Essie. We make a great team.'

'It's not sufficient reason for marriage; just because we get on fairly well as business partners.'

'*I* have sufficient reason. I know you are still cherishing romantic notions about that London chap. But I love you, Essie Connor, enough for both of us.' He had said Connor again. His next words were even more surprising. 'I have loved you ever since you bargained with me about a book on Walsall market.'

Essie jumped from her chair, indignant. 'You knew! All this time! Why didn't you say?'

'Why didn't you?' His eyes swept over her in amusement as he rose from his chair.

'I . . . wasn't sure,' she stammered, taken aback.

Joss roared with laughter. 'I will tell you the exact moment you were sure, my sweet. The day we met in Axminster.

'I couldn't believe my eyes when I saw you standing there, in Axminster market. Looking so anxious.' He smiled at her for a long moment before carrying on, as if silently reminiscing. 'Looking so anxious,' he continued. 'Then so *cross*. And with *me*.' He spread his hands in mock amazement. 'All through the war I had set my heart on meeting you again, Essie. I knew we were meant for each other. I had to pinch myself to make sure I wasn't dreaming. And you were *so cross*!'

'What brought you to Axminster of all places?'

'My guardian angel, I suspect,' he laughed, before continuing more seriously. 'A group of us were billeted on a farm at the start of the war, five or six miles from the town of Axminster, before being shipped to France. When I started trading in antiques I remembered the treasures stacked in that old farmhouse, and others like it where we were taken for training. I thought it might prove a good hunting ground.

'It did as it happened,' he added quietly, again gazing deeply into her eyes. 'I found the greatest treasure of all.' After a pause his bantering tone returned, 'As soon as I told you my stepfather kept a bookshop in Walsall you remembered me, didn't you, my lovely?'

Essie felt the colour surge into her face on a wave of irritation at him knowing all along.

'When you did not remark on it,' he continued, 'I knew there must be a reason. Now I know what it is.'

'Do tell me.'

'It is because you are ashamed of Heath End. Ashamed of your family, ashamed of your beginnings. You should not be ashamed, Essie, but proud that you have risen above all that.'

She sighed. 'You are the most irritating man on earth, Joss Berridge.'

His one eyebrow shot up quizzically. 'Sorry, ma'am. I shall try to do better.'

She wanted to add that it was not just shame she felt, but disgust for a father she wanted to forget, a childhood she wanted to wipe from her memory for ever. But she could not tell anyone, so she returned to the attack. 'It isn't fair to have pretended all this time that you did not know. And why are you calling me Connor?'

'Connor? Connaught? What's in a name? You will always be the same to me whatever you call yourself.

Although I must admit I have a preference for Mrs Joss Berridge.'

'Never. Just accept that, Joss. And please do not mention it again.'

'On one condition. That you will consider my proposal and give me your answer later.' Entwining strong hands around her waist he pulled her toward him. 'If you want me to stop asking, say you will consider.'

'No.'

'Then I shall kiss you repeatedly until you promise to give it the attention it deserves.' He tightened his hold. His mouth was dangerously close. 'Repeatedly.'

'All right. I will consider it.'

'Promise?'

'I said so, didn't I?'

'Just a tiny peck to seal our bargain.' His mouth over her own brooked no protest, one strong arm preventing escape. His kiss was unexpectedly tender, a sweet, sensuous kiss, yet so brief. She was surprised to find she felt slightly discomfited at being released so suddenly. It must have shown for he laughed softly. 'Funny little mouse,' he teased, gently pulling her hair. 'You see, I'm not an ogre. You are under no obligation.'

She felt an urge to slap his confident face, but feared it may lead to retaliation of a different kind, so she walked away from him and sat waiting in the car while he locked up the lovely house on the edge of the chase.

Her resolve to remain in disapproving silence throughout the journey was counteracted by Joss's determination to break it.

He returned to the subject of her name. 'When I heard from Joy you had forgotten to bring home the dinner because you met someone, I guessed you had seen your brother.'

'You know about *Sidney*?' She nearly shot out of her seat.

He nodded. 'I used to watch you two meeting every market day at the corner of George Street, near the crock stall where I worked. In my suspicious mind he was a black-mailer. I wondered what he "had" on you, and fancied myself one day rescuing you from his clutches . . . ' He chuckled at the youthful memory. 'Then I ran into Sid Connor in the army, early on in the war. When he knew I was from Walsall he talked about how he used to meet his sister. And why.'

Essie felt that every bit of privacy was being stripped away, leaving her totally vulnerable.

'Why are you telling me all this now?'

'I would have told you earlier, darling, but you seemed determined to make the break with your family permanent.'

At that moment she wished fervently that she had.

Chapter Eleven

Her visit to the Midlands left Essie drained and confused. The overwhelming despondency she had felt after meeting her family returned during the long drive home. It made her feel guilty.

She supposed she should feel proud of a brother who, by his own efforts, was founding a fish and chip empire, and a sister carving a satisfactory career in the face of arduous odds. But sadly she realized she could feel nothing for either of them, and when she thought of her mother she shuddered. The only people she had ever loved were Vee and Francis, and both of them had gone from her life. She had never felt so alone.

As far as Heath End was concerned she wondered if she had done it an injustice. Mary Ann had gone from the shop, but seeing it again had re-awakened memories of the Brooks and other Heath End families, many of whom she knew would be of the same opinion as those she met on the common yesterday, filled with happy memories of childhood in the village despite overwhelming difficulties and poverty.

If only her mother had shown some affection for her

children maybe they could have been happy too. If only she had been aware of, or admitted to, what was going on with regard to their father! 'She was a pawn in his hands,' Clara had said. But Essie was convinced that if her mother had shown more courage things could have been better for all of them.

Determinedly she threw herself into her work, redesigning the lay-out of the store, attending sale-rooms and auctions, studying every night. Nothing eased the torment of her need for Francis which Joss's kiss had painfully reawakened.

One day, in response to a press advertisement she had placed, she received a letter from a village called Branscombe. The writer needed to sell the entire contents of her home before going to live with her son. The cottage was easy to find, and she quickly reached an amicable agreement with the owner.

She experienced a sense of familiarity as she approached the pretty village at the foot of a steep hill, with its meandering streams and thatched cottages. Now, as she strolled across sheltered meadows tucked beneath the combe, with an hour to while away before the furniture was ready for collection, she recognized she was not far away from the antique shop she had visited with Francis.

She gave herself up to the luxury of thinking about him. The tall figure of a man in the distance invited her to imagine that it was Francis approaching, to stroll beside her in the sheltered combe, to share the silence and the tantalizing glimpses of sea ahead.

She sighed; it was total fancy, born out of an aching desire to see him.

But as the figure of the man came closer toward her he raised his hand in greeting. She found herself running toward him. Then he was running. Then they were locked in each other's arms.

'Esther! I thought you were a mirage.'

'I thought the same about you.'

She clung to him, feeling the smoothness of his jacket beneath her fingers as he gently stroked her hair, murmuring her name repeatedly.

They sank on to the springy turf. Holding her gently he softly kissed the hollow of her neck, along her cheek bone and finally her mouth. She felt her love for him taking liberties with her body. She wanted him to hold her more possessively, to kiss her more urgently.

'We mustn't,' he said.

Essie pulled away, remembering. 'No.'

They faced each other, not touching. They walked, side by side, still not touching, down to the pebbly beach tucked into a tiny bay. There they sat, their backs resting against the side of an upturned boat, listening to the swishing of sea on stones and a lone, hungry seagull.

His hair glinted almost white in the sun as at last he reached for her hand and began to talk. 'I kept away, Esther, because I did not want to cause you any more distress. But surely a loving friendship could not hurt anyone?'

There was a silence before Essie asked a question so irrelevant she surprised even herself. 'What is your wife's name?'

'Delia.'

'What is she like?'

'Oh Esther! Why torture us both?'

'I want to be able to picture your other life. What you do. What you have done before. We know nothing of each other's lives before we met at Eden House.'

'My life began on that day,' he replied. 'Everything that matters has happened since.'

She pondered before she whispered, 'Mine too.'

She would have hated him to know all the things about

her that Joss knew. She certainly did not want him to know about Heath End, Sidney, nor her mam and dad. Not even Clara. She tried to imagine what it would have been like if he had been free and he had asked to meet her family. She knew she would not have wanted that and felt that he would be repelled by it all. In spite of everything that had happened since, Long Row was always with her, deep down, and she was ashamed for him to know anything about it. So perhaps things were best left as they were.

When he pleaded, 'Just let me see you sometimes,' she agreed.

A loving friendship, he had said. That was all that it was when they met for a meal in Exeter. And later at his apartment in London, where he booked her in at a hotel as he had done before. She sat comfortably close beside him as they listened to music, or talked about canvasses he had viewed. Essie was buying modestly-priced landscapes for herself now and Francis advised her. In all their discussions the names Delia and Joss were never mentioned.

Browsing round an ancient shop one day they exclaimed simultaneously at an old locket engraved with the letter E. He wanted to buy it for her but she insisted on giving it to him. First she cut off a lock of her hair and wound it tightly to fit inside.

'More precious than the gold of the locket,' he murmured, deeply touched. 'I shall keep it always, Esther.'

One weekend when Francis was on business in the area they explored local churches and villages, Abbotsbury, Burton Bradstock, Chideock. Finally they came to Charmouth's sleepy village with its rolling downs and sweet bay. They wandered together along the sea's edge, to the boulders at the far end, where they sat, quietly content.

Perhaps because of memories of Vee and the boys on this beach, she paused to gaze fondly at the pink cottage as they strolled back to the car. His eyes followed hers.

'Delia lived for a time on that hill,' he stated simply.

'Your *wife*? Which house? Where on the hill?'

He turned away toward the car, startled by her animated curiosity, immediately regretful he had mentioned it.

'Francis! Which house?' she insisted.

'The pink cottage, tucked into the hillside,' he replied shortly, his voice sounding cold and aloof.

Essie's mouth felt like cracked lias on a hot day as she whispered hoarsely, 'By herself? Francis, don't walk away. I need to know. Please!'

His reply seemed a century in coming, yet too soon. She felt as if a black tongue of grey limestone was about to envelop her as it had the fossilized ammonites for which they had searched.

'She lived with her two sons by a previous marriage. And a friend, I believe.'

There it was. The ear-splitting rockfall. *A friend, I believe.* She let out a cry she hardly heard, yet which shattered the stillness. '*It was Vee*! Francis, *it was Vee*!'

He stood rooted, unnerved by the chalky stiffness of her face, by the wide brown eyes, which a moment before had been happily reflective, now horror-stricken, and by the panic in her voice as every bit of life drained from her.

'Esther! What is wrong?' She shook her head dumbly.

He helped her into the car and drove quickly to Axminster, as much alarmed by her stunned silence as he had been by her previous cry. She was quite composed by the time they arrived.

'Just go, Francis,' she pleaded as she stepped from the car. 'I can't see you again. Ever.'

But he followed her to her rooms. 'Please explain, Esther.'

How could she explain to him how much his wife had meant to her? Vee, her young employer, teacher, friend. How could she ever describe Vee's gentle voice saying, 'If ever you need me,' as she wrote her new name on the back of the card Essie destroyed, a name Essie did not want to know, a name that may have alerted her to all this. How could she describe Vee's lovely violet eyes filling with tears at the thought of their parting, when they climbed Stonebarrow together on Christmas morning?

She tried to explain and he listened intently, his grip on her hands tightening as she proceeded with her story.

But it was impossible to communicate the pictures flitting through her mind, pictures of herself and Vee racing together down grassy slopes to the sea, or perching close, on boulders, to take off their shoes and stockings on that first day in Charmouth; or of Vee teaching her to swim and much more besides, opening up a new world for her; or of Vee in a workmanlike overall painting window frames and helping to lay lino.

She tried to explain about the precious gifts awaiting her in her room when she moved to Axminster, and of Vee always sharing, sharing. 'He is a good man,' she had said of Francis. Essie could not allow her to share him, too.

'Didn't she ever speak of me?' she ended.

He nodded. 'At first. I think I remember her saying she wished her friend would write. But as time went on . . . no. I was away a lot, and the boys at boarding school.

'Did you speak of her?' he asked as an afterthought.

Essie shook her head. Only once, she remembered, when she had told Joss all about Vee and the boys, and Charmouth. What was it he had said? 'There is still plenty left to enjoy.' How much would there be left to enjoy after today?

'I cannot, must not, take you from her. You must see, Francis, all this has to end. Here and now. Finally and for ever.'

'No!' He sagged despondently into a chair, covering his face with his hands. 'How can you take me from her when I never belonged?'

In a choked voice he accused her, 'You love Delia, your Vee, more than you love me.'

'You know that isn't true. But she is so . . . so *perfect*! Surely you love her too?'

'Yes,' he murmured. 'I love her. Like a sister. Always like a sister, since we were children. She was in need, you must know that, and there was no one else for either of us at the time. We are good friends, that's all. She will understand.'

Tears in his eyes tore at her heart when at last he raised his head to gaze miserably across at her. Her thoughts were in turmoil, memories of her life with Vee flailing at the back of her eyelids, making her head ache.

He pulled her gently towards him. 'I never truly loved anyone until I met you, Esther. Won't you believe that?'

'I do believe you, Francis. Darling, I do.' She sank on to the rug, her arms entwined around him. 'But don't you understand? I owe her so much. It's different for me.'

'The only difference is that I love you more than Delia, while you love her more than you love me.'

'No. No!' It was agonizing to see him so unhappy. As her arms went round his shoulders she felt his tears wet on her upturned face. As usual her tears were encrusted in a painful knot round her aching heart.

'I can't live without you, Esther. We must tell her.'

'No! If you love me, Francis, you must never do that. Never.'

'Then give yourself to me, just once more,' he pleaded. 'Esther, *please love me*.'

They were the words she had used herself, that other time. How could she refuse him? 'Just this once,' she whispered.

Falteringly they made love. No magic this time for Essie; only the silent reproach of her most treasured possessions, the ones that had belonged to Vee, scattered around the bedroom, and an overwhelming sense of guilt that was never to leave her.

Aware of her lack of response, he became more insistent, more demanding. Suddenly her father's face floated sickeningly above her. She found herself fighting to be rid of the enclosing arms, aghast, ashamed, afraid. She found herself crying out in protest.

After what seemed an interminable time he drew away, contrite, apologetic, sobbing. 'Esther, my dear, I'm sorry. Forgive me. Please forgive me.'

What was there to forgive? She loved him.

But as the vision of her father faded it was still not the face of Francis she saw in front of her, but the tranquil features of her dearest friend, her violet eyes awash with tears.

Chapter Twelve

The agony of having betrayed Vee kept her awake at night. 'Oh, Vee, forgive me,' she would whisper into the darkness. 'Please try to understand. You have loved before, another man, your sons, your parents. Francis is the only man I have ever loved. Oh, Vee, I am sorry. So sorry.'

Joss, when he came, was quick to notice the haunted eyes in the alabaster face. It had not been difficult these last few months for him to guess she was seeing Francis again. Now he was just as sure that something was wrong. He invited himself for a meal in her flat. He stood at the door dividing living room from kitchen, quietly studying her as she prepared their meal. He noticed how she picked at her food when it was cooked.

'Is it over between Jameson and yourself?' he asked at last.

'It has to be, doesn't it?' she replied quietly. 'He has a wife.'

'That isn't what I asked.'

Her heart had lurched crazily when she heard Francis referred to so indifferently, but she answered calmly. 'It is over, yes.'

'The house at Brocton is furnished ready for occupation, Essie. Brocton Antiques Centre will be opening there soon. You would love it. Imagine, Essie, all we could do. Together.'

She had thought a lot about Joss's proposal of marriage as she lay sleepless. It was essential she put an insurmountable barrier between herself and Francis; and what could be more insurmountable than Joss as her husband? She had to admit that since hearing his story from Joy her trust and respect for him had grown. But was it fair to marry him when she loved someone else?

'I am not in love with you, Joss,' she reminded him now. 'I know we have a lot in common, and I enjoy being with you . . . well, most of the time. But I don't love you.'

'Surely you remember I said I love you enough for both of us, sweetheart? I need the woman I love to share my life and help me with my business. I need *you*, Essie.

'As long as you enjoy being with me *some* of the time, that will do for a start,' he added, his eyes twinkling.

'*I* have a business here, Joss.'

'And you can keep it, my love. Make Len manager, and come down whenever you like.' He chuckled. 'This flat can act as a bolt-hole for you whenever you need to escape me.

'You can still buy for me down here. You're going to have lots of business interests, Essie. Not just Connaught House, Berridge's Walkabout and Brocton Antiques, but many more besides. Together we shall work miracles.'

It did sound exciting. And if she was to live without Francis she had to have something to get her teeth into.

They were married by the special licence Joss already had in his pocket, on Essie's twenty-first birthday, two days later. Len, his wife and their daughters, accompanied them to the registrar's, and afterwards to an evening meal in a luxurious hotel at Sidmouth, with the sounds of the sea pounding below the cliffs.

There they discussed future arrangements for Connaught House. The van-hire business was booming under Len's enthusiastic handling. They decided to buy another vehicle, employ an extra driver and undertake local deliveries. Len happily accepted Essie's offer of an increase in salary to take over general management under her direction. His wife, Pauline, was willing to serve in the store, helped out by their daughters at weekends.

It was not until they had left Len and his family at the door of their cottage that Essie had time to worry about her new relationship with Joss, to realize that as her husband he would doubtless consider himself entitled to the privileges that husbands considered were theirs, making the same demands her father had made on her mother. She shuddered, as childhood terrors made gooseflesh of her back.

She watched Joss bound up the stairs to her flat, two at a time, while she followed apprehensively, shaking with nerves. The enormity of what she had done swept through her like an icy blast; Francis and Joss were about as different as two men could be.

Immediately they were inside he pulled her to him, kissing her hard on the lips. Then just as suddenly he released her. He held her at arm's length, searching deep into her eyes for a long, serious moment. 'Goodnight, my love. My wife.'

'You . . . you are not?' She flushed with confusion. 'You're going?'

'Disappointed?' he teased, his dark eyes crinkling mischievously. 'I don't think you are quite ready for a honeymoon yet, Mrs Berridge. We'll save that for Brocton.'

'A week to get your affairs in order,' he added briskly. 'I'll be back for you then.'

When he had gone Essie slipped off her clothes and sank

into bed, weak with relief. A week's grace! And after that? 'He usually gets what he sets his heart on, does Joss,' Joy Burnett had warned. 'And he's set his heart on you, make no mistake.'

She had done what she had told Ivy she would never do, commit herself to a husband. She groaned inwardly at the thought of giving up her precious hard-won freedom.

She drifted off into a troubled sleep, where Joss, lying by her side, changed into her father; she was struggling to escape through the window to the street below where Francis stood waiting for her. But in the morning when she awoke she could look her bedroom in the face again. All the precious things from Vee appeared to have forgiven her: the little regency table with its fluted trays, the neat secretaire, the gentle seascape, the samplers and porcelain, the old work-boxes and inkstands, the pretty clock.

'I did it for you, Vee,' she whispered. 'Now be happy.'

The week went all too quickly. There was much to do. She had to familiarize Len with the office, its records of stock, purchases and sales, its cash book and banking procedures. She taught him and his elder daughter how to keep basic accounts, she took Pauline with her to a housesale, she cleared all outstanding invoices.

She packed the things she wanted to take to Brocton: porcelain and pictures she had bought herself, her books and clothes, her collection of hatpins. Lovingly she separately packed the precious sampler worked by Eden Cornish in 1680, with its embroidered horse, bats and balls and trees. It would forever remind her of Francis. 'Just a little thankyou,' he had said as he passed it through the window of the moving train. Her own train was moving so fast now there was no means of escape, she thought pensively.

'Looks as if you are coming for good, Mrs Berridge,' Joss teased, as he packed her possessions in the car.

*   *   *

'You're home, Essie.'

He had carried her over the threshold and had set her down with a flourish. Winter sunshine streamed into the hall from the wide landing windows. She exclaimed with delight at golden chrysanthemums which spilled from a huge cut-glass vase placed in the centre of the silver-topped table she had transported to the Midlands herself, the tall candle-stands either side. They looked so right here, complementing the gleaming polished floor, below a crystal chandelier glinting in the sunlight.

The house felt even more welcoming than she remembered. Joss steered her gently toward the library. 'Come and inspect our home. The "shop" can wait.'

The library now housed a couple of dark-red leather armchairs, a leather-topped desk, a regency rosewood bookcarrier and Amy's library steps, lovingly restored.

'You didn't sell them?'

'I knew they would come in useful for us one day,' he chuckled.

Essie wondered why she did not feel indignant at such a premature assumption, but all she could feel was serenity. It was something to do with the effect of the house, of this room; she had such a strange feeling of belonging.

There were many books already, but plenty of space left for her own. She looked forward eagerly to spending some time in this room.

The dividing doors between dining and drawing room were concertina'd flat on opposite walls, combining the two spacious rooms. Bright fires burned in both elegant firegrates and logs were stacked in shiny scuttles.

On a magnificent mahogany sideboard were laid out cold meats, home-made bread rolls and pastry pies, cheeses and pickles, while an oval dining-table was laid for a meal, with antique cutlery and sparkling glassware. It seemed they had only just missed seeing Tom and Maggie, Joss's gardener-caretaker and wife, who lived in a cottage down the road.

Most of the furniture was early Georgian, complementing the house. It was difficult to appreciate it all at one go, but the general effect Joss had achieved was cheerful, yet peaceful; no gaudy colours, but nothing drab, the effect Essie would have strived for herself. She felt what was perhaps unjustified surprise at his good taste. He was watching her closely as she drank in the effect of how well everything went together.

In the drawing room two wing armchairs, patterned in pink on a cream linen background, stood invitingly on either side of the ancient fireplace. An elegant sofa, in rose velvet, was placed at an angle across the room and delicate matching French chairs stood against the walls.

She exclaimed spontaneously at a little sewing-table. It had a pink silk bag which operated on a moving channel beneath. Joss pulled it out to reveal a multitude of cottons and sewing materials.

Again she expressed delight when she caught sight of a dainty Queen Anne writing-bureau.

'For your own personal use, Essie,' Joss said. He indicated a tall, glass-fronted corner cupboard, completely empty. 'And this is awaiting your favourite porcelain pieces.'

'You have anticipated my every need, it seems.'

'I hope so, my darling. Do you really like it?' He was like an eager schoolboy seeking approval.

Essie stood in the centre of the room, her feet sinking into the soft Indian carpet, delicately patterned in creams and pinks. 'It's wonderful! However did you manage it, with so much else to do?'

'By thinking of you, sweetheart. Would Essie like this, I asked myself. Would she like it in this position?' She glanced round again. She could see nothing she did not like; it amazed her that he knew her taste so well.

'There is plenty of space for you to choose some more. 'You can move what there is around. Or out, if you wish.'

'Except this.' He led her to a corner of the room where a very ordinary upright pinao stood, shabbily out of place among the other grand pieces. 'This isn't rare or expensive. But it is important to me,' he stated simply. 'Bought with Rebecca's hard-earned sewing money.'

'And as such, it's priceless,' she agreed.

'I wouldn't let it go, even if the bailiffs were in.'

Remembering one of the first pieces of advice he had given her, 'There is no place for sentiment in business', she was surprised and touched. This was a side of Joss she had not suspected. Yet what was it Joy had said? 'He's as hard as a nut on the outside, soft as marshmallow within.' Could it be true?

'Quite apart from anything else,' he was saying, 'this piano is a reminder that I haven't done all this,' he indicated the rest of the room, 'on my own.'

'You loved her a lot.'

'Almost as much as you, sweetheart,' he replied, losing his seriousness. He was seated at the piano, looking up at her. His eyes never left her face as he played and sang, 'I'll be your sweetheart, if you will be mine', changing the words at the end to, 'When I was young my plan was always to marry you.' Even his singing voice, deep and uninhibited, contained an underlying chuckle.

Then, surprising her again, he played some Mozart. Essie had no means of recognizing it yet. Her musical knowledge was limited. She only knew that it was soothing and haunting at the same time, and that Joss played it with great depth of feeling. It fitted in with her mood and the mood of the house.

There was a sense of unreality about being here at all; it had all happened so suddenly. Yet there was also a calm acceptance of, and by, the home Joss had made for her. At that moment she felt that the house was inviting her to travel serenely, trustingly. It exuded an assurance that was almost tangible.

She had been leaning on the piano, absorbed, pensive, watching his talented fingers skim over the yellowing keys. As he finished playing he reached out for her and brought her on to his knee, entwining his arms tightly round her slim figure, burying his face into the nape of her neck.

'*Well*, Mrs Berridge?'

'I am very well, thank you, Mr Berridge,' she replied, deliberately misunderstanding him. 'After such lovely music how could I be otherwise?'

She tried to match his bantering tone, but he felt her stiffen and pull away from him when he would have planted kisses all over her face.

'Am I going to see the showrooms?'

'Tomorrow, my sweetheart. Today is our honeymoon. Tomorrow, business as usual.'

They carried the food they needed into the drawing room, closed the dividing doors, and ate from a low table in front of the fire. It had been a long drive, with only a short stop for tea at a cottage in the Cotswolds. They ate appreciatively at the delicious food Maggie had prepared.

Joss had filled the twinkling glasses with sparkling champagne. 'To my adorable wife. One day may she love me too.'

He looked so handsome as he stood gazing down at her, so deliriously happy, that she wished she *could* love him. Why couldn't she feel for Joss what she felt for Francis?

She was dreading bedtime. Would she be feeling like this if the eyes meeting her own were sky blue instead of passionate shades of midnight, and the man she loved was free to marry her?

* * *

215

She had enthused about the kitchen, with its rich-red terracotta floor, new gas-cooker and geyser, plain wood table and chairs and tall dresser. She had been impressed by the workmanlike office Joss had set up in the smallest bedroom, with its pedestal desk, filing cabinet, box files, reference books and catalogues stacked neatly on open shelves.

She had hung her clothes in the roomy hanging cupboard in their bedroom. She had bathed in the big bathroom, revelling in the luxury of unlimited hot water.

Now, in her white cotton nightie and wrap, she sat in front of the prettiest lowboy she had seen. Through its toilet mirror she could see reflected their large four-poster bed of carved oak, the soft woollen rugs on the floor, and the no-nonsense set of drawers for Joss. As she brushed her hair, fearful brown eyes stared back at her. A pulse beat a nervous tattoo in her throat as she tried to quell the rising panic in her chest.

It was all going to start soon: that business that went on between her father and her mother; that her father tried to inflict on herself and Clara.

Her hand froze in mid-air as Joss appeared behind her in dark blue pyjamas, fresh from his bath. Gently he took the brush from her frozen hands; gently he brushed her hair, as she held her breath. Gently he gathered her into his arms and lightly carried her across the room.

'Come to bed, sweetheart.'

She was trembling as he removed her wrap. Lying side by side in the big bed, his hand gently stroked her cheek as he made her comfortable in the crook of his arm and kissed the top of her head.

'Let's both go to sleep now,' he said.

Gradually the trembling ceased, gradually the panic receded, the pulse returned to normal. Joss's breathing became deep and regular. Her head sank into the warm hollow of his shoulders. The quiet house enfolded her, reassured her. With a deep sigh of relief, she slept.

She dreamed of Francis. She dreamed she was lying comfortably, safely, in the crook of his arm, her head resting in the hollow of his shoulder.

When she awoke in the early hours of the morning the dream stayed with her. It was as if he was by her side. She reached out to caress him. The man beside her stirred, immediately aware of her first movement. The next moment his lips were crashing on to hers in an agony of longing. They travelled sensuously down her throat, behind her ears, before their joyful exploration of her body. This was *Francis* gently removing her gown, *Francis* free to love her. And she was free to love him. Her body tingled with a desire she had not known on those previous, stolen occasions. She returned his kisses in an ecstasy of exploration and sharing. She found herself emitting involuntary cries of delight as they made love in such fulfilment that it felt as if it was the first time, for it was like nothing she had ever experienced.

Afterwards, with his strong arms still cradling her, she reached up to caress his hair and found springy curls where there should have been silky smoothness. It was not until that moment that she accepted that the most wonderful experience of her life had been shared, not with Francis, but with Joss. Joss, her husband.

As she drew back in cold comprehension, he was murmuring, 'Essie, my sweet darling girl. That was Paradise.'

Dawn was beginning to break. She could see the rugged outline of his face, the broad strength of his rippling body, and cold reality hit her like an avalanche of snow. She rolled away from him. She did not want realization of the truth. She wanted to re-live the ecstasy before it slipped away, before the dream of Francis vanished.

She had deliberately rejected the truth earlier in their love-making, when for a moment she was aware of Joss's voice. How could she hold on to the fantasy with a very real Joss reaching out to take her again?

She slipped out of bed and hurried to the bathroom. Wide awake and facing herself in the mirror one compensating fact emerged: this marriage could work, could even be enjoyed, as long as in their most intimate moments she could pretend that Joss was Francis.

Chapter Thirteen

'Six weeks old already!' Joss exclaimed. 'Time he was christened. I can't call him "Baby" for ever.'

'Do you mind if we call him Eden?'

'Like the boy in your favourite sampler?'

She nodded. Joss did not know that the sampler was a present from Francis, nor could he guess at the memories that it evoked.

'If you promise faithfully that our son won't take up embroidery for a living,' he laughed.

'How about Eden Joshua?' she suggested. That was the least she could do.

'Fine by me, sweetheart.'

Essie stroked the soft white down on top of her baby's head as Joss continued, 'Do you think his hair may change to gold, like yours?'

'Too early to tell,' she murmured.

'And his eyes?' Essie's heart missed a beat. 'They're all born with eyes that colour, aren't they? I suppose they will change to darker blue, like mine. It would be nice if he had a bit of both of us, wouldn't it?'

'They might.' Essie bent low over the baby to hide her

feelings of hypocrisy, for she was certain that the baby's eyes would stay sky-blue. He reminded her so much of Francis.

She had agonized over the possibility of it being Francis's child when she became pregnant so soon after her marriage. She recalled how Joss had reacted; how apologetic he had been, so out of keeping with her usual self-confident husband.

'Essie, I am sorry!' he had said. 'I didn't intend this to happen yet.'

'Don't you want children?'

'Not want them! Oh, my love! When there have been only two people in your whole life that you have ever felt close to, and you don't know of a single blood relation, you not only want children, you need them!'

'Well, then?'

'But how about you? I know how much you enjoy the freedom of darting between here and the Walsall store and tootling off down to Axminster. And making your mark in the homes of our customers.'

Essie did enjoy being invited to visit interesting houses, to get the feel of what customers were looking for. Equally she enjoyed helping Joy on her busy days. Brocton Antiques and Berridge's Walkabout were two such different businesses, both firsts in their own areas, both supplying a need.

Their antiques centre had been a success from the start. Essie was amazed when she first saw the treasures Joss had assembled for the opening: precious porcelain, rare pictures, antique silver and glass, all stylishly displayed among lovely old pieces of furniture. The opening had been well attended, the general feeling being one of Occasion. Glasses of port were on offer, together with home-made chocolates, and later coffee and sandwiches bulging with fillings, which appealed to the down-to-earth Midlanders who formed the bulk of their buyers on that first day. Since then people had travelled from far and wide.

The book-learning had paid off. It enabled Essie to talk knowledgeably with the knowledgeable, as well as being able to put the less experienced at their ease. Customers loved to chat with her, but she felt that much of the success of the Centre had to be attributed to the indefinable welcome the house exuded.

From Maggie, who tended the house lovingly, she learned about its previous owners, a well-known bibliophile-historian married to a pretty woman who wrote music. According to Maggie, who had worked for them since she left school, they reared four children there, with an abundance of patience and humour. 'They were such a happy family,' she reported. 'Always laughing, teasing, sharing. I never once saw the parents ruffled. Always calm and unhurried, they were, however much they had to do.'

Calm and unhurried. That accounted for the mood of the house.

Essie loved to wander slowly through its rooms, barefoot, in the quiet of early morning, her toes curling into the thick rugs, or gliding on the wooden floors. Sometimes she would stand gazing out into the garden and to the chase beyond, listening to the birds' chorus and savouring the promise of another interesting day.

And whenever she was coming home she would joyfully anticipate the moment when she could step into the hall to feel the welcome of its ancient wood-panelled walls and elegant staircase. Sometimes she would hear quiet voices of would-be buyers at the front of the house, and know that Joss was dealing with more satisfied customers.

She had made only two fleeting visits to Axminster, where Len and his wife were devoting more time to the van-hire and delivery business than to selling furniture, and she saw nothing wrong with that. They were providing a much needed service in the area. 'It will be Connaught's Chara-bancs next,' Joss forecast, chuckling at the prospect, while

Essie decided to discuss the possibility with Len on her next visit south.

Yes, this life suited her well; she was surprised at how happy she felt. It was not something she would want to give up readily. But she could always take the baby round with her, she decided, while Joss had other ideas.

'I shall organize some help for you, sweetheart,' he assured her. 'I had hoped you would have a few years' freedom before we started our family.' His black eyes drew together in puzzlement. 'It must have happened about the first time we went to bed together.'

Or two weeks before then? But surely not? That second time with Francis had been such an unhappy, faltering affair. Yet she held indisputable evidence in her arms: Baby Eden, with his sky-blue eyes, long slim fingers, long slim chin and long body, his soft white hair.

He reminded her so much of Francis it scared her. What if Joss ever suspected? She felt deceitful every time he proudly referred to the child as 'my son'. Joss, who had longed for someone to call his own. He must never know. It would be too cruel.

Each day of their marriage had brought something different. Joss had been determined to keep her so occupied there would be no time to think of Francis, and in part he had succeeded. But now here was the baby, reminding her of her stolen lovemaking every time she looked at him.

She had to admit she was enjoying life with Joss. Working with precious antiques fascinated her. She had to admit to missing her husband whenever he went away on buying trips. She missed his humour, she missed their verbal sparring, and she missed him when she had to sleep alone.

Often they took long walks, after the Centre was closed, deep into the chase, where it was possible to imagine they were the only human beings on earth. They were far enough away from the industrial Midlands to be unaware of it, yet close enough to attract its well-off collectors.

Although there was no sea, which Essie sometimes longed for, the chase had its own unique beauty: ancient trees in ever-changing golds and ambers, deep greens and yellows, all mingling compatibly. It had its own brand of tranquillity, while remaining alive with the gentle bustle of bees, birds, deer, swaying ferns, spiky shrubs, soft streams and bouncing waterfalls. They played hide and seek among the boulders near the falls like a couple of children. Joss never ceased to amaze her with his knowledge of wild flowers which grew in profusion. Rebecca had often brought him here as a small boy.

At other times they visited theatres in Birmingham, sometimes dining out beforehand, sometimes eating after the performance, perched on high stools in the oyster bar.

And sometimes, unknown to Joss, as she read in the library during the evening, she would prop open the door so that she could hear as he played his beloved piano. It was as if all his innermost hopes and thoughts were reflected in his music. It was like journeying into his soul.

And at bedtime, although he teased her about getting undressed in the dark, he did not insist she did otherwise. And if he guessed that when he transported her into Paradise she imagined she was sharing the experience with someone else, he never showed any sign.

Joss was planning a christening party and insisted she invite Clara and Sidney. 'They're the only real relatives Eden has. I never had any and always wished I had. Clara should be godmother really.'

'*No*, Joss.' Essie had already asked Ivy and Ron to do the honours; she would have preferred to keep the christening a quiet affair, with just those two. But, although he gave way to her on the choice of godmother, he was adamant about the party. He had several times fetched Clara for a visit lately. Very gradually and patiently he had won her confidence. She was no longer nervous with him, and was for ever telling Essie how lucky she was to have found such an unusual man.

Poor Clara had been obliged to give up her job at the hospital when their mother was taken ill. Despite her constant care their mother had recently died. She had always seemed old to her children; they were staggered to discover that she was only fifty-five. Now Clara was looking for a job, her previous post at the hospital having been filled, and Joss thought he knew the very thing.

It wasn't that Essie minded Clara coming to the christening: it was Sidney she objected to. He brought Una, his wife of two weeks, and kept a heavy proprietory arm round her shoulders for most of the time. Una was as tall as Sidney, as narrow as a wood-chip, with straight, tight lips which never relaxed in spite of Joss's efforts to entertain her. She moved stiffly in an almost zombyish fashion, showing no sign of noticing when Sidney's red hands lingered on her flat chest, or when he vainly attempted to find flesh to squeeze on her equally-flat bottom.

In complete contrast to Una, Sidney's rapidly-expanding waistline was emphasized by a shiny brown jacket and bulging flannel trousers, while his florid features were showing the effects of too much whisky.

Essie felt a queasiness between her shoulders at his constant smirking and sensuous touching of Una in front of other guests, Ivy and Ron, Tom and Maggie, Joy and her two lads. It was not a normal show of affection between two newly-weds, but an aggressive posturing such as their father had shown towards their mother. Essie felt physically sick; her brother was looking too much like their dad for comfort.

'Put Una down a minute, Sid,' Joy joked, as Sidney's

fingers were exploring above his wife's stocking tops. 'Come and dance with me.'

Una acted as if she had not heard, but Sidney, looking decidedly sheepish, bopped around the room with Joy to the strains from the gramophone. He resembled an elephant fried in butter, while Joy appeared feather-light and as cool as cucumber, despite her size.

The large rooms, with doors folded back, were ideal for a party. Delicious food Essie had baked was served from the dining-end. Joy's sons organized games and later Joss played the piano while Essie went to feed the baby. Eden had behaved impeccably in church, and was passed round for everyone's approval, at Joss's insistence, before they left.

It was then that Joss and Essie argued.

'My brother should never have been invited,' she protested. 'He is so crude.'

'He's very newly wed, remember,' Joss excused him, although anyone foolish enough to marry the unlovable Una deserved her in his opinion.

'What has that to do with it? He embarrassed others.'

'You are making a fuss over nothing. No one but yourself took any notice. You are exaggerating, Essie.'

'I couldn't wait for it all to end.'

'Don't spoil our baby's christening party, love. Everyone enjoyed it. Everyone.'

'Don't I count?'

'You know that's not true. Stop behaving like a child.'

'I won't have Sidney in the house again, Joss.'

'*I* shall decide that, Essie,' Joss replied sharply.

She lay awake for a long time that night, likening Sidney and Una to her father and mother. She appreciated her attitude would seem unreasonable to Joss, how could he possibly understand?

When she finally fell asleep the old nightmare returned. She was trying to escape through the window. Her dad was lying beside her, holding her back. As she struggled to get away she gradually became aware of Joss's voice and his arms around her. She was bathed in sweat and crying pitifully.

'It's all right, sweetheart. It's only a silly old nightmare.'

Essie screamed. 'Don't touch me. Get away. Don't touch me.' She had to escape. Pushing him away she slid out of bed and ran downstairs, stumbling over the last step. She darted from room to room, seeking escape. Still partly asleep and confused, she could not find her way out.

At last, as reason returned, she stood quite still, and gradually, calm and unhurried, the house reassured her. Joss had followed her downstairs. Now, murmuring soothingly, he scooped her up into his arms and carried her like a child back to their room. She lay, her face turned away from him, feeling ashamed, shut away inside herself.

'Essie, won't you tell me about it, whatever it is?' He felt her shake her head dumbly. 'It might help,' he ventured.

'You would insist upon inviting Sidney,' she accused him in a breathy voice. '*Please*, Joss. Don't do it again. Ever.'

'All right. All right,' he replied. He could not believe that this was all that was bothering her. Essie did not normally sulk if she could not get her own way. And Essie did not cry. Yet before she awoke she had been sobbing in pitiful despair. He knew there was something else, something much more serious than Sidney coming to the party. He also knew she had no intention of confiding in him.

After a while he drew her into his arms. This time she allowed him to settle her into the crook of his arm. He cradled her like a child until long after he was sure she was sleeping peacefully.

But next day he was brisk and business-like, knowing that the antidote to Essie's troubles would always be work. He had some shop premises in Lichfield to view this evening, he said, and would continue north. He would be gone for a few days, leaving Essie in charge.

'As soon as I return it will mean one of us taking over at Walsall for a few weeks, while Joy goes away for a break.'

'Joy didn't say anything,' Essie exclaimed in surprise.

'Perhaps because she doesn't know yet,' Joss chuckled. 'I am going to see her this morning. She hasn't taken even the briefest holiday since we opened here.'

'That's true.'

'I know she would like to take the youngest boy to visit London; she has friends there willing to put them up.

'So we have arrangements to make, Essie.' He paused. 'About a nanny for Eden. I know of one who could start immediately.'

'And who might that be?'

'Clara.'

'Clara!'

'Yes, Clara. We need someone reliable, someone who is not going to leave after a short time, for whatever reason; maybe to get married or have a baby of her own. Then Eden would be messed about, looked after by a variety of people. We don't want that, do we?'

'No. We don't want that.'

'There is also the fact that your brother Arthur agreed to pay the rent of the house at Heath End for as long as your mother lived; that commitment is now fulfilled.'

'You mean Clara would live here?'

'No. She needs her own place just as we do. The cottage next door to Tom and Maggie is up for sale. I thought about buying it for Clara, if you agree. She dotes on Eden and she is his auntie, not some total stranger. She would be flexible, and available when we needed her. And we would be getting a trained nurse into the bargain! It would be good for Eden, good for her and good for us.'

'Would she come?'

'I could call this morning and ask her.'

'Well! You are arranging the lives of Joy and Clara without consulting either of them. Typical!' But she had to laugh, adding, 'You have made out a good case, Joss Berridge. Go ahead and fix it.' Having someone always at hand to 'fix' things was still a new experience for Essie, and not without its advantages.

So Clara came to live next door to Tom and Maggie, who, never having had any children of their own, made a great fuss of her. She blossomed beneath the warmth of their affection, in much the same way that Essie had under Vee's loving guidance. As Joss had said, she doted on her little nephew, and rightly regarding herself as a member of the family rather than a hired nurse, did not mind how much time she devoted to him. As regards past traumas, she recognized that Essie did not want to talk about them, and as she became involved in her new life they faded from her own mind, and from her conversation.

From a quiet, contented baby Eden developed into a lively, intelligent child, tall for his age, quick to absorb what was going on around him. Essie introduced him early to the world of books; he could read by the time he was four.

At about the same time, she began taking him along when she visited local auctions and housesales, and to the other shops they had opened: another 'Walkabout' at Willenhall, supervised by Joy's middle son; a small intimate antique shop in Lichfield, and a larger one in Birmingham. She was always proud to present 'my son' to staff, customers and business colleagues alike.

Joss could always find time for outdoor games with Eden; a wonderful rapport existed between those two. Often they all went together to large open areas of the chase, where they could play cricket, football or rounders. Eden picked up certain of Joss's mannerisms, the drawing together of eyebrows when he was puzzled, the throwing back of his head when he laughed, which was often. There was lots of laughter at Brocton. Even Clara was losing her inhibitions and joked with the rest of them.

For most of the time Essie could forget that Joss was not Eden's real father.

'It's lovely to see those two together,' Clara would say. 'But they're so different, aren't they? As different as chalk from cheese!'

'That was all it needed to bring Essie back to reality. How she wished he was really Joss's, for lately she was having to admit to herself to falling hopelessly and irrevocably in love with her husband, and it was with great delight she discovered she was pregnant again. She wanted to hug the knowledge to herself for a time before telling Joss. She felt extremely fit and did not want him to fuss and worry as he had done last time, for she was very much involved in getting the Birmingham shop off the ground before handing over entirely to the bright young man they had taken on as manager. And she wanted to be quite certain about the pregnancy; there must be no disappointments.

Chapter Fourteen

It was on the day Essie decided to tell Joss the good news about the baby that it all went wrong; the last full day she had planned to spend at the Birmingham shop.

It had been exciting launching the shop, getting to know what sort of things sold best, what window-displays tempted shoppers to venture inside. The shop was in a very busy thoroughfare close to the railway station, so its customers ranged from people on a day's shopping spree, just passing through and looking for a small gift or trinket, to keen collectors.

She had done all she could and the young manager was showing such promise she felt it was time to pull out and leave things to him.

She had made sure neither she nor Joss had any evening appointments: she planned to have Eden in bed early, to cook a delicious meal and then to announce her news. She was already anticipating her husband's delight and intended to savour it to the full. This time there would be no anxiety as to whom the father was.

As she ate her lunchtime snack at a hotel near the shop she imagined how Joss would react. She could not stop smiling, hardly able to contain her excitement.

She was still smiling as she rose to leave, when she heard someone call out, 'Esther!', and Francis appeared beside her. Her instant reaction was to notice how much older he looked, his face lined and seeming thinner than before. His silky white hair was receding, his eyes were tired. But of course he had always been older, she reminded herself. It was because she was so used to Joss, youthful and brimming with energy, that she was aware of the difference.

'Esther, my dear! You look beautiful.'

While she had been studying his face he had been noticing the bloom on her cheeks, the happiness shining in her clear wide eyes, which he mistook for delight at seeing him.

She wore a fashionable, striped linen coat, straight and loose, in tan and cream, a cloche hat in matching tan perched cheekily on one side, a neat amber necklace on a plain cream dress, cream shoes, and gloves and handbag in softest leather. She looked expensive and she looked wonderful.

To her amazement Essie felt nothing beyond the pleasure in seeing an old friend after a long time. It was a great effort to drag her thoughts back from Joss and tonight, to the present and Francis.

'How nice to see you, Francis.'

'You are not leaving?'

'I was just going.'

'Oh, no! I can't allow that. We must at least have a drink together. You have no urgent appointment?'

She hesitated, caught off her guard. She had dealt with all the tasks she had set herself that morning. There was no excuse for hurrying away; it would be rather pointless, and she would like to hear news of Vee.

She found herself being shepherded towards his private suite after he had ordered drinks to be sent up. As he put his key into the lock she was about to say that they should not be doing this; then reminded herself that there was absolutely nothing between them now and it would sound as if she expected there might be. So she contented herself with saying, 'I mustn't stay long.'

Immediately they were seated opposite each other she knew she had made a mistake to come. It may be all over for her, but the flame of love still shone in his eyes, more brightly than before.

'I've searched for you so often, Esther. In every street, in every shop, in every gallery. I have haunted the south-west! Now I meet you here when I least expect it, in the centre of Birmingham! Esther, my darling! You don't know how good it is to be with you.' He took both her hands between his own; she noticed that his were as soft and white as ever.

Looking straight across at him she said clearly, 'I am happily married now, Francis, with a small son, and I am expecting another baby. I'm sorry.'

'Don't be sorry, darling. Above all else I want you to be happy.' She tried to ignore the fact that his eyes were brimming with tears, and that the hands reaching out to take hers were shaking.

'How is Vee?' She smiled apologetically. 'Sorry, I mean Delia.'

His hands dropped away then. He examined his beautifully-manicured nails minutely, trying to regain composure. 'She gave birth to a daughter a few months ago. I am afraid we lost the baby, and Delia has never been quite fit since. A bit late, I suppose, for a new baby. But it is what she wanted.' His voice dropped almost to a whisper. 'She wanted it badly.'

'I am sorry she has been ill.'

'She is meeting me here tomorrow, for my birthday. Would you like to come, to see her, Esther? We could think of some explanation.'

Essie stared at him, horrified. He would risk Vee interpreting the guilt in their eyes! 'Oh no, Francis! We mustn't even consider it.'

He sighed. 'Maybe you are right.' Then, unexpectedly, he asked, 'What did you call your son?'

She hesitated for a moment before replying quietly, 'Eden.'

His blond eyebrows shot up in surprise; a smile lit up his eyes. 'After the boy in the sampler?' She nodded. As she watched him pour out the wine all the old guilt welled up in her; guilt toward Vee, guilt toward Joss, and shame for herself. She must get away. She put down her glass after only one sip. 'I'm sorry, I must go, Francis. Happy birthday for tomorrow.'

He accompanied her silently down a flight of stairs, neither of them speaking until they stood outside on the pavement, near the hotel entrance. There was a touch of spring in the air, despite a cool breeze. Essie took great gulps of it, and smiled with relief at being out of the hotel as she held out her hand to say goodbye.

Francis groaned painfully. 'Oh, Esther, darling. I can't let you go like this. Darling, I can't live without you.' Before she was aware of what was happening he had gathered her closely in his arms. There was such a wealth of love and yearning in his face she could not bear to look.

It was at that precise moment that she saw Vee. It was at that moment that Vee saw her. She had just stepped into the road to cross over to the hotel. She stopped, hesitated, turned back, turned again as if to make sure that what she had thought she had seen was true. She took one step toward them, her lovely face contorted in anguish. The tram driver had no chance. She cried out once, at the same time that Essie screamed, before she was bounced off from the front of the tram into another moving vehicle.

Essie could not even remember darting into the road. She gathered the injured body into her arms, tears streaming down her face. 'No! No! Oh, Vee! Vee!' She kissed the unconscious face of her friend. She tried to stem the blood with her ridiculously-small handkerchief, she wrapped her coat around her, the whole of the time murmuring, 'Please Vee, forgive me. Forgive me, forgive me.' She had to be forced from her, sobbing uncontrollably, pleading to be allowed to travel with her in the ambulance.

Francis still stood like a petrified ghost, unable to grasp what was happening. He had not moved from the pavement.

Someone from the hotel drove them to the hospital. Francis, stiff-faced and silent, looking like a strange old man, sat close beside her, but all Essie could see were Vee's startled violet eyes as she realized who it was that Francis was kissing so passionately.

They sat close together on a bench in the hospital corridor, Francis continually repeating, 'She said she was coming *tomorrow*, tomorrow,' while the tears Essie had never shed before continued to fall. She did not try to stop them.

After many hours of waiting the surgeon came. 'We did our best. But I'm afraid she has very little time. She wants to see you.' As Francis rose he put a kindly restraining hand on his shoulder. 'She is asking for Essie. Is that you, my dear? You may go in, just for a moment, before her husband sees her.'

Vee's body was swathed in bandages. Her face was bruised and swollen, but the lovely eyes searching Essie's tear-stained face were full of forgiveness.

'Look . . . after . . . him,' she whispered painfully. 'He's a good . . . '

'Vee, he loves you.'

'No.' Her swollen lips were trembling pitifully. 'He . . . never . . . ' She gasped with the pain from her injuries. Essie tried to find a hand or something she could hold on to, but bandages were everywhere. She could only murmur brokenly, over and over again.

'We want you to get better, Vee. Please try.'

Vee shut her eyes against the pain, and the surgeon beckoned from the doorway. As Essie turned to leave, she opened her eyes again. 'Essie!'

Essie bent over to hear. 'Love him. Promise.'

Oh, how could she promise when her heart was filled with love for Joss? The violet eyes were troubled and pleading. 'Love him, Essie.'

'I'll do my best, Vee.'

She passed Francis in the corridor. The surgeon shut the door behind him. 'We will leave them to have a little time together now,' he said.

Suddenly, because she had only just thought of it, she asked, 'Please may I telephone my husband?' How could she have left it so long? How could she be so thoughtless? Joss would be nearly out of his mind with worry. The surgeon ushered her into an empty office. Dear God, what to tell Joss? She had no time to think of it before she heard his voice, first anxious, then angry.

'Essie! Where are you? At the hospital! Are you all right? With Jameson! What the hell are you doing with him? His wife? How did *you* come to be there? Get the hell home this minute. I don't care how distraught he is. *I* am distraught. Didn't that ever occur to you; no, it wouldn't. You have a child here, asking for his mother. Stop crying, can't you; I can't tell what you are saying. Listen. Are you listening? Stay where you are, you are in no condition to drive. Stay there, you obviously want to!'

At that the telephone was banged down and Essie collapsed on to the floor in a paroxysm of sobbing. As she did so she felt the first faint stirrings of life inside her. Her child and Joss's. Their future together. She must pull herself together. Gradually calmness and control returned.

The healing tears had done their work, releasing years of pent-up emotions. At long last she felt she could explain everything to Joss: all the traumas of childhood she had never been able to talk about, the reasons for inhibitions which had prevented her from giving herself to him entirely. Despite the heaviness in her heart her mind felt as if it had been released from prison. She had been able to cry. At last, she had been able to cry.

When she could talk to Joss quietly in the tranquillity of their own home she could explain everything. Then she would give him the news of their baby. How angry he had sounded on the telephone. What a mess all this was; so different from the day she had planned with such anticipation.

It seemed hours before Francis emerged from Vee's room, into the corridor where Essie sat patiently waiting. He sank heavily to the hard bench beside her, his grey face etched deep with guilt and despair.

As Essie's heart wept for the dearest friend she had ever known, he sobbed, 'She's gone, Esther. Oh, Esther, what shall I do without her?' His thin frame shook as he gasped, 'It is our fault she died. She came a day early to surprise me. She tried to say it was her fault. It was *our fault*, Esther. We killed her.' Oh, Francis! How could he say that. He had reached out to kiss her after she had told him it was all over.

But of course the fault dated back to long before that moment. She had to accept her share of the blame. She held his hand and stroked it speechlessly as she contemplated the horror of his statement.

'She said you would . . . love . . . '

'Yes, yes, I know,' Essie reassured him soothingly. He was like a small boy in need of a mother's comfort. He had meant a lot to her once, although she now knew that the relationship had merely been a stepping-stone to her deeper feelings for Joss. Recalling Vee's pleading she stood up to cradle his head against her body, stroking his hair and murmuring, 'Things will get better, Francis, for both of us.' She heard footsteps coming closer, but thinking it was a doctor, she did not turn round until she heard Joss's voice, accusing and bitter.

'I'm glad things are going to get better for somebody!'

Essie swung round to face him. 'Joss! Oh, Joss!' He was here; now everything would be all right. She would have gone into his arms, but he stepped away, his face grim.

'I am here to take you home,' he explained curtly.

'I'm afraid I can't leave yet.' She indicated Francis, struggling to control his distress and get to his feet. 'Vee has just died, Joss.'

'*Vee*!' The word from his lips was like an explosion blasting her brain. 'Vee! You are telling me that *he* is the husband of *your best friend*?' His disgust cut her like a knife far sharper than even her own guilt. His lips curled in distaste as he gazed down at her. 'Good God, Essie! How low can you sink?' Then, after a horrified pause, 'How long have you two been seeing each other again?'

His voice rose angrily and a white-capped nurse popped her head out to admonish him. 'Ssh! Patients are sleeping.'

'We *are* in a hospital,' Essie reminded him.

'Not for long. Get your coat.'

'I can't!' She had no idea what had happened to the bloodstained garment since she had wrapped it round Vee after the accident.

'You can't?' Joss expostulated, misunderstanding. 'You will!' He pushed her out of the way so that he could regard Francis, now standing a few paces away from them. 'Let me see this . . . this *paragon*.'

The two men considered each other coldly and silently. Francis was slightly taller, but Joss, with his broad shoulders and upright stance, dwarfed him. He looked so frail and ill. Essie felt a rush of concern.

'We must at least take Francis back to his hotel.'

'*Must?*' repeated Joss, his eyes gleaming angrily. 'Did you say *must?*'

'Please, Joss!'

'There are things to be settled before I leave here, thank you, Esther,' Francis interrupted shakily.

'Please let us wait for a while, Joss,' Essie pleaded.

'You can come home now or stay away for ever.'

Essie felt her head reeling from the gall in his voice. She trembled as she realized the shock he must be feeling, discovering that Vee was the wife who had suffered the accident; she had talked so much lately about their friend-ship. Moments before she had been relieved to see him; now she would have given the world for him not to have come.

She stood hesitating, looking first at one man and then at the other. 'Will you be all right, Francis?' she asked, taking a step towards him.

Joss put out a restraining arm. 'That is the way out,' he indicated coldly. 'If you are sure you want to come.'

Essie took one last, sad look at Francis before she turned to go. Joss pushed her unceremoniously toward the exit.

'Wait.' It was Francis, quiet and composed now. 'Be careful with her. For the sake of the baby.'

Joss's face was a mask of hurt and hatred as he turned to face the other man. A low moan escaped Essie's lips. 'Oh, Francis!' Why, oh why, had she told him her news before Joss? Then she remembered it was to add weight to the statement that all was over between them.

'I'll be careful with her,' Joss replied through gritted teeth.

He bundled her roughly into the car, Essie shivering from the night air. 'For the sake of the baby, eh?' he repeated bitterly as he jammed the car into gear. He did not speak again until they arrived home, driving through the dark night at breakneck speed. When they reached Brocton he jostled her up the stairs from behind as if she were a sack of potatoes, contempt in his every movement. In their own bedroom he faced her angrily with the words he had used last. 'For the sake of the baby, eh? Another of *his*, I presume?'

Essie cried out. 'No! Oh, Joss, no!'

'Now that I've seen him I know where the first one came from. Our blond, blue-eyed boy!' His voice was bitter.

'Where is Eden?' she asked, afraid that the commotion might disturb her sleeping son. In her confused state she overlooked the fact that Joss would never have left him in the house on his own, not even for the few minutes it would have taken him to fetch Clara.

'So you've remembered him, have you? He is at Clara's for the night. That's if you are interested.'

'Joss, that isn't fair!'

'Fair? You talk to me about being fair?' He caught her wrists in a grip of steel. '*He* is the father of that child, isn't he? Isn't he? Say it. Admit it.' He shook her like a rabbit as he shouted. She thought of Joss's devotion to Eden, his pride in him, and knew how me must be feeling. Oh, why did the explanations have to start from this point? She had planned to start at the beginning, to beg Joss to listen to it all before he judged, to tell him how much she loved him. How she had looked forward to telling him about the baby before today's tragedy. But now he was demanding an answer to this question before anything else.

'Answer me,' he demanded as he threw her on to the bed. And then, 'Oh, don't bother! It's all there, written across your face. And I apologized for making you pregnant so soon! What a fool you must think I am. You wanted a father for *his child*. That's why you married me so smartly, wasn't it?'

'It wasn't like that. Believe me, Joss, I didn't know I was pregnant. I didn't know!'

His black eyebrows shot up in exasperation. He looked so

disbelieving she ploughed on clumsily trying to explain. 'I married you because I wanted an end to seeing Francis when I knew that Vee was his wife.'

'Oh, yes. Vee. That's something else. Tell me,. did you go to bed with Casanova *after* you knew who his wife was?' He put his hand beneath her chin, jerking it upwards so that she was forced to look at him. She felt her colour rising. Why did he keep asking all the wrong questions?

'You did know!' he gasped. It was as if he had hoped she could at least have denied that.

'Just once. Only once.'

'Just once!' he repeated sarcastically. 'That makes it right, does it?'

'I didn't want it to happen.'

'You mean he forced you?' Once again that slight hope in his voice; an unconscious desire to excuse her.

'No. Oh no!'

'I see. It was his irresistible charm.'

'It wasn't like that at all, Joss. I wanted it to end.'

'Yet you went back to him! You met him today.'

She made as if to stand; to be close to him. He pushed her away, so that she was perched on the edge of the bed. He drew up a chair and sat opposite, so close their knees were touching, his eyes boring into her.

'It's been fascinating getting the Birmingham shop off the ground, hasn't it, Essie? You have said it so many times. I know now what the fascination was.'

With superhuman effort Essie kept her voice calm. 'Joss, please listen and try to believe me. Today was the first time I had seen Francis since I married you.'

'And yet I found you with your arms around him, promising things would get better! Fast worker!'

'His wife had just died.'

'Oh, yes. The "best friend you ever had". You would both be grieving for her. A bit late, don't you think?'

240

'Joss, don't be sarcastic about that,' she whispered. 'Please! I can't bear it.'

'You said on the phone there had been an accident. How did you come to be on the scene when the accident happened?'

How could she explain? She did her best. She tried to tell him how she had gone into the hotel for a quick lunch, how they had met by chance, how they were saying goodbye on the pavement.

'And she saw you together! And that is what caused the accident?'

Tears came into her eyes as she remembered how it had all happened. She recalled standing in front of the hotel with Francis reaching to take her into his arms; she was seeing Vee again, so startled, so shocked. Poor Vee. She was kneeling beside her trying to stem the flow of blood. She was pleading to go in the ambulance. 'It was our fault,' Francis had said. And it was. She began to shake uncontrollably as she re-lived the horror. Had Vee really died, or was all this part of a terrible nightmare?

Joss's voice jerked her back to the present. 'It was an afternoon session, was it?' he questioned her scathingly.

She struggled to focus on what he was saying. 'What do you mean?'

'Did you go to his room, that's what I mean.' Her failure to deny it once again gave him his reply. 'You did!'

'Just for a drink.' Why did he make it sound so awful.

'I have never had it in a hotel room, Essie. In an afternoon. What's it like?'

'Nothing happened. I told him I was happily married. I love *you*, Joss. I know I didn't at first. But I do now. So very much.' Her voice trailed away hopelessly at the disdain on his face.

'You do? You really love me, *Esther*? Let's see, shall we?'

He leaned forward and sensuously undid her stockings,

241

rolling them down to her ankles, caressing her legs lightly as he did so. He kissed her toes and her tiny ankles, her knees, her thighs, his eyes never leaving her face. Slowly he removed her dress and her underwear, pausing to caress her gently after the removal of each garment, ignoring the tears starting in her eyes. 'It will be quite a change for me to be allowed to *see* you, *Esther*, as we make love. I take it you didn't mind the daylight this afternoon?'

'Nothing happ . . . ' He silenced her by covering her mouth with his own, his tongue forcing her lips open. She found herself returning his passionate kisses as ardently as he gave them.

'One for the baby,' he quipped, kissing her stomach softly, and for one magical moment she imagined he believed her about that, until he added, 'whoever the father is.'

He piled her hair on top of her head, winding it roughly round his hand, as he planted erotic kisses behind her ears and in the nape of her neck. He turned her over and covered her back with kisses so light, yet so sensuous, she burned with desire.

It was so slow, so sensuous, bringing her gradually, but so surely, to the heights of ecstasy. All the day's horrors were pushed into the background of her consciousness. Inhibitions of a lifetime faded away as she responded to his lovemaking, until she reached the point where she ached for him. As she was begging him to perfect their union he moved slowly away from her, away from the bed, where he began to get dressed, his back toward her. Her longing for him was overwhelming.

She let out a pitiful cry. 'My darling, what is happening?'

He ignored her until he was dressed completely, when he strolled back to the bed and stood gazing down at her where she lay just as he had left her. She put out her arms to him, but his face was closed, totally devoid of emotion. Then to her horror, slowly and deliberately, from his pocket he drew out several pound notes and a handful of change. Disdainfully he tossed them all on to the bed. 'That's all I shall be requiring of you tonight, my dear.'

He walked away from her, closing the door so quietly she hardly realized he had gone.

Essie pulled the bedclothes tightly round her, feeling insulted, depraved, and broken-hearted. Finally she cried out in an agony of despair. 'Oh, Joss! What have you done to me! What have I done to you!'

Earlier she had thought she had cried all the tears of a lifetime. Now new ones fell silently on to her cheeks, and they were the bitterest of all. When she dragged herself wearily out of bed, hours later, there was no sign of Joss, no note. His weekend case was missing and she remembered he had a couple of days business up North. It was morning and she went to see Clara in her neat, quiet cottage. Clara was shocked at Essie's swollen eyes and drawn face.

'What happened to you, Essie? We were all nearly out of our minds with anxiety.'

'A friend had an accident.'

'Couldn't you have sent a message to Joss?' her sister reproved her. 'He was beside himself with worry. He went to Stafford station; your car was still there. He went to Birmingham and sought out the new manager of your shop. He was just about to go to the police when you phoned.'

'Sorry to have caused you all so much anxiety, Clara.' And then, changing the subject, 'How was Eden this morning?'

'Upset at not seeing you last night. He did not want to go to school, but I persuaded him; I thought it best. Not knowing whether you were home or not, of course.'

Poor Clara. Neither Joss nor herself had thought to let her know last night. She looked almost as bad as Essie felt; she had probably endured a sleepless night also. Essie held out her arms. 'I'm sorry, Clara. We ought to have let you know.'

For the first time ever the sisters clung together, Clara in some inexplicable way aware that there was something terribly wrong, something much more than an accident to a friend; aware also that the barrier between them was down at last. She stroked Essie's back tenderly, as if soothing a patient.

'I have to get away for a time, Clara.'

'When will you go?'

'Tomorrow.'

'Does Joss know?'

'I shall leave a note, so that he doesn't worry. And you will look after him for me, won't you?'

'And Eden?'

'I shall take him with me, of course.'

Clara took off her spectacles and gave them an unnecessary polishing with a snowy-white handkerchief.

'Are you sure you are fit to go, Essie?' she asked at last, a knowing glance indicating that she recognized her sister's pregnancy. Clara associated the trouble with that, although she could not see why. Unless? Surely not! Could it be that the baby was not Joss's? But they had seemed so idyllically happy lately. 'Are you sure you will be all right, Essie?' she repeated.

'I shall manage,' Essie replied firmly.

Chapter Fifteen

'When are we going to see Daddy? And Auntie Clara?'

'When we have had a lovely long holiday here, darling.'

Essie ruffled the boy's blond hair, not for the first time noticing that, in contrast to the smoothness of Francis's hair, it was rough and tousled. Or was she only imagining it? Lately she was always imagining she saw Joss's mannerisms in Eden. Like now, as he drew tufty eyebrows together and stuck his chin out stubbornly, Joss-fashion.

'But I want a holiday at home!' Two sad tears coursed down his cheeks as his lips trembled ominously. 'I don't like it here, Mummy. It smells!'

'That's because it hasn't been lived in for so long, but we are going to make it all nice and fresh and beautiful, aren't we?'

'But we have lived here for a long time!'

Essie laughed then and drew him on to her lap. 'Oh, Eden! Two weeks isn't a long time. Haven't you enjoyed all the fun we have had on the beach and in the sea at Charmouth?'

'That I like. But not *here*.' His head dropped on to her shoulder disconsolately.

Essie hugged him to her and hummed a little tune he liked as she glanced round the Axminster flat. It did smell slightly fusty but not nearly as bad as when they first arrived. Cool breezes had prevented her from having windows open as much as she would have liked, but she had polished and cleaned and gradually it was beginning to smell a little sweeter and look a little homelier.

She had been unable to make Eden feel at ease here however much she tried, and she could appreciate how it looked to him, with only the house at Brocton and Clara's trim, neat home to compare it with.

For her the flat was filled with nostalgic memories. Some of them flitted through her mind now as she hugged her son closer to her. Laying linoleum with Vee to hide cracks in the floor. Painting walls, ceiling, window-frames. Together. Assembling her scant belongings for her first home; finding Vee's precious things to supplement them on her first day. Finding the bicycle. Her own place; what a thrill it had been, to be followed by disillusionment when poverty loomed.

Then salvation, unrecognized, in the shape of a man she had considered arrogant and conceited when he had appeared at her stall, and only slightly more bearable when he reappeared with a sack of logs and the offer of a good meal. She thought of the business proposition he had put to her that night which had set her on the way to a fascinating new life. What a lot she owed to him and what a long time it had taken her to recognize his worth.

She recalled with what patience and humour he had taught her to drive, and with what enthusiasm he had tackled the conversion of the store and later the re-designing of her living space. When he had made her a separate bedroom and a bathroom this place had seemed like a palace, a luxury beyond her wildest dreams.

But now she could see the flat through Eden's eyes, in

comparison with the beautifully-appointed home he had known. How she missed the peace and comfort of that elegant old house. How she missed Joss! How she wished she could hear him bounding up the stairs at this moment. How she longed to see the love and humour in his eyes. She reminded herself that that love was no longer hers to claim. She must concentrate on making Eden happy.

'We shall soon have the Easter circus here,' she promised him now. 'And after Easter, a new school, and lots of new friends.'

He jumped down from her lap, ignoring what she had just said. 'Doesn't Daddy love us any more?' he asked, his lip trembling dangerously.

'He loves you very much, darling.'

'Doesn't he love you?'

Essie avoided the clear, penetrating gaze of her young son. Joss had loved her so much, of that there was no doubt. It had showed in his every action, she realized that now, however casual or indifferent he outwardly appeared. But he had made it clear by an action that spoke louder than words that he now considered her no better than a whore. The memory of that moment hurt like an open wound, the pain from which showed in her eyes as she faced Eden's curious stare.

His young arms went round her neck as if to comfort her against whatever it was he saw, but could not understand. 'Doesn't he love you any more, Mummy?'

'He is a bit cross with me at present, darling.' She tried to make her voice light. 'We all get a bit cross with each other at times, don't we?'

'Why? Were you naughty?' he whispered conspiratorily. And then, 'When may I see him?'

'One day.'

How could she promise that, when she had no way of knowing whether Joss would ever want to see Eden again, now that he knew he was not his son; she had tried to imagine the hurt he would feel about that. She had received no word since moving here, although she had left a note telling him where they would be. She had smiled wryly as she wrote, 'I am going to use the Axminster flat as a bolt-hole,' using the term he had voiced himself when jokingly suggesting she may need to escape him. And she had needed to escape. Anger she could have stood, but such cold contempt in eyes that had always shown love and laughter was more than she could bear.

If only he had made an attempt to believe her. She had needed him so badly on that traumatic night. He had never failed her before; the hurt he had felt must have been insurmountable. As hers was now.

Before she left she had visited the hotel in Birmingham where Francis was staying, her promise to Vee in her mind. A tall commanding woman had appeared at the door of his suite of rooms. When Essie explained she was a friend of both Francis and Delia she invited her in, somewhat reluctantly.

Her brother was out on business, she explained, and she had arrived only an hour ago, shortly before he left. To Essie's enquiry she replied that Francis was, 'devastated, but calm'. Now that she was here they would manage very well, thank you. She would make all the funeral arrangements and her brother would stay with her until he felt he could cope alone.

She seemed puzzled by Essie and a little resentful at her questions, answering them coolly and politely in the manner Francis would have used in similar circumstances. Essie was reminded of his coolness when she had questioned him about the pink cottage on the hill.

Because of her promise to Vee she had intended telling him where she would be, should he need help, but felt it would be most inappropriate to leave such a message with his sister, who was already looking at her with restrained suspicion. She merely requested that he be told that Esther Connaught had called.

'Were you the friend who was with him when the accident occurred?'

'Yes.'

She could fell the suspicion turn swiftly to chilled hostility as she was shown to the door, and knew that his sister was as convinced as Joss had been that her meeting with Francis was to blame. How could such an innocent meeting have produced such disastrous consequences? What a cruel blow Fate had dealt tham all on that day.

'When, Mummy? When will I see Daddy?' Her son's voice and a quiet knock on the door brought her back to the present. Eden jumped off her lap and ran to the door. Essie could not believe her ears when she heard him yell, 'Auntie Clara!'

Next moment he was dragging Clara into the room, shouting, 'Mummy! Look who I have found on the landing.' Clara was already digging into her holdall and bringing out Eden's favourite toy, a black woolly dog he had had since a baby.

'I thought you might be missing Alfie.'

Eden shrieked in delight. 'Where was he? I searched for him before we left.'

'Hiding behind the garden shed, the naughty old thing.'

The two sisters embraced as Eden danced about in excitement. Later, when he was tucked up in bed, clutching Alfie, Essie declared, 'Clara, how good of you to come. How long can you stay?'

Clara hesitated for a moment. 'Joss said to stay until . . . until after the baby, Essie; that is, if you'll have me.'

'He . . . he sent you?'

'He *asked* me if I would come,' Clara replied with quiet

dignity. 'He had been anxious about you, Essie. And about Eden. He has missed you both terribly. Won't you come home to have the baby?'

'Did Joss ask you to say that?'

'No, but I'm sure it would be best . . . '

'I think not, Clara,' Essie replied gently. She glanced around the room, wondering where Clara could sleep. She had given over her bedroom to Eden and already had a divan in the living room for herself.

'The sofa looks quite comfortable,' remarked Clara, reading her thoughts. 'Joss did say something about staying at The George Hotel; he gave me money for that. But I would rather be on the spot when the event takes place.'

'That's some time away yet,' Essie smiled. 'So how about the sofa for tonight, and tomorrow we will book you into The George until the baby is due.' Essie could not work out what sleeping arrangements could be arranged after that, but she was content to take one day at a time.

'And you are happy for me to stay?' Clara enquired uncertainly.

'Happy and grateful,' Essie replied, hugging her sister. Never had she imagined she could be so pleased to see Clara.

Eden became more settled after Clara's arrival. He loved his mummy, but she had seemed so sad lately, and Auntie Clara had come from home. She brought news of his daddy, who missed him, she said.

Now Essie could proceed with plans that had been forming in her mind. Len and the other driver, together with Len's wife and daughters, provided more than adequate staff to run the van-hire business. Second-hand furniture sales had dwindled along with customers' available funds. There was less money about, what with unemployment rising, farm wages decreasing and recession looming. Essie recognized she would have to shelve the idea of chara-bancs for the time being. She must try something else.

She had already written to a northern textiles firm she had dealt with when helping customers of Brocton Antiques Centre to refurbish a whole house or to find suitable materials for re-covering and curtaining. On one of her visits to the factory she had noticed tall wire baskets brimming with good-sized pieces of materials from roll-ends; a variety of cottons, muslins, satins and velvets, as well as heavier suitings and tweeds.

In her letter she had enquired if the firm would consider selling her a mixed batch of such pieces. The proprietor, remembering the amount of business Mrs Berridge had initiated, wrote back saying he would be glad to send the first consignment with his compliments, and if they proved suitable other batches could be forwarded for a reasonable charge.

Essie set to, making paper patterns in various sizes, as Ivy's mam had taught her. When the first materials arrived she sewed sample sets of dresses with matching knickers and hats for girls of all sizes, using pretty, sprigged cottons with plain collars and belts, or contrasting plain bodices with checked skirts. Boys' jackets and knickerbockers proved more difficult, but with Clara's help she produced a reasonable number of samples for her opening day on an Axminster market stall.

This time she had thought out the needs of the local community very carefully. The sample garments were hung on a display rail, marked clearly with the total price they cost to make.

She was not out to sell the garments, but kits, each containing a paper pattern together with the necessary lengths of materials, buttons and sewing cottons, so that industrious mothers could make them up to fit their own children.

The idea quickly caught on with thrifty farmers' wives, who were usually experienced needlewomen, impressed with the quality of the cloths and the variety of pretty colours. Each kit was numbered so that they could refer to a similar sample on the rail. Word spread, and soon she was being asked for a dozen or more kits at a time by Women's Institutes and local sewing circles.

Clara had booked a bedroom at The George, but arrived at the flat bright and early each morning. She met Eden from school, she took him to the beach, she cooked meals when Essie was busy. Once again Joss had recognized her need, in asking her sister to come. She realized how much more difficult it would have been to get her new venture off the ground without the help of Clara.

Once a paper pattern had been made it was easy to cut out several. Clara was able to help with this and Eden happily packed the kits into paper bags. Soon Essie was booking stalls on other days, at Bridport and at Honiton. The flat became a hive of industry.

Despite the longing in her heart for Joss, Essie was too busy in the daytime and too tired at night to think any further ahead than one day at a time.

She made prettily-sprigged cotton maternity dresses for herself. These were openly admired by many of the young mothers who bought from her stalls, which she continued to run throughout her pregnancy.

Time sped by and one hot summer's night at the beginning of July Essie's daughter was born, easily and without fuss.

Round and beautiful she was, with midnight-blue eyes, a shock of black hair and a deep dimple in her chin.

When Clara placed the baby in her arms Essie whispered brokenly, 'Joss! Oh, Joss.'

'Isn't she like him?' Clara breathed, undisguised relief in her voice. She had never broached the subject as to what had gone wrong between them, but she guessed it was something as serious as one of them having a lover.

'Do you have a name for her?'

'Oh, yes,' replied Essie. 'I shall call her Rebecca after her grandmother.'

Within a week, with Clara as godmother, Rebecca was christened at the local church. Essie recalled ruefully how Joss had wanted Clara as godmother to Eden, whom he then regarded as his son. Now she was godmother to his daughter whom he believed to be the child of someone else.

Essie was fast discovering Clara's worth. She had introduced a calm routine to Eden's day. Quietly efficient, like the trained nurse she was, she also loved him and valued his affection highly. She would have made such a good mother, but the past had cheated her of any desire to marry and have children of her own.

Joss she accepted as a brother, and Tom as a friend, but her attitude to men generally was still one of avoidance and suspicion. The nightmare of Caleb Connor had not yet receded for Clara.

The day after Rebecca was christened, Essie was back at her market stall, where Connaught Kiddie-Kits continued to sell like hot cakes.

One eveing, with the baby put down for the night, and Eden protesting against his bedtime, Essie said on impulse, 'How about if you and I go to Charmouth to hunt for fossils and coloured "jewels"?'

Eden whooped in delight and Clara nodded approval. Like Essie, she was aware of how much he missed the previous attention which now had to go to his little sister.

The horizon was red satin swathed between sea and sky. Golden Cap was silhouetted against clear skies to the east, while to the west a slowly setting sun weaved in and out of soft clouds turning the sea into a golden fretwork. The river Char, which separated the two beaches, was wide and slumbrous.

Essie and Eden were the only people on West beach, except for one man in the distance, seated on the pebbles, his back against the sea wall. So absorbed did they become in their search along the edge of retreating waves, that Essie was hardly aware of the man's presence until Eden let out an ear-splitting yell.

'Daddy!' Dropping his 'jewels' on to the damp sand he darted excitedly along the strip of beach between sea and stones, all the time calling urgently. 'Daddy! Daddy!'

The man had left the sea wall and was advancing slowly. Her back to the sun, Essie refused to believe what she saw, even when the man opened his arms wide and Eden ran into them, even when he swung Eden high into the air.

She stood riveted to the spot. She thought that her heart would split in two as she watched her husband and son falling over each other in delight, wrestling, teasing, laughing. At last they remembered her presence and, subdued, they came toward her so slowly, so quietly, she could be forgiven for thinking it might be a dream. Eden clutched Joss's hand tightly as if afraid he would disappear, while Essie's heart beat a deafening tattoo in her chest.

Now they were standing in front of her; Joss, despite the lingering laughter in his dark eyes, looking sad and older, while Eden gazed warily from one to the other.

'I was coming to see you tonight.'

She had longed for something like this to happen. Now that it had, she felt the weight of estrangement that his opinion of her, so cruelly manifested, had wrought. She could find no words. They walked on silently, the three of them, toward the setting sun, to where big boulders hunched together at the far end of the beach.

Eden pointed to a huge flat boulder, large enough for them all to sit, but some instinct caused him to leave them alone together. He took off his shoes and socks and they watched the imprints of his feet quickly disappearing in the wet sand as he chased toward the swiftly-retreating sea. He stopped suddenly and turned. 'Daddy!' he shouted. 'I have a little sister. And Mummy's sorry she was naughty.'

Joss studied Essie's flushed face. 'I was naughty too,' he said softly. When she still did not reply his gaze followed Eden, now jumping the lazy waves. 'Look, Daddy. Watch me.'

'You said you were coming to see me?'

'I wanted to ask you to come home, Essie.'

'With another man's son?'

'I love him, regardless,' he said simply. 'I have missed him.' His voice was husky. 'I'm sorry, about that night.'

'I am sorry, too, Joss. But are you sure you know what you want?'

'I know what I don't want,' he replied forcibly. 'I don't want Eden to grow up without a father, like I did.'He paused. 'So unless Jameson wants to marry you?'

'You would divorce me, Joss?'

'If that's what you want, and it would provide Eden with a father . . . '

Essie shook her head. 'I have not seen Francis since . . . since *that* night.'

'Then bring the boy home to Brocton. We can make some sort of go of it, surely, for his sake. It was no fun for me. Nor for Rebecca.'

'But Rebecca managed, didn't she?' Essie thought of her own rapidly-expanding market business. 'And I can.'

'So you prefer that, do you, "managing", to coming home?'

'I don't know, Joss.' It was true. Her heart ached for all that could have been, but now that the opportunity to pick up the threads presented itself she shied away from making a decision. She could only envisage his contempt the last time they were together.

'Do you think that what we are doing is fair to Eden?'

'He has missed you. He is missing Brocton,' she admitted frankly. 'But he's coping. Let's leave things as they are, Joss. For the time being.'

'Then at least let me take him back for the remainder of his school holiday.'

Knowing how much Eden would enjoy that she could not refuse point-blank. 'I will think about it,' she promised.

She lay thinking all night. Joss still loved Eden; she should have known that nothing would alter that. He had given Eden as his reason for coming. Not herself. No words of love, and no mention of the baby. Until he did, she felt she could not mention her either; it was too hurtful, the remark he had made when he knew she was pregnant. They had seemed like strangers yesterday on the beach. It had been easier to talk the first day they met.

She tried to analyse her emotions. She had longed for him to take her in his arms, while at the same time fearful lest he did. The humiliation she had felt on the night she had given herself to him, more completely than ever before, had swept through her again, drowning all other emotions. His rejection had erected a barrier between them that now appeared insuperable.

Eden had questioned her repeatedly as she drove back to the flat. 'Has Daddy come to fetch us?' he had asked excitedly. 'Are we going home soon, to Brocton? *Please*, Mummy.'

'I don't know, Eden.'

'Doesn't Daddy want us to go?' he had insisted.

'You know how busy I am here, darling.'

'But *I* am not busy,' he protested, his lips trembling. And when she suggested he might like to go to Brocton for a while, he was overjoyed.

Essie discussed it with Clara before setting off for her market stall. Clara could not understand her hesitation. It was only fair to Joss, she said, and her own cottage must be crying out for a good clean by now. She would go with them, and would see that Eden returned in time for the start of the new term.

Later that day, flushed from the sun and from exhaustion, Essie reached for her sample garments hanging from the display rail above the stall. She began to pack them in a cardboard box between spotless folds of tissue paper. It was only three o'clock and she was sold out. It seemed everyone had made their way to Axminster market today. Hoards of eager women had crowded round her stall since she arrived early that morning.

Not until she had packed the last piece of tissue did she become aware of a man, square-shouldered and confident, a man with engaging eyes and impudent smile, appraising her from behind her open stall. She thought it might be an illusion from the past, brought on by the heat, but he chose that moment to saunter casually toward her.

'I'll take the lot,' he declared with a grin that somersaulted her heart.

'Thank you, Mr Berridge, but I have decided to sell no more today.'

'Why, I saw you pack your stall sky-high this morning. And you say you have no more to sell?'

'You were hoping I would drop my prices, I suppose?'

'As if I'd do that!' He scooped up the box she had packed. 'If you won't take my money, at least let me help you with these.' He chuckled as he walked beside her through the now gradually-thinning crowds. 'Connaught Kiddie-Kits! Well, you certainly weren't selling ice cream to eskimos today, love.' His voice contained laughing approval.

'Don't call me love.'

'Then I must have a name, Miss . . . ?'

'Connaught.' She was enjoying their banter. This was something she could cope with. This was the Joss that she knew, the Joss who had appeared on her doorstep with the logs when she needed warmth, the man who had recognized that she was hungry and lonely before she had admitted it to herself, the man who had sent Clara when she was most needed.

'Connaught, eh? Fancy changing it to Berridge?'

'Oh no. Berridge Kiddie-Kits wouldn't do at all.'

They reached the flat and immediately his arms were round her, crushing her to him, his lips on her forehead, her cheek, her mouth. 'Oh, Essie!' he murmured. 'Remember that day?'

'Could I ever forget?'

'Come home, Essie.'

She wanted to stay for ever within the comfort of his arms. She could agree to go back with him. And then what? He loved the memory of her. But what of the reality? She needed more time.

He released her as soon as he felt her pulling away from him.

'Eden would like to come for the rest of his holiday, Joss. If you will take Clara too she will bring him back.'

A black eyebrow quirked upwards in the way she remembered so well. 'Your insurance policy, eh?' Then, 'What will you do?'

'I shall stay here, of course. I am quite capable of looking after myself.'

'Yes, I see that,' he replied quietly. 'And *you* are all that matters, I suppose?' The sudden bitterness in his voice cut her like a knife.

'Please go now, Joss.' She knew that Clara and the children would be back from their walk soon and, perversely, she did not want him to see the baby he still had not mentioned.

He left without a single protest.

* * *

Clara was openly elated at the thought of seeing her own little home again; Essie felt guilty at not realizing how much it meant to her, how much she had missed it.

'What a pity Joss did not see the children this afternoon, Essie,' she said as she checked the contents of her bag and Eden's case for the umpteenth time. 'I would have brought them back earlier had I known.'

'Please Clara, don't tell him how much Rebecca resembles him, will you?'

'Why ever not?'

'Please, Clara!' She did not want Joss rushing back down here just because Clara had confirmed that Rebecca was his child.

Clara sighed. 'I wish I knew what all this is about. But all right, if that is what you want,' she agreed.

The flat seemed dreary and empty after they had gone until Essie tiptoed into the bedroom to look at her daughter, stretched out in a wicker clothes-basket, rosy with sleep, her blanket kicked off. As if feeling the intensity of her mother's gaze she opened her eyes. She dimpled immediately when she recognized Essie. Her beautiful dark eyes already sparkled with fun. Just like Joss's had in the market today. Oh to be able to go back to that day they had first met and live it all again! But then there would have been no Eden, and she could not imagine life without him.

'Just you and me for a while, sweetheart,' she whispered to the baby. At that moment she felt very close to the first Rebecca. She had had Joss all to herself. What had been her secret? Essie wondered. Who had been Joss's father?

Chapter Sixteen

On four days each week Essie took Rebecca with her to the markets, using a parasol to make a shady spot for the wicker basket. Customers were enchanted with her winsome chuckles, while she revelled in all the extra attention when she was awake. She took her naps as usual, despite the raucous market noises all around her. This is how it must have been for Joss and his mother, Essie reflected, feeling an empathy with them both.

She enjoyed having Rebecca to herself, although she missed Clara and Eden. She had sent regular picture post-cards, and had received a little note from Eden in laboured, childish writing. 'It is luvly heer, having fun with Dad. I luv you a lot, Mummy.'

Essie wondered if the second sentence had been dictated by Clara, whose letter in the same envelope described the 'treats' Joss had arranged for Eden, and how she had been entrusted to hold the fort at the antiques centre on a couple of occasions while Joss took Eden riding on the chase.

Only a few days now before they would be back. Time had sped by, what with her market days, caring for the baby, keeping the flat clean, and working into the nights to prepare the popular kiddie-kits for sale. Occasionally she popped into the store to talk business with Len and his wife. They were puzzled by Essie's lengthy separation from Joss, but, like Clara, were too polite to broach the subject.

Essie supposed it was Len one evening when there was a gentle knock on her door. But it was not Len. It was Francis; a calm and immaculate Francis, very different from the dispirited man she had last seen at the hospital.

Seated opposite him Essie felt chilled, despite the warmth of the evening, as she recalled that dreadful time when they were last together.

'I caught sight of you this morning, Esther; you were driving through Honiton. I thought I may find you here. I am sorry I was not at the Birmingham hotel when you called.'

'I just wanted to make sure you were all right, Francis. I had to come away next day.'

He glanced at the table, piled high with heaps of cloth, scissors, paper patterns and bags. 'You mean? This isn't just a temporary visit?'

She smiled sadly. 'Not exactly.'

'What about the new baby?' he enquired.

'She is here with me. Joss thought she was yours, Francis.'

'Oh, Esther! Oh, my dear!'

He was concerned for her, but he was no longer declaring his love for her, she realized with a sigh of relief. He was very composed and controlled in spite of his concern. 'I must talk with your husband, Esther. To explain.'

'No!'

'Please allow me. I feel responsible.'

'No, thank you,' Essie stated firmly. 'It would do more harm than good.'

'But you love him. It was all there in your face. Couldn't he see that?'

261

'He evidently thought that what was in my face was for you, Francis.'

Francis was silent for a moment, considering. 'It must be very difficult for any man to accept what he thinks is another man's child. I could not do it.'

Essie thought of the love Joss showed for Eden, in spite of what he suspected.

'How are you managing, Francis?' she asked, changing the subject.

'My sister, a very capable lady, looks after me well, thank you, Esther.

'I work mainly from home now. I have been commissioned to write a set of books about famous artists, and I have various other commitments, writing for collectors' periodicals, local newspapers, and so on. It is a very different life, but I quite enjoy it. And I am always available if Delia's sons want to pay a visit. They come quite often.'

'She would like that,' Essie replied, in her mind's eye seeing two adored little boys, Justin, red-haired and truculent, and Robert, like his mother, unassuming and patient. She noticed that Francis had referred to them, not by name, but as 'Delia's sons'. Another man's sons.

'Esther, I wish to talk to you about Delia.' Essie waited, her breath suspended. 'There is something I should like you to know.'

'Delia would have died within a few months, Esther. She had a heart condition, and had been advised not to give birth to the baby. I learned this only recently. She told my sister she wanted to leave me someone of my own.'

An image of Vee's anguished face when she had seen them together flashed once more across Essie's vision. The information Francis had just imparted made no difference to the agony of the knowledge of how and when she died. Painfully aware of the part they had played in her death, she felt

262

horrified that he could sit here discussing it as if it was somehow inevitable.

If only she had lived a little longer they could have explained to her. Essie felt that Vee would have understood, and would have believed them when they told her they had met by chance on that day.

'The knowledge helped me. I thought it may help you,' Francis was saying.

'Yes. Thank you, Francis.' She forced herself to reply politely, remembering Vee's pleadings. 'Love him, Essie. Promise.' He no longer asked for her love; he needed her understanding. He had himself sorted out; she envied him that.

'What you and I had was sweet and lovely, Esther dear. I shall always cherish the memory. As I shall always cherish Delia's memory. Delia lives on, in her sons.' Then he said, 'They are more important than any of us, aren't they, the children we bring into the world. They are the future.'

Long after Francis had left Essie sat near the open window and gazed into the street below where couples lingered, reluctant to leave the soft night air to go indoors.

It was on such an evening that she had sat here with Joss, and he had first talked to her about his mother. 'I wasn't used to sharing her,' he had said. And recently, with regard to Eden, 'I know what it was like without a father. Don't let us do that to him,' he had pleaded. She thought of the glow in Eden's face when he had spotted Joss on the beach, and again when he was going home, to Joss and to Brocton.

What was it Francis had said to her earlier? 'These children we bring into the world, they are the future.'

'Did you send him here today, Vee?' Essie whispered into the night. For he had brought more than one message. 'It must be difficult for any man to accept another's child . . . I couldn't.' But Joss had. And she had not even given him a glimpse of his very own daughter.

Clara and Eden were due back on Tuesday for the start of school the following day. She had many arrangements to make before they returned.

A small wicker laundry basket was placed in the centre of the polished floor where a shaft of afternoon sunlight slanted down from the landing window of their Brocton home.

A key turned in the outer door. Eden darted in, ahead of his father. He almost stumbled over the basket. 'Rebecca!' His voice rose excitedly. 'It's Rebecca!' He covered his little sister's face with kisses. 'Dad! Hurry up. Rebecca's come home.'

Joss, pausing to lock the door, heard the baby's soft chuckle. He turned slowly, to be greeted by a dimpled smile as she flirted brazenly with midnight-blue eyes that were mirror images of his own. With joy and wonderment he lifted his daughter into his arms. In one rapturous moment she had captured his heart for ever.

'Welcome home,' the house had murmured as Essie carried Rebecca from room to room, on a tour of inspection, the baby alert and curious, occasionally gurgling as if she understood Essie's remarks. The little sewing-table, the pretty desk, her corner cupboard filled with precious pieces of porcelain, all shone with polish, evidence of Maggie's industry; all loving gifts to her from Joss.

She lingered at the piano in the corner, running her fingers along its yellowed keys. 'This is where you will live, my baby. Your home,' she whispered as Rebecca cooed at the soft piano sounds.

She sat for a while in the deep leather armchair in the library, strangely moved at the sight of her books stacked side by side with Joss's; there was such an enduring quality about books.

The office was piled high with papers, showing signs of a

hurried departure. She guessed that Joss would have left early to go out buying, since it was a Monday, closing day for the antiques centre.

She wondered if he had taken Eden or left him with Clara.

She could bear to look only briefly into what had been their bedroom. Memories of the last time she had lain in the big four-poster were a physical pain. Yet the house was already imbueing her with a sense of peace, and a sense of assurance that all would be right in the end. She must be patient, as Joss had been for so long. 'I have loved you ever since you bargained with me about a book on Walsall market,' he had once said. It was not going to be easy, but if he had been as patient as that, then surely she could wait.

She lay the baby on top of the bed in the room next door to Eden's, while she unpacked their clothes. From the window she could see the garden ablaze with summer flowers, and the majestic greenery of Cannock Chase beyond. Would she ever be stepping out happily again, beneath the tall firs, with Joss at her side?

She turned back into the room to watch her daughter who, delighted to be free of her nappy, was kicking vigorously. She was such a happy child, as happy as this house. 'And now, my poppet, we must get you ready to meet your brother. And your father.'

Eden threw his arms around her neck excitedly. 'You've come to stay, haven't you, Mummy? We can stay, can't we?'

She hugged him close. 'For as long as you like, darling.'

'Oh good. I can go riding tomorrow.' He darted away into the garden to chase butterflies, pausing only to shout, 'Dad, Mum says we're staying.'

Joss appeared at the kitchen door, carrying Rebecca. 'She's beautiful, Essie,' he breathed.

'And she's yours.'

'I can see that!' His eyes searched her face. 'You've come home?'

She nodded. 'For the children's sake.'

'That will have to do for now.'

He made no comment when he realized she had prepared a separate bedroom for herself.

It had been a tiring day, physically and emotionally, and Essie fell asleep immediately; but in the night the old nightmare returned. She was trying to get to the window and her father was holding her down with arms of steel. She cried out in her sleep. Within seconds Joss was beside her, cradling her gently until the deep sobs ceased. When she became conscious of his arms around her trembling body he was stroking her hair gently, murmuring, 'It's all right, Essie. No one is going to hurt you ever again. No one.'

When the trembling had ceased he carried her gently into what had been their shared bedroom. He lay beside her, her head resting in the crook of his arm, talking soothingly the whole time. 'My poor little Essie. It's all right now. You're safe.'

Gradually she drifted off to sleep in his arms. When she awoke early morning he was still there, still holding her gently. Instantly alert as always, she remembered immediately.

'Joss,' she whispered, sensing he was awake too. '*You know*, don't you?'

'Yes, love. I know.'

'*How?*'

'Clara told me the other day.'

'*Clara!*' It seemed impossible to think of Clara confiding in any man. 'You mean she told you about our *father?*'

'Yes; when we were walking on the chase. She said she wondered if it would help me to understand you. She doesn't know what went wrong between us, Essie, but she thought it may have something to do with what happened all those years ago, when you were children.'

'In a way, it did, Joss,' Essie whispered.

'Yes, I know, love.' He waited.

'I couldn't love, or trust, any man. Then Francis came along. He was so different from anyone I had ever known. I thought it was love I felt for him. I was afraid of the kind of love you wanted. But you showed me that what I felt for him was only a weak substitute for the real thing, Joss. A sort of . . . a sort of preparation.'

'And when I cried for Vee it released so many tensions. I had never been able to cry. I felt at last I could explain everything to you. All that had gone before. Then it all went wrong!'

His arms folded around her more closely. 'Forgive me, Essie.'

'Forgive you! I am the one who needs forgiveness.'

'No, I should have given you a chance to explain. I should have believed you. I was mad with jealousy. Those last few months you had seemed so happy. I thought I was winning at last. Then I found you holding Jameson in your arms and promising him things would get better! It was too much. It seemed as if you had never been mine and never would be. And when I knew you had been lovers, that Eden . . . ' His voice broke.

'I know, I know.' It was her turn to soothe him, to stroke his face and hair as they clung tightly together, hearing each other's heartbeats.

'Then when Clara told me about the traumas of your childhood, I knew the only thing that matters is to make you happy again. It doesn't matter if you can't love me.'

'But I do love you. *Oh, Joss, I do.* All that joy in my face was for *you*, and because I was carrying your child. I didn't want to tell you about the baby until I was absolutely certain. And I didn't want you worrying about me because there was no need. I felt wonderful.'

'You named her Rebecca!'

'What else was there?'

'Oh, Essie! Is it possible that you do love me?'

'Until the end of time,' she replied simply.

Oh the blessed relief of shedding the awful secret, the sense of shame and guilt that had plagued her since the days in Long Row. And it had taken Clara to bring this about! She lay thinking of all that Joss had had to come to terms with.

'After all this, you still love me, Joss?'

'From the beginning of time, sweetheart.'

From across the landing came the sounds of Eden talking to his little sister, and her gurgling responses.

'*Our children*, Essie. At least we can make sure that they are happy.'

'I've lots of things to show you, Rebecca,' Eden was promising. 'Just lots!'

Eden always did have lots he wanted to show Rebecca. Throughout their childhood she was his best friend. Almost as soon as she could walk she climbed trees with him, paddled in the streams searching for tiddlers with him, played football and cricket like a boy, and rode her small pony at his side. She was a sturdy little girl, full of teasing and fun, like her father. They could always rely on Rebecca to turn anything into a joke.

She reminded Joss of the first Rebecca, but strangely Eden never brought Francis to mind. Eden grew tall with strong square shoulders, maybe because he had always helped Joss lift the heavy antique furniture that was too precious to be handled by anyone else.

Joss, always keen that the children should travel, found time each year for a family holiday. Together they visited

Holland, Denmark, France and Germany. Once they motored through Italy and explored Rome, Florence and Venice, a cultural education that was to stay with them always.

Then there was the never-to-be-forgotten trip to Canada, to visit Essie's brother Arthur and his family. Joss could not spare the time for such a long visit, but encouraged Essie to take the children, eager for them to make contact with any family they possessed.

They spent a few days familiarizing themselves with Toronto before travelling to the prairies, where Arthur and Liddy farmed, together with their five active sons.

Eden and Rebecca immediately fell into the routine of helping out-of-doors. Essie wished that Joss could have been with them to see the young folk getting to know one another. The youngest of Arthur's boys was about the same age as Eden and they got on well from the start, while sturdy little Rebecca enjoyed the challenge of keeping up with her tough noisy cousins, relishing the attention they showered on her, in spite of their boisterous ways.

Essie would have willingly worked alongside her busy sister-in-law, but Liddy insisted she sometimes sat in the shade to read or rest, and not even Essie considered it worth arguing with Liddy. She returned to England rejuvenated, thrilled that she could picture her brother content within his family.

At home all of them loved to explore the area round Brocton, on foot, on horseback or on their bicycles, Clara often accompanying them on such jaunts. Clara did a fair amount of home-nursing now, and in her spare time had taken to reading some of Essie's books. This resulted in her joining an English Language and Literature class at a local technical college. 'Never too late' she said, when Rebecca teased her about being a mature student, 'although I wish I'd had chance to do it sooner, like you have.'

Since the day Joss had suggested Clara join them as nanny to Eden she had blossomed within the love of an affectionate family.

Essie still held the reins of the transport business down south. Although ably managed by Len and his wife, they invariably had a list of queries for her attention whenever she appeared. She combined her visits to them with hunting for suitable antiques from outlying districts, which were still a good source of supply. She loved to take the children along but Eden often preferred to stay home with Joss.

To Eden, Axminster was reminiscent of a fusty flat, of a time when he pined for Brocton and Joss, a time when his parents were estranged, whereas, to Rebecca, sleeping above the store was great fun, as were the auctions and housesales she attended with her mother. She was ever ready to accompany Essie on her visits south, if they coincided with school holidays.

Combining business with pleasure they fished for mackerel from Lyme Regis, went deep-sea fishing with the fishermen from West Bay, all of whom they now knew by name, and often climbed Golden Cap, where they would lie companionably on its topmost grassy peaks, gazing down at changing seas, miniature vessels and matchstick people; confiding, laughing, enjoying being together, just the two of them.

Rebecca also accompanied Essie on her visits to Ivy, who loved to reminisce about life at 'The Mellish', chuckling heartily as she recounted how Essie called the mistress 'Mrs Vee' to her face and got away with it. 'I shall never forget the day Essie started,' she would say. 'All eyes and no body she was. Yet she had a winsome way with her, even then.'

They were happy time for all of them, despite the slump in the 1930's bringing difficulties for the antiques trade. Fortunately Berridge's Walkabouts supplied a never-decreasing need for do-it-yourselfers anxious to save money.

And Essie's Kiddie-Kits business was expanding rapidly. It was just the sort of thing to appeal to money-conscious mums. From the day she arrived back at Brocton Essie enlisted the part-time help of Clara and Maggie, and later the skills of Maggie's neighbours in the rows of cottages nearby. In the beginning she turned the conservatory into a workroom, installing a large cutting table in the centre and several smaller individual tables, together with store cupboards, three sewing-machines, a desk and a filing cabinet.

With patience and humour, she advised her workers on the most economical ways of cutting, and on colour co-ordination, pinning illustrative charts on the walls where the conservatory joined the house. The Kiddie-Kit ladies, as they christened themselves, soon became absorbed in the project, one or two of the older ladies preferring to concentrate on packing.

Now, most of the cutters worked in their own cottages so they could fit in with school times and their men's working hours, while the conservatory continued to be used for packing, for clerical work, and as a receiving centre. Essie paid piecework for cutting, and production was always high.

She started by supplying needlework shops in Stafford, Birmingham and Walsall, but eventually she had a number of supply units of her own dotted around the area, which despatched Connaught Kiddie-Kits all over the British Isles.

With the threat of war looming large in 1939 the kits became even more in demand. In appeared that, wary of possible shortages, many mothers were prepared to lay in stocks of other things beside food. Maggie, loyal as ever, was still in the forefront of the Kiddie-Kits organization, while Clara had become less involved over the years, gradually dropping out completely, she had so much more now to occupy her time, with her new studies.

Sidney had kept in touch with Clara, visiting her from time to time, and it was through her they learned he had been gambling heavily, regularly visiting race-courses and dog-tracks. It was not until Clara had parted with most of her carefully-saved small capital that she told them about it, by which time Sidney had been obliged to get rid of three of his concerns to help pay his gambling debts, and only by Joss putting money into the Walsall shop was he able to hang on to that.

The same weekend that war was declared they learned he was in police custody for attacking his wife.

'Thank goodness she had sufficient sense to report him instead of putting up with it like our mother did,' Clara retorted.

But in Essie's imagination there arose a picture of a half-starved lad, inadequately clothed, on a freezing January day. She remembered his boils and pimples, his poor purple hands. She was haunted with thoughts of the night he had been forced to shelter in an entry, wet through and shivering, after daring to stand up for their mother, and another time when his dad had locked him in a dark lavatory.

'I must go to him,' she said.

At Walsall Police Station they sat on either side of a small table, Sidney resentful and truculent. 'Come to play the Lady Bountiful?' he asked ungraciously.

'I have come to see if there is anything I can do, Sidney.'

'Like what? Like coming to bed with me?' he leered. He grinned spitefully at her startled expression.

'You had to go with our father, didn't you? Does Joss know that, Mrs High-and-Mighty? Does Joss know?'

'It is over and done with now, Sidney.'

'*Is it*? That's what you think!' Suddenly his blustering manner crumbled; suddenly he was on the verge of tears, reminding Essie again of the snuffling, shuffling youth seeking warmth from a hot potato machine. For the first time in their lives she felt she would have liked to have put her arms around him as waves of compassion flooded over her. He looked so lonely. So alone. In spite of his bulk he seemed like a child again. He lapsed into the way he used to talk. 'I 'ad to go with 'im an' all, yer know.'

'Oh no!'

He nodded. 'After you left 'ome. He'd 'ave killed me if I 'adn't. He used to come downstairs to me in the night.'

She shuddered. 'Why didn't you run away?'

'Run? Where to? I was unfit, no money, no job. The bobby would 'ave marched me right back 'ome.' Essie knew what he meant. There had never been anywhere for her to run to either.

'Where could I 'ave gone?' he asked bitterly. 'I joined the army as soon as I could, remember? Scared to death, I was, in case they wouldn't take me. Blokes used to grumble about the food we cooked 'em. They should have been sentenced to a spell at our 'ouse. The first decent food I ever tasted was in the army. First time I'd 'ad me belly filled in me life.'

'In spite of everything, Sidney, look what you achieved when you came out of the army. You were winning. You had a lot to be proud of.'

He dropped his head into his hands, groaning. 'That was before Una. She is such a cold fish, in bed and out. I went off with the racing crowd to get away from her. Then I felt I'd like to see what it felt like to lash out at her. Like *he* did.'

'Oh, Sidney!' But again Essie felt she understood. Sidney, not able to form a normal relationship, felt the need to dominate as he had been dominated.

'She is so devoid of emotion.' His words brought back the memory of Una's zombyish expression at the christening. 'I just had to force her to respond. To cry out. Anything! It got out of control; couldn't stop myself. I've put her in hospital this time.' He groaned again, as if in physical pain. 'Oh, God, there must be something of *him* in me. What a life we led, eh?'

'There is nothing in you that you haven't put there yourself. You can get rid of it yourself. Sidney, listen to me,' Essie pleaded. 'I shall come to court and explain about our childhood; they will understand, and Joss will stand bail if necessary. You may come and stay with us for a while until you have sorted yourself out.'

'I don't want any help from you, sister,' he spat out spitefully. 'You can keep your threepenny bits!'

He was jealous and resentful, hating her for seeing him in such a state. He glared at her menacingly, and at that moment he looked like their father. Now Essie could stare back calmly, without fear. She could not condone the violence; no one could do that. Yet she felt a surge of pity for the miserable man opposite.

Sidney had, unconsciously or otherwise, chosen a woman very much like their mother for his wife, a woman without a spark of affection, and the similarity had unhinged him, rekindling the trauma of those early years. Essie was over it at last. The awful nightmares had ceased. Life had been good to her. She had Joss, who had shown unerring patience when bad memories haunted her, as they had for many years, even after she recognized her love for him and how much he cared for her. And she had the children. She felt reasonably certain that Clara was over it too, although the scars would always remain, for both of them. Sidney was the most tragic casualty of those terrible days.

He ambled to his feet now, dismissively. 'This war that's startin' will help me. They'll let me off to join up, you'll see.'

He was right about that. They fined him and let him off with a warning that if ever he came before them again charged with violence, he risked prison.

But Sidney did not join up. Back at home he consumed a vast amount of alcohol with a bottle of aspirins. He left a suicide note saying he had lodged a will with a solicitor, leaving the house and his one remaining fish and chip shop to Una.

Essie felt the sadness of failure. If only they had appreciated his need for affection. But if they had, could they have given it? All three of them had erected a barrier well-nigh impenetrable. In the case of herself and Clara that barrier had finally been removed by patience and love. Love. Something no one had ever felt for Sidney.

Despite his cynicism about wars and politicians, Joss was one of the first volunteers for the army.

'It isn't fair,' Essie's leaden heart cried out when he informed her of his intention to join up. Just as things were running smoothly for them. What if Joss was injured? What if he never returned. She could not bear it. Often those who went first were killed. Look what happened in 1914.

Memories of Vee reading the fateful telegram about Captain Vincent being killed recurred with alarming clarity. What if she had to face such a loss? Her body shook with panic. No, she could not live without Joss; she could not let him go. She tried to dissuade him.

'What about the businesses we have built up over the years? All the time and energy we have put in?'

He took her gently into his arms. 'I am leaving you in charge, my lovely. I know your capabilities. Come on, Essie, what is it you always say? "I'll manage." And you will.'

'I can't manage. Not any more,' her mind screamed, 'Not without Joss.' Aloud she pleaded quietly, 'Don't go, my love. You did your share in the last war.'

'This time there's a maniac at large, dearest,' he reminded

275

her. 'There is no future for our children, or anybody else's children, until we have put paid to him.'

She knew that was true. She must stay calm for the children. There was no changing her husband's mind, that was clear. She would just have to smile and kiss him good-bye, like countless other women, and warn the children to do likewise. She would just *have* to manage.

Chapter Seventeen

So Joss went off to fight a war and values changed almost overnight. No one wanted to risk investing their money in precious goods that may be bombed to smithereens. Essie had to adjust to the fact that trading in antiques would come to a standstill.

Very early in the war she packed all the porcelain and glassware from Brocton and the Birmingham shops into crates and transported them south, where friends in rural areas of Dorset stored them in their outbuildings for almost five years.

The young manager at Birmingham also volunteered for the forces, and the premises were rented for the duration by the Ministry of Food for distribution of cod-liver oil, orange juice and ration books, while at Axminster the Ministry of Transport took over their vehicles and employed Len as a driver.

Berridge's Walkabouts at Walsall and Willenhall managed to survive for about a year, but once all stocks of timber, hardware and second-hand goods were sold they had no means of replacing them. Joy became afflicted by severe arthritis and her sons were called up.

Essie was in danger of losing all members of her staff as one by one they were transferred into reserved occupations. It was becoming a struggle to keep the businesses afloat. But what appeared at first to be her biggest headache turned out to be her most successful wartime venture.

Salvation came in the shape of a former employee, a first-class carpenter who was invalided out of the air force owing to him losing a leg. With his carpentry skills and Essie's determination they managed to come to an arrangement with the Ministry of Supply to set up workrooms at Walsall and Willenhall to make utility furniture, which was to be supplied, in exchange for the necessary dockets, to newly-weds, or people who had been bombed out of their houses.

Once launched there was no shortage of orders, for although the furniture had to conform to a set design laid down by the government and prices were controlled, buyers soon began to recognize that the label BERRIDGE signified excellent workmanship, and the word spread.

Essie spent long hours each day supervising the factories, keeping clerical records and filling in mountainous piles of government forms, usually required in triplicate. It all helped to alleviate the mounting anxiety about Joss, who had only one leave in four years. She had to keep busy. Some days when there had been no mail from him for a long time it was almost impossible to concentrate. She had to keep reminding herself that it was for him and their children that she must keep a firm hold on herself, and on their livelihood.

At the house in Brocton were billeted a dozen or so land-army girls who were working on neighbouring farms. All the furniture from Brocton Antiques Centre had been moved into the warm dry cellars, which made a comfortable bolt-hole for the whole household during the Battle of Britain, when sirens disturbed them from their beds almost nightly.

One awful night in 1940 they could see the sky blood-red

with fires as they all trooped from the cellars into the garden after the All Clear had sounded. Next morning they heard that Coventry had been razed to the ground. The parents of one of the land-girls were bombed out that night and joined them at Brocton until the end of the war.

In such circumstances, with everyone endeavouring to be cheerful in the face of ever-recurring fears, many lasting friendships were formed, some continuing long after hostilities had ceased.

Despite every moment of her time being taken up, Joss was never out of Essie's mind, and as the war dragged on interminably a further anxiety arose; Eden would soon reach calling-up age. 'Oh, let it all be over by the time he is eighteen,' she prayed. But it was not to be. At the time when Eden would normally have started at university he was called up for the Royal Navy. She and Rebecca saw him off at Stafford station, all of them joking until the train pulled out, when Essie and Rebecca cried in each other's arms.

Now there were two of them to worry about. What if she lost them both? The horror of the possibility intruded into everything she did.

After Eden's initial training very little news filtered through from him, nor from Joss either.

Clara went back into hospital-nursing, Rebecca grew up in double-quick time, and they all three became doubly precious to one another.

At times it seemed the war would never end. But at last 1945 and VE Day arrived. With Clara off-duty from the hospital and Rebecca off school the three of them danced with their band of loyal workers, outside Berridge's Utility Furniture factory, hugging one another, laughing and crying at the same time.

'The sign for Berridge's Walkabout will soon be going up again, Mum,' Rebecca declared. 'That's if Dad doesn't keep you tied to furniture manufacture for ever.'

Uncharacteristically Essie could not care less about what happened with regard to that. All she wanted were her two men back. Safe and sound, to live in peace, whether in affluence or scarcity, with Berridge's Walkabout or Utility Furniture, or neither. What did any of it matter as long as she could hold her loved ones close again? The war had taught them all a different set of values. Peace was all that mattered now.

Back home at Brocton Essie put on a party for the land-girls, using all of one week's rations in a day, while the girls themselves made plans, some of them to go home and return to previous jobs, others to stay on the land; some already had offers of accommodation from the farmers they had worked for.

Joss, being in the older age group, was back home fairly soon after the cessation of hostilities in Europe. They held each other close and Joss shed his first tears of the war. But it was a quiet homecoming; Joss did not want any party. There were adjustments to be made. They were both older, Joss more subdued. Having survived several major land battles, he had memories not for sharing, experiences he wanted to forget. He was proud of Essie's achievements in the furniture business, and wanted to hear all about her war rather than relate his own.

Essie could only wait patiently until he was ready to take over the reins once more. They both realized, with everything in such short supply, it could take many months, maybe even years, before Berridge's Walkabout could take off again. She constantly reassured him that nothing mattered as long as they were together again. They discussed fetching their stock of antiques back from Dorset when they had saved enough petrol.

But not until Eden came home, after the cessation of hostilities with Japan, did it seem that the war was really over. He too wanted to forget. He was at last able to take up his university place at Bristol, glad to be alive, and ambitious for the future.

Rebecca sang as she moved about the house. She was delighted her brother was home safe; she had worried about him, and missed him, more than she ever admitted.

She insisted on leaving school at seventeen. 'Only experience matters,' she declared vehemently. 'Certificates count for nothing in the newspaper world until you have proved yourself.' From a very early age she had known she wanted to go into journalism; she had talked about it long ago when she had lain beside Essie on the top of Golden Cap.

Undeterred by the fact that very few females were even considered, she composed enthusiastic letters of application to all the local papers and her diligence paid off. She was offered several interviews, and was soon accepted as junior reporter on the *Birmingham Mail*.

With her burning curiosity as to what makes people tick, her natural alertness and her sense of humour, she was ideally suited to the job. She enjoyed it from the start, regaling her parents with humorous accounts of the funny things that happened at council meetings, garden parties and dog shows, the events that all trainees had to cover before advancing to more important news. But it wasn't long before Rebecca wrote her first front page, followed by her first middle-page spread. Before they knew where they were she was regularly writing the women's page.

Her newspaper sent trainees for the second half of each of their first two years to a college for budding journalists in Cardiff. During her second year she shared a room with a girl named Annette. She often chatted on the phone to Essie about her new friend, and one weekend, near the end of the course, she arranged to bring her home.

'Eden asked me to tell you he will be home too, Mum. That's because I am bringing Annette, of course.'

281

'Really? Sounds interesting.'

'I'll say. Watch out for something special between those two.'

'How old is Annette?'

'A couple of years older than me, I think.'

Essie knew that Eden had taken to motoring from Bristol University to Cardiff fairly often, but as he had always been fond of his sister she thought nothing of it. He was a handsome man, tall, with thick fair hair and a ready smile. He never appeared short of female company, although he maintained he was far too busy for a regular girlfriend.

So it was with more than usual interest that Essie looked forward to meeting Rebecca's friend.

She was busy selling a Cozens watercolour to an avid collector when she heard the girls arrive. Old customers had gradually drifted back when they heard that Brocton Antiques Centre was functioning again, along with new collectors. The Cozens was a painting of a lakeland landscape, reminding Essie of the marvellous family holiday they had enjoyed in Italy. What a satisfying life she had enjoyed with her wonderful children and Joss, who had regained all his own keenness for their business ventures.

It was in this happy frame of mind that she said goodbye to the customer with the watercolour and went along eagerly to the kitchen to greet the girls.

Rebecca was on her knees saying hello to their old dog, christened Alfie years ago by Eden, after his favourite toy dog had drowned in a waterfall on Cannock Chase.

Rebecca's room-mate, Annette, tall and graceful, stood gazing down at Rebecca, a cup of coffee in her hand, her back toward Essie's welcoming smile. Her daughter jumped up and flung her arms around her mother's neck affectionately. 'Mum! This is Annette. Annette meet our wonder mum.'

The girl turned eagerly, holding out her hand. Smiling

from a lively face were lovely violet eyes which made Essie's heart lurch as she sank into the nearest chair, her hands gripping the kitchen table, memories of Vee pouring over her. Even after all these years the slightest thing could bring back haunting memories of Vee. Francis's news that she would have died anyway had not helped to lessen the guilt and regret that Essie had not had chance to explain. Now a girl with violet eyes had made her dumbstruck. All the old guilt feelings welled up inside her.

'Are you all right, Mum?'

'Yes, of course, dear. Just a little tired, that's all.'

Rebecca anxiously searched her mother's pale face. 'Are you sure that's all it is?'

'I am perfectly all right. Don't fuss.' How could she possibly explain? She did not want to risk questions she could not answer.

'Do have my coffee, Mrs Berridge,' the girl said. 'I haven't touched it. I will make another.'

'You can make me one while you are at it, please.'

'Ah, changed your mind now you have sniffed the aroma, Rebecca,' Annette chided playfully.

'It's just that I want you to have plenty of practice before Eden arrives,' Rebecca laughed. 'He is very fussy about his coffee, I might tell you.'

The girls continued to tease one another as Essie tried to gather her thoughts and still the knocking of her heart. How silly that a girl with violet eyes could set her heart pounding like this after so many years. Just gazing into them had brought it all back.

The girls joined her at the table. 'I hope you don't mind me taking over your kitchen, Mrs Berridge. It is your daughter's fault. She said . . . ' Annette hesitated, suddenly embarrassed.

'I said if you want anything to eat or drink in this house you get it yourself,' Rebecca butted in, chuckling.

'Rebecca! But of course I don't mind, Annette,' Essie replied, trying to pull herself back to the present.

Rebecca got up to give her mother another hug. 'What I meant was that you are not one of those boring household mums who refuse to allow anyone to feel at home. You do like everyone to do as they please, don't you?'

'As long as that is all you mean, young lady.'

'She does feed us on occasions,' Rebecca assured Annette flippantly. 'In between various other distractions. Actually she is a great mum, Annette. I can recommend her as a mother-in-law.'

'Rebecca, you are impossible,' Annette countered, but she did not seem to mind the teasing.

Essie forced herself to consider the lovely laughing face. Was this the girl Eden was falling in love with, a girl whose eyes would remind her constantly of Vee and the past? She was relieved when Rebecca decided to introduce her friend to the rest of the house, and to her room. By the time they returned she had herself under control and was preparing the evening meal.

'May I help?' Annette perched herself on a stool close to where Essie stood at the sink.

'There is no need,' Essie assured her. 'The joint is in the oven and I only have to prepare the vegetables.'

'I would like to stay if it doesn't bother you. It will give us chance to get to know one another.'

So Essie gave her a bowl of fruit to prepare a fruit salad. They worked in companionable silence.

'How are you enjoying journalism?' Essie asked after a short while.

The girl wrinkled her nose. 'I enjoy writing. I always have. What I don't like is having to hound people to get unsavoury facts, disturbing their privacy, projecting myself to the point of . . .'

'Intrusion?'

'Exactly.'

'You are not pushy enough for a journalist; that's your trouble. Not like me.' Rebecca reappeared behind them, laughing.

'You are back soon,' Essie remarked in surprise.

'And why? Because I met the man of the house, very excited. Come on, we all have to go and admire Dad's latest find.'

They all gasped in amazement when they saw the beautiful Ming vase Joss had acquired for a special customer, and which he allowed Annette to handle.

'It is in perfect condition,' she breathed. 'This must have cost the earth.'

'It did,' Joss replied. 'I only hope the customer appreciates it as much as you do, my dear.'

'If not, put it aside until I can afford it.'

She wandered round the showrooms exclaiming at the quality and variety of antiques with genuine interest. Joss was captivated. If this was the girl Eden had fallen for he admired his good taste.

How could he guess at the memories and the guilt engulfing Essie each time her eyes met Annette's?

They heard the crunch of Eden's car on the drive and all ran out to greet him. He looked so happy, lifting Essie off her feet and swinging her round as he always did when he came home. He shook hands with Joss, and landed an imaginary punch to Rebecca's chin before hugging her affectionately. Only then did he turn to Annette, waiting quietly on the doorstep, in contrast to the noisy Berridges. As Essie saw the glance exchanged between those two there was no doubt in her mind that this was not just an ordinary friendship.

Clara had joined them for Sunday lunch. Now, together

285

with Essie and Rebecca, she sat in the drawing room, facing the garden, where Eden and Annette strolled, in earnest conversation, Eden's arms lightly around the girl's shoulders.

'Isn't she lovely?' Clara enthused. 'Just right for Eden.'

Essie did not reply. Rebecca, writing a letter, glanced up curiously. Her mother was acting so strangely, as if purposely restraining her natural cordiality. She was usually so welcoming; they had never had any worries about bringing their friends home.

She must like Annette, surely? Everyone did. It could not be jealousy, could it? She had always been close to both her children, but never unduly possessive. Perhaps she had been overdoing things; she appeared so strained.

Rebecca had looked forward to bringing Annette home to meet her parents; Eden's parents. But while Joss had chatted away animatedly, Essie had hardly conversed at all. There was a disturbed atmosphere in the house, so unfamiliar Rebecca did not know how to deal with it.

Essie was still staring through the window with unseeing eyes and an expressionless face.

'We shall have to let him go sometime, Mum, shan't we?' Rebecca ventured lightly.

Essie turned to meet her gaze. Rebecca was shocked at the misery etched deeply into her mother's large brown eyes, usually so lively and happy.

'What have you got against Annette, Mum?' she enquired after Clara had left.

'Nothing at all. She is a delightful girl.' There was no way of explaining the agony of the memories a pair of violet eyes had evoked.

'I'm pleased to hear it,' replied Rebecca in her frank manner. 'Because those two are head over heels in love, Mum. Anyone can see that.'

Yes, anyone could see that; they had not been able to take their eyes off each other the whole of the weekend.

Chapter Eighteen

Essie remained fairly calm as she read the contents of the formal solicitor's letter informing her that Francis Jameson had died and had requested that the two enclosed items be forwarded to her on his death, an envelope containing a personal letter, and a package.

It was when she unsealed the square package and the gold locket lay in the palm of her hand that her heart beat double-fast. It was Francis's own handwriting, unfamiliarly shaky, that brought the first tears, and the reading of the letter which caused her to sob.

'My dear Esther,' he had written, 'I am returning the locket, more precious to me than anything I have ever owned. Many times I have held it tenderly, kissed your lock of hair, and thought of the past.

'My darling, I have never ceased to wonder if Eden is my son. Yours and mine. I have liked to fantasize that he belongs to both of us, for I realize that this is possible.

'We met too late, dearest Esther, that was our tragedy. But I have never regretted one moment of our affair. Only that it could not go on for ever.

'Always my love. Francis.'

The locket dropped to the floor as Essie pushed the letter to one side, covering her face with her hands. His letter, following so closely after meeting Annette, who had reminded her so of Vee, brought back the whole miserable business of what she considered her own betrayal of Vee, and the sadness of how she died.

Downstairs Eden was letting himself quietly into the house. It always felt good to be home. He hoped that if he and Annette married they could find a place with as much character as this. His stint at university had come to an end. He was eager to discuss with both his parents the encouraging replies he had received to some of his preliminary enquiries with regard to posts in business management. But an open garage door had indicated to him that his father had already left; he may be gone for a few hours or several days. He still searched far and wide for attractive and unusual items to sell, happy to leave Essie in charge of the Antiques Centre.

A swift tour of the ground floor without finding Essie sent Eden bounding lightly up the stairs. As he was about to step into his own room he paused on the landing and an anxious frown replaced the smile that had lit up his face since jumping out of the car. From the office, next door to his bedroom, came the sound of sobbing.

Eden opened the door quietly. His mother was sobbing uncontrollably, her torment so great she did not hear her son enter the room.

'Mum! What has happened?'

Eden bent to pick up the gold locket. As he placed it on the desk in front of her his own name jumped out at him from a letter she had pushed aside. Something compelled him to pick it up to read.

'Is this true?' he asked in a shocked voice.

Essie heard Eden's voice as if from a great distance. She looked up into the bright blue eyes questioning her, and automatically nodded. She regretted that nod immediately. He had caught her at a weak and vulnerable moment. If only she could take it back.

The enormity of what she had done as she faced her son's astounded reaction silenced her sobs. What had come over her? The young Essie would not have betrayed her feelings in this way; she would never had allowed her emotions to betray the secret that should have remained unrevealed for ever. But the damage was done.

Her son was gazing at her with hurt, horrified eyes. He drew up a chair, close to the desk. 'Tell me about it,' he whispered hoarsely.

She found herself beginning with the first time she met Vee at Mellish Road. Eden already knew how she had started work at thirteen and how she had moved to Dorset to work for the same mistress. He had never realized until now how close they had become, or what a wonderful benefactress she was. He knew that when the lady married again, Essie took the room over the store, and he had been told how she met Joss in the market and how she undertook to buy for him in the south.

Now she described her meeting with Francis at Eden House, how a friendship grew into something more, how she later discovered he was married to Vee, and how she married Joss immediately afterwards.

'So you weren't in love with Dad?'

'I'm afraid not.' Her lips trembled. 'Not then.' Her voice faltered when she came to the important part of the narrative. 'I didn't know at the time, but I must have been pregnant when I married Joss . . . '

'Pregnant! By Francis. With me.' His voice was flat and miserable. 'Why did you marry Dad? I mean . . . Joss?'

'I didn't want to break up the marriage of Francis and Vee. I knew Francis would not try to persuade me if *I* was married.'

Eden strode across to the window, gazing out silently for what seemed an eternity, his back silently accusing her. At last he turned back into the room. 'I feel so much a part of Joss, Mum.' His voice broke. 'I always have.'

'And he loves you, my dear. Very, very much.'

'He knows? About the other man?'

'Oh yes. Joss knows.'

Her son sank into a chair. 'Poor sod!' he groaned. He sat staring into space, his face ashen, as Essie longed to be able to eliminate the last half-hour.

Eden grappled with the agony of what this meant to him. His parents had lived a lie toward him all these years. His father whom he adored was no longer his father. This is what hurt. Not that his mother had an affair with another man. Nor that Francis had died before he had chance to meet him. But that Joss was no longer his father. How could he change his way of thinking? They had been so close.

It was obvious he was Rebecca's father; you only had to look at her. But he, Eden, was an outsider, no longer part of this closely-knit family he had always thought of as his. Now he was on his own.

Eventually, after a long silence, he stood up. 'I need to be alone,' he stated simply.

When he emerged from his room many hours later he was outwardly calm, although filled with doubts. Did his mother love Joss now? She still held her emotions quite closely. Or did she cherish regrets for what might have been?

Essie read his thoughts. She knew there was no way she could make him understand that her tears were mainly for Vee. To him, her distress was all for Francis.

He said he must get away. Away from Annette. He could not live a lie with her, yet he was not ready to tell her the truth; it was all too much of a shock.

He must get away from all of them; they were no longer

his family. Had they ever really loved him? Did Annette love him? What was love anyway? His true father had obviously married the wrong girl; he did not want to make the same mistake.

His true father! If only it had been Joss! Yet he wondered if he had ever really known Joss.

But Arthur, his uncle, he knew. He *was* his uncle. Essie's brother. Eden remembered the feeling of stability he had felt when they stayed at the farm in Canada. He would go there for a while. He needed to sort himself out. He needed to come to terms with who he was.

Rebecca's attitude could not have been worse if Essie had told her the whole truth.

'Why has Eden shot off to Canada so suddenly?' she demanded. 'Without proper goodbyes. Just a brief telephone call to Annette and a short note to me! What is it all about, Mum?'

'He feels he would like a few months on Arthur's farm before he decided on a permanent post.'

'Rubbish! There is more to it than that. He was lining up jobs here; he told me he had several irons in the fire. Why the sudden change of plan?' Her eyes blazed angrily, reminding Essie of Joss on the dreadful night of Vee's accident.

'You broke it up, didn't you, Mum? His affair with Annette? What did you have against her? I would never have dreamed you could be so possessive until that weekend I brought Annette home. Didn't you like her? Or were you just plain jealous? There was definitely something odd about you while she was here.'

Only because she had the eyes of someone I loved and lost disastrously, Essie's heart cried out. Only because of the guilt they resuscitated. Oh, if she could only explain that Eden's hasty departure had nothing to do with her feelings toward Annette. Now her son was on his way to the other side of the world, far away from the girl he loved. What a mess! And it was all her fault. Why had she been so careless about the letter, about the locket? Why had she permitted her feelings to get the better of her?

Now here was her precious daughter, usually so loving, bitterly accusing her of causing the break up between Eden and Annette.

'I liked Annette very much,' Essie permitted herself to say.

'You had a strange way of showing it, Mum. I wish you could see her now. She is broken-hearted.'

'I am sorry.'

'Are you?' Rebecca's voice was still accusing. 'Eden has always taken notice of you, Mum. I know you have influenced him in some way. Well, I shan't take notice, ever again.'

Rebecca had never been stubborn or defiant. There had been no teenage traumas such as many mothers had to endure. Any differences between them they had always been able to sort out. Now there was nothing Essie could say in explanation.

Going to Arthur's had been entirely Eden's idea. He had happy memories of their previous visit. He had discussed it calmly and rationally. But she could imagine the hurt Annette would feel at his sudden change of plan. He had been mortified and bewildered by her revelation, and she could explain it to no one, not to Rebecca nor to Joss. There was no point in opening up the old trauma for him.

But the secret exacted a heavy price. Rebecca became 'far too busy' to visit them. They had to content themselves in reading her excellent articles in the *Birmingham Mail*. She had taken a flat near her office, and never mentioned Annette on the rare occasions she telephoned. Eden's letters were infrequent and short. He was enjoying the outdoor life, he said, and feeling fit.

The house at Brocton was silent and sad.

Joss, aware of Essie's anxiety, tried to reassure her that it was the most natural thing in the world for youngsters to want to spread their wings, but privately he was puzzled by Eden's sudden change of mind. Post-war Britain was booming; there was a wealth of opportunity for anyone with his qualifications. Why he had let a lovely girl like Annette slip through his fingers was beyond him. And whatever had happened to their cheerful, loving daughter?

The revelation she had made to Eden weighed heavily on Essie's mind. She longed to share the burden with Joss, but whenever she considered doing so she convinced herself it was not fair. He had suffered enough from that long-ago affair with Francis, so brief and yet so devastating in its consequences. It would be like re-opening an old wound that had healed.

Fortunately Joss was too occupied to ponder much on the situation. There was a new market to cater for. With more money in their pockets than ever before, ordinary people were becoming interested in collecting, particularly smaller items such as gift cups, porcelain ornaments, hatpins, antique mirrors, silver and walking sticks. Many now owned cars for the first time and Brocton had become a popular venue. Combined with a meal at one of the attractive inns scattered around Cannock Chase, the antiques centre provided an interesting round-off to a day out. Now the difficulty was in meeting demand, and Essie went on regular buying trips to the south, to supplement their stock.

Their Birmingham shop was again prospering. Berridge's Walkabouts, in Walsall and Willenhall, were now in the capable hands of Joy's sons, to whom Joss had given some shares, and they were still favourite rendezvous for do-it-yourselfers. The new carpentry factory which Essie had started was working full steam, one of the first places to produce flat-pack kitchen furniture. Homes not touched since before the war needed to be re-decorated and refurbished, and people had the means to do it.

Connaught Kiddie-Kits too, had survived and was prospering still, under Essie's guidance.

Joy, now housebound by arthritis, yet still as cheerful as ever, had retired to a bungalow on the edge of town.

'What's up, luv?' she asked Essie. 'Worrited about yer kids, are yer? They all 'ave to do their own thing. You did. I did. And Joss's mam did.' She chuckled in recollection. 'Once when I was quizzin' 'er about where she'd cum from she said she'd jumped on a train and cum as far as she could afford.

''Twasn't true, though. Rebecca was astute enough to know where the work was. And 'appen your lad knows summat about Canada we don't.'

Then on another of Essie's visits to the bungalow, 'Yoh look peeky to me, gel. Is that 'usband o' your'n workin' yer too 'ard?'

'No, of course not, Joy.'

But Joy reprimanded Joss when next he called. 'The sparkle 'as gone out 'o your little missus. Give 'er a break, lad.'

Joss had always taken notice of Joy, and the next time Essie mentioned she was planning a trip south he arranged for one of the Birmingham assistants to take over at Brocton so that he could go with her.

'Let's make it a fun trip, love. We can stay in a luxury hotel and combine business with pleasure,' he suggested.

But in the end Essie opted to stay in the flat over the store, where they revelled in ten days of pure nostalgia. They visited a couple of auctions, swam in the sea at Charmouth, went to the old Electric Theatre, now called a picture house, danced at the Greyhound and walked along the coast to Beer, where they sat side by side on Joss's coat and Essie recalled how on that spot she had told him about her friend Vee and all that she meant to her.

Joss had brought her a new car before they left. She drove him along the glorious coast road to Weymouth. Suddenly she drew up. 'Move over,' she said, digging him in the ribs. 'I'll teach you how to drive. You may be able to buy something of your own soon.' The mischief had returned to Essie's eyes; the bloom to her cheeks.

'You mean I can have a go?' Joss replied in mock wonder. 'You will entrust your precious car to me?' He had remembered her every word.

She countered with the reply he had given her all those years ago. 'I would entrust my life to you, my darling.'

From where she had pulled in they could see the quiet waters of Fleet and the whole of Chesil Bank, curling round from Portland in a grey arc which gradually changed to brown-yellow, a breathtaking scene that impressed every visitor. They sat drinking in the beauty of the scene before Joss took her into his arms, and with the sounds of seagulls in their ears they kissed with the passion of young lovers.

'My favourite pupil,' he chuckled when he finally released her.

'My favourite teacher,' she breathed.

At Weymouth they munched gingersnaps again as they explored the harbour, listened to the band and watched the sand-sculpture man perform his miracles on the beach. Joss bought fresh bread, a chunk of cheese and a pint of cider for their supper. 'We will sit by the side window and watch out for courting couples beneath the lamp tonight,' he laughed.

Len was just locking up when they returned. They chatted with him about the progress of the renovation of some garages he was organizing on a site Essie had bought on the outskirts of Axminster. They would house their new holiday coaches and hire-vans. As Len was about to leave he produced a cutting from the local newspaper. 'I almost forgot,' he said. 'I don't know whether this is of any interest. But I thought that possibly, with your daughter being named Rebecca . . .'

He had circled in ink a single paragraph which read, 'Anyone knowing the whereabouts of Rebecca Berridge, last heard of in Symondsbury in 1895, please contact Mrs Forster, The Manor House, Symondsbury.' A telephone number followed.

'1895! The year you were born, Joss. It must have some significance. Shall we telephone?' Essie suggested excitedly.

'Why don't we just go? This minute,' said Joss quietly, displaying no emotion. But Essie knew what he must be feeling.

Symondsbury was a tiny village only half-an-hour's drive away; they had passed the entrance to it that day.

Only a couple of miles from bustling Bridport the village of Symondsbury, with its ancient church and thatched cottages, was a haven of tranquillity.

A long crunchy drive wound from a small lodge to an impressive manor house, white, with stone pillars flanking either side of its entrance. A rosy-cheeked girl ushered them into a wide hall.

'Mr and Mrs Joss Berridge,' she repeated in her soft Dorset burr. 'I will see if Mrs Forster is awake. Last time I looked in she was takin' her afternoon nap.'

Within minutes they were following the girl into a huge, semi-circular conservatory, where an old lady, as straight as a ramrod, sat on a comfortable wicker settee, deeply cushioned. She was gazing eagerly toward the door. Her eyebrows were still jet black, her hair thick and white, and Essie had only to look into the midnight-blue eyes, dancing with anticipation, to know that here was someone related to Joss.

'Becky's son, without a doubt!' she declared as they came

forward to greet her. She had a firm decisive voice. 'You are the image of her.'

'You should see our daughter,' Joss grinned, immediately at ease.

The old lady patted the space beside her. 'Sit here,' she invited. 'Obviously we have a lot to catch up on.

'Find yourself a seat, my dear,' she instructed Essie, indicating the luxurious assortment of garden chairs scattered around the conservatory. She grasped Joss's hand firmly as he sat beside her. Essie could sense the excitement at fever pitch between the pair of them as they weighed each other up, each endeavouring not to show their feelings, and failing completely.

'Yes, yes. You belong to Becky, I can see that. Tell me, how is she?'

'My mother died. A long time ago, I'm afraid.'

Her eyes filled with sudden tears. 'I was afraid of that. Poor Becky.' She blew her nose vigorously. 'Forgive me. She was my only sister, you see.'

'So you are my only aunt! Wonderful!' He smiled at her disarmingly. 'I never knew I had one.'

'Your mother never mentioned me? She never mentioned her sister, Rowanna?'

Joss shook his head.

'And yet we were so very close,' she murmured sadly. 'We loved each other so much. Fancy Becky never mentioning me!'

'I am sorry.'

'I can remember the day she was born. I was eleven by then and had always wanted a little sister. Was I thrilled! We were inseparable, despite the age gap.

'When our parents died, within a few weeks of each other, Rebecca was only fourteen, and I had been married a couple of years. She came to live with William and me. We were all very happy together; he loved her as much as I did.

It was he who first called her Becky, when she was quite small. We always knew William, you see.

'Ah, she was a bright merry soul from the start. She could turn anything into a laugh, could Becky.'

Rowanna sat silent for a few moments, remembering, smiling into the past, until her face turned suddenly sad. 'One day, when she was barely eighteen, she left. Before I was up. Without any warning!' The old lady's voice held extreme surprise, as if it had been only yesterday. 'Just left a little note. I have always kept it with me.' She dug into a wide canvas bag on the floor at her feet, and drew out, from a square envelope, a yellowing piece of writing paper which she handed to Joss.

A lump came into his throat as he recognized the bold handwriting, already maturely formed. 'My darling sister,' his mother had written, 'Thank you for all you have done for me. It is time I made my own way. Try to understand and do not worry about me. I love you. Rebecca.'

'I was devastated! I wanted to inform the police, in case she was in any danger. She was so young, you see. William was as upset as myself, but he said I must let matters rest. He pointed out that Becky was a capable girl, very grown up for her age, which was true. I suppose it was because she had always had an older sister for her friend. He said she would probably get in touch when she was settled. But she never did.

'After waiting a year I enquired after her whereabouts through newspapers all over the country, to no avail. To no avail! I never could understand it. I loved her so much.' Rowanna sat silently with bowed head, now looking a very old lady, so different from the person who had greeted them when they first walked in.

Essie crossed the room to wind her arms round the old lady's shoulders in an effort to comfort her; she looked so dejected. 'I am sure your sister loved you too.'

'You are right, my dear; she did.' Rowanna quickly regained control of herself. 'I am so sorry. But it still hurts, after all this time.'

She turned toward Joss again. 'What about your father? Is he still alive, and was Becky happy with him?'

'She was very happy with the man she married later in life.'

'I see,' she replied quietly.

The rosy-cheeked maid who had answered the door reappeared. 'Would you like me to serve tea in here, ma'am?'

'No, it is getting cold. We will take it in the drawing room, please Cathy.'

Rowanna led the way, leaning heavily on her stick, taking the wide canvas bag which had lain at her feet. A fire had been lit in a gracefully-furnished room, where a small table was laid with tiny currant cakes, scones, jam and tea.

'Will you pour, Essie, my dear?'

But Essie was rooted where she stood, her gaze transfixed to a large portrait over the fireplace. 'Eden!' she gasped. An equally startled Joss joined her to stare in astonishment at the portrait. It could have been their son gazing down at them, with his dear familiar smile, his familiar quirk of brow, his sky-blue eyes and blond hair, not silky, as Francis's had been, but tufty, like Joss's. There were the same strong wide shoulders, the long slim chin, the aristocratic lift of the well-shaped head.

'You like the portrait? That was my William. Wasn't he a handsome man? I had it painted for his twenty-sixth birthday, just after we were married.'

For his twenty-sixth birthday! Eden was nearly twenty-six! Essie felt Joss's hand reach out for hers.

'I have lots of photographs of him,' Rowanna was saying. 'I will show them to you later.'

Essie searched Joss's face, very conscious that for the first time he was seeing an image of his true father, knowing for certain that Eden was his true son, William's grandson, and knowing the reason why his mother ran away from a sister she loved. His expression was a mixture of incredulity and joy.

There was not the slightest doubt that Eden was William's grandson; they could not have been more alike had they been twins. She could not tear her eyes from the portrait, remembering how she had puzzled about the texture of her son's hair, and how she had credited his broad shoulders with all the physical work he had performed. Oh, the years of agony that could have been avoided! Eden's blond appearance had not come from Francis after all, but from William.

Her hand shook so much as she tried to pour their tea that Joss took the teapot from her and completed the task.

After Cathy had cleared away the tea things Rowanna brought out a leather casket filled with photographs. They were mainly of William: William throwing back his head when he laughed, just as Eden did, William standing with his hands behind his back, like Eden. One recent studio photograph was so clear it showed up a small mole on his cheekbone, toward the left ear; Eden had inherited that too.

'This was taken a few months before William died; still a good-looking man, don't you think?' said Rowanna as she handed the studio portrait to them.

It was true. Even at eighty, the tall upright man still bore a striking resemblance to their twenty-five-year-old son.

Rowanna's face was filled with tenderness as she lovingly handled the photographs, pausing to study each one herself before passing it on.

'We fell in love when I was five and he was seven,' she reminisced, 'and I can't remember a moment since then that I haven't loved him with all my heart.'

'You grew up together?'

'Oh yes. William's father was a Member of Parliament,

away a lot, so our father managed this estate for him. We lived in the lodge by the gate.'

Her hands shook as she returned the photographs to their box. 'He was always so gentlemanly and kind, my William. I shan't last long without him, I know that.

'A few weeks before he died, he said, "Rowanna, we must make one more effort to find Becky or her children." We were never blessed with any children ourselves. I can't say that I minded; William was all I ever needed. But he was disappointed.'

She sat quietly, holding the box tightly, staring ahead, her face pathetically sad and remote from them. When she finally spoke her voice was no longer strong, but quavering and husky.

'About a week before William died . . . ' She hesitated for a long moment. 'He told me that Becky was with child when she left.' Her voice was a hoarse whisper as she told them what they already knew. 'The child was his. She made him promise never to tell me; she knew how much I adored him. And how much I loved and trusted her.'

Joss and Essie sat one each side of the sad old lady, sharing in her distress as tears fell on to the wrinkled cheeks. Why was it that every joy had to bring some sadness in its wake?

'All those years he had cherished thoughts of her! He had wondered about their child. About you, Joss. I had suspected that Becky may have left because she was getting a little over-fond of William. But I had never suspected . . . I never suspected for a moment that they . . . '

Their arms went round her shoulders on either side, feeling the terrific effort she was making to regain her self-control. When she spoke again her voice was firm.

'I fondly imagined I knew every thought in his head,' she said, with an attempt at lightness.

'We can never know all that is in anyone's head, however dear they are,' replied Joss.

Rowanna turned and studied him as she had done when he first sat beside her. 'That's true.' And then, after another pause, 'So she called you Joss! Joshua was my William's second name. William Joshua, he was.'

'And I am Joshua William,' he told her gently.

'She must have cared an awful lot for him, you know. We mustn't blame her. Becky would not have given herself if she had not cared. Poor Becky. Poor William.'

'You made him happy,' Essie consoled her.

'I wish I could be sure of that, my dear.'

'We have just been studying photographs of a very happy man,' Essie assured her.

'Bless you! I do hope you're right.' She was quite calm now as she continued. 'William said he knew he didn't have long and he would like to think it was someone belonging to him who would inherit all this.' She gestured toward the window indicating the rolling acres stretching as far as the eye could see. 'His parents were very wealthy and William was their only child. "Make one more supreme effort, Rowanna," he pleaded at the last. "For my sake. And for Becky's."'

'I don't know what made me write to the local paper, except that I thought there was a faint chance that someone local may still be in touch with her. Never thought it would reach you directly, my dears.' She smiled brightly now as she had done when they first entered the room. 'Are you surprised by all this?'

'Not since we have seen the portrait.' Essie brought out a wallet with photographs of their son and daughter on either side. 'Eden, our son, and our daughter Rebecca,' she explained, handing the wallet to Rowanna.

'Why, your daughter is the image of my sister Becky,' the old lady gasped. 'Oh, just look at my William! Exactly as he looked at our wedding. I see now why you stared at the portrait with such concentration.' She kissed each likeness tenderly. 'It's like seeing them both again. The two I loved most in all the world. Wouldn't William have been excited!

'Can you possibly spare me these, my dear?' she whispered.

'Will you exchange them for a photograph of William?'

Rowanna hesitated, reluctant to lose even one from her precious collection.

'To send to our son,' Essie explained.

The old lady passed the box to her with a smile. 'Take as many as you like, my dear,' she invited. 'You choose.'

Essie chose the recent studio photograph that was so lifelike, and a snapshot of a younger William throwing back his head in laughter. Once he had seen these, Eden would know that he was not Francis's son after all. Joss, whom he had always loved, was his father.

Rowanna understood how curious Joss must be about the father he had never seen. She told him how efficiently William had always managed the estate, even in old age, and how he enjoyed 'buckling in', as he called it, to help the farmhands when they were pushed. She told of his love of nature, of horses, flowers and birds, and Essie went on to describe how Joss had opened up a new world for her by his interest and knowledge of his surroundings during their long walks over Cannock Chase.

Now Rowanna wanted to hear about Becky. She questioned Joss at length about his mother, and he related all that he remembered about the early days when there was just the two of them, before describing the happiness she found with Arnie, Rowanna leaning forward in her chair to absorb every word about her beloved sister.

'Tell me about yourselves now, my dears,' she commanded when they had exhausted the topic of Becky.

So Essie and Joss talked about how they met in Walsall market when they were little more than children, and again in Axminster, not far from where Rowanna was living. They talked about their son and daughter, unable to keep the pride from their voices; it seemed to bring them close, discussing them with another member of the family. Rowanna listened intently and Joss looked as if he would burst with joy. He had found a member of his very own family at last, someone who knew both his mother and his father.

Cathy came in to draw the curtains against the darkness.

'I don't know who will be carrying on William's work in managing all that out there,' murmured Rowanna. 'More than six hundred acres of it.'

'I think I know who might,' Joss replied, recounting how Eden, in his last letter, had said how much he was enjoying farming, which he felt he would like to continue even after he had left his uncle's farm. With such enthusiasm and his knowledge of business practice, The Grange would provide a perfect opportunity for him one day, if he wanted it. Rowanna was ecstatic at the possibility of Eden – so like her William – taking over.

'Now, my dears. Give me your address, and the addresses of your children, William's grandchildren. I will see my solicitor tomorrow in order to arrange everything. Isn't it exciting? I wish my William could have been here to meet you; he would have been so thrilled.

'Just get that son of yours back from Canada as soon as possible. Tell him we need him here.'

'I hope you are going to be around for some time to advise him, Rowanna. If he agrees to come he will need all the help you can give.'

'So more talk about not having long to go,' put in Essie. 'Now that we have found you we want to keep you as long as possible.'

The old lady looked delighted. 'Well there certainly seems more to live for now, my dear. I must wait, at least, until I have seen Eden, musn't I? Rebecca, too.

'This place is far too big for me. I would quite like to move back into the Lodge, where we started. Has Eden any plans to get married?'

'There is someone rather special; he might.'

'Tell him if he comes they can have the house to themselves. No, I insist.' She held up her hand as Essie protested. 'I shall arrange it tomorrow. I rattle around here now like a stone in a can.'

Joss smiled; it was one of his mother's sayings.

Later, they lay side by side in the little bedroom Joss had made for her over her store, discussing the surprising events of the last few hours.

'My mother abandoned Becky, their name for her, just like you abandoned Connor,' Joss mused.

'A new name, a new life,' Essie replied, understanding.

Joss turned to take her in his arms. 'Essie, my love, can you ever forgive me?'

'Forgive *you*. Whatever for?'

'For my holier-than-thou attitude when I realized that Jameson was your friend's husband?'

Essie's heart stood still; he had not mentioned this for years.

'I was so shocked that you *knew* he was married to Vee,' he continued. 'Yet my mother knew that William was married to her own sister.'

'You must not think any the less of her because of that, Joss. It did not alter her love for Rowanna, any more than it changed my feelings toward Vee. I feel so close to your mother, Joss; I know exactly how she would feel, the terrible shame, the regrets.'

'My dear love!'

'It did me a lot of good today to know that Rowanna still loves Rebecca's memory, in spite of what she did. It has made me realize that Vee would have understood. And forgiven.'

'And I should have underst . . . '

Her lips prevented him saying any more. Tomorrow she would explain to him the real reason Eden had fled to Canada. But right now she had to convince him that nothing could ever come between them again.

Chapter Nineteen

Each day had seemed like a month as Essie waited for some acknowledgement of the photographs and letter of explanation she had sent to Eden. She could hardly contain her disappointment when her package was returned unopened, together with a letter for herself, from her sister-in-law.

'Sorry, Essie,' Liddy had written. 'Your letter just missed Eden. He is on his way home. But via the rest of Canada, it would seem. He has organized himself quite some tour! So we cannot hazard a guess at when he may arrive. We miss him already.'

Essie had so wanted Eden to receive the good news about his parentage as soon as possible. She was unable to share the disappointment with Joss, for he was away.

Turning to re-enter the house after seeing off a customer a day or two after the receipt of Liddy's letter, a crunch of wheels on the drive made her linger as a stylish, white sports car came to a halt with a flourish. A couple of silk-clad legs appeared, followed by an excellently-tailored suit, and she found herself gazing into the exquisite features of Annette.

'I do hope you don't mind me calling, Mrs Berridge. I am

on my way to Birmingham to see Rebecca and I thought . . . '

'Mind! My dear, I'm delighted. What a lovely surprise.'

As they sat together in the drawing room Essie could not tear her eyes from the graceful woman in front of her, no longer an eager adolescent, but poised and controlled. How she wished Eden was home.

'It has been almost three years, Mrs Berridge,' Annette remarked, as if in reply to Essie's unspoken thoughts. Her voice was deeper, more assured than Essie remembered it.

'Three years, yes. What have you been doing with yourself all this time? And please call me Essie.'

They were soon chatting comfortably. Annette had changed enormously. The eyes still reminded Essie of Vee, but now she possessed a firmness and business-like maturity Vee had never had, and it was all there, in her eyes, making them quite different. No longer that soft luminous look that was Vee's. 'I need a man,' Vee had said once. Essie felt that this girl definitely did not. Her voice held the confidence of a successful career woman with a sense of purpose, which was understandable when she explained she lived in central London, near the offices of a well-known magazine where she held a responsible and highly-paid position.

As the evening wore on Essie realized that neither of them had mentioned Eden. Annette helped to prepare the meal they shared, after which they settled down for more chat, snippets from Annette's childhood, incidents from Essie's busy life. The time fled.

'Is Rebecca expecting you tonight?' Essie enquired as it drew late.

'I told her to expect me when I arrived,' Annette laughed. 'Rebecca does not mind that sort of arrangement, as you well know.'

'Then will you stay overnight?'

'I would love that. Thank you.'

At breakfast Essie broached a subject she had been giving

some thought. 'It will soon be Rebecca's twenty-first birthday and we would like to give her a surprise party. Will you be able to come?'

'Try and keep me away!'

'Could you help me compose a list of friends she would like us to invite?'

'I can supply a few names, although I am not completely up to date. But as I shall be staying with Rebecca for a couple of nights I will see what I can find out and let you know.

'It might be as well to get in touch with Rebecca's editor,' she suggested. 'To make sure he doesn't have any "urgent assignment" lined up for her on the important day. Knowing Rebecca, she would regard that as being far more important than a party, even her own twenty-first.'

'Is she as dedicated as that?'

'Very much so. Hence the offers from Fleet Street.'

'Really? I didn't know.'

'I ought to have let her tell you herself. Sorry.'

'Don't worry. I'll be surprised.'

'How do you plan to get her here?'

'By inviting her to what she will think is just a family gathering. Eden may be here by then.' Essie kept her voice as casual as possible, while watching for Annette's reaction.

Annette smiled, aware of the scrutiny. 'I must confess I was shattered when Eden suddenly announced he was off to Canada,' she admitted frankly. 'But I am grateful now.'

Noticing Essie's look of surprise, she continued. 'I think we may have rushed into marriage at that stage, and it would have been far too soon. Neither of us was ready for that. His hurried departure forced me to concentrate more on my own career.'

'Are you enjoying that now?'

'Very much. Working on a monthly magazine is so different from a daily newspaper. And I don't have to go raking for unsavoury facts any more. Now I investigate only pleasant things, such as make-up, hair-dos and new clothes. I am in charge of the fashion and beauty pages.'

'Which I am sure you manage excellently.'

'Some day, when I have a bit of "life experience" I intend to write fiction. That's something I could do from home.'

'Maybe from a home in Dorset?' Essie permitted herself to hope.

'Any special men friends on the scene?' she ventured.

'Lots of men friends. But no one special. Foot-loose and fancy-free, I am, Essie. And that is how I like it.'

As Essie waved her off later Annette looked radiant, animated, confident. It was obvious she had not spent the last three years pining for Eden.

Eden arrived a week before Rebecca's birthday.

'It doesn't surprise me, Mum,' he said, when Essie told him that Francis was not his father after all. 'I always felt that Dad was . . . ' He shrugged. 'Well, definitely Dad. But you were so agitated about the whole thing I couldn't risk you being right, so I thought it best to clear off and get my own mind sorted out.'

'What can I say, Eden? I am so sorry.'

'Don't be.' He laughed as he lifted her off her feet and swung her round in the way he used to do. 'Best thing that ever happened! To think I was planning to put myself in a stuffy office for the next forty years!'

There was a timbre in his voice that had not been there before, a maturity about his bearing. He looked vitally fit. He smelled of the great outdoors; Essie felt she was taking great gasps of fresh air when she stood near him. Bronzed by the Canadian sun his eyes appeared bluer than ever.

He was eager to tell them about his travels, and even more eager to talk about the farm. He had lots of good ideas he would have liked to implement on Arthur's farm, he said, but of course he had no authority to do so.

When he heard of Rowanna's offer of farm management he was overjoyed and insisted on going straight away to meet her, promising to be back in time for his sister's birthday. There had not been time to talk about Annette. As he prepared to leave, Essie mentioned she had called.

'How is she?' he asked, pausing from his hurried re-packing.

'Very well. And very beautiful.'

'Good.'

That was all. And his face told her nothing.

Annette had changed a lot, Essie had to admit. But so had Eden. When they met again at Rebecca's party surely they would not be able to resist one another and Annette would forgive and forget. Essie mentally crossed her fingers.

Joss had been preparing the party for days. He had fixed coloured lights at each corner of the lawn, and smaller ones among the trees and bushes. Fireworks were set aside for later and a group of young musicians had been booked to play for dancing. Rebecca could decide where the dancing was to be, he said, inside or out.

'Both,' was her verdict when she arrived, together with Annette. 'A bit elaborate for a family party, eh, Dad?' she twinkled when she saw all the preparations. When she was told they were all in her honour she was deeply touched.

She had hugged Essie briefly when she arrived, and now sought her out as she was putting finishing touches to food in the kitchen. 'I have something to tell you, Mum.'

'Exciting?'

'I think so. I am moving to Fleet Street on the first of next month.' She mentioned a well-known national newspaper.

'Congratulations, dear. I am so glad. And so proud.'

'So am I. My clever little sister!' Eden had crept up quietly behind them both.

'Eden! You're back!'

'Just.'

Rebecca whooped for joy and they hugged each other joyfully after he had landed the customary left to his sister's chin. Essie felt a lump in her throat as she watched the uninhibited show of affection between her two children. They each held out an arm and drew her into their embrace. It had seemed that no sooner Eden had arrived from Canada than he had gone again, to meet Rowanna. Now, at last, he was home. Now he would have seen the portrait of his grandfather which eliminated all doubts.

Eden interrupted her thoughts. 'I brought Rowanna back with me, Mum. She insisted she wanted to come to the party. She is in the drawing room talking with Dad.'

'Rowanna! Here? All the way from Dorset? How wonderful.' Essie hurried off to greet her.

'I have been hearing about this long-lost relation from Dad,' Rebecca remarked. 'What a story! Dad's auntie practically on Mum's doorstep in Dorset, and they never knew.'

'That's only the half of it. We had better not tell you the rest in case the Press gets hold of it,' Eden joked. 'Come and meet her. She's a great lady.'

'Here they come, William and Becky,' Rowanna murmured as brother and sister walked in together. 'What a sight for old eyes.' Rebecca was intrigued. What on earth did the old lady mean? But as she met the dark eyes so much like her own, she guessed that a chat with Great-Aunt Rowanna would soon put her in the picture.

Masses of food was laid out in the dining room and dancing indoors was in full swing. Rebecca had joyfully exclaimed as guests she least expected arrived; lots of her own circle of friends, and Clara, Maggie and Tom, Ivy and Ron, Joy

Burnett and Len and his wife who had travelled from Axminster for the occasion and were staying overnight.

Essie felt a glow of pride as her two men stood in the doorway, close together. One whose dark hair was showing streaks of grey, the other as blond as they come. Yet their square shoulders, jutting chins and mischievous grins proclaimed them father and son. Why was it she could not recognize the likenesses before? Maybe because she was not expecting to find any.

Joss began to mingle with the guests, while Eden sought out one special person. Annette was dancing with a very attentive man from Rebecca's office. She looked ravishingly beautiful in a classical white dress that showed off her figure to perfection. Eden approached her as the music ceased.

Annette greeted him with a dazzling smile and they danced together a couple of times, but it was obvious to Essie that she was determined to stay within the group of friends she knew, introducing Eden to them all and encouraging him to dance with some of the girls.

But later in the evening they disappeared into the garden together. They were away for some considerable time. When at last they returned they danced together, both looking relaxed and happy and Essie noticed with delight that they stayed together for the remainder of the evening.

Rowanna enjoyed every minute, her face alive with excitement, her sharp eyes missing nothing. Joss carried out her chair into the garden for the firework display. Wrapped snugly in a mohair shawl, she sat outside until after midnight. She had chatted to many people, including Rebecca, who had promised to visit her in Dorset. No doubt with her journalistic flair she had already found out all that she needed to know.

Annette was staying the night in Birmingham with Rebecca. When everyone else had left they came together to say their goodbyes.

While Eden walked Annette to the car Rebecca clung to Essie in a way she had not done for a long time. 'I have missed you, Mum,' she stated simply, and Essie knew that, in spite of her impending move to London, their daughter had come home.

Next day Eden announced he would not be in for lunch; he had to go to Birmingham.

'That wouldn't be anything to do with the fact that Annette is staying at Rebecca's in Birmingham, would it?' Joss teased.

Eden laughed good-humouredly. 'Sorry to disappoint you, Dad. I am going to meet someone off a train. Someone special. Her name is Abbie, short for Abigail, and I hope you will like her.'

Joss and Essie gazed at him in amazement, while Rowanna showed no surprise whatsoever. It was obvious she had already heard of Eden's Abigail.

'But you and Annette ...' ventured Essie. 'We thought ...'

'Annette and I had a long talk last night. We are both very different people to what we were three years ago, Mum. She has her sights set on a highly successful career on the magazine, and is as relieved as I am that we did not rush into marriage.

'Apart from that,' he continued, conscious of their disappointment, 'Can you honestly see Annette as a farmer's wife?'

Later, when she and Eden were alone, Essie brought up the subject again.

'I am sorry, Eden. I feel I have forced you and Annette apart.'

'Now don't start imagining you destroyed a great love affair, Mum. It would have destroyed itself in time, we both realize that. Annette wishes to preserve her link with the family, and she and I will always be good friends. But that is all.'

Her son reached over and took her hand. 'Don't you realize that, but for your revelation, I would have married the *wrong girl*. Just as Francis did.

'Although that man was not my father after all, the fatalistic circumstance of his letter changed my life. It forced me to change direction and give up the girl I now realize I could not have truly loved.

'But for the intervention of that letter I could be just like Francis was, inasmuch as I might be having to pursue a love affair with someone else while being caught in the trap of a marriage that could never work.'

'Is that how you really feel, Eden?' Essie pressed, still needing reassurance. 'No regrets?'

'No regrets,' he assured her earnestly. Then he added quietly, 'Although I never knew Francis he influenced my life more from the grave than he ever could had he lived.

'So cheer up. You will love Abbie and I know she will love you.'

Essie smiled in relief. She felt a buoyancy she had not experienced for a long time. Life was full of surprises. She had agonized for three years over spoiling a special relationship. Now Annette's career was more important to her than a love affair, and Eden had a new love, a new life.

'Tell them about Abigail now,' Rowanna commanded when they were all together again.

'When did you meet her?' Joss prompted.

'We first met casually, travelling by train from Toronto to Moosejaw. Abbie was on her way to stay with her grandparents, to help out on their smallholding. She grew up on a farm in Herefordshire.

'She left the train a couple of stops before I did. We telephoned each other occasionally when we had time, and met on a few occasions at agricultural shows and the like.

315

Then we discovered we were both planning to return to England at about the same time. As soon as Abbie knew about the tour I had planned she decided she would like to join me.

'So there we were. I had gained a perfect companion for the tour and we both soon discovered we had much in common.

'And gradually we fell in love,' he concluded with a smile.

'What is your Abbie like?'

'She looks like you, Mum. Small and blonde. Energetic. Practical. Determined. *Very* determined. Independent.' He laughed suddenly. 'And she is great fun.'

'Sounds like a perfect combination,' Rowanna murmured. 'Have you popped the question yet?' she added mischievously.

'I wasn't aware I had anything to offer her until I met you, Aunt,' Eden smiled. 'Now I intend to pop the question very soon.'

'Well, now that you have us all popping with curiosity isn't it time you were away to meet the young woman?'

They followed him outside to his car in the drive, Rowanna leaning heavily on her stick.

'Do you think you stand a chance of marrying this girl and bringing her down to Dorset?' she asked, as Eden seated himself behind the wheel.

Eden wound down the window. His smile embraced them all as he replied with conviction, 'I have set my heart on it.'

Essie glanced across at Joss. His eyes met hers with a look that said, 'I love you still', as Joy Burnett's voice drifted over the years. 'He usually gets what 'e sets 'is 'eart on, does Joss,' she had prophesied.

And Eden was Joss's son, after all.